THE RETURN OF JASON GREEN

Suzi Wizowaty

Fomite

Burlington, VT

ISBN-13: 978-1-937677-72-5
Library of Congress Control Number: 2014942472

Fomite
58 Peru Street
Burlington, VT 05401
www.fomitepress.com

Cover art - Cassandra Ricard

The Return of Jason Green

BOOKS BY SUZI WIZOWATY

A Tour of Evil, New York: Philomel (The Penguin Group), 2005.

The Round Barn, Hanover and London: The University Press of New England, 2002.

For Gigi,
in memory of our brother

Richard

When the doorbell rings at 11:15 on a frigid March night, do you answer it? If you're a 270-pound introvert lying in bed watching one of your favorite old war movies, what you want to do is reach over and turn off the light. Who rings the doorbell in the middle of the night? Someone up to no good or someone in distress. I had no use for either. I wished I had a large dog. Besides, it was the front door, which opens onto the living room. Everyone around here uses their side doors, through the mudroom.

Besides that, I was watching "From Here to Eternity" for the eighteenth time and eating a bowl of vanilla ice cream in bed, because, after all, it was Saturday night and I'd spent all day listening to the financial woes of people who leave their taxes to the last minute, and I was tired and sorely in need of comfort. Without company.

I ignored the doorbell.

"From Here to Eternity" provides distraction and comfort in equal measure. It's one of the best war movies ever made, I once tried to explain to Alice who lives next door. She watched it with me one night when Max was out of town. Max is married to Alice. Alice cried at the end, when Montgomery Clift got killed, but then she was furious. What an idiot, she said. Why didn't he just stop when they yelled at him to stop?

Because then it wouldn't be as dramatic a movie, I explained patiently. Alice is a practical woman, but sentimental when it comes to movies. She turned on me: This is your favorite movie? she demanded. Yes, I said. One of them. It wasn't just the male bonding either, I told her.

She said it was a ridiculous romanticization of the army.

But you have to admire the loyalty, I said. The army is his family. He says that, to Donna Reed.

Abusive goons, said Alice. That's fucked-up. To be loyal to people who treat you that badly.

Not the people, the system as a whole. The whole package. He's loyal to the army in spite of the hazers, in spite of Ernest Borgnine. It's his friends—Frank Sinatra, and the good guys. Fairness and honor and like that.

She shrugged. Okay, it's a morality play. The bad guy dies in the end, and the guy who avenged the bad guy also dies. And the top guy who let the hazing happen, he doesn't get his commission, okay, that's fair. But what about Burt Lancaster, who sleeps with the top guy's wife and stands by and lets the men abuse Montgomery Clift? He gets off scot-free, while everybody who tries to do the right thing ends up dead. What's that all about?

I gave up. It's not a morality play, I said. It's a *movie*. It's *art*. There are mysteries of the heart.

She rolled her eyes. Oh, Richard, she said. Loyalty like that may make you a good friend, but I'm not sure it's healthy. You're hopeless, she said. She kissed me on the top of the head and let herself out.

I cannot adequately explain why I love old war movies any more than I can explain my preference for vanilla ice cream. Or Max and Alice, for that matter. Or why my red hair is as thick now as when I was twenty, or how electricity works. Some things just are.

Do we have choices? I don't know. That's Max's domain.

The doorbell rang again. With irritation, I paused the VCR, pulled on my pants and went downstairs.

I freely admit that I am a wimp, a fact established by the time I was six and made abundantly clear to me by other boys throughout my growing up. I am afraid of violence, both in life and in the movies, which is one of the reasons I love *old* movies, where the violence is minimal and benign. People kill and die but in a way that hurts your heart rather than makes you want to throw up. But at that moment I was simply annoyed. I am a wimp, but I'm big, and one of the few advantages of my size is that young males—the kind that break into houses to steal drugs, that sort of thing—tend to leave me alone. That night, it was without anxiety that I flipped on the porch light and opened the front door. I didn't think it would hurt my heart.

Through the storm door I saw a young man somewhere between eighteen and twenty-five, my height but maybe half my weight, in scruffy jeans and a down parka with a thin, ratty sweater hanging out underneath. He wore blond dreads down to his shoulders, but he was an unusually good-looking kid, though his nose was red.

"Can I help you?"

He peered at me through the glass that was quickly steaming up. His arms were folded across his chest with his hands in his armpits as if he were cold.

"Uncle Richard?"

"Excuse me?"

"Could I come in? It's like, zero degrees out here."

"Uh, no. Who are you?"

"Jason Green. Remember me? Adam's friend? We moved away after—. You know, eight years ago." He stamped his feet. His breath came out in puffs.

I looked at him more closely. *My* Adam, as I thought of him?—though of course he wasn't my son but Max and Alice's. Adam Henry, who'd died eight years ago?

He saw me thinking and looked more hopeful. "Remember? I was his best friend? I was with him on the day... We used to play in your yard?"

Then I did remember...a little blond kid who played with Adam. I remembered them sliding on a wet sheet of plastic in the back yard next door, and jumping in a pile of leaves I was trying to rake. And just running around making noise.

"What are you doing here? Do you know what time it is?"

"Um, not really. I know it's cold."

I opened the storm door and stood aside to let him into the living room. He smelled like coffee. My house is very small—a 1950s cape. Half the downstairs contains a small living room and a kitchen and sun room separated by a counter, and the other half has a small guest room, office and tiny bathroom. Upstairs has only a bedroom and bath.

"You look half-frozen," I said. "Do you want something warm, some tea?" I led the way to the kitchen.

"Tea?" He sounded disappointed.

"Yeah, tea. Or hot milk. Drinking age is twenty-one. Look, it's almost eleven-thirty. I have a long day tomorrow. What's the deal?" I filled the electric tea kettle with water and turned it on.

He looked at his hands. "I left my gloves on the bus."

"The bus from where?"

"Connecticut."

I tried to sort this out. "Is that what you want, a pair of gloves?"

"It was stupid. I fell asleep on the bus, and when we got here, I got flustered—I was having this really intense dream—and I just got off the bus and by the time I realized and went back to the bus station, the bus was gone."

"Did you leave a message?"

"There wasn't anybody there. They'd all gone home. It was like a wasteland. The bus was three hours late; we had to wait for a new bus in White River Junction." He dropped his small backpack on the floor.

The water boiled and the kettle clicked off.

"Okay, Jason. That's your name, right? Jason?"

"Yeah. Only I go by Jocko now. Do you remember, you used to call me Jason the Jock? Mr. Henry—all of you. Because I so wasn't?"

"Jocko then." I got out two mugs and two bags of peppermint tea. "It's late. Tell me what you need. If I can help you, I will. Otherwise—"

"Adam was the adventurous one and I was the one who followed him everywhere."

I handed him a mug of tea. He stood in the middle of the kitchen, looking around. "Thanks. I never was in here before."

"Let me ask you something. Do your parents know where you are?"

"Sure."

The way he said it made me doubt it. "Where do they think you are?"

"In Vermont."

"That's all? Just Vermont?"

"Well, they know I was coming up to see Mr. Henry."

"Ah!" I set down my tea with great relief. That explained it. Now I could go to bed. "In that case, you're fine. They're right next door—as of course you know." I headed toward the door, thinking to usher him out.

Now he looked uncomfortable again. He held his mug to his chest with both hands and began examining one of the prints on my wall—an oil of the U.S.S. Enterprise at the Battle of Santa Cruz.

"Wow. What's this?"

"Okay, wait. I get it. You've come back here to see Max and Alice for some reason that's none of my business, and the bus was late getting in, and their lights are off, and you don't have any place to sleep, so you came here. Is that right?" He didn't answer, seemingly engrossed in the painting. "Do you have any money?"

"I have money. This is kind of gruesome, I mean with the bodies flying in the air."

"All right, look. You can stay here tonight and go see them in the morning. I have to go to bed. Some of us work. If it weren't twenty degrees out, I'd say you could sleep in the park, but whatever. You can sleep on the couch in the living room."

"Don't you have a guest room?"

"Excuse me?" I laughed, but it came out sounding more like a snort. "You're not my guest. You're a homeless waif I'm taking in off the street as a favor to my dear friends and next-door neighbors. I'll get you a blanket. There's a clean towel in the bathroom." I retrieved a pile of blankets and a pillow and dropped them on the futon.

"You used to be friendlier," he said.

"You used to be younger. Do you need a toothbrush?"

He shook his head and began unfolding the blankets. "What is it with all these war pictures? Are they valuable or something?"

"No, just old." I turned on a standing lamp in the living room for him.

"You just collect them for no reason?"

At the bottom of the stairs, I paused. "Why did you come up here?"

"I told you. To see Mr. Henry. I want—." He gazed at the blanket still in his hand as if its yellow threads held the secrets to his future. "I—he—he needs to take me on as an apprentice."

"What?"

"You know, like in the olden days, when you apprenticed to, like, a printer, and you were a printer's devil."

I watched him carefully smooth out the blankets. What a curious kid.

He looked up. "What? You don't think he will?"

I shrugged. "How would I know? I don't even know what it means."

He'd been wearing his parka all this time. Now he took it off. Suddenly I saw him as the graceful young animal he was, not merely the irritating straight boy who was bringing out something in me I didn't care for—as if I were the aging ape whose dominance was about to be challenged. Now I couldn't help noticing how young and attractive he was. His shoulders were well-formed, his chest filled out, his arms strong. My gut tightened; an alarm bell went off somewhere far away, faint but clear enough to register.

"It's not rocket science," he said with a frown. "I need someone to clarify a few things. Philosophical questions. He's a philosopher. That's how it works, isn't it?"

"Not where I come from, but, hey, I'm old-fashioned. I'm also old and I have a long day tomorrow. As I've mentioned. Okay? You all set here? Turn off the light when you're done."

He set the pillow carefully at the head of the couch, oblivious of me. I didn't know what to make of him. On the one hand he seemed so young. Apprentice himself to Max? What in the world? On the other hand, he had an intense, bottled-up energy that affected me. I was going to have a hard time sleeping, with him in my living room. Shit. I was sorry I'd let him in. But I forged ahead with the effort to be the generous neighbor, the parental figure. Uncle Richard.

"One more thing," I said. "This is the thermostat. I turn it way down at night, okay? But if you get cold, you can turn it up. A *little*. With all those blankets, you should be fine. A little goes a long way here."

He nodded and pulled his sweater over his head. His shirt pulled up slightly over his taut belly. I looked away.

"See you in the morning," I said.

He didn't answer.

"Goodnight, Jocko." I pulled the door at the bottom of the stairs closed behind me. His voice came through softly.

"Night."

The next morning I padded downstairs about six-thirty to discover with some surprise the blankets carefully folded on the couch. I checked the bathroom, the guest room, even the basement just to make certain, and when I concluded he'd indeed left without leaving a note, I was both relieved and disappointed. But after a big breakfast I huffed off to a half-day's work, assuming the kid would easily find Max since it was Sunday, and Max would say no, and that would be that.

Max

Sunday afternoon. I made a mistake thinking I could write this goddamned book about punishment. I planned my whole sabbatical around it. I prepared for it with months of research, on top of several years' worth of casual interest. I persuaded myself that the past two years of weekly volunteering in the prison gave me a Real-Speak that would transform my overly dense style. I imagined that the excruciatingly slow, almost imperceptible evolution of my thinking gave me a certainty of voice that would lead to success. And not just success but easy success, success that would blossom naturally and extravagantly in my world like one of Richard's peonies, startling in its vibrancy and richness.

I also imagined ease of creation. And I realize now that in my heart as opposed to my brain—which is my better organ—I also envisioned a book that would succeed commercially. I would write a *trade* book, a book for the public, if not the masses. A book people would actually read, that might have an impact on the world. A tiny segment of the world, perhaps, but an impact nonetheless. All my books of philosophy—and I say with pride that I've written five—have sold under a thousand copies. Truth be told, all but one have sold under five hundred copies. Am I ashamed of this? Heavens, no. We live in an anti-intellectual world. Let it be duly noted, Max Henry is proud of his books, to wit: *Everything is Connected: a treatise on Leibniz*; *All is Light and Shadow: Platonic Imagery in the 19ᵗʰ Century*; *Henri Bergson, Master of Mind*; *An Intelligent Student's Introduction to the Philosophy of East and West*; and my big seller (887 copies) on ethics, *The Chi of Right Action*.

It is not easy teaching philosophy to undergraduates these days. Perhaps it never was. I have tried to make my courses less predictable by including poetry—but if it's raw, contemporary spoken-word poetry, students prefer it to philosophy and resent the return to the actual subject matter, and if it's older, slightly more dense poetry, they think I'm torturing them. Lose-lose. For a while I tried including stories from the prison, but I've never known how to tell a story. I don't mind their eyes glazing over when I talk about philosophy, but I can't bear it when I'm telling them about someone's life. Which is, I suppose, the problem of this goddamn book on punishment. Where the hell is the story? They say "narrative non-fiction" needs a story, a narrative thrust, but what is that?

None of my other books had it, whatever it is.

Both Alice and Richard have tried to help. Why do you care about this, they've both asked. What is it you're trying to explore?

It's this: why is it that when someone tailgates me on the highway, and then speeds around me after I've kindly moved over, why is it that when that happens, I wish he'd go off the road at the next bend, and I'd find him around the next corner overturned in a ditch?

Where does that come from? Why do I want to see him hurt?

Why is it that a visiting grandmother, upon discovering that her two-year-old grandson has drawn on the wall with markers, says indignantly to the child's mother, "Aren't you going to punish him?"

Punish him. Spank him, take away his stuffed bunny, lock him up!

In the prison last year, I came across a young man who like most people there had done a dumb thing. In his case, he'd fired a rifle across a hayfield into a tractor. He'd been out hunting with his buddies and hadn't got a deer and he was frustrated, so he shot at something else—a tractor parked in a field. But unbeknownst to the kid, asleep in the cab was a 72-year-old farmer, who was killed. It was an accident, all agreed. A stupid, foolish, irresponsible thing to do, but an accident nonetheless. When the case came to trial, the man's widow said, "I don't want to ruin his life, but I do want justice."

Justice? What is justice?

Is justice served by locking up an immature 19-year-old who wants nothing more than to farm, who could perhaps be helping that widow with her crops for the next few years, or doing something else productive—*anything* instead of sitting in jail at taxpayers' expense? Is justice served by punishing a two-year-old for creating art in the wrong place? What kind of justice? What kind of justice would be served—what kind of illusory balance created—by a reckless driver's ending up mangled on the side of the road?

In the introduction to my as yet leg-less book, I introduced a personal note: When I was a small boy, my older brother used to slug me as I walked by. I hit him back. Immediate retaliation feels natural, instinctive. People who have hurt others deserve to suffer, right?

However, when I hit my brother back, he'd hit me again. At that point, he was hitting me for having hit him, which he made clear. I learned early that I could either stop then or keep going, but in any case, he would get the first and last hits. Naturally I complained bitterly about this to my mother. Her response was, "Don't hit him back." Practical advice, maybe, but counter to my sense of how the world should be. Outrageous, I thought. *Not fair.*

Someone hits us, we hit back. Someone hurts us, we want to see him hurt. Revenge! Justice! But if the impulse is natural, how we act on it, individually and as a society, has varied over time and place. Varied and developed, evolved. Somewhere along the line, we encountered another idea, another way of looking at the world that elicits a different set of questions: Does anyone deserve to suffer? Does the impulse to teach someone a lesson really serve any purpose? Does punishing someone who has broken a rule or caused harm bring about any good, anything positive? Might it indeed cause further harm?

Just as societies have evolved their understanding of punishment, so can individuals mature in theirs. We start off with an inchoate sense of justice and its dark side, revenge, but then we grow up and things happen. We do things, things happen to us—unexpected things, tragedies and the like—and fault and blame and responsibility and even the causes of suffering become less clear, less black and white. "Punishment" begins to lose its meaning.

So here I am, having devoted almost nine full months to this project, and I have a mess on my hands. No clear plan but rather a frustrating collection of fits and starts, no closer to any kind of resolution than when I began. I begin to think the whole idea was a mistake. I never should have tried to tackle such a subject outside my area of expertise in such a short span of time, and I certainly shouldn't have tried to write a trade book. That was a joke. But, Christ Almighty, I cannot abandon the entire project now! I'm chained to it like a nineteenth-century prisoner chained to a leaden ball. I've invested too much.

I also cannot tell Alice that I'm stalled. Although passionate and loving, she is above all practical and determined and gets impatient with what she calls my overly self-reflective nature. She would tell me to stop worrying and simply do it. Just write the book. Her approach to life provides a good balance for someone who is a philosopher by nature and training, but in this case it would be unhelpful. Unhelpful because impossible. I can't tell Alice. But I can perhaps confess my failure to Richard, who, while even less reflective than Alice, often surprises me with his oddball comments during our weekly breakfasts. Besides, he loves me like a brother—not the kind who hits you but the sweet, faggy twin who helps you dress for the prom while he stays home watching movies. Although he, too, can be impatient with me, he will not think badly of my inability to advance this book. His own life is stalled out on too many levels for that kind of judgment.

Alice

WELL-MEANING PEOPLE can say amazingly stupid things when a child dies. My favorite is "You can always have another."

First of all, I was thirty-seven when Adam died. Second, we didn't want another. We wanted Adam. But that's neither here nor there. I refuse to be defined as a woman who lost her son. You never get over it, correct. This and every other trite thing people say is true. But I am like those people with cancer who don't want to be defined as a person with cancer. Yes, they have cancer, and no, you can't control what other people think, but the point is, they want to *live*. And so do I. *I have a life.*

If this sounds a little desperate, more like a plea than a statement, it's because the *problem* in such situations is what the hell are you going to live *for*? On the other hand, whether or not you come up with an answer, time rolls on. There's a story about a grieving mother who goes to the Buddha asking him to take away her pain. I came across it while researching images for a local hospice; that was a design job I would have refused, but at my firm we don't have that choice. Anyway, he tells her to bring him a feather or something from a home in which there is no grief. She goes from house to house in the village and of course she discovers that in this house the husband has died, in that house the mother is very sick, in this house the son has lost his leg to gangrene. She returns to the Buddha and thanks him for opening her heart to the suffering of others.

In real life, this takes a while. If it occurs at all. Nothing happens in real life as quickly as in a story; grief is very isolating. That's one of the first things a grief counselor tells you, to reach out to others so you don't become isolated. Especially to your spouse, because 50% of marriages where a child dies end in divorce. Something like that; I don't remember the exact figure. I remember thinking, okay, we've got a fifty-fifty chance. And also, Max did want another child.

Max has always loved children. He loves teaching, or at least he used to. He loves young people. I'm not one of those women who can say she loves children. Frankly I don't get how anyone can say honestly that they love a whole category of anything. Children, dogs, cats, old people, museums. *All* museums, even the decrepit one devoted to someone's dusty collection of Russian stacking dolls? How about the smelly, mean old person? The psychotic cat you can't touch? The whiny kid controlling his miserable mother? As Richard would say, oh, *please*.

However, this is weirdly, actually true for Max. Naturally it has created some distress between us, but I told him I was perfectly happy for him to make a baby elsewhere, if he wanted to keep two relationships going, and that seemed to take the wind out of his sails a bit. And frankly, after Adam died, he didn't have the energy for it. In any case, it's too late now—for me anyway, I'm forty-five; I suppose Max could make babies for years if he wanted, even though he's ten years older. If Max harbors any lasting rage toward me about this, he does a fairly good job keeping it in check. Usually.

Aside from having another baby, the other big thing I no longer wanted to do after Adam died, of the many things you might say I'd lived for before, was to take pictures. You could speculate on all kinds of reasons, as Max did when he was trying to get me to return to it: he said I was stuck in the world created by the photos of Adam that were all over our house, in the hall, on the shelf in the living room, on my dresser, on the wall in the bedroom—Adam and us, Adam and the dog, Adam and his friends, Adam alone. He said I'd been too limited in the happy content of earlier photos and I just needed to branch out. He suggested I'd realized the falseness of trying to fix something in time, and now I could keep going, free of illusion. He was trying to be helpful, and he was creative in coming up with ideas, but the simple reason was, I just had no interest. I never saw anything I wanted to take a picture of. It's like I forgot why one took pictures in the first place. Eventually I put most of the photos of Adam in a box in the basement.

Richard, our next-door neighbor, said I was depressed, but I wasn't. I was appropriately grief-stricken. Bowled over, weighed down, eviscerated. I'm only saying this now to get it over with, to be able to move on, because people wonder: what was it like for you to lose a child? Actually most people don't wonder. They don't want to think about it; the possibility is simply too terrifying.

So, enough of that. I am middle-aged, just turned forty-five, and fairly bitter about my stupid, wasted life—but privately, because I am by Midwestern temperament and training cheerful and pleasant. Or so I tell myself. I've never had much patience for introspection, and my recent angers—and fears—have surprised me. It's probably hormonal, but there it is. I have a mildly satisfying job as a graphic designer in a field dominated by computers and young people. Everyone left in my firm is fifteen or twenty years younger than I. This makes me feel old and worried. Not so much about my job but about my *life*. What am I contributing? It wakes me up at night. That and hot flashes.

But I'm not dead yet. I may be drying up, losing words, forgetting things, weeping unexpectedly for no reason, but then this other voice says, *Jesus Fucking Christ, you're only forty-five, get a grip!* And then this week, something happened, which brings me back to the photos.

Wednesday night I read a review of a show, a photography exhibit at a college in Massachusetts. The photo in the review was a black and white self-portrait of a woman with one eye swollen almost shut. What I imagine must have been shades of blue and purple under her eye showed up as streaks or smudges. Her whole face gave the impression of being a little smudged, worked over—not literally, the photo was very clear, you could tell she had make-up on and her hair was very beautiful, coiffed and full, but that was my impression. Except her eyes. One was a mere slit but the other was... sharp, hard, clear. I don't mean "hard" like her soul was hardened, I mean that photographically while the rest of the face gave the impression of a sort of smushed-ness, even though it wasn't technically blurry, her good eye looked at you with such a clear, penetrating focus. The fact that it was a self-portrait, so she's looking at a camera lens, made it that much more remarkable. What was she thinking? What exactly was she trying to document? Was she just trying to document suffering? I don't think so. That's not what I got from the image. I got survival, inner strength, courage. Not "This is what happened to me," but "This is my response, this is who I am." Not the bruises on the surface, the strength underneath.

In other words, a woman who has a life, who loves the world and herself. A woman who's saying "I am more than you think."

Was that why she took the photo?

The exhibit was called "Beautiful Suffering," which had to be expressing several levels of irony, or something. It couldn't possibly be a simple statement. The woman had a beauty, and the photograph had an eerie beauty, but not because she was suffering! Jesus. That's either sick or insane. According to the review, though, all the images are of people in pain—or dead. Why? What's the purpose? I want to know who took each one, what they're photos of, and what the circumstances were. I think—*I know*—there has to be more to it.

I wanted to talk to Max about it. My philosopher husband always has theories, multiple theories and explanations. He likes ideas. What keeps him from being pompous is he lets them go as quickly as he comes up with them; it's really quite endearing. But he wasn't home yet. Nor was Richard, my next-door neighbor and unlikely best friend. Richard would have no theories and profess complete bewilderment, but he'd be interested because... because he loves me.

In the end I was glad neither was home. Something is happening to me that I can't explain. The images haunted my dreams that night, but nonetheless I wanted to see the rest. The next morning I called and ordered the catalogue.

I waited impatiently all week. I snapped at Max twice and had to reassure him that nothing was wrong. I was sure the catalogue would come by Saturday. Here it is, the third week of March, cold again, below freezing at night and warming up into the forties during the day—perfect maple syrup weather. And *the catalogue has not come*! What the hell is wrong with the mail? I am so disappointed I could scream.

I could have driven to goddamn Massachusetts and picked up the catalogue myself yesterday, and then I would have had all day today to look at it. Instead I've been thinking about it all day, which is *extremely* unlike me. I have never been someone who obsessed over things—and I haven't understood people who do. *Just do it, let it go, move on,* would be my mantras if I had them, which I don't. Now I'm forced to switch my attention to making Sunday dinner for Max and Richard because it's my turn, and though I'm the one who goes to the least trouble of all three of us, having by far the least interest in cooking which I find boring, boring, boring, I may out of desperation surprise them with something other than hamburgers and green beans and potato chips.

Richard

Alice doesn't take pictures anymore. But she used to when Adam was alive, and I still have on my desk at work a photo she took of Adam and me on his birthday when he was six. I don't actually look at it very often, in the sense of really seeing it, but the Sunday after Jason Green appeared at my house, I had a bit of a harder time settling into work, and I found myself gazing at the picture.

Adam loved whipped cream, but not just any whipped cream. Whipped cream in a can. He liked the way the white plastic nozzle went *phtttt* when you bent it. He liked the sound, the squirt, everything about it. It was so deliciously male. It was one of the many ways we were in synch, young Adam and I.

For his sixth birthday, I arranged with Alice that I would provide the cake for his party, and he and I would decorate it beforehand. Exactly *how* would be a surprise. At the grocery store I picked up a simple, flat cake I'd ordered, big enough for ten children and assorted grownups, without frosting. The woman behind the counter asked why I didn't just buy a mix for a quarter of the price. I didn't feel like explaining.

"I'm a man," I said in my swishiest voice. "I don't bake."

I also bought six cans of whipped cream to cover the cake. One can doesn't actually hold that much. It's mostly air, which is why a tablespoon has only a few calories. At 1:30 I called next door and told Alice to send Adam over.

He let himself in. "Look what I got, Uncle Richard!"

"New toy? Let's see."

He showed me a contraption in each hand. "Not a toy. It's a transformer. This is a zorgmeister and this is a bugamorph. See this, you move this, this is the stabilizer, and this—" he struggled with a stubborn joint and his face got red, "this part gets stuck—there—" he fixed it, "it's a fuselage, and this is its weapon, it's like a laser."

"Ah. What does it shoot?"

"Zorgs. Or anything that comes at it. And look, see this one, the wing turns into an arm and you bend this like this and it's a robot so they can fight."

"Why would they fight?"

"Because they're fighters."

With the paper bag of cans clinking under my arm, I carried the large, flat cake box into the back yard where I'd set up a card table. Adam followed at my heels.

"Can I see? Can I see?"

"In about thirty seconds." It was a perfect summer day, if a little warm for June.

"Dad and I decorated a cake for Valentine's Day. For Mom."

"I know."

"We made a picture with candy. Of all of us." A photograph of this famous cake hung on their refrigerator. It was an unrecognizable jumble of red hots, M&Ms, chocolate kisses, sour balls, and colorful chewy animals all squeezed mercilessly into muddy chocolate frosting.

"The cake we're going to make will be all white, like a field of snow." I lifted the bare cake from its box. It was only one-layer high, but about fifteen by twenty-four inches. "Ta da!"

Adam looked puzzled.

I was eager not to disappoint him. "Look!" I pulled a can of whipped cream from the paper bag. "And this. And this." His eyes widened. He actually jumped up and down.

"Let me! Let me!"

I popped off the plastic hat from the first can and shook it. The bottle got heavier as the contents firmed up. "Go for it."

He took the can without a word, eyed me expectantly.

I nodded. "However you want to do it. Just hold the can over the cake."

He pressed the nozzle and out came a spurt of white, a softly ridged line that soon made a round little clump—accompanied by the most satisfying sound in the world. He smiled. I smiled. He zigzagged across the surface of the cake and back again. Then again, more randomly. The cream dribbled out of the can at the end.

"Shake it up in between squirts."

He shook it happily. The sloshing inside stopped at once. Adam squeezed again and moved back and forth across the cake in earnest, back and forth, covering the top. He had no system, only a free and haphazard slathering, a mad, whipped cream graffiti. It was irresistible.

"May I help?" I asked.

"Sure."

I popped the cover off another can and shook it. *Phtttt-ts-ts* sputtered Adam's can. He shook it and tried again. "It's empty."

I handed him mine and got myself another. "Cover the sides, too," I said.

Adam's aim was not great. Whipped cream spilled onto the cardboard holding the cake and onto the table. He gave up on the sides. It was more fun to make piles and mounds on top like drip castles at the beach, seeing how high they could go before they fell over.

I stood back from the cake for a moment. It was looking rather lumpy. I tried to delineate its edges with a little crenellated ridge. Adam went about adding height to the top. When he ran out, I gave him a third can.

No cake showed now. It was a mass of mushy white. In the warmth of midday, the whipped cream seemed to be melting. Adam licked his fingers, then with a sly glance at me, squirted some directly into his mouth.

"Hey! That's for later."

He laughed, and squirted his face. I ignored him. Then, as I bent over the cake in concentration, he squirted me in the face. I jumped. A line of whipped cream stuck to my cheek. Adam seemed no less shocked than I—shocked, gleeful, and wide-eyed all at once, holding his breath, wondering what I'd do.

I squirted him back. "You!"

He shrieked and leaped away, then circled back. I had the advantage, with longer arms. I sprayed a ring around his face and hair. But of course he was little and quick, able to dart in and out, the Spanish armada confronting the ancient British fleet. But then his squirt dribbled.

"Shake it! Shake it!"

He did, and got a better trajectory. When his can emptied, I tossed him mine. But when I bent down to pull the last two cans from the paper bag, he leaped on my back with a yell and sprayed my hair and face and neck.

"Aggghhh!" I shook him off and tossed him his last can. He now had a can in each hand. He danced and jumped and squirted, hopping and laughing, looping around me until the final, weak spit of the last can. I met him squirt for squirt.

"Truce?" I said finally.

"Truce." Then, "It's kinda greasy."

"Shall we wash it off?" I took his hand. Comrades in arms, we marched to the hose attached to the side of his house. I saw Alice at the window.

"Stay right there!" she ordered.

We looked at each other and laughed. She returned with her camera and a couple of towels. I knelt next to him for a pose, and then we rinsed off the slimy stuff and I dried him the best I could, while Alice took more pictures.

"I think a real bath is probably a good idea," she said finally, smiling at Adam. "We'll see you later?" she asked me.

"What about my transformers?" Adam said. He'd left them inside.

"I'll bring them over."

"What about the cake?"

"The cake will be great. You'll see."

But it was clear the original cake had drowned, not to be resuscitated. I dumped it in the garbage, showered, and rushed to the store where I bought an ordinary birthday cake with chocolate frosting and "Happy Birthday" written on it. Bland but not too goofy for a six-year-old, I hoped. At three o'clock I took it next door. Adam was busy with his friends. I don't think I stayed long. I probably chatted with Alice and another mother or two for a moment and made a graceful exit. I knew that later Alice would present the cake and everyone would sing and Adam Henry, king of all children, would blow out candles, and he and his friends would eat, noisily, happily, with no more restraint than is called for at six-year-old birthday parties. They would be silly and combative and sweet with each other in their six-year-old ways. Our game—our scrappy battle marked by the true warrior's unflinching courage and unbridled glee—was already on its way to being forgotten. And that was as it should be: Adam would grow up and have a life full of such moments.

Alice gave me a copy of the photo a week later in a simple wooden frame. I took it to work because I liked our expressions. I'm not very photogenic, and even I looked good: our faces are flushed and dirty, and we look happy. It made me think I should loosen up like that more often, have more fun. Maybe even have children—ha. I didn't need children, I had Adam.

And now here was this kid, this eighteen-year-old punk waif who had descended upon me the night before...definitely not a child, but not an adult either.

I finished up what work I had the energy to do. It was Sunday, after all. I'd be seeing Max and Alice at dinner, because we took turns cooking once a week, and even more often during tax season as they helped me out, and I looked forward to hearing Max's review of Jason Green. The two of them would have connected by then, no doubt. Since last night my conviction that Max would say no had faded; now I really had no idea of his reaction. Unknowns are unsettling for an accountant, and I wanted this one settled.

Richard

From the outside, Max and Alice's house is a mirror image of my own, with the driveways at the opposite edges of our tiny lots, small roofless porches in front and mudrooms that lead to the kitchens added onto the sides. Inside, the variation is minimal but significant; the stairway in my house bisects the house from end to end, running parallel to the street and separating kitchen from living room. Their stairway runs the opposite way, from front to back, leaving an open floor plan of kitchen and living room on one side of the house and small office and guest room on the other side. Max and Alice's house is better laid out for a family. In their house, you could have two rooms upstairs, because of where the stairs come up. In mine, you couldn't. The layout of my house makes less sense—as with much of my life compared with theirs—which is I suppose why the owner before me opened up the back wall of the kitchen to add a dining-sitting area. I call that half the sun room; through its large windows I can see into Max and Alice's back yard. So now my house, for just me, is bigger than theirs, which doesn't seem right. How did that happen? I suppose the point is that you never know how things are going to end up. I find this disconcerting and rejoice that I am an accountant rather than, say, a graphic designer like Alice or a professor like Max. In my world there is one right way for things to turn out. The columns and rows are neat and tidy, and the numbers either add up or they don't, for which I am extremely grateful.

I am regularly reminded of this awful truism—that you never know how things will turn out—whenever I go to Max and Alice's for dinner. It's not exactly a thought, but more like a sort of mental tic. I want to make clear that I don't think, *How sad, there's no family in this family-appropriate house,* or imagine how things might have been different had Adam lived. I don't think consciously about Adam at all. First of all, it's more like the kind of habitual twinge like *Oh God, I ate too much.* And second, speaking of food, my concern has more to do with dinner.

I never know what they're going to serve.

Fortunately they are big eaters; they're both big people; not fat like me, more like bears, which I've told them. I love bears. Max is big and burly with curly mostly black hair, which he is touchingly proud to still have in abundance. Alice would be more like a polar bear, a descendent of the Vikings, a Valkyrie transplanted to the Iowa plains which muffled but never quite obliterated the Norse passion.

Alice doesn't like to cook much, but her Midwestern meals with a twist are usually more than adequate. And Max is a wonderfully creative cook, even if sometimes his weird ethnic concoctions can be hard to decipher. But there it is, another of life's awful mysteries: I love them, they are my best friends, they cook good hearty meals, and yet if I am honest I have to admit that there is something about eating with them that makes me anxious.

That Sunday night, I wondered whether Max's encounter with Jason Green, a.k.a. Jocko, would have inspired him to prepare some strange Hungarian-Japanese-Ethiopian combination for dinner.

I let myself in as I usually do. Ah, relief: Alice was at the stove, stirring a big pot of soup. She leaned over to kiss me. "Hello, darling."

"Smells good. What are you making?"

She smiled. "You'll be surprised to know I *was* going to make something good for a change, but as it turns out, Max threw this together this morning before he left. I'm just heating it up. Mulligatawny—à la Max. Surprise ingredients. Who knows?"

I believe Alice *could* be a perfectly good cook if she wanted—she has all the creative instincts and skills, which she demonstrates on rare occasions—but she lacks the interest or the patience. I might have the patience but lack the creativity and skills.

"Where's Max?" I asked.

"At the university. He wanted to work on his book for a few hours today when there was no one around. He implied he was onto a new idea and needed to focus, but I actually think he's struggling. This week he didn't go to the office at all. He said he wanted to catch up on stuff here, but that's unlike him. How was your week?"

"Fine. Can I help?" I cleared off the little table that sits against the wall, half in the kitchen and half in the living room—these small Capes have no dining room—and dumped the pile of papers onto one of the living room chairs. "What are all these magazines for? *Sports Illustrated*? *Car and Driver*? Something for work?"

Alice handed me the silverware and flipped up the rounded edge of the table and secured it, so the table could seat three. Though I eat there several times a week at this time of year, they always return the table to its narrow rectangular position after I leave. That way it fits two. I always thought it was because the room is small and the table-for-three takes up more space. Alice wasn't answering my question, and in the pause it suddenly occurred to me for the first time that maybe she and Max didn't want to be reminded that they had been three and now were only two. But surely if that was ever a conscious thought, it was now likely one of those little habits of mind like mine about how things never turn out as you expect. On the other hand, I didn't know what it was like to be a parent. I didn't think about Adam all the time, but maybe she did.

Now Alice stood gazing into an open drawer, as if puzzling over which placemats to choose. Her back was to me, her strong, straight back, draped in an oversized, worn-out cardigan of Max's. What was she thinking about?

"Alice—."

"What?"

"How often do you think of Adam?"

She glanced at me. "Every day. Maybe once in a while a whole day goes by and I don't think of him till I'm lying in bed. I used to think of him every minute, every single second, but it got less. I don't suppose that ever completely goes away, but it's not here"— she pointed to the front of her brain—"but more like back here." She smiled at me.

I brought the extra chair from the hall closet, as Alice set out a third placemat matching the two on the table. It was a miniature braided rug, like people used to make to sit on. Colorful, but ratty and old-fashioned, not yet qualifying as an antique.

She said, "Why do you ask?"

"I don't know, just wondering. Never mind." Better I should let Max tell her about Jocko.

"What? I hate when people do that. Tell me."

"I was going to make a silly crack about the magazines, but I've forgotten what it was."

Alice snorted. "I wouldn't believe you except that my own brain seems to be disintegrating. I can't seem to remember anything anymore. But if you're wondering about the magazines, they have nothing to do with Adam. Oh, good, Max is home."

Max took off his coat in the mudroom and came through the kitchen door noisily. He kissed Alice and patted me on the back on his way to the bathroom amid friendly greetings. He usually kisses me, too—ever since he went to a men's retreat a few years ago—but he didn't that night. I *like* kissing Max, but I had to get used to it. I mean, this was *Max.* When he first started, I wondered if he was teasing me, or even being cruel in a way I hadn't seen before. But I concluded if he was playing a game, I would play, too. The only thing I don't like is that he sets the rules. But that's how it is: the person who says *No* controls the game.

Why didn't he kiss me hello? *Richard Lazarovsky, you are way too sensitive to Max*, I told myself. *Maybe he just had to pee. Lighten up.*

When we sat down to dinner a few minutes later, Alice said, "How'd it go today, Max?"

"Fine. Making progress, I suppose." He offered me and Alice the wine I had brought over. Max prefers beer. I held up my glass.

Alice declined. "I'm worried about my memory. I think alcohol makes it worse."

Max made a face and filled my glass. "What's progress? How does one define it? The work goes on; nothing new."

"Nothing?" I asked.

"That's a piercing look. What did you have in mind?"

Jocko! What did you say to Jocko's request? But I'm good at stifling irritation. "I don't know," I said. "A breakthrough of some kind? The March thaw makes the sap run."

Max smiled ruefully. "As runs the sap, so flows the blood and good ideas? Hey, all's well in that department. Tell us about your week, my friend. I want to hear a story."

"Let's see. There's the lesbian who's been living under the radar who just inherited a chunk of money from her family and wants to give it all away without triggering an audit. And the two guys with a civil union but *very* unequal incomes who want to adopt a child and are trying to figure out how to set up their deductions."

Max sighed. "But those aren't stories. They're outlines of stories."

I raised my fork to him inviting him to do better. Then, "Alice, the soup is fantastic."

"Max made it this morning, remember? It's all there is, though—a one-course meal. But there's lots of it."

"Thanks for the warning. Did I ever tell you about the time I went to a friend's house for dinner and they served soup, and they kept asking if I wanted seconds—everybody else was having seconds—but I wanted to save room for the rest of the meal, and it turned out that's all there was?"

"Yes, actually," said Alice.

"There was no main course," I continued. "Just the soup. I left there still starving. I thought, *Jesus, couldn't you at least tell your guests that this is all there is?* I mean, it was good, but I would have had thirds and fourths."

"Now that's a story," said Max. I acknowledged the compliment.

"A story we've heard before," said Alice. But then, kindly, "Richard, darling, are you still hungry?"

I shook my head: it was okay, my bowl was still half full.

"Not just Richard's story," said Max, "but the larger story of long-time friends who repeat their stories but don't remember they've heard them." He raised his fork back at me.

He wanted my forgiveness. For what, I didn't know, but as always I softened. I would do anything for him. "You are a master chef," I said. "The soup is delicious, and filling—perfect for a blustery-cold March night. And yes, I'll have some more."

I got up to refill my bowl. Behind me, Max and Alice ate in silence. I sat back down, and we all ate quietly for a moment, but it wasn't the comfortable silence of old friends that I was used to. What were they thinking about? They both seemed preoccupied.

"So, Alice," I said. "What about those magazines?"

"Oh, yes. I want to ask you two about this. I have this terrible assignment at work—to develop a campaign about fathers."

"Fathers?" Max and I said in unison. He raised his eyebrows at me.

"Fathers. It's this coalition of non-profit groups that's gotten a grant to do a p.r. campaign encouraging fathers to be more involved with their kids."

"Is that really necessary?" asked Max. "In this day and age? Everyone I know is involved with his kids. Much more than our fathers were."

"I guess that's a certain demographic," said Alice. "There are still plenty of deadbeat dads, dads in jail, that kind of dad."

"So you're looking in those magazines for images of fathers," I said.

"Something like that."

"Why you, Alice? It seems like, well..."

"Because everyone else I work with is twenty-five. And the guys are a *long* way from being fathers, except hormonally. They're into snowboarding and video games and getting more tattoos." She paused. "I sound like an old fart, don't I? I feel like an old fart, but I'm trying to see it as an honor. But I'm at a loss. What comes to mind? Images. Healthy, positive images."

"I have no idea. I'm not a father," I said.

Max got up with his bowl. "I'm not a father, either."

There was a silence.

"Come on, you guys. I need your help. Ideas. What do you think of?"

"Don't they have some notion of what they want?" Max asked.

"I guess they couldn't decide. Too many choices."

I said, "How's your father, Alice?" Of the three of us, she was the only one with a father still living. He never came to visit, so I'd never met him, and though she visited him in Iowa once a year, she rarely spoke of him.

"The same. Quiet, self-absorbed. Hardly has any friends as far as I can tell. Drinks too much and spends most of his time watching TV."

"Richard had a good father, didn't you, Richard?" said Max.

"Good enough," I said.

"So give me an image," said Alice. "Holding you in the air with his feet while you pretended to be an airplane? Playing catch outside? Walking hand in hand in the park? It's all so trite. And Max's father was hopeless."

"Come on, old buddy," said Max. "Tell us about a good father. How does a father raise a good son, keep him safe, teach him right from wrong, that sort of thing?"

"Whoa, nelly." This wasn't Max's good-natured teasing; it had an edge. Why was he baiting me?

"No, I mean it. I really want to know."

Had something happened with Jocko? Was he pissed that Jocko had come to see me first? Or did it have nothing to do with me? I observed him over the top of my wine glass. Sometimes I thought if Max and I could just go off and have a good screw, these strange little moments of tension wouldn't arise. But it was years too late for that.

"All right," I said agreeably. "A toast to Pop, who thought I was so different from him he wondered if I was really his son. He used to tease my mother about it. He had black hair, not red. But we had the same fair skin." I raised my glass. "If he was going to the store, my mother would tell him to take me along, and he'd look at me and scratch his head and say *This little guy? Whose kid is this?* And then he'd laugh at the joke, and I'd go running off with him. He was a simple guy. But he had a big heart."

"Okay," said Max. "That's a story, if a small one." He leaned forward with an unusual intensity. "But how did he show you how to live? How did he teach you how to be a man? How did he... *correct* you?"

"You mean how did he set me on the straight and narrow? Max, Max. I'm surprised at you. Obviously he failed miserably at that."

Max sat back and shook his head as if I were hopeless. "I'm serious, man. I'm not talking about who you sleep with."

"You probably didn't need correcting," said Alice cheerfully. "You were probably as rule-abiding then as you are now."

"You mean prissy?" I said. "Hey, he tried to teach me to box once, when I was about eight."

"He's the winner, then," Max exclaimed as he got up. "You're the winner." He got himself another bottle of beer.

His second. It's not that I care how much people drink, it just seems to be my nature to count things. I was still on my first glass of wine.

"And then there's Jacob Henry or Hertzberg or whatever he was originally," I said. "The mean old shit." I raised my glass.

"May he rest in peace," said Max, raising his bottle.

"He had his good points," said Alice.

"Indeed," said Max.

"Such as?" I asked.

"He was always nice to me," said Alice.

"More accurately, he was polite," said Max. "He was more friendly to the guy who sold him his daily paper."

"He didn't go to your wedding," I said.

"It wasn't exactly a wedding," said Alice. "I mean, he wouldn't have recognized it as such—you know, with a shiksa."

"Of course he would have," said Max. "He wasn't religious. Just stubborn." He looked at me. "You know we didn't actually invite him."

"You didn't invite your own father?" I'd always understood that he simply refused to come.

"He was a harsh, critical guy," said Max, finishing his beer.

"He loved Adam," said Alice.

"Oh, yes," Max said. "He wanted lots of grandchildren. Old world values and radical politics—manual labor and procreation. Noble pursuits, unlike the life of the mind. When I gave him a review of my first book, he tore it up."

I'd heard this story before. "So you were punishing him."

"It was out of fear," Alice said automatically. "He was protecting Max against the Evil Eye or something. Right, Max?"

"And when Adam died—" Max got up abruptly. He collected our bowls. "Okay, next topic. Who wants dessert?"

Alice glanced at me then closed her eyes.

"Chocolate mousse," said Max. He brought over two old-fashioned sundae glasses and set one before each of us. "When he died a few years later, I was glad. It was a relief."

"All right, gentlemen," Alice said firmly. Her husband had controlled the conversation long enough. Max sat down with his own dessert. "We're going to talk about good fathers now. For this goddamn project. You good, kind men are going to help me. So. Do I want a series of portraits of ordinary men, showing that fathers come in all shapes and sizes and ages and colors? Just faces, close-ups? Like twelve on a page with a line at the bottom like 'Fathers: Be a Good One'? Or a series of images that together add up to a more multi-layered message? Maybe each one communicates something different. Except that now that I'm saying it out loud I think maybe abstract is better—the faces, not specific images of men doing anything particular. You know, like the smiley face, that you can project your own ideas onto. What do you think?"

"It was unforgivable," said Max, as if to his dessert.

"Max!" Alice cried. "Stop!"

I got up then. "Thanks, guys, for a lovely dinner. Good luck, Alice. Max, I *imagine* I'll see you Tuesday as usual, and you'll be sober, which will be nice."

Alice exclaimed, "You haven't finished your dessert!" Trying to be perky, she added, "That's a first."

"Lot of firsts here tonight," I observed.

Max looked worn out. "Goodnight, Richard. See you Tuesday." He hadn't touched his dessert either. It seemed we'd both lost our appetites.

Alice sat back in her chair and crossed her arms. "I'm not taking new photos," she said firmly. "But I need to direct my assistant. If portraits, how do you capture the essence without showing the underlying pain? Where's the *joy?*"

She wasn't speaking to me but to the room generally. To herself, to her husband, I didn't know. I laid my hand briefly on her shoulder. "Goodnight, Alice."

Max said quietly, "That's good, Alice. Portraits will tell their own story."

I let myself out. When I got home, I felt lonely and hungry so I had a bowl of raw oats and milk, roughage to draw out the toxins. I wanted so many things.

Richard

I HALF EXPECTED MAX to phone to apologize before I'd gotten in the door. He was usually so good-natured; being a jerk didn't really suit him. But when I didn't hear from him that night or Monday morning, I knew he'd moved on. Max didn't brood. He might brood over ideas, I supposed, that being required by his work, but with people, he lived in the moment.

Monday was a blustery day in the forties. By lunchtime, I was certain that at our Tuesday breakfast Max would cheerfully tell me what he was thinking about, I would understand him all the better, and so I began to look forward to it as I always did.

I left work Monday evening about seven, turning my back on needy clients and thinking vaguely about Max and Alice as I drove home, hoping there wasn't some invisible strain on their marriage that would one day be revealed to me in the form of an announcement of divorce or something. But wasn't I part of the glue that held them together? Weren't we in some crucial way a threesome?

Imagine my surprise when I pulled into my driveway, already icing over from the day's melt off the snowbanks, to see someone sitting on my mudroom steps in the dark. He raised his arm to block the headlights.

"What are you doing here?" I tried not to sound unfriendly. He was wearing the same thing he'd had on the night before.

"Stalking you."

I smiled in spite of myself. "And I'm an axe murderer." I locked the car. "Did you see Max today?"

"Nah. I've been, like, checking out the scene." He stood up and stepped aside so I could get by him on the steps.

"I suppose you'd like to come in."

He shrugged. "I'm not an axe murderer, either."

"All right, come in. Wipe your feet, please." He followed me in. I dropped my briefcase in the living room and returned to find him examining the photos on the refrigerator. I also have a whole wall of photos in the kitchen but he hadn't noticed them yet.

"Who are all these people? Are these, like, your kids?"

"I don't have any children. I'm gay and single. As you must have noticed."

"You could still have kids."

Ah, the new generation. "Those are children of friends and relatives."

"You have a lot of friends."

"I'm about to make dinner. I imagine you haven't eaten?"

"It's strange that I never came in your house before. I was in their house lots of times. It's so different inside, and from the outside you'd think they're the same. Right? I remember theirs perfectly."

The kitchen seemed small with him in it. He paced around it, picking things up and replacing them.

"Jason, Jocko, could you sit down, you're making me nervous." He obediently sat at the counter. "I'm going to make a pot of spaghetti."

If he caught the slight edge in my voice, he ignored it. "Okay. Thanks."

I was trying madly to imagine what he was doing here. He suddenly seemed like a feral cat, as if he could take off at any minute. And now I didn't want to scare him away, at least until I knew what he was doing. I filled a pot of water and peeled an onion, slowly, deliberately, as if he came for dinner every night. He swiveled on his stool back and forth and looked around. Then he said, "No war pictures in here. Just friends, right?" He indicated my photo wall. "That's the war room in there and this is the love room."

I caught myself mid-laugh. The love room? But he was serious. I said instead, "So what did you do today if you didn't see Max?"

"Not much. Just walked around. Up at the university."

"Did you go to his office?"

He hesitated. "No. Not really."

"Not really?" I scraped the diced onions into a pan with olive oil and added a couple of cloves of garlic in slivers. "Why not? You came all this way."

"I was thinking," he began.

I waited.

"I was thinking it might help, it might be better if you asked Mr. Henry for me."

I stopped stirring. "Why can't you ask him yourself?"

He hopped off his stool. At the end of the counter I had a small collection of salt and pepper shakers, mostly kitschy combinations like a pair of sequined high-heeled shoes, a little Dutch couple, and the front and rear ends of an elephant. He picked up a soup and sandwich pair with genuine interest. "These are great."

I added the tomato sauce to the pan and the spaghetti to the boiling water.

"Where'd you *get* all these?"

"People give them to me. Somebody gave me a pair as a joke years ago, I don't even remember which one now. Someone else saw it and thought I collected them. And so it goes. Twenty years later... So what do you do with them? You can't give them away, they're *presents*."

"They're cool," he repeated.

"The funny thing is, I never liked them in the first place. But they've grown on me. People get an idea about you and they believe it and eventually you turn into that person after all."

He looked at me darkly. "That can't be right."

I shrugged.

"That's not right," he said again. "You aren't what people think you are. Just because you—. Those are just *thoughts*. They're not real." He grabbed a salt shaker. "*These* are real, man. *Things* are real. Objects. The things people say, the things people think—." He shook his head. He was staring at the salt shaker, a miniature stylized Matterhorn, gripping it so his knuckles turned white. "Nobody can—. You can't—" He looked at the miniature mountain in his hand bleakly and set it down as if it were a thing he had no right to touch. He put his hands in his pockets. I'd never seen someone so desolate.

If he'd been a child I would have put my arms around him to comfort him. Instead I just stirred the sauce.

"You're right," I said. I wished Max were there. Max could argue any point of view. He could persuade you the earth was flat, at least till you got home. Max would be able to help this kid.

Jocko echoed me without conviction. "Right."

But then something happened. I was used to wishing for Max's physical presence, and I was used to little stabs of longing in my chest, but this was different. This wasn't twinges in my heart, this was a fist squeezing my insides, and out of this squeezing came a squirmy dark rotten thing blooming in my chest like a hungry, mutating peony.

I'm a drama queen, but this took my breath away. All of a sudden *I wanted to be the one.*

Max had been father. He'd had a son. And he was still a teacher. He had students up the wazoo. Young people looked up to him. He taught them, guided them. He had plenty of opportunities. It wasn't fair.

I served the spaghetti in large bowls. "This is my Saturday Night Special. In March—"

"It's Monday."

"In March and April I work every day. Saturday Night Special can come any day. Lighten up, kid. "

"So will you tell him it's a good idea?"

I sat at the other end of the counter. "What is?"

"Come on, man. To take me on as his apprentice. In philosophy."

I considered my spaghetti. "Look, Jocko. You can stay here tonight again if you need a place to stay. You can stay in the guest room. But look"—I turned to him but he kept his eyes on his meal, which he hadn't started. "In terms of your apprenticing yourself to Max, *I* don't know if that's a good idea. I'm in no position to judge. I don't know what you need. How can—"

"But I do!"

"Fine. Then just ask him yourself. I don't see what's the big deal."

"So you won't help me?"

Why was he so desperate? Now he was glaring at me. "Would you please eat?" I said. "You're too thin."

He poked at his food. "He's your best friend, right?"

I didn't answer.

"You could just, like, clear the way. So it won't be such a shock. So it, so he won't say no right off." He waited. "It's just really important that he agree."

I wiped my mouth. "Okay, fine," I said.

He looked at me sideways as if to make sure I meant it. "Now? Will you call him now?"

"Certainly not. It's too late. Tomorrow." I took my bowl to the sink.

Jocko considered his fork a moment, and then, as if he had decided he could trust me, he took a deep breath and began to eat. I watched him out of the corner of my eye. Then I pulled out a loaf of bread and set it in front of him on a cutting board with a knife. It was a heavy round loaf; it felt medieval, as if I were an innkeeper serving a lost and ravenous traveler. Jocko ate in silence while I brooded. He cut one fat slice of bread, then another.

Max had everything. He had a wife, he'd had a son, and he had me who still adored him after all these years and would have given him everything and he knew it. Maybe he had issues about his father or about being a father, but hey, maybe I did, too. And now Max would get this boy-man sitting at his feet looking for the answers to the universe just because he was a goddamn philosopher and I was an accountant? It wasn't fair, and it wasn't right.

No. Max would not get Jocko, too.

Max

As with this one, during my first sabbatical fourteen years ago I'd stayed in town. Adam was only four then so I couldn't work at home, and I wanted to avoid campus for fear of being drawn into university affairs, so I holed up in a corner of the public library or one of the downtown cafes. But I missed my colleagues.

One Saturday in late September of that year I went out to tackle our overgrown front lawn, and Richard Lazarovsky, our neighbor to the south, was out putzing in his neat, beautifully manicured garden full of luscious flowers, most of which I couldn't identify. I barely knew him then except to wave and chat about the weather. He seemed quite private. I knew that his longtime partner had died of cancer a few years earlier, only months after Alice and I moved in with our new baby. Alice had taken over a condolence meal, but we were involved with our own life.

But that Saturday afternoon, feeling a little sheepish about our yard, which with its foot-high grass and weeds was in truth rather more of a meadow than a lawn, I made some joke about his calling the beautification police on us, and we began talking. He was terribly gracious about living next door to our chaos and noise. He claimed to enjoy Adam always yelling hi at him and said the occasional temper tantrum he heard through the open windows gave him hope that Adam wouldn't grow up too classically male because he was so good at expressing his feelings. He, Richard, also said that when Adam and a young friend ran through his flower garden and trampled his newly planted snapdragons, he imagined the snapdragons growing large and devouring the boys like the plant in "Little Shop of Horrors." He seemed to have no expectations of our family or me—was more amused by our unkempt yard than judgmental—and I found that refreshing.

That night I called him and asked him if he wanted to have breakfast with me the next day. He hesitated, clearly surprised, and then he said his workday began at eight. I reassured him that I wasn't asking him for free accounting advice and said I'd meet him at Fleury's, the restaurant around the corner from his office, at seven.

We've been having weekly breakfasts ever since. An odd friendship in some ways. But now he is part of my family, a brother to both Alice and me, as he was an uncle to Adam. He can be uptight and prissy at times, not to mention irritating and quirky—but who isn't? And one could not ask for a more loyal and trustworthy friend.

So here it was, the spring of my second home-based sabbatical, a Tuesday morning in March, cold and sunny. I hurried up the street toward Fleury's. I was excited because I had a new idea and I wanted to hear what he thought.

Generally I liked to change our breakfast venues, rotating among four or five of my favorites, to correspond with changes in direction in my work, and Richard tolerated this well, though he made it clear he'd be perfectly happy eating at the same place every day for the rest of his life, just as he was happy eating the same food for breakfast, which I will never understand. Thus ordinarily I would have called him on Monday night to announce a move to another diner, but I'd felt abashed enough about Sunday's dinner to wait another day before communicating. We could change locations next week.

I rushed into Fleury's a few minutes late as usual and found him already there, as usual, having claimed his favorite table next to the wall with the stuffed swordfish. The fishy décor at Fleury's includes signed photos all over the walls of men proudly holding two- and three-foot-long fish, and cheesy shell sculptures on the tables and counter, some with tiny nets and lobster cages and sea gulls. Authenticity is not a concern of Fleury's.

"Have you ordered?" I asked. He nodded, folded up his paper and put it aside.

"Good morning," he said.

"Look what I've found." I pulled the books from my backpack and spread them over the rest of the table. "Basho!"

"Basho?"

"The poet! The Japanese warrior poet."

"Oh, of course. Sit down, Max, so you can order."

The waitress I knew as Shirley appeared with a little pot of hot water and tea bag and took my order. (I'd given up morning coffee for Alice who'd read that doing so would make us live longer.) I held up one of the books. *The Narrow Road to the Deep North*," I said. I tapped it significantly. "Listen to this." I had marked places with plastic tabs. "Departing spring / birds cry / in the eyes of fish, tears.' Isn't that great? 'In the eyes of fish, tears?' It's funny, right? But also sad. Poignant. How about this one? 'Full moon / North Country weather / unreliable.' That sums up this moment in Vermont, right?"

"Does this have something to do with your book on punishment?"

I closed the book, as Shirley brought Richard's breakfast. Sausage, pancakes, two eggs, toast and home fries, along with a glass of orange juice and a glass of milk. As usual.

"Nothing," I said. "Or rather, I don't know yet."

He raised his eyebrows at me.

"I'm sure there's a connection." I sounded a little defensive even to myself.

"Hey. I'm not questioning the validity of your intellectual exploration. Just curious." He said it in a way that suggested that was exactly what he was doing.

"Ah, fuck you. You're a cretin."

He snorted. "You wish." And dug into his pancakes.

I opened the book again. "Listen to this: 'Summer hills / departing / we pray to the clogs.'"

"What does that mean, 'we pray to the clogs'?"

"I don't know, but isn't it suggestive?"

"Of what? A journey? Are you going to chuck everything and go to Japan? Is that what this is all about?"

I laughed, but something was bothering him. He wasn't his usual easy self. "Hey, what's up? Do I need to apologize for being a jerk on Sunday night, because if so, consider it done. I don't know what got into me. It's this damn book. "

He shook his head, and speared the rest of his sausage. Shirley brought my eggs and English muffin. I could put away almost as much food as Richard, but I liked a light breakfast. "All right, then, consider this: 'Fleas and lice / a horse pissing / near my pillow.' That's the downside of a journey if I ever heard one. Fleas and lice? A horse pissing near your pillow?"

"So you're not going on a journey?"

"Of course not! I'm on sabbatical, trying to write a book about punishment, for God's sake. You know that."

He looked relieved. Then he said, "It's haiku, right? We had to write haiku in fifth grade."

"Right. I doubt it sounded like this, though. Do you want to hear some more?"

"No. I'd rather you tell me...the point. You know how I like to understand you. Is it for the jail?"

"No. That is, I might use this in the jail, but that's not the main thing. There is something about the journey, though. Listen, who says you can't start a new journey at fifty-five? Basho set out for the deep north with nothing but a little backpack. The deep north of Japan for God's sake, dangerous country back then."

Richard wiped his mouth and said cautiously, "A metaphorical journey then?"

I signaled for some more hot water. "God damn. You've just given me a thought."

"You're going to write the punishment book in haiku."

"Better than that. Or worse. This book, the punishment book, is not going as well as it might. As well as it needs to. I've *got* to get a draft out by June first. It's a bitch, actually. And I'm realizing I need to approach it differently. More like a story, with a beginning, middle and end. Of course I don't know how to do that. I don't have the faintest idea, to tell you the truth. But the idea of the journey, which occurred to me the other day, even before I discovered Basho—there's something there. Maybe the universe is trying to tell me that I need to tell the punishment story as my own journey, my own intellectual evolution paralleling the evolution of the ideas historically."

"Can you do that?"

"Are you doubting my capacity or whether it's a successful strategy?"

He smiled then. "I never doubt your capacity, Max. You're the most virile man I know." Richard loves to flirt with me, and I can be silly with him back—it's like being twelve again—but not in public. Which he knows. I was stacking the rest of the books, five in all, and stopped midway. "Listen. This book is really important to me, for a whole host of personal reasons. But I have never injected anything personal into any of my books. I loathe books that do that; they have no place in serious scholarship."

He raised his eyebrows at me over his coffee.

"I know. You think the titles of my books are foolish. But you've never actually read any of the contents."

He smiled. "You don't know that for a fact."

"Anyway, I didn't choose the titles."

"I might reread your books every night for all you know. I might be totally obsessed with them."

"Unlikely. You're obsessed with World War II movies."

"That would be my cover."

I drank the last of my tea. "Listen, you know what I'm *really* worried about? That my intellectual journey would appeal to no one, would have absolutely zero interest, and that what people really want to know is the maudlin story of how a grieving father moves from wanting to punish the whole world to wanting to eliminate the whole concept of punishment. One of those reveal-all, sordid autobiographical things. The very thought makes me sick to my stomach."

"Well, for heaven's sake, don't then. It's nobody's business but yours."

Shirley brought the check and I thanked her. "Right. That's what you're supposed to say. I appreciate it. But—."

"But what?"

I got up and put on my coat, and he followed me to the cash register. It was my turn to pay. We walked outside into the bright sun and I turned up my collar.

"What if it's either that—I mean if that's the story—or nothing? Do I just give up?"

He was silent, looking at me intently. He either wanted to embrace me or slug me; I couldn't tell. He said, "In 'The Bridge on the River Kwai,' when the Japanese general thinks the bridge won't be completed on time he commits hara kiri."

This was like being punched in the gut. When I gathered my wits I said casually, "Thanks, I'll remember that. Fortunately, I'm not quite there yet."

He looked suddenly stricken. "Whoa. Wait. I didn't mean it like that. I'm not suggesting—. It's the Basho-Japan-punishment thing. It's a terrible movie. I mean, it's a good movie, but the leaders are both—."

He was so discomfited, I had to smile. "You don't think I should kill myself over this book?"

"Of course not." Now he was pissed, as if I had tricked him. "Schmuck."

"Hey, you okay? You seem a little off today. Oh, Jeez, I forgot." I dug around in my backpack, under the Basho. "I brought you these. I know you don't have time now, but after tax season." Richard has an annual ritual of indulging in mysteries for several weeks in early May, before gardening season kicks in. I know what he likes, and our local used bookstore collects them for me.

"Thanks, buddy."

"Listen, Richard. I don't want Alice to know I'm struggling with this book."

"Why in the world not? Anyway, she already knows."

"She doesn't know I'm trying to figure out what the story is, and that the story might have something to do with Adam."

"Alice tells you everything," he said sternly.

I laughed at that. "No one tells anyone else *everything*." Richard looked so guilty then, I laughed again. What an open book. In spite of his attempts to the contrary, he is one of the most transparent people I've ever known. "Even you have secrets, eh? Don't worry, you're entitled." I punched him lightly on the shoulder and with that we parted.

Alice

WHEN I GOT HOME FROM WORK on Tuesday night, I discovered
two good things. First, Max wasn't home and a voice mail message
said he was going to his office after the library closed in order to
put in a couple more hours on his book. I was glad it was going
better. Second, the catalogue I'd been waiting for, for almost a
week, had arrived in the mail. Then I was doubly glad Max wasn't
home, because I wanted to look through it in private.

I quickly ate some nondescript veggie leftovers for dinner and
settled in with the catalogue on the couch. I knew enough of its
contents not to look at it while eating. But no sooner had I finished
going through it once than I wanted to talk to someone about it
after all. It was almost nine by then, but Richard's lights were on,
so I went next door.

He looked surprised to see me.

"Hi. What's the matter, were you expecting someone else?"

"No, no, it's fine, come on in. What's up?"

I peered at him—he *was* expecting someone else, it was obvious, or hoping for someone else—and he returned an exaggerated,
theatrical glare.

"Okay, fine, none of my business," I said. "I want to show you something. Come in here." I went into his living room, moved aside a couple of pillows and plopped onto the couch. He sat next to me. I showed him the book.

The photos were in color and black and white. There were street scenes and interiors, single portraits and group shots. There was a ragged child on a pallet on a street with Arabic writing on the wall behind him. There was a thin, raggedy woman on a sidewalk holding a baby with bedding piled next to her as if guarding it.

"Oh, dear," said Richard.

"Yeah."

He turned the pages reluctantly. There were somber, bearded men with dark eyes sitting around a café table, staring impassively at the camera. There was a black and white photo of grizzled, dispirited men in a line for bread or work. There was a woman bending over a stark bathtub in a room with plaster crumbling from the walls, holding a deformed child in her arms. Richard stopped at the image of an emaciated old man wrapped in a diaper-like cloth curled up on a mattress in a dark room, facing the wall. It was a beautiful black and white photo, with muted light coming in apparently from a doorway behind the viewer, as if you'd just stepped into the room and been arrested by the sight. Richard looked at it a long time. He didn't say anything else. Finally I laid my hand across the photo to rescue him. He sat back, relieved.

"Wow," he said.

I shut the book. "So, Richard. What's the difference between these photos and, say, that painting?" I pointed to the one he loved of the battleship H.M.S. Hood, burning and smoking during its last battle on May 24, 1941. The original was in some British naval museum. "Or one of your war movies, like 'Up, Periscope'?"

"Are you kidding? You're kidding, right?"

"No, actually. I mean, in terms of the emotional impact and the art."

Richard looked like he was about to say something smartass and reconsidered. "For one thing, they're made up. Nobody dies in 'Up, Periscope.' Nobody's even injured as far as I know. They make money. They're *actors*, honey."

"Okay. What about the painting? It depicts a real event, right?"

"Sure, more or less. But—"

"Where more than a thousand men died?"

"In the actual battle, yes. But the painting is some guy's imagined version of the battle, not a picture of the thing itself. It's different."

"But they're both art, the photographs and the painting."

"These are art?" He frowned at the catalogue.

"That's the argument. It's a museum exhibit. What do *you* think?"

"Alice, you know I don't know anything about art. This painting of the H.M.S. Hood, it tells a story. I don't know if it's a good *painting*."

"Okay, well, what about your movies?"

"What about them?"

"Like 'The Great Escape.' You think it's a good movie, right? It has emotional resonance for you. Right? Why else would you watch it eighty-five times?"

"Not quite that many, but okay."

"So…"

"So what are you getting at?"

"I don't know exactly. 'The Great Escape' is based on a true story, right?"

"I think so but that's not why—"

"Hold on. All the paintings in here, all these reproductions of famous battles are actual ships sinking or planes blowing up—I mean real battles, right?"

"Right."

"And they're called art. Whether they're good art or not is another question."

"Yeah, so…?" He stifled a yawn.

"Let's leave aside the question of emotional impact, because the paintings don't do it for me. We'll assume they have meaning for someone, maybe you. But these photographs. They're disturbing, right? They're disturbing because the content is … distasteful, let's say. Upsetting. But they're made more disturbing by the fact—I mean, I'm wondering, I don't know—the fact that they're beautiful. They're beautiful photographs and so you want to keep looking at them."

Richard looked at his watch.

"I'm sorry, I know it's late, but this is important."

"Darling, I know. I mean, it's obvious. You're in a state of distress. But, sweetie—"

"Is it art or is it voyeurism? Is it documenting or exploiting? Is it compassion for the subject or schadenfreude? Where's the line between them?" I took the book from him. "How does a photographer do honest work? That's the question."

"Ah. Well." He stood up. "Now that we've established that. Which, my darling, I can see actually *is* a most worthy topic. Let's continue this conversation… over the weekend."

"You mean in April." I took his outstretched hand and he pulled me up. "You're a hopeless friend at this time of year."

"I know," he said. "But I'm seeing you on Friday night for dinner, yes?"

"I can't talk about it then. I don't..."

He held onto my hand and led me to the side door. I put on my jacket while he held the catalogue, gazing at the cover—a beautiful young Afghan woman with haunted eyes. I said, "It makes me want to do something."

"Like take pictures?"

"This is why I *don't* take pictures anymore. I don't know."

He opened the mudroom door and said rather apologetically, "Do you want to watch 'The Great Escape' on Saturday night? Free popcorn."

I love Richard, but he was failing me. "I've seen it, thanks."

He sighed. "Alice, if you were in the hospital a hundred miles away, I'd come visit you. If you got hurt in the middle of the night, I'd pull my sorry ass out of bed to help you. But as far as I can see, you just need a sounding board who's a lot more alert than I am right now—and maybe a lot smarter. You're not dying. Which I'm grateful for, by the way. But I'm happy to talk with you more about this later and offer my extremely limited wisdom, for what it's worth, which is not much. As you've been the first to remind me, many times."

I rolled my eyes at him and kissed him on the cheek. "I love you. Go to bed."

The cold air was refreshing. Richard keeps his house warmer than we do—too warm. Maybe that's why he could watch "The Great Escape" forty-seven times or whatever it was by now. Big, happy Richard with his ice cream and popcorn in his too-warm house watching stupid old war movies.

God, what was wrong with me, Richard was my best friend. I wanted to wail. The stars were bright overhead, as bright as they get over our small city. That one was probably a satellite. What would it see if it could zoom in on me? An ordinary desolate middle-aged woman, temporarily deranged? I suddenly wanted to take a picture of myself, like the woman who photographed herself with one eye swollen shut. But not me standing pathetically under the stars, a speck in the great universe. I had a different image. I wanted to create an image of myself lying on a couch like Goya's Naked Maja but with my belly sliced open like the wolf's so the grandmother and Little Red Riding Hood and god knows what else could get out.

The car was in the driveway; Max was home. I tried to remember children's books with wolf illustrations. Had I ever seen such an image or was I making it up? Did we have any old paperback picture books still stashed in a box under the eaves? But I must have given them all away. After Adam died, I was ruthless about getting trapped in sentiment. I'd seen bereaved mothers fall into a fretful, nauseating self-absorption that turned them into children, or little old ladies, anxious and demanding, aging but never growing. My aversion to such women encountered in grief groups helped me get going again. Women like that made shrines to their sons, with candles and beads and statues of the Virgin Mary, and football trophies and stuffed animals from childhood and early art projects. I would not make a shrine to Adam.

All right, so we didn't have any old picture books. It didn't matter; I didn't need an illustration of the wolf being cut open, with Granny and Little Red Riding Hood hopping out. I had it in my head. Suddenly chilled, I hurried inside.

An extraordinary urgency filled me. I didn't know why or what it meant. But it seemed to me that not only my marriage but my very life depended on it. I recognized that I was having a moment of high melodrama, as Richard would have said. Nonetheless it seemed to me at that moment under the stars that if I didn't listen, something awful would happen. I might shrivel up inside, irredeemably and forever. I would never move from this particular moment in time. I'd be stuck in the same loop, round and round, over and over till my body gave out, my soul having died along the way. I would never feel anything new or experience any more growth or light or joy. Although I had no religion nor did I need one, this was a matter of my spiritual life or death.

But what was the "this"? What was I being called to do?

Richard

As TIRED AS I WAS, after Alice left I didn't go to bed right away. I went upstairs and stuck "The Bridges of Toko-Ri" into the VCR. In spite of the wooden acting of William Holden, this is one of the all-time great war movies, not about World War II but Korea, the Air Force during the Korean War. Descriptions always highlight Fredric March and Grace Kelly, but the heart of the movie is the relationship between Holden and the two helicopter pilots who rescue him early on, Mickey Rooney and Earl Holliman. And what makes the movie stand out is the fact that, contrary to Hollywood conventions where the good guys survive, in this movie they don't. All three of the major heroes get killed at the end. It's completely shocking. You could argue that we're set up for it, and I suppose artistically that might be true. Nonetheless, the actual dying-in-war of these three guys has the same incredibility that death does in real life. You just can't take it in.

I lay on my bed and listened to the movie with my eyes closed. Where was Jocko? It was probably twenty-five degrees outside. It was also after ten. I chided myself; he wasn't a kid, he could take care of himself. And I was extremely relieved he hadn't arrived when Alice was there. I'm not sure what I would have said. She might have gotten the wrong idea about an attractive eighteen-year-old sleeping in my house. Just possibly.

Then the doorbell rang, just as it had only three nights ago, only this time it was the side door. I padded downstairs in my slippers, glad I hadn't yet changed clothes.

"Do you know what time it is?" I demanded, more brusquely than I intended.

"Hey, I didn't want to bother you earlier." He lumbered past me into the kitchen. Then with irritation, "You're not my keeper."

"That is certainly true, nor would I want to be. But it would appear that I *am* your host, and this is not an inn with the doors open at all hours."

"The doors aren't open ever. You could give me a key."

"I don't give out keys to my house. You don't *live* here, you know."

He laughed at that. "You wish."

I remembered my own similar comment to Max that morning and wondered whether I could throw Jocko out now. But he was taking off his parka and hanging it on the back of a kitchen stool.

He said then, with a transparent effort to sound offhanded, "So, did you, like, happen to speak to Mr. Henry today? Did you ask him about me?"

"I did not. And now I'm going to bed." I left the kitchen.

"Hey, man! You said you would!"

I turned back to him, surprised by his fierceness but roused to my own. "I lied."

He had followed me into the living room. Now he stood a few feet from me, his face pale, his breath shallow. A less hefty man than myself might have been knocked over by the force of his anger; I withstood the storm. But he wasn't ready to challenge me to the death evidently. He took a step backward and sank into the couch. "Shit."

I relaxed. "Indeed. Perhaps we can talk about it in the morning."

"I'll be gone in the morning."

I had nothing to say to this, though I felt a pang. I headed to the stairs.

"Could you—" he began. I stopped.

He leaned forward, gazing at the floor, with his hands clenched between his knees. "Okay, I got it. You're not going to help me. It's like Adam said once, you have to be self-sufficient." He pronounced it like sufFISHent.

"Adam?"

"So I'll just ask him myself. Only, the thing is, if this doesn't work, I'm going to kill myself."

"I don't know how self-sufficient that is."

"I was thinking about it today. When Adam said that. It was like this outside, I don't know what month, but it was colder than a witch's tit. That's what Adam said. We thought that was hilarious. We wanted to camp outside, and everyone said it was too cold but Adam had seen this show about winter camping and he was like, *Dad, we have to!* He was always the adventurous one. And you know they let him do things my parents would never let me do. Sleep outside when it was thirty degrees? Maybe it was above freezing, but anyway what I remember is when we woke up, there was frost on the grass and we could see our breath. They came out in the night and put extra blankets on us but still. Adam said he had to pee, and I did, too, but it was too cold to get out of our sleeping bags. So Adam kind of hopped over to the door and unzipped his sleeping bag halfway—and unzipped the tent just enough—and kept it kind of clutched around him so there was nothing showing but his dick. He said it was too cold to pee, but then he did anyway. We laughed so hard we fell over.

"And then we wanted to go inside—you know, we were just in the back yard—but we stayed in our sleeping bags and just kind of hopped from the tent to the side door, and inched our way up the stairs, and we kind of fell over the doorjam into the mudroom. And when we finally got up, we realized we'd left our clothes in the tent. Mr. and Mrs. Henry were in the kitchen, and we told them the problem, but Mr. Henry said, *You have to be self-sufficient.* Adam made this fish face with his lips and started repeating, *self-sufF-ISHent.* Which we also thought was hilarious. I think we were in second grade."

"Did you go back out and get the clothes?"

"I don't remember."

I stood behind the stuffed chair across from him and now leaned on the back of it. "I'd like to understand something. You've come all this way to apprentice yourself to Max. You crash here because you're afraid to go over there. You hang around town all day doing God knows what when you could easily track him down. What is it—what are you afraid of?"

He shook his head as if I were hopeless. He straightened the stack of new mysteries on the coffee table in front of him and studied a pile of magazines.

"Have you ever had sex?" I said out of the blue. Honestly, I don't know what possessed me.

"Whoa, whoa! None of your goddamn business. Step back, Jack. Is this a come-on?"

I laughed. "Hardly. The truth? I'm trying to figure out whether you're an adult."

He leaned back and opened his arms, resting them over the back of the couch. "I'm a troll, man. Trolls mature early. Way early."

It seemed the answer was *yes*. I was curious about him. "What is it you're really looking for?"

He jumped up. In two steps he stood before my little Santa Fe chest and started fingering the things in the bowl on top. It was a full minute before he spoke again. "The truth, huh? I told you. The secret of the universe. Good and evil. Is there even such a thing as good and evil? What's real? What's true? What makes a person good or bad?" He paused. "What's this?"

"It's a canoe Adam made for me years ago."

"And this picture. Is that you and Adam, with those water uzis? Cause he and I used to play with those."

I said nothing. What to do? What did he want?

"You were thinner," he commented.

"A bit," I said. "Look, I'm going to bed. If you're hungry, help yourself to food. Leave the canoe there, please."

"I don't need your help," he said, not looking at me.

I observed his profile, his erect bearing, the tension he carried in his powerful, toned young body. He wouldn't look at me. I didn't know what he needed. I knew only what I needed, to do and not to do.

"Good night, Jocko."

Later as I lay in bed, a funny memory came to me. Ordinarily I didn't think about Adam much, in the sense of having a full-out, organized remembering, first this, then that. I supposed Jocko was reminding me.

It was when Adam was about six or seven, or maybe a little older. How old are you when you start playing on teams? In any case, he was an ardent soccer player and one Saturday he came over to my house as he often did, wanting to see if I was going to his game. He told me all about it in the kitchen before I even had a chance to tell him I couldn't. I had to work. Fortunately, this was true. I did not want to stand outside in the cold for an hour or more, even for Adam.

"But it's Saturday!" he wailed.

"I'm sorry, Bo. But Alice and Max are going, yes?" We called him Adam Bobo for some reason I've forgotten.

"Mom is. Dad's coming later."

He picked up a pair of salt and pepper shakers—a soccer ball and shoe—and clinked them around on the counter angrily.

"Adam, honey, I'd like to, but—"

"I know, I know. Stop talking about it!" He put down the ceramic shoe but clutched the tiny ball as if he wanted to squeeze it to death; I relieved him of it for his sake. He was about to work himself into a snit, and I had to meet a client in twenty minutes. I knelt and put my hands on his arms.

"Adam, what would you like to do right now?"

He shook off my arms and stomped around the kitchen in frustration. Suddenly he stopped. You could almost see the cartoon idea balloon over his head. His face lit up.

I was still crouched on one knee over by the refrigerator. He stood across the room by the sink. He unzipped his pants, pulled out his little penis, and without a moment of hesitation, sent a stream into the center of the room.

I didn't move. Had he been a kitten, I would have shoved him roughly out the back door. Had he been my son, I might have been outraged and shouted at him. Instead, I just watched. His gleeful, exuberant little stream dribbled to nothing. Now he quickly zipped up his pants. The pool in the middle of the floor began to flow toward the refrigerator. He looked at me nervously.

I stood up. "What was that all about?" I tore off a handful of paper towels. "Adam?"

He said nothing.

I mopped up the pee and threw away the towels. I gave the floor another swipe with a soapy sponge. He stood watching me. "Sorry," he said softly.

Down at his level again, I asked curiously, "Was it fun?"

He hesitated, then nodded imperceptibly.

"Good," I said.

Then he broke into a huge grin and bolted out the back door, slamming it behind him. Only later did he ask me not to tell, but he must have known I wouldn't anyway. Some things between friends are meant to be kept secret.

Max

As noted, I had no interest in writing a memoir or anything remotely resembling it. However, Lazarovsky's sarcastic suggestion about writing the book in haiku rattled around in my half-empty brain, and I found myself idly wondering whether some poetic form could structure the book, or at least parts of it. The little academic inside me said scornfully, *That's ridiculous. Would never work.* The fifty-five-year-old quietly lurching toward mid-life and wanting to avoid the red convertible Porsche, the affair, and God knows what else said, *Why the fuck not?*

"Lurching *toward*" was wishful thinking. "Staggering around within" would be more accurate.

On Wednesday I sat in my office and watched the rain lash the windows. It was school vacation and the place had emptied out, so I felt free to work on campus without interruption. I'd been struggling with the chapter on responsibility. It was too dry, too academic, pedantic. The rivulets of rain on the panes were more interesting, in fact fascinating, rhythmic, like a poem. I started the chapter over, calling it "Thirteen Ways of Looking at Responsibility." The words poured out in a rush.

Thirteen Ways of Looking at Responsibility

1. What is responsibility? What does it mean? What do we mean when we say we hold someone responsible for another's death?

2. Responsibility does not equal causation. In other words, having responsibility for an event does not necessarily mean you caused it. The Israelis were held responsible for the massacre at Sabra and Shatila in 1982, even though they didn't commit it, because they didn't prevent it. When is a parent responsible for not preventing an accident?

3. *Feeling* responsible is not evidence of, does not *prove*, actual responsibility. Then what *is* the relationship between feeling and actually being responsible?

4. What is guilt? How is guilt-the-feeling related to guilt-the-legal-condition?

5. Feeling guilty is not evidence of, nor does it prove, actual guilt. Getting stopped by a cop can make you feel guilty, whether you've done anything wrong or not.

6. Proposition: A person responsible for causing an adverse event deserves a chance to provide the remedy—if the event can be remedied. This would apply to burglarizing a house, vandalizing a mailbox, jacking a six-pack, perhaps even burning down an old barn which can be rebuilt. Punishment, jail time in particular, serves no social or individual purpose.

7. But what if no remedy is possible? What if the barn was loved by many generations, the mailbox a work of art, or the thing injured or destroyed unique and unreplicable? What if a living being was killed?

8. The young man hunting with his buddies caused the old farmer's death. Responsibility is not in question. The question concerns the appropriate moral, social, ethical response. What can the kid do to "restore" justice? What, in any moral social system, makes sense for him to do? Help the widow? Take on the farming duties of the old man? Drive the tractor to get the hay in? Or shift his life to prison, where he can work in the kitchen or the fields and go to classes and write poetry and perhaps either serve as someone's "boy" or abuse someone weaker, and learn additional criminal behaviors like how to bribe guards, smuggle drugs, intimidate others with violence—all at taxpayers' expense.

9. Focus: But is the question here what to do with people who *are* responsible for a death, even though it's accidental, as in the case with this kid? Or is this example merely a warm-up, a preamble to the more profound and interesting question of whether or not—or rather the degree to which—anyone carries responsibility for any random, unlucky or tragic event?

10. Example #2: On a school outing in the Swiss alps, where off-trail skiing is widely practiced and enjoyed, a beloved teacher leads a group of students, all skilled skiers, down a mountainside. Avalanches, though uncommon, are an accepted risk, and everyone in the group has had avalanche training. Unfortunately on this day an avalanche does occur, and two students and the teacher are caught in it. The teacher and one of the students survive. The other student is found too late. What responsibility does the teacher bear? He didn't cause the avalanche. He

could not have prevented it. He could have led the students down a different mountain, or not gone out at all that day. Does that make him responsible? *Is an adult in charge of young people always responsible for their safety no matter what?*

11. Is a scout leader responsible for the safety of his scouts on a camping trip, no matter what? What if a child using a kitchen knife cuts his thumb? What if he trips and hits his head on a rock? What if he gets bitten by a snake? What if something happens and, God forbid, the child dies?

I stopped abruptly. Hold on. Too personal, and not what I intended. I took a deep breath. What would Alice say if I showed her what I'd written? We didn't talk about Adam. Nor was she much one for speculation. She left that to me; she tended to assert, where I wondered. She preferred certainty to mystery or ambiguity. When it came to Adam's death, she had a hierarchy of those responsible—the boy who was with him at the time, the boy's father who led the troop, me, herself and Adam, in that order, or maybe in reverse order, I wasn't sure anymore. She would have blamed God, too, if she'd believed one existed.

But I was oversimplifying. Alice called herself "a simple girl"—a reference to the little Puritan girl in a small Thanksgiving display her parents had when she was growing up—and in some ways this was true, but of course she was as complicated as the next person. I thought I knew her, but the occasional despair under her cheer frightened me. I worried that she would surprise me one day by announcing she was leaving me, or having an affair or God knows what. Maybe a sex change.

I wrote:

> 12. If a cat gets hit by a car, who is responsible? The driver who actually hit the cat? The owner, who could have (should have?) kept the cat inside? Did she not take on responsibility for the cat's wellbeing upon adopting it? What about the cat itself, fully grown and experienced with streets? *What does it mean to be responsible?*

My neck hurt. I dug my fingers into my shoulders to rub out the knots. Far from being fun, this effort had exhausted me. What was I thinking? I read over what I'd written and sighed. I knew it wouldn't work, but I finished it nonetheless, since I'd set out to write thirteen—thirteen ways of looking at a problem, a blackbird, anything that mattered.

> 13. A cat is not a child. If a child runs out into the street when a parent isn't looking and gets hit by a car, is the parent responsible?

It was all I could write for now. It is unfortunate that the griefs in one's life simply pile up. I mean one's own and those of others, which are easier to think about but nonetheless add to the overall weight. The widow of the farmer shot in the field, the teacher whose student died in the avalanche, the owners of the cat I ran over some thirty years ago, even Richard who lost his partner and never talks about him. Their griefs add to one's own, but… it wasn't really like stones piling up—that was wrong. It was more like a giant pool, endlessly fed by streams, that overflowed its banks and spilled down the mountainside. I was the mountainside, wearing away.

I laughed out loud at that. A mountainside? I was a mere pebble being washed down the mountain like every other pebble.

Then I felt weary. There was nothing you could do about the grief, but goddamn it, you could do something about the rest of it—the rage, the blame, the urge to hurt. Good God, wasn't there enough suffering in the world?

Max

I TOOK A BREAK FOR LUNCH and wandered around the university library, the kind of thing you can do on sabbatical and no other time. I spent a luxurious hour in the oversized folio section looking at photographs. Alice used to take pictures; she's taught me a lot about how to see. I found a gorgeous collection of dancers. My son was unusually graceful; I've sometimes wondered whether he might have grown up to be a dancer.

I returned to my office mid-afternoon. I read over what I'd written and concluded it was worthless and then I sat in my desk chair, swiveling back and forth, imagining I was meditating but in truth merely watching the sleet and wondering whether I should just go home. In my cozy, book-lined office, I often feel deliciously alone, but the weather was making me feel dreary and spent.

The knock on the door was so quiet I wondered whether I'd imagined it. Then it came again, this time with more confidence, as if my visitor had overcome some tentativeness and concluded that he did, after all, want to be heard. "Entrez," I called, and when no one appeared, I went to the door with some irritation. It couldn't be a student. When students visited, they barged in.

Indeed it wasn't a former student of mine. It was, however, a young person, and he was dripping wet. He was my height, with matted shoulder-length hair, a soaked parka and jeans, and a wet book bag. "Yes?"

"Mr. Henry?"

"Yes."

"I'm Jason."

"Jason?"

"Jason Green. You know, Adam's friend."

Jason Green? Jason Green. *What the—?* The young man's face rearranged itself briefly into a familiar, eager look and then went slack, waiting. I held onto the doorknob. Jason Green, Jason Green. Minutes passed, or mere seconds, I couldn't tell. Finally I released the doorknob and stepped back into the room.

"Jason Green. Come in, come in. I didn't –. You look different."

He took off his dripping parka and hung it over a chair. He ran his hands over his wet head and flicked them so the drops flew off. I handed him some folded brown paper towels. "Jason Green all grown up. Have a seat. It's, ah, it's been a long time."

"Eight years." He remained standing, wet paper towels in hand.

I blotted drops from the edge of my desk. "Of course. Well. What brings you back here? You left the state, I believe." On the papers spread across my desk, tiny wet circles of blurred ink appeared. I took the remaining paper towels from Jason's hand and pressed them against the wet spots. It was useless. I dropped the towels in the trash and took up my seat behind my desk. "Where do you live now?"

Jason hadn't moved. He looked around my office, giving me a chance to observe him more closely. In his ratty, oversized sweater, collarless shirt and his torn jeans, he resembled my students. But my philosophy students tend to have a lean, undernourished look, like scrawny 1950s intellectual beatnik types, and this fellow, this new version of Jason Green the almost-adult, looked like, well, more like a man. It wasn't his physical stature; he was tall but he hadn't filled out completely. His face had a mature cast, but it wasn't that, either. It was the way he held himself. Now that I had a chance to gather my wits, I observed that he *felt* like a man. Not an equal certainly, but a physical peer, a challenger among the great apes. This was a feeling I almost never had about *students,* but that I had experienced regularly with the young men I'd met at the jail. *Hey, man, I'll take you on.* At the same time, beneath that power often lay uncertainty—*how do you manage the world?* Such boy-men might pick a fight and expect to win, but fall apart if you said the wrong thing. The contradiction was touching. And tricky.

This observation came to me in seconds, as did the memory of Jason as a confident, energetic kid. Adam had considered him his best friend. But from my perspective back then he was also a little... not exactly scary but suspect, as if he might be capable of torturing cats or setting out thumbtacks in your driveway. Alice and I had talked about him often. Was he a good kid or not? But Adam had loved him and never reported anything untoward. Before Adam died, Alice and I had concluded Jason probably just had a sensitive, brooding nature. Afterward, we didn't know what to think.

"You have a lot of books," Jason said now, running his fingers along them.

"Jason Green. You're an adult! I always remember you as ten. You—you look well." I made an effort to be polite.

"I'm still in high school. I mean I was. How come your books aren't in order? Hemingway, Cather, Nietzsche. Like what kind of system is that?"

"Why don't you sit down? Stay a while?" It was a poor attempt at lightheartedness, and Jason didn't smile.

"Is there a system? I used to, like, work in the library at school."

"There is a system. My own."

Jason seemed genuinely engrossed in examining my books.

I said, "You must be a senior now." Of course I knew this better than I knew my own birthday.

"I was. I got expelled." He said it matter-of-factly.

"What for?"

"Just drugs. No big deal. I mean, what a crock of shit. It's like everybody does it, only I got caught."

Jason dropped into the easy chair over the back of which hung his parka. If the seat was wet, he didn't mention it. "I mean, it's not like it was cheating or stealing or anything."

"Ah."

"I didn't hurt anybody. Don't you think there's like a hierarchy of wrongdoing, Mr. Henry?"

"What are you doing here, Jason?"

"Like I said, I got expelled. It's no big deal—I've been expelled before, from other schools—but my dad—" he hesitated.

"How is your father?"

"Fine, I guess. He always said that after high school I could do what I wanted and he'd help. I mean, I could go to college or something else, like flight school or art school or whatever, and he'd pay for it. But I gotta get through high school."

"That sounds reasonable."

"Yeah but see, the problem is like no high school where we live will take me anymore and Dad won't pay for any more private schools. Shit, I don't want to go back to private school anyway. They suck."

"What *do* you want?"

"I want you to teach me." He had continued to study the bookcase nearest his chair and now he looked at me for the first time.

I had an almost physical reaction, bile rising in my throat. "What do you mean? You want to sit in on one of my classes at the college? But what for?"

"No, no. I can do that anywhere. I mean—you know how it used to be, you wanted to like learn blacksmithing, you went to the blacksmith and he made you his apprentice? I want to study philosophy. Like be your apprentice."

I leaned back in my chair, as if to get as far away as possible. Jason jumped up and went back to inspecting the books up close.

"How curious," I said. "Why philosophy? Why me? I don't really—. There are many other teachers I'd think you'd be more... comfortable with. For that matter, a dozen other disciplines you'd find more suitable. In other schools."

"What, don't you think I'm smart enough? I'm screwed up, not stupid."

I smiled in spite of myself. I wondered whether Jason was the kind of young man who attracted women.

"You were a smart boy, yes. I remember the games you and Adam used to make up. But what have you been doing since? What have you been reading?" I swiveled casually back and forth, clutching the arms of my chair.

"I don't know if that's any of your business. But I'll tell you one thing I wonder about is good and evil. That's philosophy, isn't it?

Right and wrong, moral dilemmas, fate and free will. Shit like that. Why do certain things happen and not other things? They don't talk about that in regular school, that's for sure."

"Does your father know you're here?"

"What does that have to do with it?"

"In other words, no."

"I'm a free agent."

"What does he think about this... plan of yours... to study with me?"

"He said if I could like find a teacher for three months until I'd ordinarily graduate from high school, he'd agree. He'd even pay for it. Then at the end of three months, I'm home free. He said you wouldn't do it."

I stopped moving. "Why would he say that?"

Jason stood in the middle of my office, unsupported by bookcase or chair, and his voice was strained. "Mr. Henry, you've got to teach me. I've just—. You've got to."

Was he pleading or threatening? I didn't care for either. I said, "Let's look at this logically. What is it you really need? To take the GED?"

"What? The GED? No, man, I could've taken that years ago and passed it. I told you I was smart. It's not about that, it's about--"

"What?"

"I don't know. Look, it's got to be you and not some other bozo."

"Why is that?"

"I don't know. I just know... Oh fuck it. I shouldn't have come. Thanks for nothing." He pulled his jacket from the chair.

"Tell me something. Why did your father say I wouldn't teach you?"

"Come on, man. Like you don't know? Like you don't know how a person might feel when you're his best friend and then suddenly one day you never want to see him again? Gimme a break. I know you hate him. You hate us. He didn't have to tell me."

I stood up then. The sudden turn of the conversation was immensely distasteful to me. I wanted Jason to leave.

"I don't hate you, Jason," I said carefully. "Or your father. I'm sure he understands why it might have been difficult for me to see him immediately after...Adam died. It's a friendship I regret losing. Please tell him that, but it won't change anything. In any event, I can't possibly take you on as an apprentice." I stepped around the desk to show Jason out. But he remained immobile, a foot from the door, wet jacket in hand.

"I know. It was a stupid idea. It's strange, though. I had this vision. It was so clear, it's like it was real. I'd come to your office every day and we'd talk about life—you know, like about what matters. What no one else wants to talk about. You could tell me about Aristotle and Plato and what those guys thought—I mean, if it was relevant—and we'd discuss it. You know, like, I don't know, like..."

"Look, it's impossible. First of all, I'm on sabbatical. Second, I don't teach ethics anymore. I wouldn't even be on campus if it weren't school vacation. And frankly, if I ever *were* going to take on an 'apprentice' as you call it, with all due respect it wouldn't be you." Suddenly I was exhausted.

Jason narrowed his eyes, appraising me. We stood a few feet apart. Finally he spoke. "Right. So... what am I going to do?"

"I don't know. Ask your father. He was a good father."

"He's a terrible father. He hates me. I can never do anything right. He's been that way for years."

I didn't have the energy to argue. "All right, he's a terrible father. And a worse scout leader. As long as we're telling the truth."

I should have just let Jason go. It was an uncharacteristic little jab—something I might have done to Alice or Richard, but not to someone I didn't know, and certainly not to a student. The last thing I wanted was to prolong this little drama. But I was worn out. I wasn't myself. I was a bear cuffing a cub, turning it over to expose its underbelly. The sleet ran in rivulets down the windowpanes.

"But that's not true," Jason said. "He was a good scout leader. It wasn't his fault Adam was killed."

There. He'd said it. He was gazing at the door. Jason Green who was with Adam when he died. On the mountain. Eight years later here was Jason Green in the middle of my office talking about that day. The scene I never saw, the scene I had imagined a thousand times, rose up before me. Ten-year-old Adam—

"Whose fault was it?" I asked quietly.

"Look, if I could just, like, observe. I don't have to be your apprentice. I'll just go to your lectures, sit over on the side and just listen while you're meeting with students, I won't say anything, I'll just listen and I'll figure it out."

"What happened that day, Jason?"

"You've thought a lot about right and wrong because you're a philosopher, and that's what you do for a living, right? So you know why things happen and what's worth worrying about and what isn't. Right?"

"Where were you when Adam fell? Where was your father?"

"He fell, okay? I've told you before! He just fell!" Jason grabbed the doorknob. He turned on me furiously. "It was *your* fault!" He fled, and the door banged against the wall behind him.

I closed the door and returned to my desk.

The little punk. I sighed. *My* fault. What did he know about being a father? About responsibility? I wondered at myself, snorted at the absurdity. Why had I asked him that in the first place? What was I doing? My fault. Jason's fault. No one's fault. Useless roads to go down, and yet… Here he was.

Eventually the rain stopped and I thought vaguely this was a good thing because Jason didn't have a raincoat.

Jason Green. Jason Green.

I'd never expected to see him again. I hadn't thought about him in years. Eight years after Adam's death, here he was, appearing out of nowhere. Jason Green. Who wanted me to take him on as an apprentice. What madness. It was laughable. It was frightening. Insane. Perverse. So perverse as to be… completely unthinkable.

And yet.

Richard

Ordinarily I can block out the muffled sounds from my waiting room easily, but I recognized Max's voice. What was he doing here? He had only come to my office a handful of times over our nearly fifteen-year friendship; hearing his voice now, urgent and low talking to my receptionist, filled me with dread. Freddie, my receptionist-assistant who double-checks my returns, typically does an excellent job of calming frantic or demanding clients. But I had no one in my office at that moment so I opened the door.

"Max! What is it?"

"Sorry to bother you, but have you got a second?" His lined face, which only got more handsome over the years, looked strained.

I ushered him into my office. Freddie raised his shoulders in apology. I waved him off.

Max stood at the window. My office is small, with just my desk and two chairs in front of it. The windows run the length of the room so it feels larger than it is. "Such a nice view," said Max absently. "The trees and all."

"Yes. It's stopped raining."

He said nothing. I stood waiting, observing him, hiding my anxiety. *Relax,* I told myself. *You haven't done anything wrong.* But now Max seemed to have forgotten why he'd come.

"Max, what's the matter?"

He turned to me. "I'm not sure. I don't know if I've just done something… inexcusable. Or if I've just missed an opportunity for, I'm not sure, really a once-in-a lifetime… or just been selfish and narrow, maybe even cruel. Or what." I'd never heard him ramble like this.

"Jesus Christ, what happened?"

"I wasn't prepared. I was taken by surprise. But that's no excuse."

"Max, what *happened?*"

"Right. Richard, remember the boy who was with Adam when he died? Adam's best friend, they used to play together all the time. His name was Jason Green. You may not remember him. He came to my office this morning. He's eighteen, and he wants to study with me."

He was obviously mystified by this. But without accusation: he didn't know I'd seen him.

"What did you say? Look, have a seat. No one's due for another ten minutes." I moved to my own chair behind my desk.

"I said no, of course. I was surprised, reacted badly. Jason Green?" Max ran his hand through his hair. "I don't know. I upset him." He remained glued to his spot by the window, watching the world. "He's tall, as tall as you or I. Almost an adult but not quite. Good-looking kid. Not charismatic exactly but has a magnetism that struck me when he first walked in. He wants to study *philosophy*, for God's sake."

"Is that so weird?" If he'd seen my face he would have seen a contorted attempt at bitter irony, but he didn't look.

"For an eighteen-year-old? Yes. I—. It's great that someone would want to study philosophy, ethics in particular, even he,

82

I guess, but why? That is"—he ran his hand through his hair again—"I know why. Obviously it has to do with Adam. I just—. Not *him*. But then, why not? Of all people, why not he more than most?"

I didn't know what to say. I picked up a pencil. But Max, goddamn him, is preternaturally sensitive to the smallest gesture, at least when not astonished into complete self-absorption. He became immediately apologetic.

"I'm sorry, Richard. I know you're busy. But you know I can't possibly tell Alice. I don't know *what* she'd do. She's so angry. I don't even know what *I'm* going to do."

"But you told him no."

"Yes, definitely." He sighed. "I think that was probably a mistake."

"I doubt it."

"You don't think so?" He searched my face with great intensity. "You think I should reject a sincere request by a young person to study in such an intimate way? Listen, I wanted to kill him, to knock him across the room and throw him out the window. But I also feel like a jerk, and I have a hole in my gut, and I, I, I have this, I have a, a..."

"A longing?"

He gave me another piercing look, as if afraid I was mocking him. But it was like a puff of smoke that quickly dispersed. He had so much doubt in himself he couldn't afford to doubt me. "Yeah."

I nodded. I knew longing, and he knew I knew. I smiled to reassure him. "I'm sure it was a good thing to tell him no. Don't worry. You have plenty of other things to do." Now Jason would leave town and things would go back to normal, his brief presence a mere ripple on the surface of our lives. No major upheaval. No big drama. That was the best outcome. He had no right to come back here anyway.

Max gazed out the window again. I was ready to get back to work. I said, with some impatience, "So what are you going to do?"

"Find him."

"*Find him?*"

"It shouldn't be too hard. We're connected. He's magnetic and I'm…determined."

"Wait, I thought—"

"Look, this isn't easy. I've been through a lot in the past hour. It was shocking to see this kid who, who might have been Adam. I mean Adam might have been him. Of course he's not. Obviously. But what a strange thing that he should come up here now." He turned to me again. I bit my lip.

"Thanks, old pal," Max sad. In such a setting he would ordinarily have given me a quick hug—he was so physical—but I had positioned myself behind my desk, and now it was too late. He was hurrying through my waiting room and out the door.

In any case, if we had embraced I might have tried to squeeze him to death. Or get him in a headlock and tried to break his neck.

From the window I watched him cross the street below. The wind blew coffee cups and paper over the sidewalk. He buttoned his coat. He never wore a hat unless it was below zero; he was vain about his thick curly hair. He strode up the hill toward the university; I supposed that's where he expected to find Jocko. My big doughy self strained after him like a dog after its master.

I was a pathetic specimen compared to Max. The great irony was that my house, my office, my work all were very neat and tidy compared to his, but my body, my heart, everything that mattered was a sloppy mess, which is reason enough to hate someone. But Max didn't seem to think I was pathetic. I knew he loved me, and for years that had saved me from a certain amount of self-loathing. How could I hate him? *You don't hate Max, you love Max.*

I hate Max.

How I wished we could communicate without words.

And Jocko? My erstwhile houseguest? The young man who had felt comfortable coming to *my* house, for whatever reason? And then came back—three times! Who gave up on trying to get me to approach Max for him—rightly. But the idea of Max taking him on as an Adam-substitute who would sit at his feet and understand the meaning of life? It was ridiculous!

I know about ridiculous, I have a corner on ridiculous. I spend my free time watching old movies whose lines I can repeat by heart, my work is as narrow and unimaginative as is possible to get outside of taking tolls at the New York Thruway, my two closest friends are a straight couple to whom I pretend I'm essential, I haven't had another serious partner since Hecky died—casual sex doesn't count—and I'm middle-aged and fat and lonely. *I know ridiculous.*

I took a deep breath. *Get a grip, old girl,* I told myself sternly. *For heaven's sake.*

Fine. And what do you think Max will say when he finds out that Jocko's been here since Saturday night and you didn't tell him?

But Max had rejected him. Very possibly Jocko was on his way home to Connecticut at this very moment. Too late, Max. With any luck, none of us would ever see him again. Everything would be okay. Max and Alice and I would settle back into our spring routine of dinners at their house and occasional movies at mine, none of us would have any secrets from the others, and Max would never know I'd ever laid eyes on the returning Jocko. We would all go on as if nothing had happened.

But as Hecky, my old partner, said when first diagnosed, I had a bad feeling.

Alice

On Wednesday night Max phoned and said he'd be late coming home again—he had some things to do on campus—and would I mind just picking up some sushi from the grocery store since it was his night to cook. I didn't mind. I'd left work early thanks to my disastrous day and I had plenty of time. An hour later I was setting out plates when Richard arrived. I was glad he was there first, not because I necessarily wanted to tell him *before* I told Max, but because I wanted to tell them separately. I didn't want to have to respond to a double-barreled reaction from the two of them.

So Richard came in, we kissed hello—Richard is a good kisser, he has soft lips—and he immediately started helping. He pulled up the table edge for three, but then instead of getting the third chair, he stood gazing at the table. I handed him the silverware and chopsticks and he set them around the table, setting the lone fork at my place. As the artist in the group I'm supposed to have the best eye-hand coordination, but I never mastered chopsticks.

Richard is usually pretty talkative, but that night he was clearly somewhere else. I know him so well it's almost as if we grew up together.

"Richard, I have something to tell you, but you're so quiet. What's up?"

"Nothing." He got an additional cloth napkin from the drawer and set it at his place. "What do you want to tell me?"

"Did you have a hard day? Nasty clients? Is the pressure bothering you?"

He smiled. "I have only reasonable, calm clients. Everyone loves this time of year. It brings out the best in people."

"Did someone give you a hard time? You look worried."

"Mmm, no more than usual, I don't think. I really do have pretty good clients, you know. It's mostly lesbians and non-profits. That's why I'm so wealthy."

"No gay men? Rich architects, lawyers?"

"A few. Mostly they're social worker types, preschool teachers, like that. The only reason they need me is because they're civil unioned, so they have federal and state returns that are different and they don't want to hassle with it themselves. But work's fine, Alice, really. I don't know why I look worried. I'm just tired. What about you? What did you want to tell me? Where's Max?"

I handed Richard a bowl of nuts to munch on and sat on the couch, pulled my legs up under me. "He'll be a little late; he had something to do on campus, he didn't tell me what."

Richard sat at the table, in my seat. He still hadn't got the third chair—very unlike him, he's the most linear person I know, one task after another till it's done. He said, "I *am* feeling a little pressured in terms of time. Maybe I'll just eat and go. Would that be all right?" He eyed the platter of sushi in the middle of the table.

"Okay, sure, but first, listen a sec." I came over and sat at the table opposite him, in Max's seat. "I got taken off a job today. It's the first time that's ever happened to me."

He set down his chopsticks and gave me his full attention. "I'm sorry, Alice. What does it mean?"

"I'm not sure. It could mean I'm on the downhill slope and I'm going to be fired, maybe sooner than later. Or it could mean nothing. It was the fathers job. It could just mean they thought a middle-aged gal wasn't the right fit for that project. They should have thought of that earlier, of course, but whatever."

"Well, arc you upset about it? I mean, you seem kind of relieved."

"I am, in a way. I don't know. Relieved, terrified... maybe it's a sign." I heard Max in the driveway and got up. Richard started to get up, too. "No, stay, stay, I'll get the chair." I brought the third chair from the closet.

"You know, I'm not feeling all that well. I think I'll just go home after all."

"Richard! Really? How can I help? Wait, do you want some chicken soup instead? I have some in the freezer I can thaw out. You do seem a little off."

Max came into the mudroom and took off his boots and coat. Richard stood in the middle of the kitchen looking pale. Max opened the door to the kitchen and said, "What's going on?" He looked from me to Richard and back, Richard standing there strangely and me hovering like a worried mother.

"Richard's not feeling well," I said.

Max was immediately solicitous. "There are all kinds of bugs going around, they can come on just like that." He scanned Richard's face as if for signs of serious illness. "But unless it's a stomach bug, it's good to eat something. Have you guys eaten already?"

Richard let out a deep sigh as if he'd been holding his breath. "I'll just wash my face," he said, and disappeared into the bathroom. It was as if he was afraid of Max. I'd never seen that before.

Max said, "Alice, this has been a strange day."

"Yeah, I agree. Why for you?"

Max hesitated. "I expect the weather. It's got everything all topsy turvy. Sorry I'm late." He washed his hands and sat down at his regular place. Richard emerged from the bathroom. I wondered what was going on with him. He and I sat and when I passed around the sushi he took his normal, large helping. So did Max. So did I, but I didn't know whether I was ravenous or not hungry at all.

I said, "So. Guys. The topic of tonight's conversation is rage."

"Rage?" said Max and Richard together.

Then, "Oh, dear," said Richard.

"Max," I said. "I got taken off the fathers job today."

Max considered this. "And that makes you feel rage?"

"No, it doesn't. Should it?"

Richard laughed. It made him half-choke on a piece of sushi. Max whacked him on the back. But Richard kept laughing as if something had been released. It was infectious, the kind of pure laughter that makes you want to laugh, too, and Max and I smiled at each other but we didn't quite laugh, and shortly Richard wiped his eyes. "Sorry, guys. It wasn't that funny." He looked completely like himself now. A little red-faced but sparkly. He kept hiccupping sporadically with an irrepressible silliness. Whatever was making him feel sick before, whether it had to do with Max or not, was history. Good, because it was my turn.

I said to Max, "It's a little worrisome, I guess, but like Richard said—I was telling Richard this, Max, before you got here—it's kind of a relief. I didn't want to do it anyway. But still, it's a loss."

"Did they give you a reason?" Max asked. Ever reasonable himself.

"Not really. Giving it to someone else."

"So where does the rage come in?" asked Max.

"I was just thinking about it. What is it? Maybe it's not rage. Maybe it's terror. What is it when it goes much deeper than throwing things or wanting to kill someone? I was thinking about how we express it. Do you want to know what it is I'm thinking this rage or terror—whatever it is—is about?"

Richard, serious now, glanced at Max, but Max continued to eat as if he thought he knew the answer and didn't need to hear it. But he didn't know. I'd never talked about it before and he only knows what I tell him. He lacks intuition.

I said, "I feel whatever-it-is about the fact that I'm getting older. That my memory is going. That I sometimes can't call up words."

"You're only forty-five," said Max mildly. Max is fifty-five.

Richard looked more concerned.

I thought, *If Max doesn't get this, I will have to leave him after all. After all this.* I said, "Max, listen to me." And then I didn't know what to say. "Richard understands, don't you, Richard? Richard knows what it feels like to have an empty life."

"Hey!" Richard made a face. I hadn't meant to wound him; I really thought he *would* understand. "I beg to differ," he said. "My life is rich and satisfying in every way." He held up a slice of California roll to prove it.

Max said, "Alice, I can understand why you'd be disappointed over losing an assignment, even if you didn't want it in the first place, but I hardly think it means your entire life is a wasteland."

"You're sounding pompous," I said.

"What are you forgetting, Alice?" asked Richard kindly. He'd forgiven me already. "Is it events, or just words?"

"Just words. But words aren't 'just' words."

"No, but there's nothing pathological about it. It's a natural part of aging."

"But I don't see you losing words, and you're fifty-five."

Richard smiled. "That's because I deal in numbers. I never had any words to begin with." Richard forgives me easily because he doesn't love me the way he loves Max. I know he and Max have a special bond. That's all right, because although Max loves us both, he *sleeps* with me.

Max said unexpectedly, "I'm familiar with rage." Richard stopped chewing, on alert again.

Men. It's all about them. I wanted to scream. But we were having a civil dinner, and I was working on being more patient. I said, "Okay, give us an example we don't know about." I was certainly not afraid of Max's rage. He was the father of my child; no two people could have shared a greater rage-or-whatever-it-is than we had.

"The time I tried to build a sukkah."

Richard snorted. "I remember that. A construction nightmare."

I thought, *You're kidding. The sukkah?* But I said, "I know you scared Adam half to death. You never told me what happened."

"You never wanted to know before."

I said to Richard, "But you weren't there, were you?"

"No."

"Yes, you were," said Max, suddenly teasing, with a sort of big brother glee. "You were watching the whole time from your little perch in the sunroom." He whacked Richard on the arm with affection.

"I wasn't *participating*," Richard corrected.

Max swirled the water in his glass with a rueful smile. "What a disaster."

"Never mind," I said. I didn't want to hear it after all.

Max said, "It was my father becoming a dybbuk and getting inside me. Speaking of fathers. He was such a hard son of a bitch. And Adam was so sweet. I'll be atoning for such moments for the rest of my life." He gave a short laugh to show us he was kidding. Richard and I both knew he wasn't.

"Well," I said. I got up to clear the plates. "I just want you guys to know that something is bubbling up in me. *Now.* I don't know what it is. But don't be surprised if it's something awful." I could feel their eyes on me, and Max's alarm.

"Like what? You're not going to leave me, are you?"

I put the dishes in the sink and returned to put my arms around his neck. I felt his rough cheek on the side of my face and thought of the photo from the catalogue of the thin old man with a couple of days' stubble, staring at the camera. Who was caring for him? It wasn't Max's fault that his sandpaper skin hurt my cheek. I kissed my husband's scratchy face and released him. "Worse than that. I'm not going to kill myself, or kill someone else, but I might make a lot of noise, and you'll have to still live with me."

"Time for me to leave," said Richard. He got up and put his glass in the sink. I hugged him and held on a little longer than usual. Richard is big and fat and offers a steadier, less demanding kind of comfort than Max, more like a sweet older brother who's already gone through his meanness by the time you come along. I said, "I'm glad you feel better."

"Yeah," he said, sounding like he wasn't at all sure he did feel better after all. "Keep that rage burnin', baby."

Which was rather an odd thing to say, and he seemed to think so, too, frowning at himself. But then he shrugged and smiled and touched my face. He's a sweet man.

After he left, and I turned back to Max who was at the sink washing the dishes, Max said, "Alice, where are the old pictures of Adam?"

That is why I would never, ever leave Max.

Max

The next morning, I returned to my office on campus early. I planned to look for Jason Green again a little later, when I imagined a teenaged boy would be up and about, if indeed he were still around which I somehow sensed he was. But first I wanted to get down some thoughts that had troubled my sleep. I needed a more rational lens through which to look at my memory than a nighttime brain allows.

Every father must have a long list of regrets, things for which he cannot forgive himself, if he's reflective at all. Words spoken in anger, thoughtless acts, even good intentions gone wrong. I don't know why some of the lesser mistakes are the most haunting. These are not a matter of good and evil; no rational person wishes to harm his child. These lesser mistakes, which may cause tiny but irreparable psychic damage—or no damage at all—have to do, rather, with such things as fear and betrayal and the like. I once badly frightened my son.

It was unbelievably stupid, an insult to my rational mind, thanks to my own father who rose from the dead to belittle me. Or, perhaps I might more accurately describe it as an insult to my father, whom I conjured up in my frustration, which I then stupidly took out on my son. Because of an irrational urge to observe an ancient ritual.

I should explain here that I did not grow up in a religious family. My father was culturally Jewish and my mother an ex-Methodist. Both my parents were passionate atheists. We lived on the border of a Jewish-Italian neighborhood in Brooklyn and I didn't even realize my father was Jewish until I was in my teens. I may remember it incorrectly; it's possible I took his Jewishness and mine for granted. I'm quite sure the subject rarely, if ever, came up.

When I met Alice, I told her I was Jewish, but not very. She said she was nothing. The way she tells it, she asked me whether I needed to have Jewish children and I said it would be up to them. I wouldn't impose any religion on them. They could choose what religion to observe, if any, when they grew up.

But the way I remember it is this: very soon after we met, Alice asked me how I felt about children. She was always very direct—feisty and prickly at times but always able to talk about important things.

I said, "Depends. Whose children?"

"Yours and mine. I'd like to have children."

I said all right, and she kissed me in a way that made me want to make a child right then.

I told her I wanted to be a traditional father. A secondary parent. It was 1980; by then fathers were expected to share in the work of childrearing. But I wanted to read and write philosophy. I didn't want to change diapers or be up all night with a sick kid if I had to go to work the next day.

Alice considered this; it wasn't what she'd had in mind. She asked if I'd support the family until our children were in school and I said of course, that was how it worked.

She said, "I want you to be interested in my day when you come home. I don't want you to treat me like a housewife—or have affairs because I'm not glamorous."

I teased her. "What will you do to make your day interesting?"

She said, "*I'll* have affairs." And we laughed, and I swung her around because even though I was a philosopher I was strong and macho and very much in love in a way that didn't eat me up inside. Finally, after two unsuccessful and childless marriages, I'd found the right match.

Then we had Adam. I'd had no idea how much I would love my son. The fact that this experience is so commonplace made it no less intense or for that matter surprising. I wanted to comfort him in the night; I didn't mind changing his diaper. When he was sick, I couldn't sleep anyway. I was not at all the distant father I'd expected to be—as my own father was. And then, as he grew from an infant to a toddler to a little boy, it became strangely important that he know my traditions. Except that they weren't really my traditions.

The first winter after Adam was born, Alice wanted a Christmas tree. We hadn't had one before, hadn't wanted to contribute to killing trees, but suddenly she wanted Adam to see the lights and to feel the magic she'd felt as a child. It had nothing to do with religion, she said, it was a pagan ritual, the tiny colored lights a cross-cultural symbol of hope. I didn't mind. I loved the smell of the tree, and we had fun buying silly ornaments. Alice sewed and decorated stockings for each of us, and it was all very sweet.

Then in the spring of the year Adam turned four, my father, the Jewish atheist who by then was more of a curmudgeon than ever, died fairly suddenly. Nine months later, I felt the need to add

Hanukkah to our family celebrations. Inexplicably, really; my parents had never observed Hanukkah. I told Alice that Hanukkah wasn't religious either, but historical.

Alice snorted. "Miracles are historical?"

"Military victories."

The next year we went to our first seder as a family. It was the *next* year, when Adam was six, that is the point of this rumination. That was the year I determined to put up a sukkah.

A sukkah is a little open-air hut for the Jewish holiday of Sukkot in the fall. I of course had never built one before. I'd never belonged to a synagogue. I'd never known anyone who had a sukkah in their backyard, and I'd never eaten in one. But I'd seen pictures. I knew it needed three sides and an open roof. Beyond that, as I understood it, anything went. I didn't actually care much about the holiday itself; I was interested in the family ritual, what you might call the cultural-religious trappings.

"It's a harvest festival," I told Alice.

She rolled her eyes but smiled. Everything strange and uncharacteristic made sense when you thought about Adam. She said fine, but she wasn't going to eat in it if it was forty degrees. She didn't think it was a tradition designed for New England. "Do they eat outside when it's forty degrees in Tel Aviv?" she asked.

"They don't build sukkahs in Tel Aviv. They eat in restaurants."

I started with a simple sketch, which I showed Richard next door. Of course he didn't know a thing about it and declined to help, he's even less handy than I, but I hadn't expected his actual assistance, only his moral support, which I can always count on. I didn't think I needed his help anyway, as I planned to get Adam to help me. After all, it was for him I was doing it. I imagined myself a true Vermonter in my red and black checked overshirt, showing his six-year-old son how to wield a hammer.

But when the time came, Adam was playing happily with a visiting dog, a fat, short-legged yellow mutt whose family had gone to California for a week, and his new friend, a scruffy, energetic blond boy who'd recently moved to town.

Imagine our yard, the grass overgrown as always, long enough to lie flat under the weight of colored leaves. It is October in the Champlain Valley; half the leaves are still on the trees. The yard itself is medium-sized, about fifty feet wide and forty deep. At the back an overgrown hedge of spreading roses creeps further into the yard every year. There I am, laying out plywood and two-by-fours on the grass—my first sukkah, in honor in some perverse way of the Jewish childhood I never had. It is an act of penance and retribution the complexities of which I can only suggest to Richard when he asks. I say cheerfully, "I don't know. It's for my father. He would have hated it."

And indeed I feel cheerful. Richard retreats inside to read in the sun like a contented cat while I proceed with my vigorous activity, knowing he'll get pleasure from occasionally glancing out his window at the progress of my work. We have an interesting relationship, Richard and I. I enjoy performing for him, like a child for a mother, or a man for his lover. Yes, there is that element in our friendship. We are not lovers, never have been. All I can say is, it's okay. It goes deeper than that.

So I laid out a ten-by-ten room, with eight-foot sides. Lacking a circular saw (or any other kind), I'd had the boards cut at the nearby lumberyard in advance and delivered. I laid the plywood flat with the two-by-fours on top. Then I took off the two-by-fours and lined them up on the grass and laid the plywood on top. I hooked one end of the tape measure over the plywood, where I could see the two-by-fours underneath, and stretched it to the other side. I had only to draw a line and I'd know where the two-by-four was, presumably to nail it in.

Meanwhile my son was playing with the dog and the other boy. The dog had a sweet, frisky nature and weighed about the same as the boys. Adam ran ahead of her calling her name and the other boy gave chase. When Adam turned to run backwards, he fell, and his friend tumbled over him and the dog leaped on them both. It was straight out of Norman Rockwell.

The metallic end of the tape popped off the plywood and the tape began to close. I dropped the tape box off the edge of the plywood onto the grass and grabbed the other end, pulling it out again and snagging the tip once more over the plywood. I could just hold it, but I'd left the hammer and box of nails a few feet away. I needed help after all.

I called my son.

He didn't hear me. Roughhousing with the dog like littermates, the two boys were making too much noise to attend to a grown-up. *Let them play.* I released the tape gently and it stayed in place. I retrieved the hammer and nails myself and returned without having to adjust the tape measure. Success. But I admit that at that moment, watching Adam and his friend across the yard, laughing, shrieking, I wondered for a moment whether what I was doing was worth it, when pleasure was so easy to come by in other ways. Still I carried on.

I hammered a nail every few feet the length of the tape measure. I actually managed to repeat the whole process three times without incident and stood to admire my work. What a guy.

I'd figured out that if I attached the three plywood panels with hinges, I could fold them together, then stand them up as one and unfold them—presto, a three-walled structure. I had not figured out how to attach beams for a roof, so I planned to lay a few extra-long two-by-fours across the top, which would have the advantage of allowing us to tie gourds or herbs or chotchkes to the beam *before* lifting it overhead.

After nailing the two-by-fours to the three panels, I turned over each panel with some effort so I could properly attach the hinges to the insides. I lined up the plywood sheets in a row. Attaching the hinges wasn't difficult, although an electric screwdriver would have made it easier. It was immensely satisfying to produce something so concrete when my usual work is so abstract, but by then I was getting a little weary, ready to finish—and the boys and dog had disappeared, which I suppose in retrospect made me feel I was missing the fun. I kept listening for them, but they weren't there.

Dutifully I attached the second set of hinges and again inspected the work. It was good. I lifted the end of one panel and walked it inward, folding it over onto the center panel, and then tried to fold over the third side. This didn't work because the middle section was now too fat. I was annoyed but undaunted: I could handle this. I considered the problem. I could either cut off a foot from the other side, or I could replace the hinges to this third side with the kind that folded either direction, which would be easier since I lacked a saw. I could manage replacing the hinges. Honestly I was a little surprised that it worked as well as it did. On the other hand, I'm a logical man and I had planned it out well, except for the folding-and-storing part, but who could have imagined that in advance? I waved at Richard, or at least at his house, but couldn't tell if he saw.

At that point the boys and dog returned from the front yard, the dog galumphing on her short legs and oversized body. I felt happy to see them. I felt happy with the world. Here I was, an able father who had just succeeded in building a sukkah, almost, for his family. His wife was inside doing something productive and his bright, active son was romping with a friend in the yard on a gorgeous crisp fall day. What could be more perfect?

How different my son's life was from my own, I thought. I'd never played in the grass while my father built something nearby. I'd never romped Kodak-style with a dog in a yard. What was a yard? We'd played in the street.

Of course our yard wasn't exactly a neat, proper, suburban yard even then, when Adam was alive, but that made it all the better. We joked that it was more like a yard-style place, like kosher-style food. Now that we've essentially abandoned it, I suppose you'd call it a meadow. But then it was comfortably *expressive*, a bit wild but alive with possibility.

And then out of nowhere I heard the voice of my father. I imagined him shaking his head in bafflement, in barely veiled scorn: I, his son, had become a goy, with a goyishe wife and a goyishe son, who wasn't even circumcised, God forbid, playing with other goyim. What game was I playing?

But what difference did it make, I argued, if Adam wasn't Jewish anyway? And since when did you teach me to be proud of being Jewish?

And then this, my father went on. *What's this?*

It's a sukkah. Or it will be when I'm done.

You call this a sukkah? This piece of junk? Is this how the goyim do it?

And I felt an old rage well up in me. In truth my father had never talked about the goyim like this; where did his scorn come from? Maybe it was *his* father, left behind in Lithuania in 1930 and never seen again. Maybe it was genetic.

The three panels together were heavy. I lifted one end and walked the construction upright. Leaning it against my shoulder, I opened the top panel and walked it out.

The dog had found an old tennis ball somewhere and Adam was trying unsuccessfully to wrench it from her mouth. His friend joined him—two against one—but the dog held on, growling and wagging her tail. Was there no end to their silliness? Suddenly I couldn't remember any such carefree moments in my own young life. But this was exactly what I had wanted to provide my son.

But then, why was I building this ridiculous, ugly, amateurish box, testament to some ancient totemistic religion?

With two sides now standing at right angles, it stayed upright by itself. The bolt from one of the hinges had worked its way up and I pulled the hammer from my belt to whack it back in place.

I wanted to have a sukkah for my son, I tried to explain to my father. For Adam, playing so joyfully with a foolish, ill-conceived dog and a friend.

My father snorted. *Look at him. What does he know from sukkas? My own grandson. What kind of a father are you with your goyishe son?* I felt the blood rush to my temples.

"Adam!"

Adam didn't respond.

I called more sharply: "Boys! Come here, I need your help."

Lying on his back with the dog on top of him, Adam glanced at me but didn't seem to register the request. The other boy tried to drag the dog onto his own chest. They were like a trio of puppies rolling around on the hummocky lawn, over the leaves and the high, bent grass—

"Adam!" I roared. Something snapped in me. I let go of the sukkah and headed for the boys. Behind me the sukkah, unbalanced from an inadvertently violent push, fell over in slow motion with a soft thump.

The boys looked up to see the sukkah collapsing and me bearing down on them in fury, wielding a hammer. They shrieked, scrambled out from under the dog and ran for their lives.

The other boy ran to the right, around the house into the front yard. Adam ran to the left screaming, "Mom! Mom!"

"Adam, stop!" I dropped the hammer and caught up with him just as he got to the driveway. I grabbed him from behind. He screeched and struggled. I dropped to my knees, gave him a shake—out of anger that he had run from me and hadn't listened, hadn't come when I asked, and out of fear. Afraid of my son, afraid of his terror in that moment, afraid for myself as if I were the child chased by an enraged father. I shook him and then held him close as he wailed.

Alice burst out of the kitchen door. "What happened?"

"Nothing. The sukkah fell over. I—he got scared."

The dog trotted up and nosed Adam from the side, trying to get in. Alice came down the steps and knelt to take over. Reluctantly I released Adam who had been stiff as a soldier in spite of his crying. Now he clutched his mother around the neck and cried more loudly.

"Sh, sh, sh. It's all right." She picked him up, rocked him. "It's all right."

She glared at me. I stood helplessly for a moment then returned to the back yard and surveyed the flattened sukkah.

What had possessed me to try this? We didn't need a sukkah. I didn't want a sukkah. And now what was I going to do with it? I marched around the house to get Richard's help, but he was sitting on the curb talking to the other child. I'd forgotten momentarily about the other boy, who was tear-streaked but obviously fine now. Alice appeared with Adam in tow and herded both boys inside for a distracting treat. Richard agreed to help me carry the damn sukkah down the street to leave in a neighbor's dumpster. I knew they wouldn't mind as their renovation had just been completed a few days before. He didn't ask why. We carried the awkward thing half a block, with both of us walking sideways rather than either one walking backward.

"Equal is always better," Richard said. "Gay people learn that early. It comes from having flexible roles." He was trying to cheer me up. "Some of us are meant to work with our brains and some with their hands. Of course strong hands are nice. Strong glutes are even better."

He chatted on, allowing me to feel morose and defeated without having to admit it.

That night, when I tucked Adam in, I didn't know what to say. I could simply have apologized. *I didn't mean to scare you, honey.* That's what Alice would have said. But I didn't call him "honey." I called him Sport, Bud, Big Guy.

Instead I ruffled his hair. "Everything okay, Sport?"

"A-okay, Dad."

I kissed him goodnight—my father never did that. But I always did. I kissed him goodnight, and I hoped to God that he wouldn't remember today. I imagined him talking to his shrink in twenty years about all the ways we'd failed him as parents and this wouldn't even make it on the list. I convinced myself that he was fine—after all, he was healthy and completely beloved—and it was such a little thing. He had all his growing up to do still and I had plenty more mistakes to make as well as a lifetime to make up for them. Everything would be fine.

And it was. I mean of course that it *would* have been. Or it *might* have been had he lived. In any case, Adam's death was not divine retribution, because, first of all Sukkot and Christmas and every other religious ritual notwithstanding, there is no divinity, only the *idea* of divinity. Second, to imagine that Adam's death was a punishment for my or anyone else's sins is a foolish, solipsistic, even obscene conceit. As my students would say, Adam's death wasn't "about" me, or Alice. Punishment is merely an idea. Good and evil, childhood, love and friendship, loyalty and betrayal are all merely ideas. Ideas are useful, but they are not truth.

Was this sukkah story the kind of personal narrative I would need to include to make my punishment book accessible to the general reader? To make it sell? A personal journey like Basho's travels to the deep north?

I had to smile at myself.

I could never include this in a book. The very thought was absurd. What in the world could possibly be the value in laying out one's pain for others to see? I had no need for that kind of exposure, nor did I believe in its value aesthetically or psychologically and certainly not pedagogically. Imagine the response of my colleagues. Furthermore, the tell-all, bare-your-soul memoirs of the late twentieth century, the reality television shows of the decade following, none of which I'd actually seen or read, I admit, made me cringe. Imagine joining that crowd. Nothing but self-indulgent, commercially driven claptrap, to put it politely. I'd put a gun to my head first.

My shame, my grief, my despair were my own. No one, not even Alice or Richard, might know their depths.

Richard

Alice knows I don't take a lunch break this time of year, but she made it sound so urgent and she's right, she doesn't ask me for much. Except love and support and undying loyalty, but hey, what the hell.

Nonetheless her call Thursday morning left me with a pit in my stomach. I felt guilty. But that was unreasonable; what had I done? Nothing! Certainly not to Alice. Would Alice be telling me something about Jocko, God forbid?

It wasn't fair not to tell Max you'd seen him, said a voice in my head. *If you wanted to compete for the kid, you should have done it fair and square. And you should have told Alice, too.* All right, maybe I should have. But confidentiality is crucial to my business. It's a habit. A requirement. Besides, what difference did it make in the end? Max and Jason met. Max said no. As I expected. And it was over, right? Ah, hell.

I hurriedly ate my lunch and made notes to finish up what I was working on later. Whatever Alice needed me for probably had nothing to do with me—or Jason-Jocko. After last night's revelation of her midlife angst, she could be telling me she was having an affair for all I knew. Then of course I felt worried for her. *Please don't be having an affair*, I thought. *Please don't have breast cancer, or anything else. Please be all right.*

Once you go with someone to hear a horrible diagnosis, you always expect the worst. Hecky only lived eighteen months after his.

Alice picked me up outside my office. I lowered myself awkwardly into the passenger seat of her messy little car where I always felt crowded. "What's up?"

"Let's do something fun this summer. I need a distraction. Something *fun*. Wild and crazy."

"Camping?" I asked, and immediately regretted it.

She frowned. "Camping? I don't think so."

I hadn't meant for her to take me seriously. It was a bad joke. We hadn't been camping since Adam died—nor did I want to. Too close to the dirt. Gardening was one thing, with gloves, proper tools, the bathroom a short walk away. Camping was another. For the sake of a kid, all right. But for adult pleasure?

"I was thinking somewhere more like the ocean," Alice said. "Someplace warm and sunny."

"Alice, honey, do you remember to whom you're speaking? I hate the beach."

"You went to Kingsland Bay with me once, remember? And you go to Florida every year."

"That's different."

"Because you sit around with a bunch of old fags and ogle young men?"

She was teasing, but something was wrong. "Alice, where are we going?"

"I had an idea early this morning. You know those pictures I showed you? They've been really bothering me and I have this strange feeling, I mean like a really serious knowing, that I've got to drown them out. Which fits with this other awareness I've got about making noise. You know, being bigger. So I was lying in bed about four o'clock this morning—you know I have a hard time sleeping sometimes—and I was listening to the rain and I had this idea."

"Okay."

"Okay, so I want to buy an *instrument*."

"You mean a musical instrument?"

"Right. Of course. What do you think, an instrument of torture?"

"Wait. For this you need me? Alice—"

"It's a big decision. I can't tell Max till after I've done it. He could dissuade me. I'm actually thinking of buying something pretty unusual."

"What, like a didgeridoo?"

She smiled. "Did I ever tell you about the time in elementary school I was told not to sing?"

"No. You have a good voice." It was true. She sang easily, and her voice was clear and strong. Resonant.

She pulled into a small parking lot. "Maybe I've gotten better. All I know is the teacher made us sing row by row, and then after she heard the row I was in, she made half the row sing, and then the other half, and, you know, kept narrowing it down until it was just me. She said, 'You! Don't sing. You can mouth the words.'"

"You're kidding."

She turned off the engine but made no move to get out. "I can still see her glaring at me. She said I was too loud."

I thought of several funny things to say but it was one of my better moments. "You're not too loud," I said simply. "And you can sing fine. She was wrong."

Alice studied me. "Maybe I am too loud. But the thing is, I'm always trying to be quiet. I think I've felt… constricted… all my life. Like I'm supposed to be smaller, quieter than I am. I think that's why I loved it when Adam wanted to play the trumpet. It's such a loud, taking-space kind of instrument. Maybe I wasn't meant to be a mother, but maybe I was meant to be loud. *Really* loud." She got out and slammed the door.

I could only nod. Every gay man of my generation knows the pressure to be *less*, in spite of decades of resistance. Maybe a general repressiveness was a Puritan thing, or an Anglo-European thing, but it was worse when you added being gay.

I pulled myself out of her car with difficulty. It might be fine for Alice though she is tall and big-boned, but it's too damn small for an *extra*-large person.

She waited for me to catch up, with her hand on the door. "Sometimes I think everything hurts me."

"You mean like fibromyalgia?" I huffed.

She laughed. "Oh, Richard. Fibromyalgia? I'm not talking physically. I'm talking about life."

If Alice had been a man, she'd have been the kind of gruff older brother type who's always cuffing you on the head. "Oh, that," I said. I followed her into the store.

I don't know what I expected—I suppose some version of a chain bookstore or a video store, with loud music and shaggy, pierced salespeople who look about twelve. Instead, the place was carpeted, quiet, with a Mozart piano sonata playing softly in the background. A store for grownups, I thought. Or maybe parents buying for their children: there were shiny electric guitars and basses against one wall, and along another, acoustic guitars and banjos and a couple of small violins.

In a second room were displays of flutes and piccolos, and what looked to me like oboes and clarinets, and, opposite, a wall of brass instruments. Nary a fingerprint on a single gleaming surface, only our faces reflecting back at us in a leering distortion. It was a large store: one large section was full of darkly polished upright pianos, another full of drums—kettle drums, bass drums, drum sets, African drums. We were the only customers. Alice wandered around touching things, seeming glad for the privacy.

A sleepy but not untidy young man approached from the rear of the store. He noticed her hand on the piano.

"That's a nice piano," he said. "Electric. You wouldn't believe the sound." Leaning over to the keyboard, and ignoring the Mozart in the air, he played two bars of a Bach suite. (I may be a Philistine, as Max says, but my mother played the piano.) He had long, graceful fingers and played easily—as if he were seated and the room were silent and he'd been playing for years.

"How do you do that?" Alice said.

"Well, see, you can make it sound like a concert grand, or have a pop tone, or change it to vibes or harpsichord." He demonstrated each of these as he spoke. It wasn't what she meant.

"I'm looking for an instrument. For me. What makes the most noise?"

"Noise? You mean like the loudest sound?"

"Yes, yes. Noise, sound."

"Sorry, it's just that if you're a musician, you—"

"Okay, *sound*. The loudest sound."

"Well, with amps you can make anything pretty loud."

"I can see you're not going to be much help," said Alice.

He looked at her sideways, as if he couldn't decide whether to get pissed off or to play along. Alice's eyes strayed to the trumpets. He strode to the wall and pulled one down. "Yeah, okay. There's always one of these."

"Not a trumpet," Alice said firmly.

He cradled it in his arms. "You know, you can rent instruments when you're just starting out. That's what I did. With the oboe, I mean. And the French horn. Of course brass instruments are pretty hard." He gave a great blast and played a piercingly pure scale, ending with a little riff on the high notes.

"Very nice," Alice said. "But I don't want a trumpet."

"No? Well, that's wise. They're pretty hard to master. I mean—," he paused delicately, "as an adult."

Alice glanced at me; I couldn't suppress a smile.

"I mean," he went on, awkwardly, "the piano is easier to take up from scratch. Or maybe you played the piano as a kid? Lots of people did. And they can get really loud."

"Are you saying I'm too old to learn?"

"Well no, it's just that, I mean—."

Alice interrupted him, speaking carefully as if to someone who spoke a different language, "I played the trumpet as a child, and I used to play with my son. Which, you're right, was a long time ago. But right now, I'm looking for something else."

I jumped in then. "Look, Alice. How about the drums?" I tapped my fingers against the surface of one. I'd wanted to play the drums as a kid. But I was kidding, you understand.

Alice perked right up. "Richard, you're a genius. How did you know? That's amazing. But why not, right? Anyone with rhythm and energy can play the drums. Right?"

"Sure, sure," said the boy. "Although they say it's good to practice on a drum pad first before you—'

"Do you have like a beginner's set?" Alice asked, excited now.

I left her to haggle with the young man over which drums would suit her best. I went outside and walked around the parking lot in the chilly March air, wondering what I was doing there. I had so much work to do! For a moment I tried to imagine being Alice, forty-five, female, without children, afraid—as she said—of drying up. Drying up was such an interesting concept, so female, the fluids and all. I've never thought of myself drying up; was it because I was a man or because I'd never had that kind of creative liquidity to start with?

I'd always thought Alice was a beautiful woman in her way. I thought about the time she'd mentioned, when she and I had gone to Kingsland Bay State Park, on Lake Champlain. It was in the summer a few years ago, a Saturday afternoon when Max was off doing something with students.

Not being terribly outdoorsy, I'd never been there, but she loved the place. A long dirt road led between fields and woods down to the park. There was a single row of cars parked along a wooden fence, and on the other side a broad, gently sloping lawn that ended at the lake. Very civilized. There were maybe twenty other people spread out across the grass on blankets or towels and three or four large sailboats anchored in the tiny bay. You could swim across the bay to a wooded point if you were Alice. The lake itself was quite narrow here, she told me. New York State was less than two miles away, directly across. The Adirondacks loomed in the near distance. In between, according to Alice, the water was over three hundred fifty feet deep.

"Big and deep like you," I said, and she rolled her eyes at me.

We lay on our towels, for Alice to absorb the sun and me to nap. It was the end of July but the temperature was in the low seventies. Alice wore a black swimsuit and I wore khaki trousers and a white T-shirt. I hate the sun. Maybe if I were a plant instead of a pale-skinned human…

After a while, Alice practically leaped up. "Let's go swimming. You can go in your clothes."

"I don't swim."

"Last one in is a rotten egg!"

I followed her to the water—weren't you supposed to have a buddy when you swam in wild places? She dove off the concrete dock and came up gasping. Swimming around the dock were a few children but no other adults. I touched the water with my fingers. It was glacial.

I hate to see people dive into strange places. I'm afraid they'll hit their heads on rocks and die. I knew someone who did that when I was a child. People said it was a freak accident. Where's the comfort in that? What accidents aren't?

I stood there watching Alice, wishing she'd come back. She was a good swimmer, her strokes confident and easy, but every stroke that took her farther away made my stomach hurt more. I thought of Adam trying to swim across Maidstone Lake years before. That memory of Adam was as clear as if it had happened yesterday. And here was Alice, swimming away from me in the same way. *Turn around. Okay, okay, that's far enough, turn around. Come back. Come back now.* She swam halfway to the point, maybe a hundred and fifty yards, then floated leisurely for a moment and started back. The knot in my stomach began to loosen, and suddenly I felt like weeping with relief. Then I felt pissed. I headed back up the hill.

She climbed out and called my name. I turned around, and she came running at me with her arms open as if to hug me with her icy, dripping body. I backed away and she laughed and chased me up the hill, finally grabbing me from behind. I shook her off; I try not to shriek in public. She flopped down on her towel like a teenager. I looked down at her and my irritation evaporated. This was her natural environment, outside in summer, with the sun on her wet, goosebumpy skin. I had not seen her this easy and relaxed in a long time. I still remember the rush of love I felt for her, and an odd pride that this handsome woman, so different from me, was my friend.

I settled on my own towel. Alice lay with her arms behind her head and her eyes closed. I allowed myself to admire her as I rarely had a chance to do. The fair, middle-aged skin of her limbs was generally unmarred, unlike my own where a thousand freckles have blended into tannish pink, mottled with age spots. Her legs were solid and strong and her upper arms lacked that flabby shelf some middle-aged women have. Her body type was firm, not soft like mine. Firm and sturdy, of body and mind.

But her skin also had tiny wrinkles, which she had showed me before. On her neck and above her ankles. Around her knees. I smiled to myself. It was like having a little secret—the window into the soul is not through the eyes, which display all the usual things, but through the miniscule folds of skin inside the elbow.

And now it was March, and chilly and damp, and this old friend who hadn't drowned in the lake, hadn't needed me to rescue her then or ever, for some reason thought she needed me now. I checked my watch; after walking around the parking lot for five minutes exactly—enough exercise for one day—I returned inside. Alice was standing at the counter.

"Oh, good. Richard, what do you think?"

"About the drums?"

The young man said, "You can bring them back within thirty days—if you change your mind. If they're not banged up or anything."

"What do you think Max will say?" she asked me, handing the boy her credit card.

Alice was a big, independent woman, but she usually talked over important things with Max *before* she did them. This was a departure.

The boy glanced up from her card and said, "Oh, that's why you—. You're Adam's mom, right? When you said trumpet. I guess you don't remember me. I knew him—Adam—in elementary school."

Alice didn't.

"No? Well, no reason why you would, I guess. Sorry."

Sorry about what? That Adam had died? That Alice didn't remember him? That he'd mentioned her son? There was a small moment of silence while he finished, and it occurred to me suddenly that this was my chance to tell her: *Hey, by the way, I've been meaning, I keep forgetting, do you remember a kid named Jason Green? The strangest thing happened—.*

"Here you go," said the young clerk. "I'll get the boxes from the back and bring them out."

Alice leaned into me briefly. The moment passed. When we got in the car with boxes of drums filling the trunk and back seat, she said, "Thanks. I couldn't have done that without you."

I laughed, because I hadn't done anything useful besides walk around the parking lot. "Well, congratulations. I look forward to hearing you pounding away at odd hours."

"I hope I didn't make a mistake."

"Like he said, you can always take them back."

"I may be just kidding myself. This may not be what I want at all. Other people just go out and have an affair." She sighed. Then she hit the steering wheel. "Agh! I've just gone and bought a *drum set,* for God's sake. What am I doing?"

"You're breaking out, girl."

"How is this going to address the suffering in the world and let the light in and bring joy and all that crap? It's so *aggressive*!"

Alice was impossible. I watched sadly as we drove past my office on the way home; I'd told her I'd help her unload it if she'd bring me back to work afterward. I felt exhausted by the events of the past hour. I needed a good meal.

"Alice Henry, you are a strong, capable, independent woman with many talents who used to play the trumpet, which by the way I never knew. I only heard Adam. But of course you can play the drums. Wild and furiously. Make the earth rock." I put my head back.

She patted my thigh. "Poor Richard. I've worn you out with my drama, haven't I? You *are* a good sport." She pulled into her driveway just behind Max, who hopped out. He looked so happy, I knew he'd found Jocko. My heart sank.

Alice opened her door. "Max! Guess what?!"

"Can you believe this weather?" Max said as he approached. "It's finally turning spring." Indeed he had on only a light sweater over a turtleneck. The snow was gone but for a small berm alongside the driveway. He gave Alice a frisky kiss. "Should I be worried?"

"It depends. I bought a drum set." She got out of the car and slammed the door again, unnecessarily it seemed to me.

"What?"

She repeated it.

"What for?"

"To play, of course. The kid in the store thought I was too old."

"A drum set?" Max said. "Well, good for you. We all need a new project once in a while." He glanced across the car at me, too obviously I thought, but Alice didn't notice. I tried to smile.

"Max, listen to me," she said. "Something's happening to me, and I don't know what it is."

Max took her arm gently. "It's okay, Alice. I don't mind that you bought a drum set." Alice had popped the trunk. I picked up a medium-sized box.

"It's not the *money*, Dagwood," said Alice. "It's that I want to make noise. I think. Can you help Richard?"

Max and Alice each grabbed a box and we headed inside. Max said, "Noise?"

"Noise. Noise!"

"It's okay, I was just curious. You said that last night."

"I don't know why," she went on. "Because I'm forty-five and I never have. Because it's spring. Because if we had a teenager, he would be. Who cares why?"

Max's face flickered and then rearranged itself into a smile, so fast I could have imagined it. He glanced at me again, colluding with me against his wife. It was what straight men did all the time, but I felt as perversely gratified as if Max and I were having an affair.

Alice said over her shoulder, "I could run off to Mexico with one of my colleagues, except they're about twenty years too young.

I could buy a gun and take potshots at people from the rooftops. I could become a compulsive shopper. Some women do that."

Max raised his eyebrows at me for support. I shrugged. *She's your wife.*

He said gently, "It's fine, Alice. I want you to be happy." Then, even more quietly, "I want things, too."

At the door Alice took my box from me and then told Max she was running me back to work. We rode in silence the ten blocks to my office. By the time we got there, Alice looked resolute, as if she were steeling herself for a hard road ahead.

When we got there, I said, "You can do it, Alice."

She patted my leg. "We'll see. I hope the pounding doesn't drive you out of the neighborhood. Thanks again."

I kissed her cheek. I felt strangely like an accomplice to a crime. But what was the crime? Buying a drum set wasn't a crime, nor was taking on a troubled kid as your apprentice, if that was in fact what Max had done. Nor was not telling your neighbors everything that went on in your own house. I was not responsible for Alice's happiness, for heaven's sake, or Max's.

I *was* responsible for getting tax returns filed by April 15th, however. I hurried back up to my office.

Richard

By five o'clock that day, I'd had it. I am extremely good at concentrating and shutting out distractions, but Alice's lunchtime excursion had thrown me off, and a warm front blew in, throwing me off further. That Thursday afternoon, the temperature reached the low fifties. A sign hanging outside the bank catty-corner from my office spelled out the increases all afternoon, and it made me restless. From my office window I could see people below in T-shirts. It was one of those blustery days at the end of winter that say *Yes, spring will come.* By then we've all but given up, and we know we have at least another month of cold, and yet comes this gift.

Since I had no appointments, because I like to leave a few hours on Thursday evenings to actually work on returns, I went home early. I'd work all weekend instead.

I want to say something about music and gardening—and Adam.

I am not musically talented, although I *appreciate* music very much. I was forced to play the harp in sixth grade—not the autoharp, mind you, the *harp*—because I was the largest kid. No teacher who isn't a closet sadist would make an oversized gay boy play the harp. No elementary school should have a harp at all, but the principal's cousin gave it to the school upon retiring from the state symphony. At the other extreme, in college I played the recorder, briefly, because my first real boyfriend played the guitar and envisioned us playing folky duets. Embarrassing to recall, but it was a time when all things seemed possible.

A better instrument for me would have been something like the triangle, if I could have played just that and not every other percussion instrument. Something simple and quiet and not called upon very much, like the far outfield where the ball never comes, you hope. Unlike most boys, I was not a child who liked to make a lot of noise. What I liked was pulling weeds alongside my mother when she gardened, making the borders neat and tidy, or quietly daydreaming while she practiced. I liked helping my father by putting his tools back and organizing his workbench. I loved it when I was given something broken like a watch or a toaster, to encourage my maleness, you understand, and I could take it apart and line up all the odd-shaped pieces in some kind of order—size, quantity, even color. I had no interest in putting them back together; I showed no signs of being an engineer or an inventor. I just liked lining them up. I got pleasure from creating order.

This is not a trait universally admired. Soon I longed to be more wild and creative. Later, when I was very young, in my twenties but before Hecky, I had a boyfriend who'd gone to Yale who called me, disparagingly, in one of his many sneering moments, the Harold Bloom of accounting. Who was Harold Bloom? I knew nothing of literature; I'd long been on track with numbers. (War movies came later.) I looked up Bloom in *Who's Who* in the library and then in the *Index to Periodical Literature*—one of the many skills we no longer need—and I fell under Bloom's spell at a distance. My version of Bloom, that is. Bloom fancied himself Falstaff. I fancied myself Bloom—but secretly, privately. By then I longed to be big, bigger than life, bigger than my little self. Inside I was lusty and full of life. Outside I was... the little Polack wimp, just grown up and bloated.

Ah, Bloom.

What was Bloom? First of all the name. Bloom—a huge, overgrown flower, a crimson peony, heavily petaled, barely able to hold itself up, drunk on its own beauty. Then there was his size, his physical bearing—large, loose, casual, frumpy, spilling over itself with uncontained, unabashed, celebratory bigness. His full lips, large head, wild mane of hair, or so it looked in the one grainy photo I saw on microfilm, another outdated technology.

Finally there was his intellect, vast and expansive, a mind that ranged broad distances, grazing in far-flung corners, swallowing everything with his inexhaustible appetite.

The boyfriend didn't last, but Harold Bloom did. It astonishes me to admit that after all these years, remnants of that fantastic longing still linger. Except for the fact of our shared size, I do not look like Bloom; I have a broad face with a small nose and even smaller chin, and a ruddy (that is, pale and splotchy) complexion, reflecting my Polish-Anglo roots. He is a slob and I am carefully coiffed. He is brilliant; I have a small, well-ordered mind that stays properly penned up within its given borders. He would not recognize in me any kindred spirit, I'm quite certain. I link us as fellow strugglers in the sea only because I imagine that he knows what it is to want.

And I notice as well, some thirty-five years later, something else we share. Bloom has remained married to his wife for more than fifty years. I would have done the same if Hecky had lived.

Instead I have been faithful to Max and Alice.

And there is my garden. Thanks to Hecky.

When Hecky and I bought our house over twenty years ago, there were no flowerbeds, only a row of straggly, overgrown lilacs. But we had grand plans. In the first couple of months, before Hecky got sick, we removed two lilacs and cut back the other to a few inches. We built a large, kidney-shaped perennial garden that curved from the porch alongside the driveway, and Hecky planted Japanese iris, lupine, and delphinium—all purple—and violet astilbe. I planted peonies. I favored true red, the redder the better, mixed with pink and white. I never went in for subtlety. I read once that the plants that need moths for pollination are generally pale in color—light yellow or white—while the plants that need butterflies (that would be me) have brighter, more vivid flowers. Gradually over the years I've replaced all Hecky's perennials with peonies.

That Thursday afternoon with the trees whipping about in the warm wind, I raced home, rushed to change clothes and grabbed a rake from the garage. Of course it was way too early for any sign of real spring in my gardens. There were no buds on the branches yet, no crocuses pushing up through the mud. It would certainly snow again. But I'd get a jump on spring and start clearing the old leaves from under my front bushes. They accumulate in the late fall after all gardening energy has been exhausted and then hide under the snow all winter, a wet and soggy mass.

I was excited about this first ritual of spring, invigorated by getting into the garden this early. True, there were still patches of grainy ice here and there, but I'd work around them. I sent sympathetic wishes to Max and Alice's untended, overgrown yard, repeating guiltily a silent promise I made to myself every year: *Someday I'll get to you, too.* Unlikely, but hope springs…

As I raked, I found I was still thinking about Alice saying she wanted to make more noise. Why didn't I? I'd never been the kind of guy who liked to bellow at the beach for no apparent reason other than declaring his dominant ape-hood. Okay, that's obvious, but was I lacking in some crucial male gene that makes you want to leave your mark, piss on the tree? I hadn't even wanted to have kids in order to leave something behind, like some gay men. My own secret desire to *be somebody,* my impulse toward bigness, which first stirred in adolescence when I began to embrace hunger and sex, felt more like a baby groundhog peeping from its hole than a gorilla claiming its territory. It's not a coincidence that I'd become at the same time aware of the pressure to *tone it down, baby,* in order to pass. I'm not complaining. It wasn't me who wanted the drum set. But I wondered.

Adam, on the other hand, liked to make noise for the sheer joy of it, not because he was particularly aggressive but because he was endowed with exuberance and bravado—in short, an ordinary heterosexual boy. But with his relatively civilized parents, he learned at an early age that he was not supposed to bellow and shriek for no reason. Thus when the urge overtook him, he disguised it by claiming he was doing something with purpose, like being a hungry lion or a really big truck.

I dumped the wheelbarrow in the small strip of woods behind my house and began on the front kidney garden. Imagine my astonishment when under the first rake-full was revealed a cluster of reddish peony shoots. I wanted to shout. Adam thought peonies were silly mistakes: *What's the point of a flower that can't hold its head up?* True enough, but oh, that luscious, extravagant explosion.

One fall night many years ago, when Adam was little, Alice called to invite me to go with the three of them to view a meteor shower they'd just learned about. It was laundry night at my house, but I had one clean shirt left to wear the next day, so I went. This is why I don't wait until the last minute; things come up.

I sat in the back seat with Adam, who was cranky. It was past his bedtime, and he'd had a long day, according to Alice. He leaned toward the window as far as the seatbelt would allow. "I don't see any! Where are they? Mo-om! I can't see!"

We drove to the end of Shelburne Bay where the LaPlatte River comes in. There was a large gravel lot at the boat ramp for parking. Five or six cars had arrived ahead of us, apparently with the same idea. When we turned off the engine, we sat for a moment in the still October night, listening to the clicks and pops of the engine and the tiny waves lapping the shore. Even Adam was quiet.

A small grassy area next to the lake was unoccupied. Alice had brought blankets and an old-fashioned sleeping bag that opened all the way up and a tarp, which she now spread on the ground with our help. We lay in a row on top of the sleeping bag and pulled the blankets over us, squeezing together like teenagers—Max, Alice, Adam and me. It was cold. Alice and Adam had the warmest spots, but I was lucky to have Adam against my side, warm as a little hot-water bottle.

"Everybody comfortable?" Alice said.

The ground was hard and cold. I wished I'd brought a hat. Max had his arm around Alice.

"Just great," Max said. Adam agreed.

"It's so beautiful," Alice said after a moment. The city lights were only a few miles away, and the horizon was only half-dark from their reflection, but the top of the black bowl overhead was bright with stars.

"See anything?" asked Max.

"The Big Dipper. Cassiopeia," I said.

"I know that," said Adam.

Another car drove up, its headlights strafing the trees and other cars. Its lights seemed exceptionally bright and its engine exceptionally loud. When it quieted and darkened, no one came out. Most people seemed content to watch from within their cars—or maybe, it occurred to me, they weren't watching the stars at all. Then some soft voices let me know at least one couple was lying quietly on the hood of their car.

"Whoa, did you see that one?" said Max softly.

"I saw it! I saw it, Daddy! Did you see that, Uncle Richard?"

"I did, Bo. Oh, wow. Look!"

"Cool," said Adam.

"Double cool," said Max.

"Triple cool," said Alice.

We watched for another few minutes before any of us saw another. Then came another lull.

"Knock-knock," said Adam.

"Who's there?" Max and I said together.

"Star."

There was a pause, as if Max and I were each letting the other play. I said, "Star who?"

"Star light, star bright, first star I see tonight—"

Alice clapped her hand over her son's mouth. "Remember, Adam. Don't say your wish out loud!" She removed her hand.

"I wish that I would see all the shooting stars in the world for-ever and ever!" Adam yelled at the top of his lungs.

"Shh!" Max and Alice said together.

"Toot da do-o-o!" he yelled, just getting warmed up. "Toot da do-o-o!"

"Adam!" Max said. "Stop. Now it's time to be quiet."

Adam let out a tremendous sigh as if he'd been told he could never have any fun again. "I was just playing my trumpet," he said softly.

I worked in the garden for two hours, till past seven when it got dark and cold again. I hated to quit, but my fingers were getting stiff. That's when I thought of Jocko. I realized that I'd half-expected him to show up. That I'd even been waiting for him. It seemed like perfect weather for a handsome young waif to appear in my yard.

Then I thought of Max, and for once I did want to bellow.

Alice

The old pictures of Adam. Where were the old pictures of Adam, Max wanted to know.

Which old pictures? There were a few framed photos around that I never looked at. Richard's house actually had many more photos of Adam on the walls and counters than we did. But I had taken thousands, not just of every Halloween costume or Christmas present-orgy or school event, but documenting every facial expression and gesture, every change of season as he experienced it by jumping in the old leaves or helping Richard in his garden, every joyful or silly moment I could capture of him and his friends, as well as hundreds of shots where he either didn't know I was there or he ignored me—where he's lying quietly curled around a visiting dog, or reading on the couch with the morning sun on his hair, or yawning over his arithmetic homework. I had boxes of photos from his first few years, and a couple of albums I'd put together when I resolved to be more discriminating and organized that covered when he was five and six. I had a separate box of copies of the photos I used to make a special book for my father on his seventy-fifth birthday, when Adam was ten. In between, there were a few dozen boxes of envelopes with dates written on the front in black marker: Aug. – Sept. 1985, Thnxgvng 1987, etc.

Where are the old photos of Adam?

In the basement. In the storage area under the stairs. Why?

Just wondering.

I let it go. Max and I had an uncanny way of being in sync, whether by coincidence or natural inclination. We had not spoken of the pictures I'd taken of Adam in years—I couldn't remember the last time the subject came up—and I had no idea what prompted him to think of them now, but the fact that he had didn't completely surprise me. I had been thinking of them, too.

Not that we are *always* in sync. I love my husband very much, but sometimes I look at him in the middle of a conversation and think, *Who is this guy?* At his core he is a mystery to me. Maybe all women feel this way.

On my lunch break that Friday, I went to the public library without any exact plan. I thought vaguely I might get an introductory book about drumming. Instead I headed toward the basement.

On my way past the desk, I glanced into the main reading room and briefly saw a young man who looked familiar, not in the way of someone I might have seen on the street—that happens all the time in a small town—but someone I felt I should have known but couldn't place. It was a fleeting thought, and I paid it no more attention.

In the basement of the library is a permanent display of used books for sale, as well as stacks of free magazines. For some reason there are always whole boxes of *National Geographic*. People must keep them and then decide all of a sudden, *That's it, too many, time to go.* I went straight for those. I spent forty-five minutes flipping through dozens of issues, and I found several that had what I was looking for. The *National Geographic* always has exceptional photos of ordinary people, even when the people are starving or

130

broken. I wasn't sure these photos were actually *real* in the sense of honest—I no longer trusted the integrity of any contemporary photos—but still they were less commercial than any others I knew.

In fact the museum catalogue had included a few well-known *National Geographic* photographs, and one of them was central to the exhibit, but those were all at least a few decades old and thus more likely to be true. It was probably always possible to deceive a viewer, but these days, an honest photograph is rare. I'm not talking about what you can do in the developing, with light, contrast, focus, that sort of thing. I'm talking about grossly, blatantly altering the content. By "true" I mean one that is not artificially, digitally manipulated—to remove the zits on a teenager's school picture, for example. If you're going to manipulate a photo, you should do it in a way that's transparent, where the viewer can see what you're doing—blurring the edges, playing with contrast. If you hide the process, you cheat the viewer of part of the experience—the part that requires using your brain and not just your heart. Manipulating the viewer secretly is cheating. It's sleazy. Cheap. It lacks artistic and personal integrity.

I thought the photos in the catalogue that kept haunting me *were* honest, at least in the sense I'm talking about. Whether it's *ethical* to make art from someone's suffering is a whole other question. What makes a photograph art, anyway? The woman with the bruised face who took the self-portrait, was she making art?

I knew as a young photographer there was no such thing as a mere observer. We learned this in college anthropology: any observation changes the thing observed. I think that's a law of physics, too. So you can't just observe, by definition, but you can be a participant-observer, which acknowledges that by observing you're participating in the event somehow. Which means, in the case of war photography, for example, that you're colluding. That is, if you're trying to make art. If you're bearing witness to suffering, maybe that's something else. But then, is it art?

I wish I had taken a picture of Adam in the hospital. It would have been unthinkable at the time. The idea of anyone taking a picture of Adam when he was dead, least of all me, would have been completely appalling. I know it's a tradition in other times and places, but I would have thought it ghoulish and perverse. Still, I wish now that I had. Why? I'm not even sure. Is it so the image of him lying inert in the hospital bed would have been transferred to a piece of shiny paper that I could obliterate, allowing me to quit seeing it in my head? I don't think so. That wouldn't have worked anyway. Then why? Maybe I'm just wishing for more, and any new photo would do. Any picture that came into my life now, after eight years, would be like getting a tiny piece of Adam back. Crazy thinking, I know. But it would be a gift, like the occasional dream of him. Or I could be deceiving myself.

On my way out with the magazines I didn't know what I was going to do with, I thought again of the young blond man I'd glimpsed on the way in, but he was no longer there. Who had he reminded me of? Maybe I'd imagined it. I wished I could remember.

Max

On Friday afternoon, I kept checking my watch. When I finally had run into him the day before—surprisingly perhaps, but I'd been confident I would—I didn't get the sense he was entirely pleased. I saw him in the distance simply walking across campus and called to him. Perhaps he didn't completely trust me. That was understandable. Perhaps I was more gruff than I meant to be. Also understandable. In any case, when I asked him whether he still wanted to study with me, he said yes. And when I said he'd have to study damn hard, he shrugged, as if that was fine with him, no big deal.

But would he show up? I'd been more certain of finding him than I was now of his following through. But at two on the dot he knocked on my office door. I called to him to come in, in English this time, and he did. He was wearing the same parka and sweater, probably the same jeans and shirt from the look of him. I wondered if he'd had a bath.

"Good. I wasn't sure you'd make it. Welcome."

"I said I would." He took off his book bag and jacket and hung them over the back of a chair.

"So you did. Come in—and don't get too comfortable, philosophy is a rigorous discipline."

Jason didn't smile. He seemed to take me literally and remained standing. He looked around the office. "You have a lot of books." He ran his hand along the shelves as he had the first time he was there.

"So you've said. See any you've read? Or would like to read?"

He withdrew his hand. "I don't know."

I wanted to set him at ease; if I was going to do this, I wanted to do it right. "So. Here you are. Where would you like to start? With the Greeks, the first philosophers? Or with how to think about thinking?"

He returned his attention to the books. My shelves are full and appear chaotic in spite of their internal order. At the end of the rows, volumes are piled on top of each other, and additional titles are squeezed in on top on nearly every shelf. Jason said, "Have you read all these?"

"Pretty much."

"Are they, like, your friends? I read that one." He ran a finger down the spine as if he were stroking it.

"*Beloved*?" I was surprised.

"We had to read it for school."

"What did you think of it?"

"It was okay. It kept me awake at night. How come you have it here?"

"It's an extraordinary book, a—"

"But I mean, it's fiction."

"Yes."

"But you teach philosophy."

"I'm still interested in ethics, good and evil as you call it, even though I don't teach it anymore. *Beloved* is—"

"It really bothered me. It's supposed to be this incredible book, right, but I mean, it's kind of upsetting. I mean like I couldn't sleep. The whole thing about—well, you know."

"What was upsetting?"

"Well, I mean, she killed her baby."

"Right. Of course the child comes back as a young woman."

"But it doesn't matter, does it. For the mother, I forget her name. She's still done this awful thing."

I said, "Don't you think it's partly about forgiveness?"

"Forgiveness? I didn't get that from it."

"Sethe—the mother—meant to kill her child. She did it on purpose. But why, do you think?"

"You have this book because you teach it?"

"No. I'll tell you my journey another time. In fact I have taught a course on philosophy and literature, but not this book. It's too—. Look, let's start with something less complex—for my sake if not for yours. Parents and children, love and despair, the sins of the fathers, that'll be our advanced class. Why don't you sit down?" There are two chairs in my office besides mine. On Wednesday—was it only two days ago?—Jason had sat in the chair close to my desk, where students usually sit. Today he chose the one farther away, an easy chair in the corner, flanked by bookcases on both sides.

I went on. "The pre-Socratics were concerned about the nature of the universe. Thales, for example, was—"

"Okay, wait. How about we talk about good and evil?"

I stopped. What was the best approach here? I wasn't accustomed to being interrupted all the time. But okay, directness was good; it was good to get right to the point. *Go with the flow,* I told myself, in imitation of my students. "Right. What is it about good and evil you want to know?"

"What is it, for a start. Like how do you define it."

"You mean, how do *you* know? As opposed to my defining it for everyone? Because each of us has his own sense of what's evil to him. Even those who commit premeditated murder often don't think they're doing something wrong. I'm talking about real people, not fictional characters."

"Fictional characters are real people."

"Ah. What's real? I'm not qualified to talk about literature or the nature of reality from a literary perspective, whatever that might be. Shall we stay with good and evil?"

He shrugged. "By the way, I go by Jocko now."

That threw me off. Jocko? I was having a hard enough time connecting this guy with the little Jason Green. But I could rally. "All right. Jocko, then. You're a different person from the one I knew. Where were we? Human beings have a built-in sense of right and wrong."

"Wait—"

I leaned back in my chair, anticipating his question. "How do you know whether your own sense of right and wrong can be trusted? You don't."

"I—"

"That's why we study ethical systems, to discover the logic inherent within them, to try to understand. For example, Confucius—"

"So there *are* answers. You said 'ethical systems.' I thought so."

"Only in one sense. Of course, it would be nice to have *the* answer, but..."

He gave me a rather scornful look. "Now you sound like a shrink."

"A shrink? Hardly. Psychology looks for answers within human beings. Philosophy..." I hesitated, watching him. He walked his left hand along the shelf as far as he could reach from where he

136

sat. He nudged each book so they all lined up perfectly a half inch from the edge.

"Look," I said. "It helps to have *reason* behind your idea of what's good and what's bad. Confucius, for example, believed that social harmony was the greatest good, and therefore measured action against that question: does it enhance or disrupt the community? For example: if I steal your umbrella, you get upset. Let's say a fight ensues. That upsets the community. Now if I steal your wife, you get even more upset. You may even to try to kill me. Thus even greater social disruption, more disharmony. In this way we establish a hierarchy of evil."

Jocko suddenly lurched from his seat like a jack-in-the-box as if he could bear to sit no longer. He hovered next to the books beside his chair.

"But here's the problem," I said quickly. "Here's the question it comes down to: Is social harmony the greatest good? What if *my* happiness depends on having *your* wife? What if I love her terribly, and if I can't have her, I'm going to be miserable?"

"If my wife left me to be with some other guy, I'd—"

"What would you do?"

He pulled a book from the shelf. "I don't know."

"But think about it. What would you do? Throw a fit? Hit someone? Kill? Toward whom would you direct your anger? Which of the two—or yourself?"

"I wouldn't kill—"

"Why not? For the welfare of the community, because it's disharmonious, or for some other reason?" I'd come around my desk by then and I gently took the book from him and replaced it.

"I wouldn't do any of those things." He looked suddenly deflated.

"Why not?"

"It would make me feel worse."

"And the wife, assuming you killed the lover? How would she feel?"

"I wouldn't kill the lover."

"So then—"

He raised his voice. "I told you! I'm not going to kill anyone. I don't even like to fight."

"Of course not. Nor do you have a wife, as far as I know. I'm speaking hypothetically. But you can see the tension here, right? The community versus the person—what's good for the polis, the community, versus what's good for the individual. Or what the individual *thinks* he wants. You, for example, may be an individualist."

Jocko blew out his cheeks and sat down, as if with relief, having found something that made sense. "Definitely."

"I mean in philosophical terms. An individualist looks inside himself to find out what he wants, whereas a Confucian looks to see what society expects, in order to know what to do. When you're young—"

"Excuse me, Professor Henry—"

"You can just call me Max."

Jocko shook his head. "If my wife wants to go with some other guy, and she *tells* me—you know, rather than sneaking around, if she's out there, like, this is the deal—then it seems like it's a sad thing for me, but nobody's doing anything wrong. It's not evil."

"You're not hurt because she left you?"

"Well, yeah, but I mean."

"What?"

"She didn't do it to hurt me. I mean if she didn't. If it just, like, you know, happened."

"Do you think things like that just happen?"

"Yeah. I mean, sure. Girls are, you know—" He stopped.

"No. What?"

He shrugged. "I don't do anything but they like me anyway."

"We're not talking about one-night stands here, right? We're talking about profound engagement, where the consequences of an action might have an enormous impact, as with Helen of Troy, when Paris was madly in love. You know the difference, right?"

"I don't have a girlfriend, if that's what you mean. I'm too… whatever. Anyway, it doesn't matter. It's weird, like they want to rub up against me. You know, like cats. Things just happen."

I couldn't help but smile. "Let's get back to the problem at hand. If your girlfriend is stolen away—"

"It used to make me uncomfortable, but now."

"Now?"

"Now I just go with it. I figure if they want to, why not?"

"You're talking about sex."

"I'm just saying things happen. Bad things, good things, you just go with it, you know?" He drummed his fingers on the arms of the chair—surprisingly long, graceful fingers in such big hands. I had a fleeting impulse to mention safe sex but thought better of it. We were here to discuss—what? My mind went blank. *Everything except Adam.* Everything except Jason's possible role in my son's death.

Wait, wait. Wrong track! This is not about Adam.

But Jason was there. And I wasn't. And I should have been.

"Mr. Henry?"

I took a deep breath, ran my hands through my hair. *Things just happen.* "Okay, look. If your girlfriend is stolen away by someone else by force—if he comes into her bedroom and kidnaps her—

then there's no question, right? Breaking and entering, kidnapping, they're wrong as well as illegal. What's more difficult in life is assigning blame—not blame, I don't mean blame, I mean responsibility—when things are more complicated. Fixing blame is never hard. Let's say your girlfriend—"

"Could you leave me out of it? Because trolls don't really have girlfriends." He rose to look at the books once more. But now I wanted him to stop fidgeting and concentrate. Listen.

"Hang on, Jason, I'm trying to help you."

"I don't want you to *help* me. I just want to learn."

I wrestled with myself for a moment. Finally I said, "That's what I meant."

He said, "And it's Jocko. I told you."

I nodded. "All right. Let's address a less loaded subject—no murder or sex. Something simple. Let's say you adopt a cat from the Humane Society and you've agreed to keep it inside. But the cat seems to really want to go out, so after a year or so you let it. For a while it's okay, but then one day the cat gets run over and killed. Are you responsible?"

Jocko hesitated. "The guy driving the car—"

"Do things like that just happen?"

"Well, yeah. ...

"Bad luck, eh?"

"Excuse me, is this philosophy? Is this what you teach?"

I ran my hands through my hair; the conversation was too personal. My fault. I made a last attempt to steer it back. "The point is, people have very different views of the world and how it works. That's what you learn in philosophy. There are no absolute—."

"So, like me and my Dad. Or you and me."

My voice rose in spite of myself. "I'm not talking about fathers and sons. I'm talking about Thales who thought the world was made of water. Heraclitus who thought it was made of fire, everything burning, burning up. Impermanence. Everything changes, nothing lasts, everything is in conflict with its opposite, and this conflict, this eternal masochistic grating of flint on rock, creates a, a *conflagration*."

"Whoa."

I took a deep breath. "That's enough for today, Jason."

"Jocko."

"Jocko. We'll take up where we left off, on Monday."

"Who are those guys you just said?"

I pulled a book from the bookcase. "Never mind. Old dead white guys, Greeks, but we're done with them. Here, read this. Confucius, *The Analects*. No, actually, read this. Basho, *The Road to the Deep North*."

"By Monday?"

"Do you have anything else to do? Look, not the whole thing, just jump around in it."

"Right." Jocko took the book and slouched toward the door, where he hesitated, as if reluctant to leave. "So, do you believe in divine retribution?"

"I'm a philosopher, not a theologian."

"Well, how about justice?"

"Justice. What is justice?" I gathered up the papers on my desk. Our first class, if that's what it was, had not gone very well, but I thought I could do better. I regretted my outburst. "I don't know. Let's talk about that on Monday." *Just come back*, I thought.

When he left, he closed the door quietly.

I sent thoughts after him like little spears, harpoons with ropes attached. *Just come back on Monday.*

Richard

THE WARM FRONT LINGERED into Saturday. I'd been invited to a party that evening, but I'd seen clients all day and felt I'd had enough of people. Besides, I really wanted to go through my peony catalogues before watching a movie.

For gardeners in Vermont, where spring comes so late, one of life's pleasures is poring over catalogues at the end of winter and planning the summer's garden. Gardening is a wonderful occupation for a solitary man. You could say I garden to see things grow and I watch movies to escape, but of course the truth would be more complicated. One can escape into gardening and grow through repetitive film-watching. For that matter, you can *say* anything you want, but saying doesn't make it so. Which is why I make my living as an accountant and not a philosopher or a designer or anyone else who has to deal with ambiguity.

Along the driveway, I have a few other tall things mixed in with the peonies for variety, like snapdragons and hollyhock. In one corner of the back yard I have a memorial garden for dead friends and family, where I plant zinnias and dahlias and the like, including purple things for Hecky. And as mentioned, in the front we kept a few bushes. But everywhere else, the yarrow, astilbe, baptisia, sedum, bleeding heart and all the rest have given way over time to a careful cultivation of peonies. They bloom almost all season long because of their staggered times. This takes some doing—and it is for this reason that I like to hunker down with a glass of wine and my catalogues. This is the time of year when I indulge in the fantasy that I am not a straight-laced accountant with clumsy, uptight hands in a small, constrained life but rather the Harold Bloom of gardening, not overly imaginative perhaps but fully inhabiting a world of rampant sensuality, riotous color, unrestrained joyful exuberance. Pretending is different from ambiguity.

Most people don't know that you can get peonies that bloom at different times or that some varieties have a fragrance. John Harvard, for example, is a single red early bloomer. Cherry Hill is a semi-double, purplish crimson peony that also blooms early. Coral 'n' Gold, pink with a yellow center, blooms early to mid-season. Bridal Shower, a double white, blooms mid-season. Nick Shaylor is another double white, but it blooms late, and its buds have carmine streaks and the interior of its blooms starts out pink and fades to white. Edward Flynn is a mid-to-late double red, and Ann Cousins is a late- to very late-blooming double white.

I know there's nothing especially unusual about my gardens; I have acquaintances whose gardens are much more complex and sophisticated. Those boys know what they're doing: in their yards, textures and shapes and sizes mingle and startle and you feel like you're in another world. But aside from Hecky's help the first year, I planted all my gardens myself. They may not be breathtaking or original, but here's what I've noticed: it turns out that even ordinary, uninspired gardens can be beautiful.

That Saturday I spread out my three favorite catalogues and the maps I keep of my various gardens, showing what grows where, along with my codes at the bottom that indicate blooming times, color, size/age, fragrance or lack thereof. I was happily sketching out an addition to the front, playing with what I might do with an extra two or three feet, erasing and re-creating, when the phone rang. It was Alice, asking me to come help her put together her drum set. *Entreating* me. Hadn't I assembled complicated science-kit-type constructions as a kid? Wasn't I expert at such things?

What, following directions? Where was Max?

Oh, *Max*. *Max* couldn't help, he was no good at that sort of thing. Please would I come, it was too much for her—too many little parts, she couldn't bear it. "I know it's a big favor, but I'll owe you one, and I'll send you home with a chicken I just picked up. Fully cooked, still warm? Let yourself in, I'm in the basement."

I set aside my catalogues with an enormous sigh for no one's benefit but my own. The truth is I was intrigued. I wanted to see up close the drums I never got to play.

I slipped on my shoes, grabbed a light sweater and locked the door. It was still probably forty-five degrees even though the sun was going down, great weather for the end of March, when it could just as easily have been thirty-three and raining. The dirty berms of slush alongside the driveway looked softer in the dusky light.

I let myself in as instructed and was surprised, and slightly annoyed, to find Max in the kitchen, cooking. It smelled wonder-fully of sautéed onions and garlic. "Sorry, I would have knocked. I didn't think you were here."

Max stood in front of the stove, stirring. "I found him."

I didn't know what to say. I'd guessed that earlier but hoped it wasn't true. "You don't sound all that happy about it."

"I'm having transference issues already."

"That would be the danger, yes."

"You have no idea."

I hate it when people do that. *Actually I do have some idea, but no, I'm not you, and guess what, you're not me, so you have no idea what I know.* It's so irritating.

"Well, congratulations. You can tell me *all* about it on Tuesday, as I'm sure you will. For now I have a date with your wife." I headed for the basement.

"Richard," Max said. I stopped, a few feet from him. "Do you know what it's like to look into the future and see yourself as a childless, bereft old man?"

I raised my eyebrows. He smiled. "I suppose you do."

For a moment we stood there, two fifty-five-year-old childless men in a small, brightly lit kitchen that smelled comfortingly of garlic and onions, I aware of Max's physical nearness and warmth and he musing about God knows what, holding a wooden spoon in the air. The sheer domesticity was romantic. He looked at me and it was one of those brief cracks in time where anything could happen. But like most such moments, it passed without event. Max suddenly turned back to the onions and stirred them vigorously, and I opened the basement door.

He said to my back, "I don't know if I can do it." I knew he was referring to Jocko.

"Well, don't then." I started down the steps.

"I have to. I have no choice." But he was talking more to himself than to me. And he sounded so goddamned earnest.

What, it's a life and death matter? I wanted to strangle him. *I* was supposed to be the drama queen.

"Thanks for the sympathy!" he called after me.

I found Alice in the basement as she'd said, sitting cross-legged on the rug.

"What was Max yelling about?"

"I don't know. It's a guy thing." I was getting better at deception all the time.

Spread around Alice on the floor were four drums, three cymbals, and a little family of things in plastic bags, some of which she had opened, which turned out to be drum heads, rims, tension rods (also called drum lug screws she told me), legs, spurs, claws, hoops and other masculine sounding names. We were in the half-finished side of the basement, where drywall covered the peeling cinderblocks and fluorescent lights buzzed behind a low ceiling of transparent plastic panels. A worn-out oval rug covered half of the cement floor. I don't sit on floors, so I pulled up a chair from the long worktable and set to reading the directions. *It's not Alice's fault,* I said to myself.

"I've already figured out which drum is which," Alice said.

"Great, but I want to start at the beginning."

Alice leaned back on her hands. "Bass drum, tom, floor tom, snare. Those two cymbals go together, they're called hi-hat, and the other one is a crash cymbal. You start with the bass drum."

"Did you check to make sure all the pieces are here first?"

She sighed. I already knew she hadn't; her way was to jump in. Mine was to read the directions.

Having done so, I felt disappointed that they were so straightforward. They even seemed to be written by a native English speaker and didn't require additional translation, which was half the fun.

But reading all the steps calmed me down. "Alice, honey, this is easy. You don't need me."

She looked doubtful.

"All right, fine. We'll do it together." I did like Alice, after all. I *loved* Alice. It was her husband…

After ascertaining that all the pieces had arrived in the box and hadn't got lost as a result of Alice's enthusiasm, I began fitting and attaching—spur mounts to spurs, drum heads to drums, rims to drum heads. I tried to engage Alice in the process, but having turned it over to me, she gave up any participation. "I'll just watch you." She pulled her knees up and rested her chin between them. It seemed like she wanted to talk about something, but was waiting for the right time.

I immersed myself in this project cheerfully. It was good to have something detailed to focus on rather than Max and Jocko, about whom I now had a vague but intense sense of dread. I finished all four drums in short order, attached the small tom to the top of the bass, and tightened the lugs around the drum heads in the same way you tighten the bolts of a tire, as if you're drawing a star. There was something terribly satisfying about it. Accounting is more concrete than philosophy—at least the numbers add up and the results are verifiable and visible—but growing this drum set… this was a physical contraption capable of creating sound that went on and on. Maybe it was a tiny taste of what it felt like to make a baby. I urged myself on: *You go, girl!*

Alice said, "Richard, can I ask you something? Why is it you never found anyone else?"

I'd almost forgotten she was there. "You make it sound like I never will."

She looked at me over her knees. "Tell me about Hecky."

"Why?" She didn't answer. I said, "He was a brilliant architect, handsome—cute, really—and funny. He had a dry, sarcastic wit. And he died raging. Not one of those reconciled, peaceful deaths."

Alice pondered this or whatever she was thinking about, while I worked on the cymbals. I set up the stand, threaded the crash cymbal onto it between a washer and cymbal-felt on each side and tightened the wing nut. I started on the hi-hat cymbal. Then she said, "Were you monogamous?"

"The first few years, no. It was the time; we were young. The last ten or so years we were—or I was. Why? If you're having an affair or even thinking about it, I do *not* want to know. I mean it, Alice. I'm not kidding."

Alice smiled sort of ruefully as if she wished she were but never would, and I thought, *Well, thank God for that.*

She said, "When Max and I were courting, I told him I wanted to do something big with my life. I didn't know what it was, I just felt like there was something in me waiting to break out. Something exciting I didn't know about yet. He said he'd be my coachman and I could drive the coach."

"And?"

"And then I had Adam. And now I'm childless and coachless."

"What does that mean?" I made sure the top cymbal was between its two felts and slid it over the pull-rod. I tightened the clutch wing nut. Lacking a tape measure, I had to eyeball the three-quarter-inch distance required between the two cymbals. This made me anxious, but I did it.

"I don't know," she said finally. "I just wish Max and I could have a project together."

So she didn't know about Jocko. Or maybe she did but wasn't interested. Not likely. More likely, Max was keeping it a secret, the jerk. Should I tell her? But it wasn't up to me. I ripped open the plastic bags containing the hi-hats and slid the bottom one, inverted, onto the stand.

"You know," she said. "If it's too annoying, don't do it."

"Do what?"

"Put the drums together. You look annoyed."

"I'm just concentrating."

"Because if it's too hard, we can just take them back."

"Alice, it's fine. I'm enjoying it." I stopped. "Do you *want* to take them back?" When she didn't answer, I kept working.

After a pause, she said, "We probably should have had another child."

I tightened the wing nut and set a height I imagined would work for Alice. Or me, since we're the same height.

She went on. "But I thought one would be enough. You know I was already *thirty-seven* when Adam died."

"That's not too old. I know lesbians who adopt in their fifties."

Alice rocked back and forth. "It was too old for me. It was too much: should we have two in case something happened to the first? People actually said that to me—that we should have had two. I would have been near sixty when the child was twenty. And Max would've been near seventy."

From my position at fifty-five, sixty didn't look very old, but on the other hand, *I* wouldn't have wanted to raise a child at my age even if I had wanted one earlier, which I didn't. "Hand me that last little bag." It held the drum key, which is like a wrench for tightening the lugs. I moved to the drum seat. The directions said to tune the drums to "what sounds best for you." My heart sank: artsy vagueness. I had no idea. It wasn't like choosing peonies, after all. Drums have a *pitch,* that has to work with other instruments presumably? But what did I know. Maybe there was even more chaos in the world than I thought. A horrifying idea. Maybe I'd leave this part for Alice.

Alice said, "The world is so hard now. It's got to be hell for a teenaged boy."

"I wouldn't know about that."

She said, "You're right, you don't. I'm sorry, darling, but you're old. The world is so different now."

"Oh, please." I gave her a look. "I was a fat gay teenager?" She was doing to me what Max had done an hour earlier: *You don't know how it feels.* Agh! I turned my attention to the tuning, which overall seemed a less daunting task than trying to understand Alice. I tapped the small tom and tightened the lugs—cautiously as advised, so as not to overtighten. But what tone was right? What pitch? I shook my head. Ah, what the hell.

"I wish I'd known him," Alice said.

"Who?" I began another careful crisscross through the lugs, tightening and tapping.

"Hecky!"

"Oh. Well, I'm not sure you would have liked him. He was a pretty *out there* kind of guy."

"I probably would have adored him. I wonder whether you guys would've ever had children? You know, adopted."

Not knowing what I'm doing does not ordinarily make me jump into an activity—or enjoy it once I'm there. I'm not a jumper-in even when I do know what I'm doing. But the little tom was coming to life as I tightened the lugs. I had total control over the sound. The power was going to my head, made me feel reckless. I knocked the head with my knuckle until it seemed right.

"Not likely. Even if we'd wanted to, it wasn't possible back then." I moved on to the floor tom, flexing my arms as I did.

The floor tom was tight enough now to make a decent sound. I compared it to the small tom—not different enough. I set to tightening it further.

Alice uncurled herself as if released. "Richard, I'm worried about Max."

Uh oh. Here it comes. I paused to listen to my new tones. The exhilarating sense of power was slipping away as inconspicuously as it had arrived. I tightened, knocked, listened.

"He's distracted. He's had this book project, you know, that he's been working on all sabbatical, and it's had its ups and downs, and going to the jail takes a lot out of him. I suppose it gives him a lot, too—he likes working with those guys. But this week…"

I gave the drum one final whack. It seemed all right.

With a drumstick she'd retrieved from the floor, Alice whacked the two toms and the hi-hat.

"What about it?" I said.

"It just occurred to me this week—. I'm afraid—. There's just a certain kind of preoccupation I've never seen before. I mean—. Richard, do you think he could be having an affair?"

I quieted the cymbal. "No."

"Would you tell me if he was?"

I was almost finished. "Alice, there's all this stuff about rings and overtones that I'm ignoring for now. You can get different heads of different thicknesses. This part is the head, you know that, right? But that's for later. For now we'll leave it like this." I gave the bass a couple of thumps with the foot pedal. I didn't know if it sounded the way it was supposed to, but that was all I could do.

"So you're saying you wouldn't tell me."

"Honestly? I don't know. I don't know if Max would tell me if he was. On the other hand, men like to brag about these things, so it's probably safe to say he hasn't. Anyway, I don't really think he's the type, do you?"

She returned to the futon and flopped down like a teenager. "I wouldn't have thought so. Loyal to *morte*, like you. But something's going on, and he won't tell me."

"Max adores you. You know that." I'd left the snare for last. I'd tightened the heads already and now I set about tightening the screw apparatus they call the strainer that holds the wires under the drum. The wires were what made the snap sound that characterizes a snare.

Alice pulled a pillow in front of her chest and held it against her. "I've had the worst thoughts lately. I've even wondered if we've been staying together just to prove we could."

"Alice! You two are made for each other!"

"It's just that our marriage feels kind of fragile all of a sudden."

Goddamn Max. What was he doing, keeping this from her? *Just tell her, for Christ's sake.* But now I certainly couldn't tell her; it would be as if confirming a betrayal. She was right, he was having a secret relationship. "You shouldn't be talking to me, you should be talking to a marriage counselor."

"Maybe. But you know us; you know our history. What do you think?"

"I think you should get your camera and document this momentous event—the completion of your new drum set. Look at it, it's beautiful. Or let me take a picture of you sitting at your new drums."

She shook her head. "I don't even know where my camera is."

I helped her up and led her to the drums.

She admired them properly but made no move to sit. "You first," she said.

I shook my head and guided her onto the stool. I handed her the drumsticks.

She said, "Didn't you want to play drums when you were a kid?"

"That was then." If it was too late for Alice to make babies, it was certainly too late for me to play the drums. "You're the one who wants to make noise now. I prefer to be quiet and invisible."

She poked me in the belly with the drumsticks. "Right, I forgot." Then to my complete surprise, as I'd have expected a more tentative beginning, she attacked the drums with a fury—an unrhythmic, chaotic melee without any redeeming feature. After a whirling moment, she paused, breathless. I took advantage of this to bend down and kiss her cheek.

"Don't worry, darling. I'm sure you'll get better."

She reminded me to pick up the chicken on the counter. Max was nowhere to be seen, but the chicken was wrapped up in a dish. When I let myself out, Alice was still pounding away below, relentless and punishing.

I went home, unwrapped the chicken and took it upstairs to eat while watching "Midway." "Midway" has the greatest scenes of airborne fighting and a less touted but equally significant subplot about a father and son who are both courageous and highly skilled pilots. But the best thing about the movie, the most shocking and strangely satisfying from a plot perspective, is this: In the end, after

154

the son has been badly burned in the battle (but we know he's going to make it), all the fighters are returning to the carrier. The father's plane, badly damaged, is the last to come in. (This is Charlton Heston, young and handsome.) We're sure we're about to see a terrific narrow escape, maybe the plane bumping and smoking a bit but settling so Heston can claw his way out of the cockpit wounded but alive, embodying the final triumph of a victorious America! Instead, the plane skids on the carrier, careens around for a second or two—and explodes. End of Charlton Heston.

The first time I saw it, I was so stunned I couldn't move for several minutes. Wasn't it Icarus, the son, who died in the fiery crash? Not the father! Now when I watch it, I wonder whether the end seems inevitable because I'm old and cynical or because that's the way the world really is.

Max

Sunday afternoon. Notes for the punishment book, which by the way still lacks a title. Under consideration: *The Myth of Punishment. Why Punishment Doesn't Work (and Why We Wish It Did). The Secret About Retribution.* Or something more personal like *A Philosopher's Delayed Response to His Son's Death?*

A bad joke.

How do I talk to him? How do I talk to the young man who is also the boy who was with my son when he died? How do I help him? Do I want to help him?

I've made endless notes about the history of punishment, but the point suddenly eludes me. Hammurabi's "eye for an eye, tooth for a tooth" must have been radical in its time. Otherwise there would have been no reason to inscribe the idea onto stone pillars that have lasted three thousand years. Hammurabi must have known he had arrived at a new, potentially transformative idea.

Not that it succeeded in transforming the world. Justice around the world still takes the form of furiously disproportionate retribution. You kill my son, I'm going to wipe out your entire village.

Jason didn't kill my son.

But even if he had, such an extreme response is not rational.

No one could logically, dispassionately defend it as fair. Still, the impulse is interesting to me. The idea of balance, where the punishment equals the crime in severity, has a certain elegant appeal. Yet clearly the determination of balance depends on where you stand. What's equal severity? I could very well believe that the lives of a whole village add up to the life of my son. It's unlikely anyone in the village is going to share that view, however, so if you're going to have a system that's universally acceptable, you have to get agreement on the definition of balance or fairness.

What's fair?

What's fair, Jason Green?

Take teenaged boys from different cultures. What if in my culture, a dirty look is a grave insult, perhaps equivalent to a slug. So, if you look at me wrong, I hit you. But in your culture, an unprovoked slug (as you experience it) requires a return punch, so you hit me back. And so it goes.

Scorekeeping, as any married man will tell you, is a no-win game.

What I said to Jason is true: the questions matter more than the answers. But don't we look to history, the history of ideas, for elucidation of the questions? Philosophers, social historians, psychologists have all contributed usefully to the discussion of punishment: why we do it, why we believe in it, why it does or doesn't work. Defenders have historically fallen into two camps—those who, looking forward, believe that punishment is good for the offender or the society or both (utilitarians) and those who, looking backward, believe that criminals *deserve* to be punished because of their crime (retributivists). In the first case, also called consequentialism, the punishment helps the offender by showing him the error of his ways, giving him a chance to repent and improve his chances for entering Heaven, that sort of thing, and it helps society by providing clear consequences and thereby strengthening the social order.

In the second case, also called deontology, those who have committed a crime deserve to be punished on moral, not social, grounds. Because they did something "bad" they deserve to suffer. There is no room in retributivist thought for the idea that suffering produces bad acts and thus augmenting suffering serves no purpose—or no purpose that can be morally justified. Punishment is a goal in itself, required by justice.

But does anyone deserve to suffer? Isn't my life as a teacher about helping students understand the world so they suffer less? Or is it? Do I care about their suffering or just their mastery of the material?

Do I want Jason Green to suffer? Of course not, but then if I'm honest, yes, I do. Because he was there. Because he lived and Adam didn't. Because I hurt and therefore so should he. But that's irrational, and so, no, I don't. Because I have a mind that can reason.

I doubt I can interest him in any of this intellectual history. I don't know his background, and he may find the material pretty dry—and yet, it *matters*. It matters that Hobbes asked where the right to punish comes from, as far back as 1651. In 1690, John Locke wrote that the right to punish exists within the social contract but should be limited to reparation and restraint. In 1764, the Italian thinker Cesare Beccaria, well known in the field of penology if not otherwise, argued that the purpose of punishment is to deter criminals and others from doing harm, and therefore punishment should be proportional to the crime. It should make a strong impression and yet "inflict the least torment on the body of the criminal."

Look at American jails. At the end of the twentieth century, we still have to point out that excessive punishment (excessive even by the standards of those who believe punishment can be effective) simply creates angry, embittered people with greater criminal skills. Prison teaches criminality.

Some people must have known this even before Hammurabi. Wise men likely have known it since we as a species began to think. Wise men and mothers. But in any case Jeremy Bentham expressed it in 1781 in a book called *Introduction to the Principles of Morals and Legislation*: "All punishment is mischief: all punishment in itself is evil." I wish we could leave it there—I wish that were the end of it—but nothing is that simple. Bentham went on to argue that punishment might at times serve a purpose and to propose when those times might be: "[Punishment] ought only to be admitted in as far as it promises to exclude some greater evil."

There's the rub. How would it do that, "exclude some greater evil"? And "promises"? The danger is obvious. Anyone can make promises. I could promise that by torturing Jason emotionally I could offer him redemption, but... Even extreme punishments can be justified by this argument. Cutting off the hands arguably prevents a man from stealing. Cutting off his head prevents him from maligning the king. Whether or not stealing or maligning the king are greater evils than cutting off hands or head depends, naturally, on whether you're the king or the owner of the head and hands. Bentham's wisdom lies in his earlier recognition that punishment in itself creates suffering.

Which brings us, if we stay with the Brits, to John Stuart Mill. Mill argued that *nothing* justifies inflicting suffering in response to suffering.

A veritable Buddhist. Never mind that Zen priests whack their students; no doubt that's to save them from the greater evil of continuing on the path of illusion.

So where does that leave me?

On the one hand I see men in prison who shouldn't be there. I see examples everywhere of humans wanting revenge, wanting to create suffering in each other in the mistaken belief that this would mitigate our own pain. I see Alice and me dancing around each other trying to avoid each other's pain and clinging to each other and trying the best we can to avoid causing more pain.

And now I have this kid, whom I've wanted to kill, who I've wished had died instead of my own son, but who has borne his own burden all these years—and I'm not sure what to do with him. I *don't* want him to suffer. I don't want to cause anyone suffering, ever. There's enough suffering in the world, I know. Adam's death wasn't Jason's fault, I know that, too. I think I know that. I believe he wants me to forgive him., to absolve him of responsibility. I could do that. I could say... something. I have no idea what, but after all, words are easy, I dwell in words. But would it change anything? Would it actually matter?

Yes. It matters. For some reason it matters profoundly. Nothing in the past eight years has mattered to me as much. This makes no sense, but I believe—how can I say this without sounding melodramatic?—my own redemption depends on my rescuing him.

What if he *had* died instead of Adam? What if Adam had carried around this weight, this horrendous, crushing guilt, whether he was responsible or not, for eight years? Wouldn't I do absolutely anything I could to relieve his suffering? Of course.

What does this have to do with my punishment book? I don't know yet, but it's more than an academic exercise. It's my way in.

It's not just about my brain, it's about my heart. I may not be able to write the book—and in the end who cares about the book?—but perhaps, just perhaps, I can reach Jason.

Alice

I sort of wished Richard weren't coming for dinner Sunday night. I love Richard, but I wanted to talk to Max. We're so busy, sometimes we rarely see each other. On the other hand, Max had been working on his book all day at the university, so he'd be in his analytical mode which wasn't really what I wanted, so I concluded we might as well have a pleasant dinner together, the three of us. Maybe we'd plan our next big trip as a threesome, to Darfur or Syria or some other happy place.

Actually our trips together have worked well. A few years before, we'd gone to a film festival in Toronto, and before that we went to New York for a packed weekend to see three performances where musicians improvised scores to go along with classic films like *Potemkin*. We all liked that, for different reasons. Richard liked what the music added to the movies he already knew really well—because while he's an expert on World War II movies, he knows an amazing amount about other old movies, too. A hell of a lot more than I do, anyway. Max liked the idea of a new experience playing off an old one, and then he went off on a tangent about the circularity of time, and something about how even though we couldn't tell, the music and the film might actually be interacting in real time, rather than the film being fixed and the music being live. I didn't really get it. What I loved was the sheer creative energy in the hall. The music, the focus and stamina, the intensity of the musicians blew me away.

That Sunday night before dinner, remembering how alive I'd felt at that concert, I wondered why I hadn't done anything about it when we came home. It seemed to me now that the experience had slipped away as if it never happened. Curious.

In any case, now I was determined to finish paying the bills and balance the checkbook before dinner. By then, Max had made his black-beans-and-couscous dish, which Richard loves, with zucchini, tomatoes, onions, garlic, raisins, and lots of curry and cumin. I came into the kitchen just as Richard arrived, breathless, bursting through the door with uncharacteristic energy.

"Sorry, guys, I got delayed by a phone call from an old client who just found a little pile of 1099s she'd misplaced and she was sorry-sorry-sorry. Plus her brother's got prostate cancer which I had to hear about, because I've also known him a long time, but it's okay because he's going on a three-week bike trip in Vietnam this summer." He ignored Max and kissed me. "How's the drumming?"

"I haven't touched them."

"No? Why not?"

Max handed Richard a plate. "Here you go."

Max and I got our plates and we all sat down. The subject of my drumming was dropped in favor of discussion of the meal. Max liked to hear whether we noticed a new ingredient or a new spice. I waited for the right moment. Then Richard said, "Alice, have you gone on one of your periodic cleaning jags?"

Richard is the observant one. Max hadn't even noticed. But I said, "How do you know it was me? It could have been Max."

Richard smiled. He's so diplomatic. He could have said, *Max?! Are you kidding?* Instead he said, "Because you're the one who likes to stack and clump and move things from horizontal to vertical surfaces, and I can see new things tacked to the walls. Looks like some nice photos. Are they yours?"

"National Geographic."

Max gave me a quizzical look.

I reached behind me to the little card catalogue we use as a table and pulled the postcard from behind the lamp where I'd stashed it. "Max, look what I found when I was cleaning. I didn't know you still had it." I set it on the table against a candlestick, facing him.

He grimaced, picked it up.

"What is it?" Richard asked.

Max held it out to him. "Remember? I told you about this."

"Oh, yes. Your Italian trip. Over Christmas."

"And New Year's," I said.

The first December after Adam died, we'd gone to Italy. It was our first European trip since before Adam was born, and we wanted to do something really different. Neither one of us had any interest in celebrating Christmas. Without Adam, what was the point? Christmas, Halloween, Easter egg hunts, the Jewish holidays that Max had been slowly introducing one after another—they all disappeared. I suppose we could have resurrected Christmas—Max probably wouldn't have minded—but we go out for Chinese instead and give each other presents on our birthdays. But given everything else, that Italian trip was a good one and we'd told Richard all about it.

"You stayed in a convent outside Florence," he said now.

"It was cheap," I said.

Max smiled. "The nun tried to cheat us."

I nodded. "The wee nun."

The place had narrow single beds, overlooked by a wooden cross nailed to the wall. The first thing we did—Max, actually—was try to remove the cross, but it was too firmly attached, I suppose to prevent theft. Then every night we moved the mattresses to the floor, so we could sleep together. We were so wrapped up in our own grief during the day that we were like strangers, but at night it was as if we left off being Max and Alice, Grieving Parents, and became anonymous lovers—anonymous but appreciative and familiar.

To make space for the mattresses on the floor in that little convent room, we had to move the beds against the wall, and I insisted we do this as quietly as possible so no one would hear us. I also insisted we return the mattresses to the beds in the morning. We argued about this: Max said it made him feel like a child and the place gave him the creeps. After a few nights, he'd had enough. He managed to figure out the phones, which wasn't easy, and he found us a small hotel in the middle of the city.

But when we were leaving the convent and I was negotiating the bill with the nun in my halting French (our shared language), it got worse.

"What's the matter?" Max said.

"She's trying to cheat us. She says we have to pay for four nights." We were leaving a day earlier than planned, but it wasn't as if they'd had to turn anyone away; the place was almost empty.

"What!?"

"Never mind, Max. I'll deal with it. You take the bags outside, okay?"

"That's perfect. You tell her we're not paying a damn cent more. And the accommodations were lousy to start with." Not knowing the language, there was little he could do.

"Religion is evil," he said to me later that night over dinner. He'd gone outside and thrown his suitcase in a rage. A tribal fury filled him; that's how he described it. He imagined a Nazi flag hanging behind him from the roof, and he saw himself turn back to the house, unsling his Uzi and spray the front of the building.

That struck me as really funny, it was so unlike him, and I laughed. And then he laughed. We laughed together at the wee nun, and moving the beds, and my childish insistence on escaping detection, and the wee nun trying to cheat us, and the idea of Max going berserk with an Uzi, and something shifted. We laughed until we cried, and we held hands after dinner. I thought then we would be okay.

The little hotel where we stayed the rest of our ten days had equally small rooms and an uncomfortable double bed, but the little balcony overlooked a garden and the Duomo a half mile away; it was all very sweet. We made love without worrying about making noise. On New Year's Eve we were awakened at midnight by the sound of fireworks, and we stood arm in arm at the window and watched fireworks explode over the city, lighting up the Duomo and the bell towers and the clay tile roofs.

I'd remembered all this when I found the postcard in my clean-up. But I remembered the other stuff, too. "I bought it for you, remember?" I tapped it with my fork.

I said to Richard, "I don't think we told you this part." I glanced at Max. He continued eating. "Max didn't want to spend a lot of time in museums getting saturated with art he didn't care about.

So on the flight over, we made a list of what we wanted to see. In the Uffizi, five paintings. The morning after we moved to our new lodgings, we got to the Uffizi early and only had to stand in line a few minutes. That's the good thing about going in December. And it was fun. Remember?"

Max said mildly, "Do you remember how we spent twenty minutes comparing three paintings of the Virgin and Child? Neither of us could see why one was so much better than the other two, which the guidebook claimed. As I recall, all three left us cold."

He left out that at that moment he'd put his arm around me and said, inexplicably, "This is why I married you." I'd rested my head on his shoulder and my eyes welled up. I remembered this because it was an extraordinary moment; we were so separate in our grief.

We spent time with Botticelli's *Primavera,* and the *Birth of Venus.* We looked at Leonardo's unfinished *Adoration of the Magi* and I got to point out which figure some people thought was a self-portrait of the artist as a young man.

"And then there was the room of Caravaggios," I said now to Richard.

"I wanted to see the *Bacchus.* That was on my list."

Richard picked up the postcard to examine it more closely.

Max said, "That's not the *Bacchus.* That was on an adjoining wall."

"I remember," said Richard. "You told me about it. The *Akedah.*"

"Good memory," said Max. He took the postcard from Richard. He had a strange look on his face.

I don't remember much from that first year after Adam died, but many things about that trip are exceptionally clear. The convent, the fireworks over the Duomo, the Uffizi. Especially that painting.

It was large, about four feet by five. It depicted the sacrifice of Isaac, which as Richard noted Jews call the *Akedah,* the binding of Isaac. Somehow, though completely un-religious, Max knew this.

In the center of the painting, a balding old man with a full white beard leans over a boy, slightly older than Adam, maybe twelve or so. The old man has one hand on the boy's neck forcing him down and in his other hand he holds an upraised knife. He's looking away from the boy toward a third figure, a beautiful young man leaning into the scene, who has just grabbed the old man's wrist as if to keep him from using the knife. With his other hand the young man points toward something else, presumably the ram whose head hovers just above the boy.

The skin of the old man's hands is tanned and wrinkled. In the lower third of the picture the curly-headed boy, pressed against a slab of stone with his arms pulled behind him, looks out at the viewer in anguish, his mouth open.

It is a dark painting, all shades of umber and red. The old man wears a sienna robe draped with a swatch of deep vermilion around his waist. The light falls on the boy's face and shoulder and on the old man's face, and on the shoulder and hands of the angel. Of course it is an angel. In the background, dark trees with almost no texture stand in front of a Romanesque church or abbey on a hill with tall poplars. Another hill rises in the distance. It looks like Florence.

It is a beautiful, awful painting.

Now Max set the postcard against the candlestick and leaned back in his chair, still gazing at it.

"I've never understood that story," I said. "It's horrible." I appealed to Richard. "But Max was transfixed. I had to leave the room; it was claustrophobic. I left Max there and wandered around, came back about ten minutes later and he was still there. I told him I'd meet him in the museum store, but I was there a long time. I looked at everything twice. Finally Max arrived when I was coming out."

Max said, "And you'd bought the postcard. Just when I thought I was done with the painting."

"I was being the supportive wife."

Max gave a half-laugh. Then he said thoughtfully, "It doesn't really capture it though, does it?"

"I suppose not."

Richard was intently observing Max, as he often does. Max looked pained.

"Where did you find it?" Max asked.

"On your desk, stuck in one of those cubbies. I was looking to see if I'd missed an oil bill I couldn't find a record of having paid. Why do you still have it?"

"You gave it to me." Max shook his head, and turned the post-card face down. "I don't know."

"I can't think why I ever bought it," I said. "The image is just awful."

"It's a beautiful painting," Richard offered.

"Right." I tried to keep my voice down, but I wanted them to understand. "I've been looking at photographs this week— *National Geographic*, and this museum catalogue I got. I haven't had a chance to show you, Max. One of the *National Geographic* issues was about families in different countries. Family portraits, maybe with a mother at the center, or it could be the father, or even one of the kids, placed in different ways in their different garb. They might be touching each other or not. Once in a while the picture tells more of a story, like the kid is off to the side, sullen, or maybe the babies are held by the older siblings and not the mother, stuff like that. Those are the ones I've tacked on the walls so I can see them. The point is, for sure families are complicated. But this *painting*. It's not exactly subtle, is it? I know it's not real, but, I mean, can you actually imagine a father doing something like that?"

I looked from Max to Richard.

"It's just a story," said Richard rather anxiously. He tried to scrape up the last bit of sauce from his empty plate.

Max got up to open another bottle of wine.

I couldn't let it go. I could see Max was getting upset, but I pressed on.

"How could a man be willing to *murder* his son? I don't get it." I took a deep breath; I didn't mean to sound accusatory, I was trying to be reasonable. "How did he know it was God talking, even accepting for the moment that he believed that there was a God and He could talk. How did he know it wasn't the Devil? Why would he think a voice telling him to kill his son was *God* of all things? To kill his son?"

"Because he has murderous impulses?" Richard said.

Max stood at the table cradling the bottle.

I couldn't stop. "And if it really was God—if he *thought* it really was God—why did he let an angel stop him so easily? Does he just do what anyone says when it comes to the life of his son? He has no will of his own, no overriding loyalty to his own son? No instinct to *protect*? What kind of a father is that?"

Suddenly Max raised his arm and smashed the bottle against the edge of the table. It didn't shatter, but the bottom broke off and wine splashed onto Max and me and all over the floor.

I jumped up. Richard yelped but stayed pinned to his chair. Max was frozen, with his eyes squeezed shut. Then Richard calmly shook the wine and little slivers of glass from his hands and got up. He reached for Max.

"For God's sake, Max," he said softly. "Get a grip." He pried the broken bottleneck from Max's hand and led him to the sink like a child. He turned on the tap and rinsed Max's arms and handed him a towel. Max dried his hands and then wiped his face. I watched this silent activity with one hand over my mouth.

Richard said, "Max, Alice, why don't you guys go out and get a cup of coffee, or walk around the block or something, while I clean up here? Would you mind? I'd really like to."

Max went obediently to the door and let himself out. I went upstairs. What had I done?

Richard

Max went obediently outside. Alice went upstairs without a word.

I sponged off the table and chairs and the floor. A bit of wall was already stained pink. My hands trembled, now that it was over. I had a hard time squeezing the sponge. I worried about shards of glass going down the drain and clogging it and kept picking up small pieces from the sink with my fingers. I swept the wet glass on the floor into the dustpan and deposited it in the trash. Finally I cleared the table but left the dishes in the sink.

Outside, Max was standing in the driveway with arms crossed, his ungloved hands in his armpits. He would have been smoking had he smoked. I joined him, zipping up my jacket. It had been a warm day, but now the temperature had dropped again. It would snow during the night.

"She hates me," Max said.

"No she doesn't."

"She blames me for Adam's death: I didn't love him enough. But she's afraid she didn't love him enough either." He was very calm.

"What's enough?" I said, tired now. "What is ever enough?"

Our breath made puffs of steam. After a while he said, "I'm afraid I'm going to lose her."

It was his even, sad tone that alarmed me more than the words themselves. Then he said, with the stubbornness of a shipwrecked sailor clinging to a small stick, "But at least I'll have Jason."

"*Jason?*" I croaked. "Max! What are you saying?"

Max uncrossed his arms and shoved his hands deep in his pockets. It was clear that now was not the time for rational conversation. I stood there helplessly, unable to comfort him, and then Max said, "I guess I'll take a walk after all."

I touched his shoulder. "See you Tuesday."

Perhaps I shouldn't have been surprised to see Jason Green sitting on my mudroom steps when I came around the house. It was as if Max had conjured him up. It was late, cold; where else would he be?

"You again. Well, well."

He stood up. "Didn't you used to have a cat?"

"Yes. He got hit by a car a few years ago."

"You shouldn't have let him out."

"Excuse me?" I stood at the bottom of the steps looking up at him. This was too much. The heat rose up my neck. "Would you kindly get off my porch?"

He spread his hands in a conciliatory gesture. "Hey. Sorry. It's just that—never mind. *Sorry,* okay? Jeez."

I shook my head in disgust. I climbed the steps, unlocked the door and left it open. He followed me in. I thought, *Start over.*

"I bet you're hungry," I said.

"Maybe."

"Help yourself. I've eaten." I took off my jacket and hung it in the mudroom. Then I sat on a stool at the counter, determined not to wait on him anymore but curious about what he wanted. He began opening cabinets and the refrigerator, and eventually he pulled out some leftover roast beef and bread and made himself a thick sandwich; he even put it on a plate. I watched this with interest, noting that he cleaned up after himself as he went along, used the chopping block so as not to mar the counter, and re-wrapped the roast beef carefully. So it was just his clothes that were sloppy, presumably by design. He was wearing the same thing I'd seen him in before. But he moved with ease, comfortable in his body in a way I could only imagine. In fact, it wasn't much of an exaggeration to say his whole demonstration was like a dance. *The dance of the midnight snack.*

It was a little like looking through the glass of a pastry shop when you're on a diet.

"How's it going with Max?" I asked.

"I don't know. We've really only met once."

"And?"

"And what?"

"What did you talk about? Any insights into the workings of the universe?"

He looked at me with narrowed eyes over the top of his sandwich as he took another bite.

"I'm serious," I said. "I'm interested."

Teenagers are very good at communicating scorn and condescension with a look. Like gay men. Then he said, "You know, this is actually important. Most people are so shallow they don't give a fuck about what matters most."

I nodded. "And what is that?"

"If you don't know…"

He was getting worked up. I said, "Hey, chill. It's your business. I'm just making conversation."

He took a deep breath and shook his hands out at his sides. He blew out the air. "You're right. I'm not pissed at you. I'm just trying to eat."

I sighed. I should just go to bed. But—what about him? "So, where are you staying?"

He shrugged. "I met this girl when I was looking for Mr. Henry; she gave me her phone number. So I was staying with her. But her roommate's kind of weird. She took a class from Mr. Henry—the roommate—and she's like in love. I mean like obsessed."

"Is that right."

"She found out I was his apprentice, and she was like, *Whoa, not fair.* Like she was jealous. It was too weird, so I left."

"Okay. So now what?"

He paused. "There's lots of places to crash on a college campus."

I waited.

"Or you can walk around all night. And there's always bleachers and dugouts."

I laughed at that.

"Not too bad unless it snows," he insisted. "But rain's worse."

"A little cold this time of year," I agreed. The idea of him sleeping outside was absurd. "All right, yes, you can stay here. It's too late to be looking for an empty dugout. But maybe you should rent a room for a month or something."

He couldn't bring himself to say thank you, but he nodded. It was clear he didn't want to be beholden to me—and yet it was equally clear that for whatever reason he felt more comfortable imposing on me in this way than on Max. Of course, even if it were arguably more appropriate for him to stay with them, tonight was not the best night for that. Alice didn't even know he was around.

Okay, but thinking of Alice standing there aghast with her hand over her mouth, and Max staring at the floor covered with wine and broken glass, as if wondering what in the world he'd just done, gave me a pit in my stomach.

Still I needed to ask. "I'm curious why you don't just ask Max if you can stay there."

He shook his head.

"But why did you come here?"

He'd almost finished his sandwich. He said, "First I came here because…" He trailed off. "Then…" He trailed off again and shrugged. He grinned unexpectedly.

I said, "That was informative."

He put his plate in the sink and turned to me. This time he said steadily. "I can't go there because it's too…" He either couldn't find the words or lost his nerve.

"Too much at stake?"

"Maybe."

"And you don't care if I like you or not."

He smiled again, a refreshingly genuine smile that made him look younger and made me realize how little he smiled ordinarily. "Something like that. But it's nice of you."

I shook my head at this crazy scenario. The truth is, I was delighted he wanted to stay with me. Or at my house, anyway. I loved having him in my kitchen, eating my food, sleeping in my guest room. I felt triumphant, even if a little guilty, like when I was ten and the cat slept on *my* bed and not my sister's. On the other hand, I was still a little afraid of him, afraid he wanted something from me that I was unable to give. He was unpredictable. I didn't trust him, but I could be more hospitable.

"Do you want to wash your clothes while you're here?"

"Are you trying to get me to take my clothes off?"

I snorted. "You look like someone who hasn't had a bath in a week—"

"Just my clothes," he interrupted. "I use the college gym."

"Well, that's something. The washing machine and dryer are in the basement, and you're welcome to use them if you know how. Just keep yourself decent; don't walk around naked, for the sake of the neighbors. I'm going to bed."

He followed me into the living room. I stopped at the bottom of the stairs and turned around. "Yes?"

"Thank you."

In that moment, standing there without pretense, he seemed suddenly like an adult, grave and gracious. I could have looked at him for a long time. Instead, I waved him off. Already I was imagining him in my kitchen in his underwear, or doing his laundry naked. It was much too dangerous to think of him as an adult capable of adult choices.

He's a kid, I said to myself as I climbed the stairs. *He's just a kid. In a man's body, maybe, but still a kid.*

Nevertheless, I lay down on my bed and indulged in an erotic fantasy for a few minutes. I thought it would be best to just get it out of the way. So I imagined him in my kitchen in his underwear making a meal. His youthful skin, his taut chest muscles, erect nipples, strong thighs. No longer troubled or sneering but openly seductive in the way he stood, the way he looked at me over his shoulder. The challenge I'd already seen in his eyes now overtly sexual. Resting the knife on the chopping block and turning toward me. Removing his bulging underwear while holding my eyes. Moving toward me.

I don't have erections every day. It was lovely.

Later, in the bathroom, I thought, *Okay, that's that. Now put that aside and think of the kid you remember, so you can remember that he* is *a kid.* Not Jocko the 18-year-old hunk but Jason Green the ten-year-old friend of my quasi-godson, Adam. I dutifully called up memories of Jason and Adam running around the back yard with sticks—that was a strong image; probably Alice had a photo of it somewhere. I remembered them making a snow fort with many chambers. Playing in my pile of leaves in the front yard in fall. Sliding on a wet plastic sheet that Alice made for them. I thought of how things could have turned out so differently. Children survive so many dangers.

Adults naturally want to protect children. I did feel slightly protective of Jocko as he was now, but I also felt many other things admittedly less admirable, like possessive, and predatory, as in "I want *that*." Okay, fine. But I knew what it was like to feel purely protective because I'd felt that way with Adam.

And then I thought of a time I'd cordoned off in my brain, a time years ago at Maidstone Lake, when something scared me half to death. I could have been in Jocko's shoes, spending my life seeking redemption. The earlier events of this evening had exhausted me, but I didn't want to think about Max wandering around alone in the cold or Alice hoping to be asleep before her husband came in—or Jocko in my guest room. So I went back to my scariest adult experience, with respect to a child.

It was the summer Adam was about to turn eight, between second and third grades. His family was going camping, and he wanted me to join them. Back then I did many things for Adam's sake that I'd never consider doing otherwise, and haven't done since. We drove way up to the northeast corner of the state where the state park sits at the undeveloped end of the lake. Remote and very quiet.

Actually two things happened on that trip.

We arrived Friday night and set up our tents. It was early in June, when normally mosquitoes and black flies are at their worst, but it had been an unusually cold spring and thus far a cool summer. The lake might be too cold for swimming, but we hoped it would be less buggy, and we were right.

Adam slept with me—a treat to sleep with Uncle Richard. I had a fairly good-sized, four-man tent which I'd borrowed from a friend. Adam could stand up in it. But I learned quickly why Max and Alice were so eager to have him share my tent rather than theirs. He thrashed and rolled about so much that I ended up sliding off the air mattress altogether and wedging myself like a tomato between it and the edge of the tent, where the ground was cold and hard but where I was protected from flailing limbs.

Saturday morning I was awakened by a cheery high voice. "Knock, knock."

"Who's there."

"Canoe."

"Canoe who?"

"Canoe tell me some knock-knock jokes?"

"Ho ho ho. What time is it?" I struggled back onto the air mattress, which didn't have all that much air in it. I found my watch in the pocket of the tent: five-fifteen. From his happy tangle of sheets and quilts, Adam eyed me.

"I have to pee."

"Go outside and pee at the edge of the camp."

"There might be a porcupine," he said slyly. We had talked about porcupines last night.

"Let me look." I unzipped the triangular screen door and poked my head out. "No porcupines."

"Come with me." Though his mother sometimes considered him unnecessarily timid, Adam was a relatively fearless child by my lights, but he liked company. Whizzing with a friend was more fun than whizzing alone.

"Not a bad idea. Give me a minute to wake up." It seemed to me that all around us birds were chittering and calling. I'd never heard such a racket. I wanted to lie still and listen to it.

"Okay. Knock knock," Adam said.

"Who's there?"

"Wayne."

"Wayne who?"

"Wayne, Wayne, go away, come again another day." Adam hooted in delight. I saw him suddenly as an old man telling silly stories, throwing his head back in exactly the same way Max did, guffawing with pleasure no matter how many times he'd told them.

"Ha, ha," I said.

Sounds of waking came from Max and Alice's tent twenty feet away. "Shh!" I said. "Whisper. I have an idea. Let's sneak out, *very quietly,* and we can be the first ones to take out the canoe."

"Yeah!" he whispered back.

"And if we're really quiet, we might hear loons."

I pulled on the khaki pants and buttoned-down shirt I'd worn the day before. Adam wore nylon shorts and a T-shirt, which turned out to be a good thing, and the red cap I'd brought him from Toronto when he was four, which he still called his Tonto hat.

Max and Alice had bought a small used canoe the year before, and with lots of stops to rest our hands, Adam and I managed to carry it down the dirt road past other campsites, where most people were still sleeping, through the woods, to the small beach. We put on life jackets—the full jacket kind that actually buckle around your chest, not the old fashioned kind that slip over your head and rest on your front. Adam wore the kind of sandals that can get wet; I took off my loafers and waded in barefoot over the stones so I could push off the canoe, feeling very butch.

The water was damn cold. But the sun was warm and a light mist rose from the middle of the lake.

"Do you know how to paddle?" I asked, as I climbed in, rocking the boat dangerously.

"Sure. Mom showed me."

Adam sat in front. I imagined I could figure out the steering from the rear. Had I ever been in a canoe before? Of course. About forty years earlier, as a fifteen-year-old on a small lake in Michigan, during some group event that involved continually, purposefully tipping over. I had a vague memory of its having been both fun and terrifying.

It was a clear, crisp morning, stunningly beautiful. We headed out along the shore. We didn't hear any loons, but soon we caught up with a family of ducks swimming along in a row. Adam called to them heartily ("Hey, Jack, Kack, Lack, Mack, Nack, Ouack and Quack!"), but they ignored us. Out on the lake drifted a few fishermen in small powerboats; supposedly one could catch trout here.

"Do you know about the J-stroke?" I asked.

"Mom told me."

I couldn't think of anything else to teach him so I relaxed. We made small talk and then paddled in silence, listening to the splash of our paddles, and occasional birds. That is, I paddled, while Adam paddled and dragged his oar and smacked the water and trailed his hands and feet in the water happily. There is nothing like drifting on the water on a cool morning in the sun.

"What are you thinking about?" I asked him once.

"Lobsters."

"I don't think there are any lobsters here."

"I know. They live in the ocean."

Shortly one of the motorboats revved its engine and headed for a new spot, parallel to the shore like us.

"You don't want to be hit by someone's wake because you can turn over," I said.

"Mom told me that."

"Well, she's right. But in this case, I think the boat is too far away. The wake shouldn't affect us." As if on cue, the boat gathered speed.

"You're supposed to go across the wake," Adam informed me.

"Right. So I think we'll just turn a little bit toward it, just in case." Then everything happened at once. I tried to turn the boat unsuccessfully. The wake of the motorboat came at us. Somehow it hit us exactly wrong. The canoe lifted up, and slowly tipped toward the shore.

From the front of the boat Adam turned to look at me with wide

eyes. In the tiniest fraction of a second I felt a biting rush of fear
and an equally strong awareness that I was the adult. I smiled as if
this were the most fun thing in the world.

"Here we go!" I cried. I held onto the sides with both hands,
the freezing water lapped over the side with a gentle but significant
wave, and we slid out. The water was ridiculously, shockingly cold.

"Whoa!" yelled Adam, looking to me again for reassurance.

"That was fun," I said, my heart pounding. Even though we
were only twenty feet from shore, I couldn't touch the bottom, at
least with the life jacket holding me up and digging uncomfortably
into my underarms. Adam bobbed and splashed like a little pup.

"Swim in. Swim to shore, and I'll bring the boat."

Here the shore consisted of flat, rocky ledges. Adam reached
them quickly and climbed out in the sun. "I still have my hat," he
called.

"Sun yourself like a turtle," I instructed. "I'm coming in."

But the canoe was now full of water, and pulling it took some
doing. It must have weighed several times what I did. No doubt I
thrashed and grunted more than necessary, but finally I made it to
the rocks, pulled the canoe up and managed to dump out the water.

"That was something," I said cheerfully. I felt stupid and
incompetent, a failure as a camp counselor. On the other hand,
we hadn't drowned.

"Let's do that again," Adam said. I was half-frozen, but he
seemed fine.

"Tell you what. I bet it's time for breakfast. Let's get back and
see what we feel like later, what do you say?"

It didn't take long to paddle back. The sun was higher and
warmer, and I took us beyond the put-in for another quarter of

an hour before turning around, hoping to dry him out completely before confessing our mishap to his parents.

After we landed, he raced up the road ahead of me. I dawdled. By the time I got there, he was helping set the table for breakfast. His clothes had indeed dried, thank God, but he was still full of our adventure.

"Sounds like you had some excitement," said Max mildly.

I just smiled, all confidence. "Piece of cake," I said. That went too far—Max knows me too well—and he raised his eyebrows at me. I slapped my forehead. "Just kidding!" I said. "Actually I'm a top-notch bumbling uncle. But it was great." Max shook his head and smiled. He didn't care that we'd narrowly avoided death as long as Adam was safe. For whatever reason, he trusted me. Alice, on the other hand, would have been upset, but she was attending to Adam in that moment and never had any idea that I'd been genuinely frightened—and I'd never tell her. She took a picture of Adam and me, calling us Big and Mr. Big. I changed into a dry pair of khakis, and the rest of the day passed without incident.

But I still felt the need to redeem myself with his parents, and the next morning when Adam again woke up early and started chattering, I said, "Shh! We don't want the enemy to hear us—or they might discover our hiding place." I would do a good deed and remove us from Max and Alice so they could sleep another hour.

Adam's eyes widened with happiness. He loved to pretend. "Okay," he whispered excitedly. "Why are we hiding?"

"We know where the gold is. We have the map. And you're the scout. But we have to get dressed first—in our camouflage clothes." I pulled on my weekend khakis and shirt, while Adam decided jeans and sneakers were better for a scout.

We followed a different gravel path down to another beach, shallow but longer. Again the lake was still. Steam rose from its surface further out. Adam and I stood for a moment like sentinels listening to the sounds of the quiet world waking up. Then we heard it. We turned to each other, wide-eyed. I held my finger to my lips.

"What is it?" said Adam. "Let's shoot 'em!"

"It's a loon. You can't shoot loons."

His face fell. I amended quickly. "Anyone can *shoot* a bird. But loons are sacred. The greatest feat of courage and skill is swimming up to them and plucking a feather from underneath, when they're not looking. Let's see if we can get closer without disturbing them."

We tiptoed along the shore toward the reeds at the end of the beach. The loon called from further out on the lake, but around a bend so we couldn't see it. Adam looked at me. I stopped, held up my hand. He moved on, as stealthily as a seven-year-old could. When a branch cracked in the woods to his right, he froze. When a gull squawked overhead, he paused. The morning bustled around him with great buoyant wake-up energy not unlike his own, but he moved with concentration, as if it were the middle of the night.

"Oh, my," I said suddenly. "A pileated woodpecker. Look, Adam." I knew only a tiny handful of birds and this was one. "You hardly ever see those." Adam glanced back at me for explanation but then he stopped. By now we had reached the reeds.

"Uncle Richard!" he shouted. "Get down!"

Obediently I crouched on the beach. Up close, the small pebbles proved to have their own shapes and colors. Who knew? I thought, *This is what being with children is like.*

At that moment, a merganser burst out of the reeds in front of us. Adam jumped back.

"There were babies," he said excitedly. "I saw them. Right there! They're gone now." He moved as if to forge his way into the reeds.

"Wait." I should try to keep him dry at least until breakfast. "Remember the map?"

He looked back at me doubtfully. "We have to capture them."

"They're a decoy sent by the enemy. A red herring. Know how you can tell?"

"How?"

"The mother just flew off."

Adam looked puzzled. I probably looked puzzled, too, having come to a dead end in my explanation. I knew there was a connection there somewhere but couldn't quite find it. I tried a different tack.

"The map, remember? The treasure is back this way."

"We have to catch the babies first," he insisted, "and bring them back. To the Snake King."

"But the babies have gone under water to their secret lair. They're invisible now. Wait. I know. We can take the Snake King a feather to show him we were here."

"Okay." Now Adam splashed into the reeds, sneakers and all. "I got it!" He tried to tear a reed without success. Instead, he pulled off the brown, furry head and waved it at me. "I got it!" He raced off down the pebbly beach. "Come on!"

I trailed after him. Suddenly he stopped again, fifty feet ahead of me.

"Uncle Richard! Let's go swimming!"

I had two thoughts. One, it was way too cold—for me if not for Adam. Two, we'd have to go back to the tent to get his swimsuit, which would wake up Max and Alice. I caught up with him. He hopped up and down in his excitement. I bent to feel the water. Maybe it had warmed up since yesterday.

"I don't know, Adam. I'd call this frigid."

But Adam was tearing off his sneakers, socks, jeans. Maybe a short swim, I thought. What could that hurt? He could swim in his underwear and put on his dry clothes when he came out. It was too cold for me, but I was a big fat wimp. Adam Henry was a red-blooded American kid, and children ran hot anyway, didn't they? He hadn't been cold yesterday. He'd be fine.

"Don't go too far, and if you get cold, come right in."

"Come with me," he called, throwing off his shirt.

"No way. Someone needs to keep a lookout for enemies."

He hesitated only a minute, as if considering enemies, but then he said, "Can I?" so quickly I nearly missed it, and I realized he spoke out of some unexamined, spontaneous instinct to politeness, acknowledging my non-parental status as an afterthought. He would not have asked permission of his parents, trusting, I suppose, that they would simply stop him if they wanted to. I had noticed long before that out of wiliness or sheer natural exuberance, Adam tended to barrel ahead and seek absolution later, rather than obtain permission in advance, as if following an instruction manual for managers. Rather like his father. Or maybe all children were like that. I didn't know.

I thought about all this afterward. At the time, I simply laughed, and he ran gingerly but enthusiastically over the stones into the water.

Adam knew how to swim. He had taken to it naturally as an infant, or so Alice said. She'd enrolled him in a mother-toddler swim class at the Y. Certainly he never evinced any fear, and Alice, herself a strong swimmer, had taught him the different strokes during the summers. They swam in Lake Champlain, where the temperature reaches the mid-seventies after a warm spell. This is hardly what normal people call warm.

Now I watched him with admiration, and a little envy.

They say fat people don't feel the cold as much. Either this is another foolish stereotype or simply not true in my case. I hate the cold and as I may have mentioned I dislike the water. I don't swim very well, I find the different sense of gravity disconcerting, and I feel like a clumsy beach ball bobbing about, unable to direct itself. I am afraid of drowning. Besides that, like a lot of middle-aged men, I feel unattractive in swim trunks. The whole experience is unpleasant.

"Don't go too far out," I called.

Adam didn't answer. He was, in fact, swimming directly away from the shore.

I stood at the water's edge. "Adam! Hey, Bo! Over here!"

He didn't hear me.

By now he was seventy-five feet off shore. Where in the world was he going? "Adam! Adam! *Adam!*"

He stopped, bobbed around, waved.

"Come back!" I kept the fear out of my voice. I didn't want to frighten him.

"Okay!" he yelled.

I watched him anxiously as he turned back. He had about fifty feet to go when he veered off course, curving away from me. Within another ten feet, he was swimming parallel to shore. I called to him again, but he didn't hear me.

By now I had waded into the water up to my ankles. In my

loafers. It was cold, even colder than the day before, I thought. The wet seeped up my pants. Again I called to him, and he didn't hear.

I had been walking parallel to him, stumbling a bit over the larger stones even in my shoes. I was afraid they were going to come off, which would make walking on the stones only harder. My pants dragged against my legs. I headed out toward him.

"Adam! Adam!"

His strokes were less certain now, his thin little arms flailing a bit.

"You're off track! Come this way!"

I was getting closer, but I was weighed down by my shoes, my wet pants. I was foolishly trying to keep my shoes on, and I was afraid to take my eyes off Adam. It got deep surprisingly fast. The cold took my breath away.

Adam raised his head and stopped swimming. He saw me, turned, but then stopped again. What was he doing? Were his limbs going numb? I couldn't tell. He was still thirty feet from me. I pounded through the water the best I could, up to my chest now, running against the water, beating it with my arms. My wet clothes pulled at me like seaweed. I kicked my shoes off, one by one.

"That's it! This way! Swim to me!"

But Adam wasn't swimming. He just stopped.

The bottom fell away beneath me. I swallowed water.

"Swim, Adam! Come on, buddy!"

He wouldn't, or couldn't. His head disappeared, and then he bobbed back up again. Was he playing? Resting?

"Float! Turn on your back!"

He struggled, bobbed, flailed. Finally I reached him.

"It's okay, Bo. Now hold on. Just hold on."

I got him onto my back. He clung to my neck with his arms; his hands might have been numb. He added very little weight. I kicked and pawed at the water, my version of a dog paddle. In a few minutes—probably a few seconds, but it felt much longer—I was able to stand up. I swam-walked, and shortly the water retreated. When it was waist-high, I pulled Adam around in front of me and held him in my arms. His lips were purple and his teeth were chattering. His whole body was bluish.

"I know you're freezing. We'll get you warm." I wrapped my arms around him the best I could, pressed him against my own cold front. He didn't cry. He kept his eyes open. He didn't look frightened, but, rather, surprised. I picked my way over the stones in the shallow. "Ooh, ee, agh!" He was quiet, even when I faltered and swore, which ordinarily would have made him laugh.

I stopped long enough to pull on his dry T-shirt and work his arms into the sleeves. Then I scooped him up again and hurried toward our campsite. Along the grass next to the gravel path, past the bathrooms, then only a few hundred more yards on the gravel road. I vowed to buy some water shoes.

"It's okay, Bobo. We'll get you warm in no time. That treasure's just waiting for you to find it." I chattered on, comforting myself as much as him.

Alice and Max were fixing breakfast. When she saw us, Alice came running.

"What happened?"

"It's a little cold for swimming," I said. "I didn't realize."

She took him from me angrily.

"He's okay. Just cold."

She ignored me. "Max! Max! Get some clothes for Adam." She

carried him up the short incline to the campsite and sat at the picnic table. She peeled off his wet underwear and dried and dressed him as if he were a baby, while he stood before her shivering. Max and I rushed around like nurses. I brought a quilt to wrap him in. Max dried his hair with a towel as Alice lifted him onto her lap. Max brought him a steaming cup.

"What is it?" Alice said.

"Coffee. It's what's hot." Max held it to Adam's lips. "Careful."

Adam drank some. "Yuck." It was the first thing he'd said. I smiled.

"It's good for you. Full of milk," Max said.

"What happened, baby?" Alice said.

"I went swimming."

"I see that."

"First I thought I'd swim across the lake, then Uncle Richard said come back so I did"—Alice glared at me—"and then I couldn't feel my legs and I got tired and then Uncle Richard came and got me."

"Thank you, Richard," Max said. He handed me a cup of coffee. "You're a little pink, yourself. Don't you want to change clothes? You're shivering."

"I'll go get his clothes. They're still on the beach. Got any extra flipflops?"

Max gave me his and I put them on. I shambled down to the road, my vision suddenly blurred. Barefoot, Max ran after me with a jacket. "At least put this on." I couldn't look at him. He gave me a wordless hug.

"It was fun," I heard Adam say behind me. "I'm going to swim across the lake."

"Richard!" Alice called after me. "Breakfast in ten minutes. I brought those nasty pork sausages just for you."

Max hurried back to his family.

"Dad, Dad. Knock-knock."

Later that morning the three of them went out in the canoe, and Alice documented the event with her camera. I declined friendly offers to accompany them, preferring to read safely on shore. On the way home in the car, Adam complained to me that they'd been unwilling to tip the canoe. "It was more fun with you."

"Sorry, guys," I said to Max and Alice. But they didn't mind.

"I bought a new pair of loafers."

A week later, Adam presented me with the little carved boat that now sat in a bowl of keepsakes in my living room. He called it a canoe, though it looked more like a four-inch piece of balsa wood with a hold gouged out of the middle. He happily pointed out the bow and the stern. And then, with quiet pride tinged with apology, as if he had been responsible for our misadventures and not I, he said, "And I didn't cut myself once."

I was the responsible adult then, and I was the responsible adult now. Jason Green aka Jocko was certainly not eight, or ten or twelve or fifteen. He was eighteen and sleeping with a girl he'd just met. Maybe he "hooked up," as young people called it, with guys, too—I honestly couldn't tell from the signals he was giving me—but he was under my protection, having sought refuge under my roof. Or was he? What *was* he doing here anyway? I wondered whether he'd done his laundry after all, and whether he was sleeping naked. I hoped I would not find out.

Alice

WHEN I WOKE UP the next morning, Max was sitting up in bed next to me, not reading or writing, just sitting. It alarmed me.

"What is it?" I asked.

"I'm sorry about last night."

I'd heard him come up the night before but we hadn't spoken, and finally I'd fallen asleep facing away from him, feeling bereft. Now I didn't know what to say.

"I'm sorry, too." We hadn't touched all night, and I still felt wary, but I slid closer to him so that I could feel his stretched out leg against my side. "What was going on?"

He said quietly, "Why were you goading me?"

"Oh, Max." I got up, opened the curtains—it was a clear, bright morning with streaks of orange—and grabbed the robe at the foot of the bed. We don't heat our upstairs so it's toasty under the comforter but not great for hanging around. Max remained in bed. I stood at the top of the stairs. "I didn't mean to be goading you, as you say. I was upset. I've never liked that painting—well, that's an understatement. I loathe that painting. And I don't know, something else. I've been thinking about suffering—"

"Alice—"

"—and the depiction of suffering—"

"Alice—"

"—and what happens when you make it beautiful, or try to—"

"Alice, stop!" He got out of bed and came over to me. "I don't like the painting either. Or the story. I was raised with this story, you know. It's one of the foundational myths of my supposed tribe. It haunts me."

I removed his hand from my arm. "Let's go downstairs."

Max made strong Irish tea while I sat on the couch. Richard had done a nice job of cleaning up. There was barely a sign of last night's event, except for the remains of a pink stain on the wall. Max handed me a cup and sat across from me in the easy chair.

"You know what I really hate most?" he said. "It's not all the obvious problems, like what happened then, after Abraham released him? What was the nature of their relationship after that? Can you imagine? Can Abraham ever look Isaac in the eye again? Does Isaac fear his father the rest of his life? Does he want to kill him? When I was growing up, I always imagined they floated around each other for the rest of their lives like two ghosts. I thought Abraham might as well have killed his son."

"Okay," I said. None of these "obvious" problems had ever occurred to me before.

Max stood up. "The thing is, Abraham *didn't* kill his son. And yet, he had to have been as consumed with guilt as if he had. Because he was willing to. He didn't stand up to God—the voice he thought was God, as you pointed out. He had to be rescued by an angel." He sighed and looked out the window over my head.

I closed my eyes. I did not want to share this with him. I was not a philosopher and I was sorry I'd brought it up. I knew that what we experienced, when Adam died and since, was different. What I'd felt and continued to feel, though it had changed over time, was more visceral and wordless. I didn't feel *guilty*. Responsible but not guilty, any more than you can feel guilty over losing an arm or a leg. Max's pain was different. Maybe it was more complicated, maybe he tried to understand it more. But I couldn't help.

Max said, "Isaac *lived*. He didn't die, Abraham didn't kill him. He wasn't a ghost, not really. *Adam* is a ghost. Where was the angel when Adam was falling off the cliff?"

"There aren't any angels," I murmured.

"I know." We finished our tea in silence, and then he took my empty cup and put it on the kitchen counter. He came back and reached out a hand and helped me up, and we went upstairs to dress. Max went into the closet to get a clean shirt. I dropped my bathrobe and pulled off my nightshirt, chilly as it was. When Max emerged from the closet, I put my arms around his neck.

"Come back to bed," I said. It wasn't that I felt close to Max in that moment, but I needed to connect with him.

He hesitated. "What time is it?"

"It's early. Do you have a breakfast appointment?"

"No, but there's something I want to tell you about."

"Tell me later." If he was going to tell me he was having an affair, God forbid, I didn't want to hear it then. So we made love; I was surprised at how ready I was. Not long afterward we took a shower together.

"Hot water in winter is one of the wonders of the world," I said. "It washes away all our sins. What did you want to tell me?"

Max put his arms around me with his face facing the shower and the water flowed over us both. "Never mind. It's not important."

Richard

On Tuesday morning spring arrived for real. You could smell it in the air. It was April, robins were everywhere, and the front page of the local section carried a photo of a bluebird seen in central Vermont. April is both delicious and excruciating for Vermonters because spring appears in tiny bursts and then retreats behind wet, gloomy shadows for days at a time. It's also quite a slog for accountants.

I considered backing out of breakfast with Max, but every time I imagined telling him that things had piled up at work, a perfectly reasonable excuse given the time of year, I also imagined the beat of silence on the other end of the phone, in which he'd communicate to me everything he believed he understood: that I disapproved of his violent outburst, that I was taking sides with Alice (hadn't I helped her set up her drum set?), and that, most importantly, in this time when he needed a friend, I was abandoning him.

Perhaps I was abandoning him. But why would I, after all these years? I didn't understand, myself.

Of course Max would never *say* any of those things. He might not even think them. He would collect himself quickly and say something like, "Right-o. See you Friday."

In the end I went—out of guilt, or curiosity, or just the habitual concern for his well-being that was as much a part of me as my insatiable hunger. Loyal to *morte*.

In any case, Tuesday brought an exhilarating April morning, frosty with that hint of warmth that tells you the day will heat up deliciously in the sun. The light was different, and because the air was different, the sounds were different—the birds, the wind, and outside of human hearing the squiggle of worms and crunching of insects in their miniscule shells, which I believe we can sense even though we can't consciously process the sound. By the end of the day I'd be able to smell the earth around my house. I thought about my peonies fighting their way through the muddy crust, and all the tiny creatures busily aerating the soil and struggling for life in the underground, and how in a matter of weeks I'd get my own thick hands into that glorious dirt on a regular basis, and I managed to ignore the dread I felt about seeing Max.

He'd sent me a message about meeting at Marco's, a change of venue that honored his work with Jocko, no doubt. Marco's was a step up from Fleury's, larger, with booths lining the interior wall and the street side under the windows. Hardly upscale—it was half restaurant, half bar—but Max liked places that were just this side of seedy. And I liked going with Max to places I'd otherwise feel uncomfortable in. Though I've been a big man for four decades, the timid faggoty twelve-year-old in me still cringes before the particular aggressive energy of men in places like this, which used to presage beating up people like me.

When I arrived, Max was already there, for the second week in a row, which might have been a record.

"I've changed it to five days a week," he said without preliminaries. "At least, that was my idea over the weekend."

I sat down. "Good morning, Max."

"It interrupts my work on the book, but it seems important." He leaned back in the booth and smiled. "So he came yesterday, but he's coming back today."

The waitress, a slim older woman (our age) arrived with my coffee. I hadn't seen Jocko since Sunday night. As usual, he was gone the next morning before I got up.

Max said, "Although, I think we should take it day by day. He's...mmm..."

"Unpredictable?"

"How did you know?"

"Just a wild guess." I'd tried not to worry about where he might be sleeping. Presumably it was with the same girl. Or perhaps another. I hoped he was practicing safe sex. I hoped he was safe. I hoped I'd see him again alive and well. "When are you going to tell Alice about him?"

Max took a deep breath. "I was trying to tell her on Sunday night, before she brought up that goddamned postcard. And then yesterday. It's tough." He ran his hands through his hair. "Listen, Richard, can I tell you something? I don't want to talk with Alice about suffering. I'd love for her to start taking pictures again, I think that would be a good, healthy thing, but I don't want to—I can't—go *backward*. I can talk about Adam, but I don't want to talk about Adam's death. I've had my last conversation about it. I'm done. It's over."

"That's why you can't tell Alice about Jocko? That's what you're afraid of?"

He nodded. "How did you know he went by Jocko?"

I bit my lip. "You must have told me. Listen, just tell her it's not about Adam."

He shook his head, then he brightened. "Hey, I brought you a present." From his backpack he pulled a paper bag and a tape, and set them next to each other. "Sorry I didn't have time to wrap it."

"What's the occasion?" Was he trying to make up for Sunday night—the second strange Sunday night in a row? Or his general instability of the past ten days? Ordinarily this would have pleased me, but now I was keeping secrets from him and he was giving me presents. Great.

He smiled and shoved the bag toward me. "Open it."

From inside I withdrew a tie, folded in thirds. It was a fine, soft, Italian silk, a rich, deep blue. The color of the lake in summer. I collected ties—Adam had even made me a couple—but I had none like this. I stroked it with one finger. "It's beautiful. But—?"

He smiled. "I never gave you a birthday present."

That was true. My birthday is in November. Alice often made me a special meal, and I did the same for her, but Max and I had long ago agreed that ritual gift-giving among friends was burdensome, and so we only gave each other things when the spirit moved us, sporadically.

"Lovely. But you gave me some books last week. And this?" I indicated the tape.

He looked suddenly shy. "I, um, taped the session I had with Jason yesterday. I thought I might like to have it later. He doesn't know I did—I suppose I should have asked him—but it's just for me, my personal use. Then I thought, maybe I could ask you... I thought, when you weren't doing anything, you might..."

I shook my head, spared from having to answer by the arrival of our breakfasts. I'd ordered my usual pancakes, eggs, home fries and sausage. Marco's home fries are the best. I realize I am not getting thinner, but it's too late. I added orange juice for vitamins.

Max said, "I'm anxious for you to hear this. He's just so… interesting. And I have such a curious response to him."

I concentrated on my breakfast. Were the sausages soft enough? Good.

He said, "I'm not ready to tell Alice—not yet—and I need your—"

"You know, Max—"

He held up his hand. "I know, it's not really your thing. But just see if I'm on the right track."

"For what?"

"Does he seem interested, am I using good examples, how does it seem to be going?"

"I don't get it. You've been teaching for what, thirty years? What's up?"

He considered. "I know I'm a good teacher. But—. " He sounded doubtful, ran his hand through his hair. "Look, you don't have to hear the whole thing. Maybe I ramble a bit. Just some of it."

"You do know it's April, right? And that I'm working twelve, fourteen hours a day? I'm here now; tell me about your conversation if you must."

Max slapped the table. "Of course you are. I'm such an asshole! How's it going? Sounds like you're swamped. How're you holding up?"

I smiled in spite of myself. "Fine. No worse than usual. Not enough hours in the day. But my home front's not stressing me." That gave me a little twinge. I'd meant to give him sympathy, but it came out sounding bitchy.

But Max didn't mind. He turned on me his guileless, unaffectedly open expression that made it hard for me to look at him. For a second we could have been sitting across from one another in an empty locker room about to kiss. I sucked hopelessly at my empty coffee cup, eyeing him over the rim. Whatever mixed-up, antagonistic feelings I'd been having drained away, squeezed out by the more familiar, equally complicated mix of tired longing, lust, and friendship.

"Go ahead," I said now, with exaggerated resignation. "Tell me your conversation."

He hesitated, as if to make sure I meant it, then he said, "We talked about suffering." He picked up the tape and made it dance like a little puppet.

"I thought you didn't want to talk about suffering." I added more syrup to my pancakes.

"Correction: we talked about answers—I told you he's looking for answers—and whether books contain them. He wanted to know if I was a Buddhist. I'd given him the Basho. Remember I read you some?"

"A horse pissing by a pillow."

"Old pond, leap, splash—a frog."

"In the eyes of fish, tears." That was my favorite.

"Parting, clutching straw for support."

"We pray to the clogs."

"You remembered." He smiled as if I'd given *him* a present. "Well, it didn't much speak to Jason, although he liked the idea of a journey. I would have thought he'd be the perfect age for it, classic hero tale and all."

Eating helped me listen to this.

Max went on. "He wanted to know why I keep my books arranged as I do, and he kept taking titles off the shelf to look at them. He didn't understand why I'd have a system nobody else could use."

"Ah. Imagine that." We'd discussed this before; he knew I found his "system" ridiculous.

He smiled. "No one else uses them but me, so it's moot."

"It's not a system, it's a memory test," I said on cue.

"He told me about a kid who gave away all his stuff and went off to the wilderness to live but ended up starving to death in an old school bus."

That was mildly alarming. I could imagine Jocko doing something similar. "What was the point of that?"

"He's very intrigued by it, that romantic ideal of living according to your principles. Extreme Thoreau, with no going home on the weekends to do laundry. And how something so well-intentioned can go so wrong. He's very concerned with unpredictability and justice—the why-bad-things-happen question."

"Makes sense," I said. Then I wanted to shake Max: *What are you doing?* Instead I watched him finish his two eggs and toast, and I asked the waitress for some more sausage.

"There's one more thing," he said. "I was telling him about the ring of Gyges. You may have forgotten this story." I gave him a look. Of course I'd never heard of it. I've tried to tell him before that his delicacy is unnecessary—we non-intellectuals are much less insecure about our brains than he is—but for him it's habitual.

"A shepherd finds a golden ring, the ring of Gyges, that can turn him invisible, which he discovers pretty quickly. To make a long story short, he goes to the local castle and uses the ring to get in, after which he seduces the queen and kills the king, and then takes over the country."

"Like Oedipus."

"Yes, sort of. Glaucon, the Greek philosopher, says, according to Socrates, that anyone would be a fool not to do what the shepherd did. Glaucon's question is, why in the world would anyone act differently?"

"And?"

"Of course Socrates argues that only those who act ethically can be truly happy--"

"Of course." But suddenly I didn't care about Socrates or Glaucon or the ring of whoever-it-was. I wanted Max to stop talking about it. We were not laughing together over his students' comments like we used to. We weren't having fun. In fact, *we* weren't doing anything. I could have been anyone! And it was Jocko's fault. Jocko had sucked the joy out of our conversation. Jocko was the problem, not Max. I stabbed my new sausage with my fork.

Max was saying now, "But wait. I'm telling Jason about this, right? I go through the whole story trying to make a point, and then he tells me about a book he read, a novel called *Fade*, about a boy who discovers he can become invisible. The first thing the boy does is sneak into his girlfriend's house, only to discover the girl is fucking her twin brother."

Max looked at me expectantly. I waited.

He said, "Do you see?"

I didn't; my mysteries were more straightforward. Like, would I ever have sex again before I died, or was I losing my best friend?

Max said kindly, "Well, I'm not sure I get it all, either. But Jason's feeling was that he'd rather not know all the things going on around him, if they were sordid. He didn't use that word, but that's what he meant. The unseemly, disappointing acts of regular, flawed human beings. I challenged him: was he sure he'd rather not know that the world is full of betrayal, injustice, sadness, as well as the good stuff—loyalty, love, kindness?" Max paused as if remembering. I stole a look at my watch. This time he didn't notice.

Max said, "I could tell he was getting worked up, but—you know, it's so rare for a student to care so much, and of course I was caught up in it, too. But he was really upset. That's what I missed. He said—yelled, actually—*Why does everyone want to know what's going on inside you?*"

He stopped and I had to prod him. "And then what?"

Max looked out the window. "He left rather abruptly. I believe he shouted. I believe he said *Fuck you*, or something to that effect. It's all here." He tapped the tape. "What do you think?"

My stomach was in knots. I'd eaten too quickly. I poked at the streaks of maple syrup and melted butter on my plate, left over from my second set of sausages and wondered where the sausages had gone. Soft, warm, juicy and salty with a touch of sweet—and I'd missed them.

"I think I'm getting an ulcer."

Max laughed. I signaled for the check.

"It's amazing you get paid to do this," I said.

"Well, not this time. I wouldn't take any money from the kid even if his father did want to pay me. I couldn't. He's like a son to—"

"Oh, *God*, Max. Stop. Jesus." I stood up. "It's late."

He picked up the tape, and when I shook my head firmly, he replaced it in his backpack with a sigh. "It's such a puzzle."

"It's not a puzzle at all. It's way too obvious. And you're ruining our nice breakfasts." *And maybe our friendship*. He's *ruining our friendship*.

"Don't you like him? I mean the sound of him." Max stood up and put on his coat. He followed me to the counter and waited while I paid the bill. Once outside I turned back to him.

"It's not about Jocko—Jason Green—it's about your infatuation. It's unhealthy. It's blinding you to the rest of your life. What about your book? What about Alice?"

Max tilted his head at me. We looked at each other and I didn't know what to think. I felt as though I were warning him against the dangers of razor blades in apples. Surely he already knew, he could see the trouble ahead. He turned up his collar, then turned it down again; it was warm. In that moment he looked tired. I wanted to smooth the lines of his face with my fingers. I wanted to hold him and tell him it was all right, he was a good teacher, he could reach Jocko and comfort him, and relieve himself. But then this strange little resentment gnome, my new friend, slid its nasty fingers into my gut and gave a little twist. I tried to ignore it. I said, "Your conversation is crazy-making, you know. No wonder he's frustrated. It's completely non-linear."

Max laughed. "He's not an accountant. It's a dance." Then he surprised me, as he often does. "We're all in pain, you know."

He made my chest hurt. *That's not it!* I wanted to yell. *It's more complicated than that. Don't you see?*

But fifty-five-year-old men don't stand on the sidewalk in the middle of downtown yelling at each other about things that matter, even if they're gay. I couldn't possibly have explained what I felt or thought, anyway, so I just shook my head. "You're hopeless."

"He just shows it more," Max added. Then he grabbed me in a quick bear hug and said, "Hey, I've been self-absorbed, sorry. I won't talk about him anymore. Listen, have a good week—only two more to go. We'll make you a good dinner Friday night."

With that he headed up the street. I watched him, his strong, lumbering stride and his curly hair wild in the wind. I had a sudden vision of young Adam walking next to him with a ten-year-old's version of the same swaying stride. Two bears, one great and one small.

I called after him, "Thanks for the tie!"

Max

On Tuesday afternoon I tried to broaden the discussion with Jason by acknowledging the existence of the many distinct ethical traditions in the world in addition to the Western tradition that began with the Greeks. It was a rather unsatisfactory hour. But it is extremely difficult to have an intelligent conversation about any ethical topic without placing it in a broader context; that's how you end up with people inanely trading position statements about things like abortion or animal rights. Jason in particular tended to get side-tracked by concrete examples, so I'd thought backing up to give him some general background might help. But he became even more restless than usual. Finally, I stopped mid-sentence and asked him whether he'd like to go with me to the jail tomorrow. I surprised myself and him.

"What's it like?" he asked, without a whole lot of enthusiasm.

"Interesting, scary, sobering, infuriating at times. Sad, but also heartening. At least I think so. I don't know how you'd find it."

He thought about it briefly and agreed. After he left, I called the jail superintendant, whom I knew, to explain the situation since there wasn't time for a regular volunteer security check, and that was that.

I'd offered to pick him up on the way, but he said he'd come to my office. Thus on Wednesday afternoon I drove the two of us the few miles to the prison that sits on a busily traveled corner in town yet manages to be invisible to most people.

"Why do you do this?" he asked now.

"A couple of years ago the college was pushing for more faculty involvement in community service. A friend of mine who'd taught in the jails suggested it. I'd never been in a jail before. Have you?"

"Of course not."

"Why of course not? Because you're white and middle class? You said you got kicked out of school for drugs. You're lucky you didn't go to jail."

He looked out the window.

"I'm not criticizing," I said. "I don't think anybody should go to jail for a drug-related offense. It's a ridiculous waste of taxpayers' money. I'm just saying that class and race play a role. In any case, most of the guys you're about to meet are white."

He was silent a moment. Then he said, "I meant, *why* do you do it?"

I had to think. People have asked me that before, and I had a standard answer: generally the students in jail want to learn, and they have something real to say, and I find that refreshing after my college classes. What else did Jason want to know?

"I suppose," I began carefully, "when it goes well, I feel like I'm making up for something. I feel like I'm giving them something that they should have gotten in school, but most likely didn't. Very small, but still..."

"What's that?"

"Something like... the chance to express themselves without being told they're a worthless piece of shit. A little encouragement. A glancing encounter with someone who believes in their basic goodness."

After a long pause he asked, "What philosophy is that?"

"Ah. I should have warned you. It's not philosophy at all. I wanted to do something far away from my field." Suddenly I felt almost shy.

"Yeah, so what is it?"

"Let me make clear that I'm not there as an expert, more like a facilitator. From their perspective, I'm just a community volunteer. The educators there don't care what I do."

"Okay, so what *do* you do?"

"Poetry."

"Aw, man, *poetry?* With criminals?"

"You'd be surprised what they come up with. Raw, original stuff. Anyway, this winter I tried haiku. Basho."

"Like you gave me. Poetry for screw-ups."

I ignored that, and we passed the rest of the brief ride in silence. As we got out of the car, I said, "I should tell you that I never know who's going to be there, or how many. There could be three guys or fifteen. We'll just play it by ear."

I showed my volunteer badge at the window and got one for Jason, after the receptionist checked out my story with the superintendent. We signed in, locked up my car keys in a locker, and waited for Lisa, the head teacher, to appear.

"A lot of working in the jail is about waiting," I said to Jason. "I think it's an institutionalized way to reinforce powerlessness."

Five minutes later, I introduced Jason to Lisa, who then led us to the first set of metal and glass doors and pressed a large button. A guard in the control room buzzed us through, into a tiny security space. "I think we've got a pretty good group today," Lisa said. The door behind us clanged shut, and the next door buzzed open.

We crossed a small open area in front of the control room. Several doors led off from here to other rooms or hallways. We waited at one of them until that door buzzed open. Lisa went through first. I glanced at Jason, but his face showed nothing. If he was only half as uncomfortable as I was the first time I'd come, he was doing well.

We continued down a hallway to a door which Lisa unlocked. The door had a keyhole but no knobs. Two inmates approached from the far end of the hall. One of them banged the cement wall with his fist, cursing about something I didn't quite get.

We followed Lisa into the room and she shut the door behind us. It was a windowless classroom with several round tables and four or five chairs each, and a row of computers along one wall.

"I'll call the units if you want to set up the chairs," she said.

"I like to pull the tables together so it's more like a circle," I told Jason. Lisa left the room through another door. "That leads to a bathroom," I explained. "There's another door on the other side of that, which leads to her office, so it's more like a hall. There aren't any locks on those doors." Jason helped me move the tables and chairs and then distribute paper around the tables. He hadn't said a word.

Suddenly there was a loud banging on the door from the hall. "The door locks when you shut it," I said. "Only Lisa can open it, but we can always get her if we need her." In the meantime she'd heard the banging and came in. She opened the door to the hall.

"Hey man, is this poetry class?" It was someone I hadn't met before.

"Come on in," I said.

A moment later two men I knew, Skipper and Keith, arrived, along with two others who were new to me. Skipper, older than the rest, with a gray beard, acknowledged my greeting, while the others ignored me. One went immediately to the bookcase, another flopped onto a chair. His buddy arrived and they fist-bumped. "Hey, man, wassup?"

"Can we use these computers?"

"What's this, poetry?"

A couple of more men arrived. I let them mill around, and after another minute I said to no one in particular, "Do you know anyone else who's coming?"

"Too late. Window's closed."

"Let's get started then. Anderson, could you close the door?" I passed around the sign-in sheet. They knew the routine; they had to be accounted for. "And I'd like to know your names."

It occurred to me suddenly that Jason could pass for one of them if he wanted to, and I wondered whether I should let him decide how to present himself. But then I thought, no, he's my guest. I'd ordinarily introduce a guest, and so I introduced myself and then said, "And this is a student of mine, Jason Green, who's come to observe."

I knew he preferred to be called Jocko, but "Jason" seemed safer in this setting. I was probably being over-protective, but...he seemed significantly younger to me than these men, though almost all were probably under twenty-five.

They announced or mumbled their names—sometimes last names which was the custom in the prison, and occasionally their first names. I wrote down whatever they told me. One young man I hadn't met before, a blond kid named Denny, seemed vaguely familiar. I thought I remembered seeing his picture in the paper, but for what?

"Any of you ever written poetry before?"

"Yeah."

"Sure. Twinkle twinkle little slut, how I want to go up your butt."

The men laughed. Skipper said, "Asshole." The others laughed again. A man named Johnson said, "Hey, I been writing poetry all my life. Before I got here, I was slam king."

"No shit?"

"No shit. I'm telling you—"

I said, "All right, good. You're in the right place. So last week we wrote some haiku, and this week we'll do some free verse. Slam, spoken word, rap, call it whatever you want. Poets have been telling their stories in their own voices forever. Just tell your story."

Two men, James and Bristol, looked at each other as if to say, *What's this shit?*

"Cool," said another.

"What story?"

"What's haiku?"

"Seven syllables, five syllables, seven syllables," said Johnson. "Don't you know nothing?"

"You can write haiku if you want," I said, "but my invitation to you today is to try something different."

"You know that poem, 'Thirteen Ways of Looking at a Blackbird'?" asked Keith.

"What's a syllable?"

"Oh, man," said Johnson.

"It's a cool poem," said Keith.

"I never know what to write," said another.

"Just write something, dickhead. It ain't rocket science."

"If you want a prompt, write about what you'd be doing today, right now, if you weren't here," I said.

Denny, who hadn't said a word, began to write, along with Skipper and Johnson.

James and Bristol looked at each other again. Bristol tapped his pencil impatiently. The man who'd called himself Xavier got up. "I'm not into this. Can I go back to my unit?"

"No. You can read if you want. Or just sit there."

"Aw man, this sucks."

"Remember, it doesn't have to be true. You can always write in the voice of someone else. In other words, you can make it up."

Xavier stood at the bookcase and looked at books. James crossed his arms on the table and put his head down. I wondered whether I'd given a poor prompt; maybe it was too hard to think about they'd be doing on the outside. But there were so many factors I had no control over; there could have been a lockdown that morning or they could have gotten really bad news. I'd had success starting them off with benign suggestions like "Write about a smell" or "Write about a place you liked to be alone as a kid." These tended to work better than asking them to write about their first fight or a mean adult or a death. At first I'd been curious about their experiences of mean adults and first fights and the like, but if I was ever going to get them to write about such things, it would be later. For now my goal was to get away from simple memories to some expression of imagination, to imagine their lives differently. Was that so hard?

Jason glanced at me. Was he expected to write something, too? I nodded encouragement. I was curious to find out whether he'd take on the role of the resistant inmate so full of anger and fear he couldn't participate even though he wanted to or the inmate fiercely seizing a quiet moment in order to express something—rage, hope, shallow regret, bleak cynicism, or a story of a bird helping a rabbit fly. I was often surprised at what they came up with.

I ignored the continued muttering and turned my attention to my own paper.

"Remember, it doesn't have to rhyme. It's just a story. What makes free verse different from a story is just the way it's laid out on the page. It's a poem because it looks like a poem."

"Aw, man." Johnson crumpled his paper and took another sheet.

James raised his head, reached for a pencil and began to write. Within another few minutes, everyone but Xavier was writing. Even Jason.

I never wanted to know what crimes they had committed. I didn't want to know whether they'd burglarized a house, stolen a car, beaten up their girlfriends, or worse. Did they deserve to be there? Who knew? Did anyone deserve to be *punished* for a misdeed? Or was there a better, more constructive response that allowed restitution, giving back, making up for one's crime to the extent possible?

What was Jason writing?

The kid, Denny, had done something much publicized but not, as I recalled, worthy of imprisonment. Jason observed him, too. They were probably the same age.

Twenty minutes later, everyone had finished.

"Let's hear what you've got. Skipper, you want to start?"

We went around the room. Denny read third.

"It's too early for haying but what I like to think about is farming and haying is my favorite thing. When I get out I'm going to work on my family's farm till I get my own farm. People say they don't like the smell of farming but I love everything about farming and the smell's just part of it. I love the smell of farming." He said "hayin" and "farmin"—a real Vermont farm kid. Of course. Now I remembered him.

"Yo, man, that's deep."

"You *like* that punk smell? Whew."

He was the one who'd fired his rifle at a tractor across a field and killed the man sleeping in it. My poster child for unnecessary punishment. He hadn't intended to harm anyone; he was just a thoughtless kid with a gun who did something stupid and had colossally bad luck. And here he was a couple of years later, in jail.

Now I said only, "Nice. Next?" Bristol began to read.

A guard opened the door: head count. Bristol stopped reading as the guard, who knew all but one of the men, called their last names and checked them off. "What's your name?" he asked the man he didn't know.

When he left, Bristol continued reading his poem about ice fishing, and getting sloshed in the ice hut with his buddy. "That's true friendship, hot and cold," he concluded.

"Nice," I said. "All right, in the interest of time, let's wait to hear the others and write one more. I want you to think of an experience. Just think of it, don't say it out loud. Think about how things could have turned out differently if one little thing had changed. This isn't a particularly helpful exercise in real life; there's no point in looking back and thinking 'If only I'd done this' or 'If only I'd done that.' But I'm asking you to do something a little different. I think. Let's try it anyway. Use your imagination. Some event that happened that you wish had gone differently. By the way, I'm not talking about your crime. This will work better if you think of some small thing, like if it hadn't been raining on a certain day or if you'd said something differently to someone, or hadn't missed a catch. Or something big if you want. But write it like it really happened that way."

"Aw man, that's too deep." James threw down his pencil and leaned back in his chair.

"And remember, if you don't like the prompt, you can always write whatever you feel like—or nothing. It's just a prompt."

Xavier had returned to the table. He took up his pencil and began to draw.

Bristol tapped his pencil as before.

"I'm done," said Keith.

"Me, too," said James. "Can we go?"

"Not till head count's over, wimp," said Johnson.

Denny doodled on his paper. Jason stared at his paper with a particularly black look, as if he'd like to kill someone. *He fits right in,* I thought.

I sighed. It wasn't the first time I'd had a lousy idea. "No go, huh? Bad idea."

"No, man, you can't rewrite history."

"Tha's right. You got to make amends."

"It's like that movie. You ever see that movie, with, like, parallel tracks?"

"That's lame."

"Naw, man, it's cool. You got one set of things happening, then you got an alternate universe happening right alongside. Like if you stayed in bed a half hour longer and got up and did all the same things, none of the same shit woulda happen."

216

"That's bullshit. You do the crime, you do the time." Xavier got up and headed toward the door. "Thanks, man."

I glanced at the clock on the wall; I hadn't noticed it was after three. Prisoners never lost track of the time. I reminded them about the next week as they waited by the locked door. Lisa came through the bathroom door at the back of the room. "How'd it go?" she asked, unlocking the door to the hall. The inmates filed out, mostly ignoring her and talking to each other about other things—chow, an upcoming hearing, a complaint about another inmate. ("Prick stole my book.")

"Fine," I said. I collected the unused paper and the pencils and moved the tables back with Jason's help. After the last inmate had left, I said to Lisa, "That kid, Denny. He's the one who killed that guy in the tractor, right? How long's he in for?"

She told me.

"God, what a waste. It's not going to bring back the guy. What possible good can it do anyone to lock him up?"

Lisa shrugged. "Do you want me to walk you out?"

"No. Thanks." Nonetheless she walked us to the end of the hall. I explained to Jason, "I remember this case. In the paper the widow was quoted as saying something like, 'I don't want to ruin his life, *but…*' She meant, 'I don't want to ruin his life but he should suffer.' He should suffer because I'm suffering. It makes no sense!"

The door buzzed open. Lisa said, "Seems pretty normal to me."

I held the door open for Jason. "It may be *normal* but it's illogical. And unnecessary. You don't think when something bad happens like that, the person feels lousy? You think he needs to be *punished?* Like that guy who was driving the boat drunk, where the two kids drowned? What in the world could possibly make him feel worse?"

Lisa shrugged. "Yeah, well, some of these guys, you want them to feel worse."

I shook my head.

"You might feel differently if you were those kids' parents," said Lisa. "Or that guy's wife."

I *was* a parent. Had been, anyway. "Maybe," I said. The door closed behind us. Jason and I crossed in front of the control room, pushed through the door when it buzzed, and waited at the next door.

"What do you think?" I asked Jason.

"About what?"

"This place, that kid I was talking about who's probably your age. Anything."

We emerged into the lobby, I collected my keys and we signed out. I said, "I think the whole building should be razed."

"I don't know," said Jason. "That guy who said, 'You do the crime, you do the time.'? He seemed like he was, not glad, but like...*comforted* to be there. Like he thought it was fair."

I didn't know what to say to that. Outside it was warm and the air was light. Did Jason know what he was saying?

In the car I said, "You know, offenders often—or this is the stereotype, anyway—often have a very black-and-white sense of morality. You break a law, you go to jail. At least after they're sentenced. Before they're sentenced they're more likely just to be pissed that they got caught. I used to try to talk to them occasionally about alternate forms of societal response—you know, like restorative justice--but they couldn't engage with the idea."

"You think they're dumb."

"Not at all. Maybe... intellectually unsophisticated."

"Or you could be wrong. Maybe they know something you don't."

"Such as?"

"What it feels like to be them! How could you possibly know what it feels like to be them? Since you're not them and haven't committed a crime. Or had their lives."

"I understand your point, Jason—"

"Jocko. Jocko!"

"Sorry. Jocko. The reason I—oh, never mind. Look, I appreciate your point. But your suggestion that just because a man feels guilty he should be punished may make *psycho*logical sense, but it's not rational. By the way, where can I drop you off? Where are you staying?"

"It doesn't matter. Anywhere."

"All right. Downtown then. I'm going to do some errands. Hey, did you keep your poem? I'd love to see it."

"No. This is fine. I'll just get out here." We were stopped at a light. He opened the door.

"I'm glad you came with me," I called after him. "I'll see you tomorrow."

"Right."

Instead of doing errands, I drove to the lake and sat in the car looking out at the gray water and the darkening mountains on the other side. The lake had failed to freeze all the way across again this year. I wondered if it ever would or if those days were over. I felt immensely sad. Jason-Jocko thought that suffering more would make him hurt less, and that's wrong. Did he think it would help if he spent time in jail, for God's sake? Or worse? That was madness. I did not want to share my sadness with him—it was not his burden—but I was at a loss how to help.

I realized I would have to include in my book a history of

horrible punishments, and I dreaded that. It was not the best
day of the year.

Richard

WHAT IS THE SADDEST story ever told? Is it about the crumbling of empires, families sinking into despair, lovers betraying one another? Is it the fall of a man who worked himself up from nothing to a pinnacle of power but trusted the wrong people, or loved the wrong daughters? The story of the oppressed woman who throws herself under a train or on a pyre, or simply lives a miserable life, impoverished and alone?

Hecky, brilliant Hecky, used to talk about this. He read me the first line of a book that begins this way—"This is the saddest story ever told."—and then he'd argue for those other stories, none of which I knew except Madame Bovary because I saw the movie. And King Lear, because everybody knows about fathers who love the wrong child.

But who cares? It's the wrong question. Max is right that we all have sad stories, but nobody's own story is the saddest story ever told. That's just plain pathetic. The self-pity goblin creeping around the corner, trying to grab you by the shorthairs before you see it coming. You have to be vigilant, cut its throat and toss it without remorse onto the highway and hope it gets flattened beyond recognition like roadkill. That's what I think.

On Saturday morning, July 29th eight years ago, two weeks before Adam's eleventh birthday, I went over to Max and Alice's to drop off the plastic container in which I had carried home some of Friday night's leftovers. Alice and I had dined alone because Max and Adam had gone off with some other boys and another father on an overnight camping trip to Mt. Fury, an ironically named, gentle hike a half hour away. By habit she'd cooked enough for four instead of two so I'd taken the rest. Alice never liked leftovers.

It was a cool, blustery morning with a gusting wind and dark shifting clouds that were expected to blow away later. But it was early and I expected Alice to be sleeping in, taking advantage of her solitude. Adam tended to pop awake happy and full of energy, *early*; with the windows open I could often hear him shouting all the way to my house. I intended to let myself in with my key, leave the container on the counter, and slip out.

But Alice was up. I found her sitting in the living room in the blue and white Japanese kimono she uses for a summer bathrobe, with the windows open and the white curtains flapping wildly like sails. It seemed she had taken advantage of the boys' absence (she called them "the boys"): the plastic building toys often spread around the living room floor had been put away in a plastic box and the painted toy soldiers gathered into a defeated heap. Clothes that might have been strewn around over the backs of the chairs and couch were piled together across the arm of the large armchair. Random sneakers had collected by the kitchen door. The long shelf above the music cabinet was piled high with newspapers, schoolwork of Adam's, a drawing sticking out between books, a child's sweater, a package of photographs, oddly shaped wooden sculptures that might have been

222

small pieces of driftwood, and a dozen other little things that stack up when one has a high tolerance for chaos—or a child.

Alice had a mug in one hand and the morning paper on her lap. She smiled at me. She looked happy. It was the last time I would see her looking like this for a long while.

"I love this weather," she said. "It's romantic, don't you think? I bet they're having a good time. It didn't rain last night, thank goodness. Although we do need rain. Maybe this storm won't blow through like the last few."

I said something about it's being a good summer with respect to mosquitoes, because it had been so dry and windy.

Then the phone rang. Alice picked it up and I waved goodbye, having made my delivery, but she held up a finger indicating I should wait. I stood by the side door. I was eager to begin my own day—to get through my errands and into the garden before it got too hot.

I remember the next moments as if they happened an hour ago. I was examining the floor, wondering whether Alice had washed it the night before as she usually did. It looked so clean, cleaner than my floors ever looked. It was such an odd combination—extraordinary clutter and an obsession with spotless floors. I wondered whether I should finally replace my old linoleum with the same fake wood. I glanced up when I heard an odd note in her voice.

"Ed?" she was saying. "What's wrong? Where's Max now? Where's Adam?"

There was a long pause. The curtains billowed behind her.

She made a choking sound. She held the phone with both hands. She turned away from me so I couldn't see her face. She hung up and turned toward me.

Her face was white. "That was the other father on the trip.

There was some sort of accident. Max is on his way to the hospital with Adam right now. In an ambulance."

It took a moment for this to register. She was looking at me as if for explanation.

"Shall I come?" I asked. "Yes, I'll go with you. Where are your keys?"

She didn't move. She held one hand to her mouth.

"Alice, why don't you get dressed, and I'll get my car."

I led her across the room to the bottom of the stairs.

"I'll meet you outside in a few minutes," I said. "Okay?"

In the car she sat still as stone. We didn't speak. She held her arms close to her chest with one hand at her throat. Tears dropped onto the front of her shirt. It was too early on Saturday morning for traffic and I drove quickly. Would we beat them there? Where were they when Ed called? When did the ambulance get there? How did you get help in the middle of the woods?

What kind of accident? How badly hurt was he?

Surely it was nothing serious. A sprained ankle or a broken leg maybe. Maybe a collarbone. "What did he say?" I asked finally. But she didn't answer.

At times like this—but there are no times like this. They say time stops, but the truth is more shocking: time doesn't stop. The sky should have been still, cloudless, but instead clouds whirled about full of a breathtaking wild beauty. People drove in their cars, waited politely at lights. A woman in red shorts walked a black dog. A man in bright bicycle tights worked on his upside-down bicycle.

At the emergency room, I told the triage receptionist we'd come to see Adam Henry, if he was there yet. Alice stood behind me. "He's a child," I added.

224

"Are you his parents?"

"Yes," I said without hesitation.

A nurse led us to a bright, windowless room with two beds, one empty with the curtains pulled back against the wall, and one containing Adam. There was nothing attached to him, no tubes, no I.V., nothing to monitor his vital signs, though the room was full of equipment. He lay motionless on top of the sheet with his eyes closed. My first thought was that he looked like a doll; maybe the real Adam had been replaced with a doll and this was all fake, a sort of practice emergency routine for parents like the exercises the Fire Department goes through.

Max sat in a chair next to the bed holding Adam's limp hand. He raised his head from the bed but didn't get up. He looked exhausted. Old. I wondered whether the boys had kept him up all night.

Behind me, Alice entered the room. A low wail rose from within her, a hoarse, scraping howl. She gathered Adam in her arms and held him to her. Max's face contorted. I left the room.

A nurse asked if she could get me anything. I said no.

When I returned a half hour later, Alice was lying on the bed next to Adam, stroking him as if he were asleep and she could wake him. Max sat where I'd left him, his head in his arms. Now he got to his feet.

"Thanks for staying."

I put my arms around him and his body shook. After a moment he stopped. I sat at the end of the hospital bed on top of a pale blue, cotton blanket, where I could hold onto one of Adam's feet, still clad in his dirty sneakers. The blanket was neatly folded. Beneath the sheets a plastic cover crinkled when I sat down.

"What happened?" I asked.

Alice held Adam and petted his hair. Max could hardly bear to look at him.

Max said, "Early this morning, Adam and a friend climbed over a guard rail at a lookout. We don't know what happened, maybe they were horsing around, who knows. Adam fell. It wasn't that far, maybe twenty feet. He should have been able to come out with a broken arm."

"A broken arm," repeated Alice.

"They'll do an autopsy," Max said. "It's required in cases of child trauma."

"How did you get him here?"

"Ed Green found the park ranger who called an ambulance. It was his son, Jason, who was with him."

"With Adam."

"Yes."

"Was he—" *Was he already dead*, I wanted to ask. What do you do with a hurt child in the woods? Do you stay with him, or leave him in order to get help? I could not imagine the desperate waiting, the nearly unbearable anxiety and fear. Unless Adam was already dead.

"They got there pretty fast, the rescue guys. He was...when I found him, he was...crumpled. They said he must have hit his head."

Adam's body did not seem beat-up. This little person looked peaceful, but unnaturally so. Not asleep as people sometimes say. He looked remarkably like Adam, with the same scar just inside his right elbow where he'd stabbed himself on a wire fence and the same scab on the right shin where he'd fallen off his skateboard last week. He had Adam's full lips, like Max's. But Adam was never this still, nor was his skin this strange pale color.

Still I watched his face to see if he would breathe again. His dark hair fell away from his forehead revealing a tiny cut at the right temple. His dark eyebrows were at rest, and his dark lashes starkly visible against his graying cheek. I remembered that the hair keeps growing after death. How long would his already dramatic eyelashes eventually grow?

Adam wore his green T-shirt inside-out—a fashion among his friends—and the reversed design didn't make sense, at least to me. His arms seemed thin at his sides. Perhaps in motion they gave the appearance of more bulk. His denim shorts were smudged with dirt. How much had come from yesterday's climb to the top of Mt. Fury through the woods, and how much from the fall?

"Do you want to say anything to him?" asked Max.

I shook my head. I felt they wanted to hear something about him, that Max at least wanted me to speak for him, to say anything that might express the tiniest fraction of what he felt. But I couldn't.

"He knows I loved him," I said instead. "Don'tcha, pal?" I gave his inert foot a little shake.

Some minutes later I got up to go. I kissed the top of Adam's head as I always did. His hair had the same outdoorsy, little-boy smell.

Alice had barely acknowledged my presence, but now she looked up at me. "Don't go, Richard. Please."

There was nowhere else to sit in that small room. I returned to my place at the foot of the bed.

A man dressed in street clothes came in and introduced himself as a chaplain. Did we need anything? Could he help? The hospital had counseling services. Did we need help arranging anything? Max said we were fine, thank you.

After we'd been there over an hour, Alice said she was ready to leave. "Does he have any stuff?" she asked Max.

"Ed will drop it off at the house later. He took the other boys home."

But she lingered by the bed stroking Adam's face, brushing the hair away from his forehead over and over. She kissed him. Then she looked at us. "I can't go."

I thought surely Max and she must want to be alone together. I embraced Alice, and she wept again. I left the room and Max followed me out. He embraced me, held on almost desperately. Then he turned away.

"She won't touch me." He seemed utterly defeated.

"Alice?"

He looked at the floor. "What can I do?"

I shook my head and wiped my eyes brusquely. "I don't know."

A few minutes later, I stood in the parking lot watching the clouds. My mind had been emptied; now images crowded in. I remembered Adam outside in the yard the day before, telling me—excitedly, slyly—about the surprise he was getting for his birthday, which he couldn't tell me about because he wasn't supposed to know. I'd contributed to a new bike and wondered how Adam knew, or if he knew. I thought of how he liked to play outside and how he must have loved the camping trip with his friends, how they would have tromped and whacked and complained and had a damn good time. I thought of the two camping trips I'd taken with him and his parents to Maidstone Lake and the time he almost drowned. I thought of Alice holding him in her lap after I brought him back shivering. I thought of Alice running and sliding with him on a sheet of plastic, wet by a hose in the back yard, and Alice taking pictures of him outside and at school events and whenever the mood struck her. I saw Alice in her kimono on the phone this morning with the curtains billowing softly behind her, and sitting next to me in the car, crying silently as if she knew. And Max. I couldn't get rid of the image of Max I'd first seen when I came into the room, Max sitting next to the bed with his forehead pressed against the sheets and his hands clutching Adam's hand, as if he were praying.

Halfway home I realized that neither Alice nor Max had a car at the hospital, so I turned around and went back inside to wait for them. I didn't really want to go home anyway.

Alice

It was Thursday evening when Max got the call. I was in the back office paying bills, and he was in the living room reading about, as he put it, "horrible punishments." He'd started to tell me the range over dinner, from the physical (whipping, lashing, beating, cutting off body parts, branding, etc.) to the mental (shunning, incarceration, solitary confinement, etc.). Then there were those punishments specific to cultures or subcultures (keelhauling, burying up to one's neck in sand, etc.). I stopped him mid-way. *Why in the world would he want to read about that?* He said he had to, for his book. Well, I didn't want to hear it, that's for sure. He didn't have anything else to tell about his day—nor did I about mine—so we spent the rest of dinner talking about where we might go for our next big vacation. He suggested Japan, where they used to practice hara kiri.

"Max!" I said. But he was kidding. He told me about a warrior poet he'd run across recently named Basho, who'd taken a journey to the "deep north."

After dinner I was paying the bills while vaguely thinking about Japan—the old women who worked in the rice fields, the awful contemporary cartoon art, ancient Zen temples, images superimposed over one another as in a photo collage, and why was I even thinking like that? When the phone rang, Max answered it. As soon as I could tell it was his dean, I got up and closed the door, not to give him privacy but so I wouldn't have to hear a conversation that was likely to go on for half an hour. Hearing one side of a phone conversation has always made me anxious.

But it didn't go on for half an hour. Max's voice rose quickly—he was clearly upset—and very shortly he hung up. I waited a moment and when he didn't come in, I went to the living room.

"What is it?"

Max was sitting on the couch looking shell-shocked. "That was the dean."

"I know. What did he want? What happened?" I was still standing at the edge of the room.

"You won't believe this. *I* don't believe this."

"What? Tell me."

He shook his head and gave a little laugh. "I've been accused of sexual harassment."

"What?" I sat down across from him. "By whom? What happened?"

"A student, I gather. He wouldn't tell me the details. But Alice, this is almost worse. He was suggesting I consider taking the early buyout."

"Wait. Early retirement? I thought—wait. Go back. What about the student?"

"He said a student, a female student, had left a message on his voice mail—it might even have been anonymous, that wasn't clear—accusing me of sexual harassment. Not a formal complaint, mind you, just a wild accusation." He stood up and began walking around the room in growing agitation. "Alice, do you have any idea how outrageous that is? She probably doesn't even know what it means. Whoever she is. God! Me, of all people. You should see how some of the faculty flirt with their students. I don't touch them, I don't flirt with them, I don't even look at their breasts which I'll tell you is goddamn hard these days when they're hanging out all over the place."

"But, Max, why do you think she was complaining?"

"Alice! You don't think there are actually grounds, do you? *I* don't know why she called the dean, I have no idea, but anyone can *say* anything, you know. It doesn't make it true, for God's sake." He ran his hand through his hair, which he does when he's worked up.

"Of course I believe you." I went to him and put my arms around him. "It's okay, honey. It's all right." He couldn't have been having an affair with a student, he was so transparently, genuinely shocked.

He took a deep breath and relaxed a little. Then he pulled away. "I'm not sure it is all right." He filled the electric kettle with water. "Tea?"

I shook my head.

He went on. "I know I haven't harassed anyone. There is no question about that. There is simply no way anything I've ever done could possibly be misconstrued by a student, I don't believe that for a minute, but—"

"Do you think you treat male and female students differently?"

He frowned at me. "Of course I treat them differently. They are different. They treat me differently. Anyone who claims the opposite is disingenuous or lying. The first thing we notice about people is their gender."

"Well, then—"

"But do I create an unsafe environment, a hostile environment?

232

That's *ridiculous!* I don't humiliate students or diminish them in any way or even tease them. And I have *never* pressured, or asked, or even mildly intimated sexual interest in a student—male or female. I am absolutely clear about that. The accusation is disconcerting, but it's hogwash."

"Do you think he wants you to retire, and he's using this as a threat, maybe even a made-up threat, to pressure you?"

Max studied the kettle. The water boiled and the kettle clicked off. He ignored it and came and sat back down on the couch. I sat next to him and put my arm around him.

"I've never trusted him," Max said.

"Oh, Max, that's not true. You've liked him fine."

He shook his head.

I removed my arm gently and moved to the end of the couch so I could face him. I slid my feet under his thighs. "Maybe it's an opportunity. Maybe you should think about retiring."

"What are you talking about? I'm only fifty-five."

"I don't mean stop working, I just mean from teaching. Maybe you should think about doing something else."

"Like what? I love teaching. I don't know how to do anything else."

"Really? Since when? Didn't you say just last year that you were tired of teaching? Tired of philosophy, tired of the university? Being on sabbatical isn't teaching, you know, it's being on vacation."

"I'm working!"

"I know you're working, but you're not *teaching.* You might be thinking about teaching so warmly because it's been almost a year since you've interacted with students. Which does make it a little weird that you'd hear about a sexual harassment complaint now, actually."

"Exactly. Anyway, I may be tired of it, but it's *my life.*"

"Well, just think about it. I've got to pay a couple more bills."
I got up.

"Alice, even if I wanted to take the buyout, I couldn't now, because it would look like I was doing it to escape a lawsuit."

"Is there going to be a lawsuit?"

"I don't know. I couldn't get that from him. Maybe he doesn't know."

"Well, if there was, I don't think it would matter if you were retired or not. But I could be wrong. You need more information. Let's sleep on it, okay? Can you let it go for the night?"

"No."

"Well, go for a walk or something."

"It's raining."

I left him then and returned to my tasks. A few minutes later he appeared in the doorway.

"I'm going next door. I'll be back in a bit."

"Don't be too late. I'm going up soon."

Richard

IT RAINED on Thursday night. I was sitting at the kitchen counter going through my mail, half expecting that Jocko would knock on my door at any minute, late as it was. I hadn't seen him since Sunday night; my anger at him had passed and now I just wished he'd come. Imagine my surprise when I heard the mudroom door open and in walked Max instead. He was wet and kept on his wool jacket, but he ran his hands through his black curly hair and flicked off the rain like a teenager.

"Max!"

"I know it's late, my apologies, but I saw your light was still on."

I glanced at the clock over the door. "It's all right. What's wrong?"

"Nothing."

"Nothing? What, you just came over to borrow a cup of sugar? At nine-thirty?"

"Have you got a beer?"

Max knows I don't drink beer, but usually I have some on hand for others. But I didn't then, and also I didn't want him hanging around, in case Jocko came. "Sorry. What's up?"

Max closed the refrigerator door and rubbed his hands together to warm them up. He wandered over to the wall of photos and stood there as if he hadn't already seen them a hundred times over the years. It's a nice, orderly wall. All the pictures are in three-by-five wooden or plexiglass frames. There are ancient photos of me and Hecky, and some old friends of mine, and various relatives including my three sisters and their children over the years, and of course pictures of Max and Alice and Adam and sometimes me, in various configurations, most often taken by Alice. The photos by Alice are black and white (her preference) and thus naturally more stark, but they also stand out because they're more dramatic in the way they capture the light and people's expressions. I waited.

Max said idly, "How'd your day go?"

"It was fine. Busy. How was yours?"

"Hey, I don't remember this one. Where'd you get this?"

It was a photo of Adam and Jocko, maybe ten years old, sopping wet, with huge water guns held at their sides. We called them water uzis. "I was looking up an old file and I found it." That was true, but I'd framed it to show Jocko.

"That's odd." He gave me a funny look.

I ignored this. But I was getting more and more anxious. "Hey, Max—"

"Oh, wait. I wanted to show you something. You've got a minute, right?"

I looked pointedly at the clock, but he ignored me.

He said, "You know I started doing poetry in the jail a few months ago, after philosophy wasn't going over very well. I took Jason with me yesterday. But that's not the point. The point is"—he hesitated—"I wrote a poem for you. Or rather, in your honor."

"Really?"

"Do you want to hear it?"

236

I hesitated only a moment. *Oh, what the hell*, I thought. "Sure."
He read,

"At the back of Uncle Richard's closet
is a secret door
to a hideout he lets me play in.
But yesterday I stayed in the closet.
It was dark.
I pretended I was a blind boy
feeling my way.
Uncle Richard has 87 ties
hanging on eight wooden poles
all in order.
I only meant to feel one.
But it was soft like cat fur.
I only meant to wrap a few around my head
but they felt so nice
like birthday ribbons and ice cream.
I didn't hear them yelling for me.
I didn't hear them come upstairs.
When Daddy and Uncle Richard opened the door
I said, Look, Uncle Richard,
it's like the sea.
Daddy's face got red.
But Uncle Richard snatched me up
and twirled me around.
Ties flew everywhere like rainbows."

He looked at me expectantly. "Well? What do you think?"

I had a complicated reaction I couldn't begin to describe. "Well, yeah. So... I'm pleased you wanted to share it with me."

"But what do you think?"

"You mean, as in, is it a good poem?"

"Yes."

His eagerness for my approval distressed me. "I have no idea."

"Oh. Well, I know you're not a scholar, but you were there, so..."

"Yeah."

"So you'd have a sense of whether it's, you know, *true* or not."

"I remember it like that, more or less, yeah. You called Adam to come down and he didn't hear you. You started to get pissed off and went upstairs to get him—you were ready to go—and I was right behind you. And there he was, in my ties."

Max smiled broadly. "Yes. A little king."

I couldn't join him. I was confused. Something wasn't right. I was touched by the poem but it hurt me, gave me a pain in my gut. My stomach was in knots. And I really didn't want to think about it because I was so anxious about Jocko possibly arriving while Max was there. I was about to implode.

"So what's the problem?" Max asked.

"I'm not sure," I said, playing with the salt shaker in front of me, the triangular sandwich Jocko had played with. "I... I guess I've always thought of that little event as mine somehow. Like it's my story."

He looked genuinely perplexed. "It's not your story. If anyone's, it's Adam's. But it's not Adam's really, it's no one's."

"You have so many memories," I began.

"It's not a competition," Max said, puzzled. He folded up the poem, rather forlornly.

"The thing is," I tried again, but faltered.

"You don't need to explain. It's fine. Really. It's just a poem." He put it in his back pocket. "I'm sorry to bother you this late."

"Wait, Max. Hang on. Let me tell you something I never told you before. About that night."

He turned back from the door, his cheerful face now impassive. I'd hurt his feelings and I was sorry. Suddenly I couldn't bear the gap that was opening between us.

"The reason I remember that night so well is after you and Adam left, I thought about it for a long time. I thought about fathers and sons—the way you looked when you lifted him off the bed. Do you remember that you were furious at first and I stepped in and rescued him from your wrath? He was about to cry and I picked him up and twirled him around like you said in the poem, till I got dizzy, and then I put him on the bed, where he started to jump. The ties were still hanging off him—my gorgeous, expensive Italian silk ties. He'd done a pretty good job decking himself out. When you lifted him off the bed, you had this look on your face, like you got a kick out of him. You'd been annoyed, really pissed, and then you… it was *delight*.

"What I'm trying to say is I was thinking about fathers and sons— you, Adam, my father—and I had a lot of mixed feelings. And I decided that night—." I hesitated, losing my nerve. But I wanted to tell him. "I decided I could be a miserable bitter old fag forever mourning his dead boyfriend, or I could be"—I paused again, to make a joke out of it—"a fairy godmother, a fairy uncle, to this kid. I could have a role. Because, don't you see, I had *rescued* him."

"From me? I wouldn't have hurt him."

"Of course not. I know that. That's not the point. It's what I meant—what I hoped I meant—to Adam. I can't explain it any better, and maybe you can't get it since you are a father—were—and you had these protective feelings all the time. But I thought some part of you got it that night."

His eyebrows were knitted; he was trying hard to take this in.

"Maybe you never did, and it doesn't matter now. I'm just trying to explain why your poem…" I trailed off. I didn't know what else to say.

"Why it doesn't sit right," Max finished. He looked at me with… what? Pity? Compassion? Curiosity? Love? My whole body ached. He said simply, "I know you loved my son."

I looked up and met his gaze and we looked at each other and the distance between us closed. If we'd been women, we'd have held each other. If he'd been gay, we'd have had sex, though it would have spoiled the moment which was more intimate than sex—but that would have been the point. It would have relieved the pressure, and I'm just shallow enough to have wished for it. Max looked away first, and he left without a word.

I had the fleeting thought that he had come over for another reason and never got to it, but it passed quickly. I went into the bathroom and jacked off. I'd forgotten about Jocko and now I remembered him in a rush.

I made myself a bowl of ice cream and went upstairs to seek oblivion in a movie.

I chose "A Bridge Too Far," somewhat randomly. It's too recent and too gory for my taste, but I own it because… it's an epic film that captures so beautifully the madness and confusion of war. Often you can't tell exactly what's happening. Tanks, bridges, entire landscapes blow up, men get killed right and left. There are dry, admirable Brits and stupid, cheerful Brits who treat it all as a game—all in good fun, you know. There are idiotic, self-absorbed Germans and respectful, courageous Germans. And then there's Dirk Bogarde, in one of his prissiest roles. But what makes it worth watching is the relentless, inexorable unfolding of events toward a tragic end. From the title and the beginning scenes where a number of players express doubts, you know the mission is doomed. What remains only is to discover how awful it will be. You know the back-up forces aren't going to make it to the bridge, and you know the German panzers are going to inflict serious damage on the 35,000 Allied paratroopers, if not wipe them out completely. You expect moments of crazy courage and loyalty and tiny triumphs, and you get them.

But it's a long movie, and halfway through, I turned it off. The beauty of watching a movie a dozen times if it's really good is you see new things every time, or at least see things differently. The downside is your life begins to resemble the movies you watch.

The plan to reach Arnhem, the stupid mission, fails for a number of reasons, some of which have to do with poor planning and hubris, and some with simple bad luck. Human error. But what I couldn't bear watching that night was the absurd lack of communication. In spite of everything else, the Allies might have prevailed if they'd been able to talk to each other. Watching the various generals and such trying unsuccessfully to reach each other was heartbreaking. They just wanted to know what was going on. *What's happening where you are? How bad is it? Can you make it?* We know they're all trying their best, but nobody knows what the others are doing! In war as in life, you've got to be able to communicate—to avoid disaster.

I needed to tell Max, and Alice for that matter, about Jocko. They were bound to find out, and the longer I waited, the worse it would be. I would never be able to explain that I wanted Max *and* Jocko. (*What are you talking about?* I chided myself. *You can't "have" either one!*) I had a dreadful sense of being in one of the movies where everyone dies. But talking to myself with such melodrama didn't lighten my mood. It wasn't enough of an exaggeration.

I no longer wanted Jocko to come that night, but where the hell was he? The rain was still coming down hard, and I'd stayed up much later than I should have watching just *half* the movie. I fell asleep worrying and had a disturbing dream about a man who started out as Max and turned into Jocko, while looking like neither, and then morphed into someone who looked like Hecky. When I said, "I thought you were dead," he said no, he'd just been staying somewhere else. I was very happy to see him.

Max

I spent Friday morning working on my book. I abandoned the horrible punishments chapter and then dispensed quickly with deterrence. We know the threat of punishment has virtually no deterrent effect except on some white collar crime, and even then it's not punishment per se but the public shame of getting caught that keeps some people, though clearly not all, from, for example, insider trading. Neither does it seem to work very well as a check on inappropriate sexual activity on the part of public figures (although there's no way to tell except from self-reports how much behavior might have been successfully restrained). Nor, apparently, does it prevent students from making wildly inaccurate complaints of sexual harassment. But that's my point. Few people think about the repercussions of their actions. In other words, the potential repercussions do not deter them, perhaps because no one thinks he'll get caught. But that's speculation. What would seem to be fact is the threat of punishment is at best an ineffective deterrent.

I believe this is what Jason wants to understand, as well: the question of consequences. To what extent are we responsible for the repercussions of our actions? Accepting that our actions have consequences—the law of karma—does not necessarily mean that we are responsible in the Western moral sense for everything that happens as a result.

But back to the book. Dispensing with deterrence brings me closer to the heart of the matter, which has to do with retribution, the belief on the part of many people that others deserve to suffer. The question is, does anyone deserve to suffer?

Intuitively one understands that for the public, if not rational public policy, anger drives punishment. And yet, notwithstanding the human desire for retribution, the history of punishment shows a steady development of a rational, even compassionate approach to those breaching the moral and social codes. True, this has been anything but a straight line, with public eruptions of rage at certain well-publicized events regularly setting back progress. But even in our punitive culture, "lock 'em up and throw away the key" has replaced such practices as public flogging, stoning, beheading and crucifixion.

The tension between the historical development of a more compassionate theory of punishment, involving restitution or reparation, and the countervailing public need to inflict pain interested me. But tracking events in the polis and relating them to the development of punishment theory was more than I was prepared to undertake. What was it I was really trying to say? I felt overwhelmed, and honestly a little distracted by personal concerns, and so I spent lunchtime walking around the campus in order to clear my brain.

The idea of punishment evolved over time, and that evolution shed light on where we were now. But where were we? It is difficult to have any real perspective on one's own period. Still, I thought it fair to state that our current thinking concluded that *punishment* as was typically conceived *did not work*. It created more harm than good, both to the offender and to society, *even if* one considered the value of revenge in appeasing the populace.

But, beyond a few geeks and policy wonks, who cared? I sighed. How could I write a popular book about this? It was hopeless. I simply didn't know how to frame the questions in a way that would be interesting to an ordinary reader. I couldn't even get the men in the jail to be interested. Or Jason, for whom I'd have thought such exploration would be crucial. But he had said to me more than once, "This isn't it." But if the question of responsibility for one's actions wasn't the issue, what was? What was I missing?

Jason arrived on schedule just before two. He looked a little peakéd, as my mother used to say. He also looked worn out and scruffy. Was he all right?

"This is a miserable climate," he said, by way of hello. "Raining all the time in fucking April."

"It's not raining today," I said, trying to cheer him up.

"I think I'm getting pneumonia."

"I hope not. How about a cup of coffee?"

I made us each a cup from the small machine in the corner of my office while he sat and looked around the room. He actually seemed less morose than usual. I handed him a cup. "What do you think is the most important philosophical problem? I mean, to you?"

He considered his coffee, then said fiercely. "*There is but one truly serious philosophical problem, and that is suicide.*"

Whoa. I returned his gaze.

"Camus," he added.

I set down my cup. "I know who wrote it. And do you believe that?"

"Sure. Why not?"

"I'm curious where you came across it."

"A teacher. Trying to shock us."

"But did you read the essay?"

"I don't know. What essay?"

"The myth of Sisyphus. It's about—"

"Oh yeah, the guy with the big rock."

"Your quote is only the first line. He goes on to say, *There is no fate that cannot be surmounted by scorn.* Surmounted by scorn: in other words, I spit in the eye of tragedy. And he says, *The struggle itself toward the heights is enough to fill a man's heart.* The struggle itself. Life is struggle, effort, a journey, but it fills your heart. And finally he says, *One must imagine Sisyphus happy.*"

"But he wasn't, was he? He didn't want to push a rock up a hill forever. He had to. That sucks."

"Okay, so…" I stop, change tactics. "How could the story be changed to give Sisyphus's life meaning?"

"Let him do something else."

"All right. How? What would that look like?"

"After he rolls the rock up a few times, and he sees he can't do it, he says, I'm outta here, and he goes off and builds a boat or something. He and his girlfriend sail off to a desert island."

"That's one approach. But let's say he's stuck with this, because that's life. Things happen and you deal with them. You're given a task, let's say by the universe, and all you can do is make the best of it. Sisyphus's task is to push rocks up a hill. So Taylor says that when Sisyphus discovers the large stone doesn't work, he could push smaller stones, which presumably would stay on top, and, once he'd collected enough, he could do something with them—say, build a temple."

"Hey, I finished that Basho. More or less."

246

"Good. But let's stay with this for a minute. Do you get where this is going?"

"I don't know. Have you got a Kleenex?"

I handed him a box from a drawer in my desk, and he blew his nose. He was running out of steam, but I thought we were getting close to something, so I pressed on. "Is there anything that can make his repeated action significant?"

"Why does it have to be significant? Not everything has meaning. Some things are just a waste!"

"But what if that's our task? To find meaning? Or make meaning?"

"I know, that's what I'm saying. But where is it?"

"I can see you're not feeling well, but stay with me here for a minute. Imagine you're Sisyphus pushing the rock up the hill. You have to do it, so is there anything that can make your life meaningful?"

"No, man, it's torture."

"Okay, it's torture the first three weeks, maybe the first six months. But you still have to do it. Then you say to yourself?"

He shook his head. "What, I don't know. Look at my biceps getting stronger. Look how cool this stone looks rolling down the hill. I don't know."

"Exactly! Couldn't it be that it doesn't matter what significance you attach to it? Maybe the point is just that *somehow* you find meaning in the activity. Any activity, any life, can have meaning *if you can only see it.*"

Jason stood up. "No. This isn't it. Sorry. Plato and Basho, this Sisyphus shit. It's not what I'm looking for. It's garbage, it's crap, it's all *talk*, man."

"That's what philosophy is—talk, ideas. Would you mind leaving the books alone?"

"Fuck the books! Do they just sit here or do they tell you any-thing? Where's the important stuff?"

"Sit down, Jocko. Hang on. What are you worried about?"

"I'm not *worried* about anything. I thought you—. Never mind. I'm done." He sneezed a few times.

"Bless you."

"What?"

I continued, somewhat desperately. "Okay, look. Sisyphus is a symbol of futility, right? The kind of futility you're talking about, the sense of a meaningless life. But we can also see in the story the idea that nothing is good or bad unless thinking makes it so. Which Shakespeare also knew. This is fundamental to understanding the history of philosophy. What you *think* matters."

Jason said, "No, about--. People say 'bless you' because they think it keeps your soul from coming out of your nose when you sneeze. And keeps the devil from coming in. Is that why you say it?"

"Heavens, no."

"Then why do you say it?"

"Good question. Habit, I suppose. I probably shouldn't. To get back to the quest—"

"Do you believe in God?" He sneezed again.

"Bless—sorry. God is outside my domain."

"So you don't believe in God?"

"I neither believe nor disbelieve. I am not very interested in the question. Do you see what I mean? The question frames the answer."

He persisted, interested now in something. "Well, do you believe in fate?"

"Fate! What do you think fate is, Jason? Jocko."

"When something happens because it's meant to happen. Like the stone rolling down the hill, I guess. Or if someone dies. Early, I mean."

"Who means for it to happen?"

"God, I guess. The gods."

"The fates?" I asked.

"Whatever."

"Let's take this up on Monday. I don't know why bad things happen. You just deal with the cards you're given. But certainly the concept of fate is interesting, particularly as it relates to the idea that actions have consequences. Not unrelated to Sisyphus's search for meaning, by the way. But you need to go home and go to bed. Is your house warm enough?"

"What house?"

I started packing up. I felt disconcerted and off center. "Where you're staying. I assume you're staying with friends."

"I guess." He blew his nose again.

"Would you like a ride?"

He shook his head.

"I'm not in a hurry, let me give you a lift. It's rather blustery out."

"I'm not going anywhere! I've got no place to go!"

"What do you mean?"

"Nothing. It's no big deal. I'm sleeping outside is all."

Jesus Christ, no wonder he was sick. I finished packing up my own books, awash in feelings of irritation that I tried not to show. Why hadn't he told me earlier? "You're sleeping outside," I said.

"I do it all the time. It's not illegal, you know. Besides, it's spring." He gave a half-laugh.

"Because you want to?"

"Sure, man. Choice, free will, and all that. Under the bleachers. It's my fate."

"Free will and fate are antithetical."

"Whatever."

"For heaven's sake, Jason, you can't sleep outside. You're sick. Look, you can stay—." I picked up the phone to call Alice, then reconsidered. "Look, there must be someone you can stay with."

He didn't answer.

"Another relative. A friend then. You must have lots of friends."

He looked at me as if I were an idiot. "We moved away, remember? Nobody knows me anymore."

"All right. Look, here's a hundred bucks. I'll take you to a motel, and we'll figure out what to do later."

"Excuse me? I don't need your money. Fuck you! With all due respect."

"Wait a minute, Jason. Wait. Perhaps you should go home to your parents. I can drive you down there."

He snorted. "To Connecticut?"

"I'm sure if they knew you were sick…"

"Don't you get it? I can't go there; he already thinks I'm a failure."

I came to a decision. "All right, you'll have to come home with me. I'll just call—"

"That's okay. I like it where I am."

"Goddammit!" I slammed the desk. "That's it! No more discussion. A decision has been made." I took a deep breath. "My apologies. I don't want your death on my hands—especially if you're going to continue to study with me. Let's go."

"Is that a threat?"

"Not in the least. Consider it an invitation. I'm sure you'll find the accommodations satisfactory. Alice will be glad—Mrs. Henry—will be glad you're... not sleeping in the rain. I hope."

Alice

ON FRIDAY NIGHT, I got home a little late. It had been another hard week and I stopped at the Y to swim. Not only did swimming make me feel better, it helped counter the worry that at the same time Max was being pressured to retire (or face a sexual harassment lawsuit?), I was being edged out of my job.

Last week it was the fathers issue, this week a local flap around snowboards. It wasn't even our account. But for a few days everyone was talking about the controversy over the "appropriateness" of the violent graphics on the undersides of the boards. Did they demean women? Of course, cried the vocal minority, mostly women. (I among them. Good lord, what century were we living in?) But the young guys I worked with thought it was a lot of hoopla over nothing; they had only admiration for the designers who'd managed to generate this kind of publicity. In fact, the two young owners *were* talented and had a good eye and a good instinct for marketing, but they thought they owned the world. And maybe they did. They talked about TV shows I didn't watch, laughed at jokes I didn't get, and went to new local hotspots I'd never heard of. It was true they always had, but something seemed to have shifted. Was it me, or them?

I hoped it was just me, the irritations of aging. Buying the drums hadn't helped. I never played them and I was going to take them back; I felt silly having bought them in the first place. I'd thought making a lot of noise would drown something out. I thought if my spirit naturally inclined toward the bleak, looking suffering in the face would spiral me downward into a black hole, and therefore what I needed was an activity, a project, something to nudge me upward like one of Richard's peonies, toward the light.

But maybe I wasn't a sad, dark woman at heart. This summer would be eight years since Adam's death. Maybe I was finally thawing out; I felt raw, but at the same time I could look at the photographs in my catalogue in a way I couldn't have even a year ago. They weren't too much, and I cared about other people's suffering in a way I couldn't before. I was Little Red Riding Hood crawling out of the wolf's belly—only after a sojourn of eight years rather than eight minutes.

On the other hand, the youthful inexperience (and, I can't help it, the shallowness) of my colleagues at work, which had given me strength as recently as a year ago, now made me impatient. I was probably giving off bad vibes, too. Whereas I used to feel like an older sister, a little out of it but respected, recently I'd begun to feel more like a sidelined and dispensable *mother*.

It would be humiliating to be fired. Maybe I should just quit. But then what?

On the flip side, it was inconceivable Max could be having an affair with someone as young as my colleagues, let alone a student. The idea was just too silly.

I ruminated over all this while swimming, which nonetheless cheered me up considerably. Fuck the drums, I looked pretty damn good in my suit and I could easily swim a half mile without strain. And when I walked in and saw my dear husband making dinner when it was really my turn, I thought perhaps I'd jump his bones later.

I dropped my things onto a chair and slid my arms around his waist from behind. "What are you making?" It seemed to be one of his creative veggie stews that include everything and taste mostly of cumin, which I love.

"Can I get you a glass of wine? Richard's not coming."

"Oh? Why not?"

"I think he's working late."

"All the better." I nibbled on his ear. He doesn't really like that, but I can't help myself sometimes. He pulled his head away. "Sorry," I murmured, but I held onto him.

Max put down the spoon he was using to stir and undid my hands. "Alice, honey, there's a boy asleep upstairs in my office."

I used the spoon to taste the juice in the pot. Delicious. "A boy?"

"Well, not a boy exactly. A student." He stepped sideways to a bowl on the counter, which I now saw was full of another of his specialties, ground beef mixed with onions and spices. He scooped out some of the ground beef, rolled it between his hands and formed patties.

"A student?" I echoed. It was not all that surprising, although a first. Max was prone to helping students in unconventional ways, buying one a bicycle helmet or paying another twice the going rate to shovel our driveway when that was one of the few domestic tasks Max enjoyed.

"Well, not exactly a student. A young man. But younger than my students. He seems very young at times. But he *is* one of my students."

"One of your students is asleep upstairs?" Mostly I was disappointed that we didn't have the house to ourselves for a raucous evening of after-dinner sex. Scratch that plan.

"Yes. That is, I believe he is asleep, yes. He seems rather worn out. It is my impression that he hasn't been sleeping well."

There was a container of olives on the counter. I got out a bowl to put them in, a small blue bowl we'd bought in Florence that year. "What is one of your students doing here?"

"He has nowhere else to go, apparently. His parents may have thrown him out."

"Why isn't he staying at the college?"

"He doesn't go to the college."

"All right. But ask me next time first, okay? How long is he staying?"

Max set the patties in the frying pan; each one hissed furiously. After a moment, he said. "He's still in high school. Or he would be, if—. I'm tutoring him."

"Tutoring?" Idle conversation-enhancing behavior suddenly gave way to genuine interest: why hadn't Max mentioned this? He was on sabbatical. He must have missed teaching more than he admitted. Such an interesting man. I watched him pour me the glass of wine he'd offered earlier: handsome, too. Why was it some men got more handsome while women mostly sagged?

Max handed me the glass. "In philosophy. He's interested."

"How curious." I raised my glass to him.

"What, that someone would care about the vital questions of human existence?"

"A kid, yes, plus the fact that you're on sabbatical."

Max began slicing tomatoes; he was especially focused on this dinner. "I admit I thought so too at first. But this is no ordinary kid."

"Need any help?"

He shook his head and I took my wine over to the couch. "Why is it so dark in here?" I turned on a lamp; it was the kitchen that I now realized was a little dim.

"One of the bulbs burned out and I broke it trying to change it… I've been working with him for two weeks. At first it was three times a week, but now every day. He's very bright. Very motivated. Well, I mean, as kids go. Though to tell you the truth, I'm not sure what his motivation is."

"Well, good. Can I change the subject? Max, listen, I think I'm going to have to find a new job."

Max turned to me then very seriously. He said, "Alice, the boy I'm tutoring is Jason Green."

I must have looked completely blank. It was as if he were speaking a foreign language; I couldn't take it in. "Jason?"

"Adam's friend."

"Is asleep upstairs?" I put down my glass. "Jason Green?"

Max wiped his hands on a towel. He set the bowl of sliced tomatoes on the table, which he had set with the embroidered linen tablecloth we'd bought in Florence. Was that why we were having such a nice dinner?

"That's who you're tutoring?"

Max turned his attention back to the stove. He flipped the fancy burgers onto their other sides and pulled whole wheat buns from the toaster oven. "It's hard to explain. He came to my office. Do you want something else to drink with dinner? Let's sit down."

I sat at the table. But I wasn't hungry. Max ate, and commented appreciatively on his cooking, obviously trying to make this a normal night. He kindly gave me a few minutes to digest this information. Then he said, "Are you upset? I should have called you to warn you. I was afraid you'd—."

"It doesn't matter."

"I should have told you two weeks ago. But I—"

"Yes, you should have, but it doesn't matter now. It's all right."

"Why are you so upset?"

"I don't know. Will you be quiet for a minute? I don't know! I don't understand what he's doing here, or why you brought him. I wish he weren't being *thrust* on me like this. The house isn't even clean. Were the sheets clean?"

"The sheets? He's just on the couch."

"Why has he come back here? Why you? Why us? Why is he—" I stopped.

"Why is he alive?" Max offered gently.

"No, no. Just, why is he *here*?"

Max resumed eating. "Why don't you go peek in on him? I'm sure he's sleeping."

"Why did you put him in Adam's room, instead of down here in the guestroom?"

"What do you mean? He's in my office, on the couch. It hasn't been Adam's room for years."

Okay, I thought. *Okay. It's no big deal. It's just a surprise, that's all.*

Max said, "You could take him some hot soup. I bought a couple of cans on the way home."

"Jason Green." I was trying to make sense of it.

"He's got no place to stay, Alice, and he's sick. It's raining."

"So rather than take him to the infirmary, you brought him here." I wasn't accusing, I genuinely wanted to understand.

"The infirmary. I never thought of it. That would have been better, wouldn't it? Then you wouldn't have even—. But he's not a real student; I don't know if—" He trailed off.

I managed to eat some spoonfuls of the veggie stew. I told Max it was good.

Then Max looked over my shoulder and I turned around, and Jason Green emerged apologetically from the stairwell with one hand on the doorjamb.

"Excuse me," he said.

The kid I'd seen in the library. Of course. He was surprisingly tall—but he would be, he was eighteen after all. He looked rather like a hungry young street musician with his dirty-blond, matted dreadlocks. He wasn't a particularly attractive young man, at least to me, but he was arresting, in a brooding, unfocused way. Mainly he looked like a young person with a cold who needed a good meal. Max jumped up.

"Jason! How are you feeling? You remember Alice, Mrs. Henry."

He came forward, almost shyly. He held out his hand. "Mrs. Henry. It's been a while. You look great. Um, thanks for letting me stay here."

I smiled at the absurdity of it in spite of myself. I looked great? What training in politeness had produced that? I responded a bit stiffly. "Please—join us."

Max said, "Let me get you some dinner. Would you like a hamburger?" He bustled about, while I observed Jason who sat gazing at his lap. It was clear he didn't feel well. His training in politeness didn't extend to making conversation under these circumstances. Neither did mine. Max set a full plate before him, and he immediately dug into the hamburger.

After a moment, Max said, "How is it?"

"Good."

Max and I exchanged glances. I got up to put on tea water and came back. Max and I watched Jason eat. He was either too out of it to notice, or comfortable being observed.

A few minutes later, evidently restored somewhat by food, he said, "It's strange to be in Adam's room after all this time. Everything looks different."

"We gave most of it away," said Max.

"I remember he had these cool posters of Bruce Lee and other karate guys."

"How are your parents, Jason?" I asked.

"Fine, I guess. I go by Jocko now." He sneezed twice.

"Jocko," I repeated, trying it out. The kettle clicked off. "Tea, anyone?" I asked. Max shook his head. I made myself a cup.

"It's kind of like a joke," Jason-Jocko said. "'Cause I'm so not a jock. And there was a book about this guy, kind of like a Robin Hood character. In middle school." He took out a handful of wadded up tissues from his pocket, blew his nose and put them back in his pocket. "I saw you still have those toy soldiers. I remember when we painted them."

"We brought them back from Europe," Max said eagerly.

"Nobody else had any like them."

"They were lead," said Max. "I don't think they make them like that in the U.S."

"We used to play with them for hours."

I got up again and brought out a roll of toilet paper from the hall closet. I set it on the table in front of him. "Do they still live in Hartford?" I asked.

He looked at me.

"Your parents."

"Oh, yeah. Sure."

"Does your father still lead boy scout troops?"

Max said sharply, "Alice."

There was a small silence. "No. He gave that up."

"I suppose that's a good thing. And what about you? Do you do any camping these days?"

Max said then, "Alice, could I talk to you a minute? Excuse us." I followed Max into my study and closed the door.

I was incensed. "How dare you speak to me like that in front of him? Calling me out like a child."

"For Christ's sake, Alice, he's our guest!"

"He's not *my* guest. I didn't invite him here."

"Alice, Jesus, get a grip. What's the matter with you? You're being irrational!"

I took a deep breath. "Max, I hate you right now. I hate when you say that. But this is not the time for this conversation, okay? This whole thing is humiliating enough. Let's go back in, you can be pleasant, and I'm going to bed. I don't know what else to say."

Max put his hand against the door so I couldn't open it. "Alice—"

I waited.

"I'm sorry I didn't tell you he was here. But this, this is an opportunity." He grabbed my arms. "I'm not asking you to take care of him. We're just going to let him stay here a few nights until I can make other arrangements."

"Fine. I'll stay with Richard."

"Alice, please." He put his arms around me. I was too worked up to relax, but I didn't push him away.

Jocko had finished his meal when we returned. I stood at the table behind my chair, looking down at him. "My husband tells me I was being rude, but I don't think so. Do you think so?"

Jocko examined his plate.

Max was shaking his head at me sadly, but I went on. "And I really don't think—."

But Jocko had interrupted me with an intense fit of coughing, to the point of choking. He pushed away from the table. Instinctively I reached to pat his back. He coughed and tried to catch his breath, and I patted his back as I would have done for Max or a stranger sitting next to me in a train station. I patted his back, and it was like a little bird escaped from my chest, and my eyes welled up. Eventually Jocko caught his breath, and Max handed him a glass of water. Jocko wiped his eyes and excused himself and went into the bathroom. Max and I looked at each other. We listened to Jocko cough a little more and blow his nose.

I said, "Put him to bed and make sure he has plenty of blankets so he doesn't catch pneumonia."

"Where are you going?" Max said.

"To get some cold medicine. I know we don't have any."

"I'll go," Max said. He stood up.

"No, I need some air. It's okay. But put him in the guest room." I kissed him lightly, grabbed my bag and left the room before Jocko reappeared.

Alice

THE NEXT MORNING, I got up early, before Max, made myself a cup of tea as quietly as I could and retreated to the basement. The *National Geographics* were where I'd left them, naturally—Max never came down here—and I brought the stack over to the futon couch. I would have preferred to spread them out on the floor, but the goddamn drum set was in the way. I needed to disassemble the thing and take it back—I could hardly ask Richard to do that, too—but that was a chore I dreaded. I hated to acknowledge a failure without anything to replace it with.

I needed something *added* to my life, not taken away.

I set aside the issue devoted to family. All the good photos from there were now upstairs in the living room. I went through the next issue methodically, but without a clear sense of purpose. When I came to an image that had arrested me before, I tore out the page. I ended up with three pages. I went through the next issue the same way and found two more. I hesitated over a third image, of a vast Tibetan landscape with some figures in the distance, but decided against it. What was I looking for after all? The others were all portraits, but something about that open mountain range spoke to me. Why? I spread out the five portraits in front of me. I left the page with the landscape propped open. Okay, yes. I tore it out, too.

I had a roll of newsprint leftover from a newspaper. It used to be the case that you could go to a paper's back entrance and ask for these ends of rolls. A painter friend who moved away got them often and she'd given me one. It was thirty-four inches wide and endlessly long, so you could roll it out to make a banner or simply cut off a large piece. Now I tore off a sheet and taped it to my worktable, made from an old flat door and deeper than most worktables.

I set out the five portraits. I picked one, a mother and child in colorful, embroidered Nicaraguan dresses. The mother was holding the child, who looked about three. I cut away the background. The next one was a portrait of a dark-skinned, exceptionally wrinkled old man in a nondescript, brownish gray shirt who could have been Roma or anything from eastern or central Europe but apparently was Tunisian. I tore off the bottom so I had only his shoulders and head and kept part of the village behind him.

Whether worn or smooth, all the faces were exquisitely beautiful. Maybe more accurately, all the photographs were beautiful, even though the subject might be missing teeth or have a disfiguring scar along a cheek, or in the case of a squat, older woman dressed in classic European widow's black, present a mask so impenetrable it hurt your heart to see. It might have hidden rage or despair or longing or a ferocious religiosity. Whatever it was, was none of the prying photographer's business. And yet she had allowed herself to be photographed, to be viewed all over the world. What did that require? Was it self-assurance, apathy, a generosity toward the photographer, or something I couldn't imagine?

The other photos came from Burundi and Inner Mongolia. I cut away everything in the original photos I didn't want. Then I returned to the pair of Mongolian brothers, whose horses I'd excised. They would go in the center. But they didn't look right. The old Tunisian man, then. I liked his background but his face needed a frame, so I drew a circle around his head with a yellow highlighter and filled it in like the halos of Giotto, which we'd seen at the Ufizzi.

The halo was fine, but now the old man couldn't go in the center. I thought of the three paintings Max and I had looked at together, three images of the Virgin and Child; the Nicaraguan mother and child could go in the center. But no halo. No. Instead I cut that image in half, on the diagonal through the face of one and body of the other. I rearranged the pieces; they needed to be even more fragmented so I cut them into smaller shapes. Yes. I glued those to the paper.

Now I had a focus. I placed the other photos around the mother and child. I included the Tibetan landscape in shards at the top. I left space around the images. I didn't want them all on top of each other; this wasn't a piece about those images but about something else.

I became aware of voices upstairs. I'd heard footsteps earlier but ignored them. Now Max and Jocko were both awake. With any luck, Jocko would take off quickly, but of course he was sick, so maybe he'd just go back to bed. Agh, Max could deal with him; he was Max's project after all. This was mine.

In the back of a shelf under the stairs were old art supplies left-over from Adam. The boxes of Adam-photos that Max had asked about, which I'd never done anything with, were also under the stairs, but not relevant at the moment. I dug through paper of various sizes and weights, markers, colored pencils, cardboard, a box of rubber stamps, a basket of dried-up paints, until I found a box of wax crayons in primary colors. Perfect. Now I drew a thick black border around my creation, and then I turned the whole thing on its side, to better ignore the images. Using my left hand, I drew on the page, as if it were blank. Of course I couldn't ignore the photos completely and no doubt their placement influenced me, but I tried to draw as a very young child might draw on a wall, oblivious of the surface. With every new thing I drew—a sun, a cat with stick legs, a rainbow, a stick flower with two leaves—I shifted the page further until I'd gone full circle. Finally, over the center, but at an angle, I drew a mother and child holding hands.

I colored in my drawings, trying to make them as garish as possible. I scrawled and scribbled, fiercely, freely, and pressed too hard so that one of the crayons broke. I laughed out loud.

By the time I had finished, it was quiet again upstairs. I hadn't heard the outside door shut, but then I wasn't sure I would have. I sat and looked at my creation for a moment. I observed the shapes and colors, the bits of the original photos that peeked out from behind the layers of waxy color. Was it garbage or art? I smiled at myself. Who cared? I thought Max would be pleased. Suddenly I was hungry, in fact ravenous. I'd have breakfast and then take apart the drum set.

Alice

When I came up from the basement, there he was, sitting at the table. I stopped in the doorway: it was like seeing a ghost. More than one. There was Jason Green, the eighteen-year-old that Max had brought home last night. And there like an image bleeding through from underneath was the ten-year-old child he was eight years ago, who was Adam's best friend and with him when he died. And there for a second—this is the weird part—was a teenaged Adam having breakfast. I grabbed the doorframe for support. It was like déjà-vu except that it wasn't like it had happened before but like I was seeing into a world that existed on another plane of reality. And déjà-vu doesn't make you feel like the floor just dropped out from under you.

I don't believe in other planes of reality, and I don't believe in ghosts, even metaphorical ones like the kind Max talks about. Things are what they are.

Except that you can't help but wonder sometimes. Max and I saw a movie once about two parallel tracks of reality, the supposedly real one and one that would have unfolded if the character had left his house a few minutes later. Everything that happened was similar but different—and got increasingly different. You walk down the street and a tree falls; you're either under it or, a few seconds later, you're not. You step too close to the edge of a cliff and you fall off; you take one step backward instead… Max and I left the movie theater and drove home without speaking, and neither of us ever said a word about it.

In any case I only thought about all that later. At the time I merely held on and the moment passed but left me scowling at our guest.

"Sorry," he said. "I didn't mean to surprise you. I didn't know anyone was home."

"Of course I'm home," I said. "I live here."

He said nothing. It seemed he'd finished breakfast and was merely reading the newspaper like an adult.

"How are you feeling this morning?" I asked. "Better, I hope."

"Yeah, thanks."

"You've had breakfast, I take it. I'm about to have an egg. Would you like anything more?" He was so thin. But he declined and folded up the paper as if to leave. He pushed his chair back and stood up.

As much as I hadn't liked seeing him moments ago, now I didn't want him to leave. "Where's Max?" I asked.

"He went out to get some coffee. He said he'd be right back."

"We don't drink coffee in the morning. Just tea."

He hesitated. "I guess he's getting it for me."

At least he had the grace to be embarrassed. I could have mercifully released him to the guest room at that moment, but… I didn't. "So, Jason, we haven't seen you in a long time. How's your life, what are you doing, and what are you doing here, with Max?" I abandoned the idea of a good breakfast just now, hungry as I was, and stuck a frozen bagel into the toaster oven instead.

He stood awkwardly in the kitchen with his hands in his pockets. "I, um, had this idea—"

"I know, of studying philosophy, Max told me. But why?"

"It's kind of a long story."

"I've got time."

I didn't exactly mean to be challenging but he took it that way. He tilted his head at me and said, "This thing happened to me when I was a kid…"

"Happened to *you*?" I echoed, shaking my head. He gave up on me. Our house is small, and he was at the door to his room before I collected myself. "Let me ask you something," I said to his retreating back. He turned. "Do you expect to have children?"

The question surprised him. He dropped his hand. "I don't know. I try not to make babies, if you know what I mean."

I smiled in spite of myself. I'd been going to ask him, to press him, about being a parent, but suddenly I thought, *He's very young.* Instead I said, "What are you going to do after this? After high school?"

He remained at the end of the short hallway. I moved back into the kitchen to get my now-thawed bagel in the hopes he'd return. He took a few steps closer and hovered at the edge of the living room-kitchen space. He said, "I don't like to think about the future. It's kind of bleak. The whole planet's deteriorating."

"True enough." I sat at the table and indicated an invitation for him to join me. He took another few steps into the living room but remained standing.

"Everybody has too much stuff," he added. I nodded.

Evidently he felt a need to explain himself. "The past is a drag, but at least it's over. The present isn't much better, but at least it's always changing. I mean it's like there's now, and then *now* is gone, and now, and now, and every second there's a new present. Adam and I used to talk about that. When we were *ten*."

I smiled tightly. I wasn't sure I wanted to hear about Adam and him. "Tell me something about yourself. What did you do in Connecticut?"

But he had other ideas. "We made a fort once in the woods behind my house where there used to be a quarry. One time Mr. Henry paid us to rake leaves and we made a humongous pile—we did your yard and next door—and we played in it. We made a snow fort next door once, too. Once we camped out in your back yard and we almost froze to death. We stole a chocolate bunny from Ben Franklin, and this man came running after us—."

"Wait. Adam stole something?"

"Well, actually, I did. I mean, he was like the lookout, but I was the one who put it in my pocket. Kind of a shitty lookout—"

"That's why he never wanted to go into Ben Franklin. He'd just stay in the car. How else were you a bad influence?" I pulled my knees to my chest and perched my heels on the edge of the chair.

"I wasn't a bad influence. He was the one who wanted to do it. He always said he wasn't scared of anything. He said being the lookout was harder. I never figured out till later why he'd make me go first. Like skateboarding down our hill where we lived. I was afraid of cars. But we did it and it was *so fun*. That was the best."

"What else?"

Now Jocko moved restlessly around the living room, picking things up and putting them down. "Those little lead soldiers you've got in his room? The room that used to be his? He was obsessed. He used to set up these incredibly elaborate little wars, these whole strategies about who did what and who moved where. And then we liked to blow them all up in the end, kind of scatter them around the room. We thought that was hilarious, the best part."

"I used to find strays under the bed."

"I remember when we first painted them. We wanted to paint them different colors so we could tell the armies apart, and Mr. Henry got this special paint, and we were supposed to spread out newspapers on the floor because there were so many of them, and be really careful—."

"I remember."

"And I was amazed that you guys didn't get mad. In our house art projects always ended up with someone getting in trouble."

"There's still paint on the floor. It's just covered up with a rug."

He fell silent then, gazing at a photograph I'd recently tacked to the wall. "How come you don't have any pictures of Adam? You have all these other pictures stuck on the wall."

"You haven't said why you wanted to study philosophy with Max."

He turned back to me. "If you can't understand without explanation, you can't understand with explanation."

I got up. "Sounds like anti-intellectual bullshit to me." I turned on the water at the sink full blast and began washing the dishes. He murmured something I didn't hear. I didn't respond, and he took a step farther into the kitchen. He stood a few steps behind me.

"Mrs. Henry, I'm really sorry to impose on you but he made me come here. Mr. Henry."

I turned off the water. "He made you? He tied you up and forced you?"

"He wanted—. I told him I was fine out there and he ignored me. He's... trying to help me."

270

"Very kind of him."

"Well, I mean, it's been raining. At least when it snowed, I—"

"And of course now you're sick and have no place to go, and you don't even have a hat."

He was silent a moment and I felt a rush of remorse. Good Lord, I was bullying a child, who was a guest in my house and sick besides. I turned back to the dishes.

He said, "Mrs. Henry, I'm sorry about Adam."

I turned slowly to him. We looked at each other, but whatever he saw in my face was not what he'd hoped for, and he fled.

I finished the dishes, a monster disguised in yellow rubber gloves at a kitchen sink. I could only hope Max would make other arrangements for his protégé soon. I didn't know what he was getting out of this, but that was his business. I wanted nothing more to do with it. My own lack of compassion, the rage I'd thought I'd let go of years ago, was choking me.

Richard

On Saturday I saw clients all morning. When I took a break around one p.m., I discovered I'd left some papers at home. I could rearrange my schedule and do that work tonight, or go home and get some lunch at the same time. I had no appointments till three, so I went home. I made myself two good-sized sandwiches and was just putting the papers into my briefcase when the doorbell rang.

I was glad to see him, invited him in. I still had a good hour. "Where've you been the last few days? Where you been sleeping? Against my better judgment I worried about you."

"Next door."

That took me aback. "Next door?" I felt the heat rush up the back of my neck. If I'd been a cartoon character, as indeed I often felt, steam would have shot out of my ears.

Jocko said, "Sleeping outside made me sick, if you can't tell. So he said—"

"Why were you sleeping outside? Why didn't you shack up with that girl, or find somewhere else?" I stopped. *Why didn't you come here?*

There was a silence. Explaining—maybe even thinking—seemed to require too much effort. "I don't know."

I took a deep breath. "Well, so how's it going?"

Jocko pulled a handful of tissues from his pocket and blew his nose. "Mrs. Henry doesn't want me there. I think she hates me."

I nodded. That seemed entirely possible, if a bit exaggerated.

"She thinks I'm responsible for Adam's death."

"Are you?"

He glared at me. "Shit," he muttered.

"I don't mean were you really, I mean do you feel like you are?"

He rolled his eyes. I said, "Okay, next topic. How's it going with Max?"

"We talk about old philosophers, and this guy Basho who went on a journey and wrote poetry. Sometimes he reads me some, like about frogs and plum blossoms and fleas. It's pretty funny."

I nodded.

"We talk about seeking meaning, which is philosophy, versus making meaning, which is the purview of literature. He likes that word, purview. We talk about things like God and fate and responsibility, but not really. It's hard to keep him on track. You know, focused."

"Really?" Max was one of the most focused people I knew. On the other hand, his thinking was non-linear, more like a dance, as he once said. Jocko didn't answer.

"Do you know what you want?" I asked him.

"I've already told you. Jesus, doesn't anybody listen around here?"

I'd made him a sandwich while we were talking and now handed it to him. "You know, Jocko, everybody's got sadness in their lives of some kind of another."

"Tell me something I don't know."

"Maybe you got your share a little early is all."

He finished swallowing and he said, "After Mrs. Henry left, I was just, like, poking around the house. Just looking at stuff. Maybe I was looking for stuff that reminded me of Adam. So I go down in the basement, and there's this really cool drum set—"

"Do you play the drums?"

"Nah. I'm not musical. I don't do anything like that. But I thought, why do they have this? I don't remember these. They must have got them *after* Adam died. But why would you get a drum set for a kid after he died? That's pretty weird. Anyway, so then I see this strange sort of collage-y art thing and right next to it there's this whole box of pictures of Adam. Photos. And guess what, some of them are of me and Adam."

"I'm not sure you should be poking around in their stuff."

He frowned. "There were pictures of *me* and Adam," he repeated.

"Right. But they're not your pictures. Never mind. Look, I've got to get back to work. Take the rest of that with you."

"There was this one picture of Adam coming out of a leaf pile. He's got his arms thrown out like this, and there's leaves flying and he's laughing. It's like a Happy Kid commercial, you know. So I put it in the middle of the collage."

Had I heard right? He'd been in Alice's private space, gone through her photographs, and then messed with what had to be her creation?

"I didn't glue it," he said defensively. "I just set it there."

"Oh, well then." The cartoon-me was jaw-dropping astonished. Saying Alice would be displeased was like saying God was displeased with Sodom and Gomorrah. I said nothing.

"And I borrowed this one." He pulled it out of his back pocket. It was the two of them, grinning, with their arms around each other's necks, outside in summer or maybe early fall. Dark-haired Adam and blond Jason. They were wearing jeans and T-shirts with designs on them, one of a dripping skull and the other some kind of explosion.

"More Happy Kids," I said. He nodded.

Oh well, I thought. What the hell. Maybe Alice wouldn't notice. "Can I drop you somewhere?" But—what if Max or Alice saw him in my car? I asked casually, "Do Max and Alice know you were staying here?"

"I don't know. I guess not. Does it matter?"

There was no reason it should matter to him. I shrugged. If he hadn't mentioned it yet, perhaps he wouldn't. Certainly I couldn't ask him not to. It wasn't fair of me to involve him in my little drama. Furthermore, I wasn't sure that he *wouldn't* tell them as soon as he knew I didn't want him to. He was a complicated kid, and I didn't trust him for a minute not to wreak havoc, if not completely intentionally then out of some preternatural certainty that this was how life was supposed to work. How long had disaster trailed in his wake? Since Adam's death, or all his life?

"Let's go," I said.

He put on his coat. Standing in my tiny mudroom while I waited in the kitchen for him to open the outer door, he said, "You asked me before why I came here."

"Yeah."

"I remembered you." He paused. "Sort of like Santa Claus."

I raised my eyebrows. I made a move to usher him out but he stood his ground.

"One time I was over at the Henrys' and Adam had this dog we were playing with. It was somebody else's. We were just running around, you know, playing, and Mr. Henry got upset about some-thing and chased us with a hammer. It was terrifying, man. We were screaming. I ran into the front yard but then I didn't know where to go. I couldn't run home, it was too far." He examined his fingers. "You were sitting on the front porch. I remember I was crying and you came over and talked to me, and you showed me how to blow a blade of grass."

"Ah."

"I never knew an adult who would do stuff like that or show a kid."

"I remember now."

"My father was all about tying knots and merit badges—you know, helping people and shit. Scouting stuff."

"I was a boy scout." I don't know why I felt a need to defend his father. I didn't want him to think I was a cool, non-scouting grown-up when I was really a goofy Harold Bloom wannabe.

He said, "You're shitting me."

"Well, only a cub scout," I had to admit. "For about a month. Then somebody probably realized I wasn't scouting material. I would have liked to have been."

"Because you were gay."

"Possibly. I don't actually remember."

"That's not where you learned to blow grass."

"No. My sister taught me that."

He laughed, one of his rare genuine laughs. I was charmed.

"True," I assured him. There was a silence.

"I'm not gay," he said.

I smiled. "I don't hold that against you."

He nodded. "I remembered all this time how it felt to be, you know, all upset and crying, and, like, *little*, then be able to make this incredible shrieking noise."

"Let's go," I said again. I opened the door and followed him out.

It was only later, sitting at my desk working on tax returns and finishing a large bag of chips that I realized how pissed I felt at Max. That was an understatement. My conversation with Jocko, which could have soothed something in me or reassured me that I had succeeded in reaching him, connecting with him, or whatever it was that I wanted—and I wasn't sure what that was—instead had made things worse.

I took off the new blue tie Max gave me and put it in my brief-case. I'd never before met with clients without a tie, but I couldn't stand it around my neck right now.

I wanted to fight with Max. I didn't want to punch him, I wanted to squeeze him to death the way a two-year-old squeezes the new baby, or a sumo wrestler his opponent. The tightness in my groin was disconnected from my brain. Something in me was merging Max and Jocko; my reaction to the one was inflaming something toward the other. I didn't understand it, but it gripped me. It wasn't jealousy about Jocko anymore, it was about Max himself. I loved Max deeply, but it was as if all those years of teasing and pleasant accommodation and restraint on my part—and resignation—in the end turned out to be a thin cap on a volcano. Maybe I wasn't a rational, reasonably decent if repressed accountant, but a frustrated fat man exploding with predatory desire.

Alice

On Saturday afternoon, it began to snow again, likely the last storm of winter, the heavy wet kind of snow that strains your back to shovel. In the early evening I went to the store, and when I got home, I was relieved to find the house still empty because it left me free to call Richard while putting away the groceries. I tried him at work but he didn't answer. With a client, I thought, and without his receptionist. I called his house to leave a message, and he answered.

"Richard!"

"Hi, Alice. What's up?"

"I'm surprised you're home, but I'm *so* glad you are."

"What's the matter, darling?"

"Quite a few things. For starters, it's good you didn't come over for dinner last night."

"Why is that?"

"Do you remember the kid who was with Adam when he died? He was Adam's best friend, a little blond kid named Jason Green."

"Yeah?"

"He's *staying* with us."

Richard obviously didn't know what to say to that. After a pause he said, "And you're not happy about it."

"That's for sure. I'm very confused. Max—oh, never mind. Hey, is this an okay time? Can I talk to you? I mean, why are you home? Are you all right?"

"Yes," he said firmly. "I'm having a little tumult in my own life, but I can't talk about it right now. Anyway, big picture, I'm fine. I'm home mainly because of the storm. Go ahead. It will make me feel better to hear you talk."

"Okay. So, this kid is here and he makes me uncomfortable. I'm sure there are lots of reasons and I can't begin to tease them apart— you know, *he's* here and Adam's not and all that. The obvious stuff. Except that he's eighteen and that makes me, I don't know, sad, angry, whatever. Then there's the fact that I could lose my job any minute, or I feel like I could, which is complicated because although it would be humiliating to be fired, it might be also be great to get out of there. And Max, well, I don't understand what Max is doing. And I feel completely ridiculous about having bought those drums!"

Richard laughed gently. "Oh, Alice."

"It was a total mistake to get them. I haven't even touched them. One night I went down to look at them, and you know they're beautiful just sitting there. They're like, full of potential, like an empty theater or a page before you draw the first line. You know what I mean?" I heard Richard's tea kettle going off, and that seemed like a good idea, so I put on ours.

"I think so," he said.

"I looked at them and tried to visualize myself sitting on the seat, and practicing, and getting pleasure from the sound, and I couldn't. I couldn't even find the fantasy. Instead, I saw Adam there. Not what he might be now, I can't imagine that. I mean, you know, Adam at ten, the way he was. *He* liked to make noise.

So I'm thinking about Adam, and I thought how I—." I had to stop.

Richard waited. After a moment he said, "Alice, are you okay? Would you like me to come over?"

I pulled myself together enough to talk. "No. I just—I just have to tell you, remember those photographs from the catalogue I showed you? *Beautiful Suffering*, or whatever it was called? I keep thinking of them. That woman with the bruised face who took the self-portrait, and the old man lying on the pallet in the corner. It's just like I—I know this seems weird, but I can't help feeling… it's like I…"

He waited again.

If I could just get the words out. I choked, "Like I wasn't a good enough mother." I held the phone away from my mouth so he wouldn't have to hear me crying.

"Ah," he said. "Well, that's just crazy. You were a fantastic mother."

"You don't know that."

"Of course I do. I saw you interact with Adam a hundred times, a thousand times. When he was cranky, when you were cranky. A million times."

"I wasn't cranky a million times." I laughed, between tears.

"No," he agreed.

"But I'm afraid I didn't love him enough." I wasn't crying now, just sad.

Richard was silent. "Enough for what?" he said finally.

"To keep him alive, I guess."

Richard sighed. "It's funny, I used to have the same thought years ago. Not about Adam, about Hecky."

I nodded into the phone.

He went on, "But it's just wishful thinking. What do they call that, you know, when you want something to happen?"

"Magical thinking?"

"See, you've still got a brain. You're not drying up, even if you were to get fired and can never play the drums."

I blew my nose. "Well, I'm just sorry I made you go with me on that stupid errand. Sorry, sorry, sorry."

"You didn't make me, darling. It was an interesting excursion into another world—of girly madness."

"Richard, did you love Hecky as much as, as much as you love Max?"

There was a little silence, after which he said, "I hate Max."

I laughed. It was the last thing I expected.

"Anyway," he said. "It was very different."

"Of course. You *are* a dear."

"And you're a goose."

It was an old joke between us. "Thank you, Richard. Hey, will you tell me what's going on with you when the time is right?"

"Perhaps."

"Perhaps?"

"Okay, probably. How's that?"

"That'll do. When will we see you next?" We left it that he'd call when he got a break, and otherwise we'd see him after the 15th, which was less than two weeks away. I hung up amid a rush of love and gratitude for such a friend.

Thus fortified, I took my tea down to the basement. What would my little creation look like, how would it appear to me, a few hours later? Would I feel pleased or want to throw it away? I was eager to see.

I sensed immediately that something was wrong. My house may be a mess, but I'm very sensitive to spatial relations—it's what makes me a good designer—and I noticed it from across the room. There was a picture of Adam in the center of my piece. I walked slowly around the drums and picked it up.

Max would never have done that. He knew better.

The shock disassociated me from my body. A voice in my head incongruously sang, *Someone's been sitting in my chair. Someone's been sitting in MY chair. Someone's been sitting in MY chair, and he's broken it!*

Jason Green as Goldilocks the intruder, the instrument of careless destruction.

What the hell was he doing in my space? Rifling through my photographs. Messing with my creation.

I could hardly breathe. I knew I was overreacting; my brain told me this was no big deal, just a kid screwing around, but my body was hot, then cold, and I trembled all over. The box of Adam-photos sat on my worktable where he had left it. I heard Max and Jason come in from outside. Before I knew it, I was upstairs.

"Hi, Alice," Max said as I emerged from the basement. "We've just been picking up another shovel. Our old one needs replacing anyway and it seemed like a good time to have two. Jason can help dig us out from this storm."

"What's wrong?" Jason asked me.

"What were you doing in the basement?"

"Nothing. I was just looking around."

"What is it, Alice?" asked Max.

"How dare you go through my stuff?" I barely managed above a whisper.

"I wasn't. I mean, I was just looking through some pictures. I didn't hurt anything."

Max looked back and forth between us.

"You have no right," I said.

Max said, "What happened?"

I couldn't answer.

Jason collected himself. "Hey, sorry. Sorry! I was just looking at the pictures, okay? I don't know what your problem is. But whatever. Hey, I know you don't want me here—it was a mistake for me to come—so I'll just go next door. Sorry for the *inconvenience*. Thanks anyway, Mr. Henry." He headed for the door.

Max frowned. "Next door?"

"Yeah, he doesn't hassle me this way."

"Doesn't hassle you? What do you mean?"

Jason opened the door.

Max said, "Wait a minute. "How long have you, when did you run into Richard?"

Jason waved him off.

"Jason, I'm asking you a question."

"Who are you, the police?"

I could see how upset Max was. My own distress dropped in the face of his. "Max, it doesn't matter."

"Of course it matters."

Jason turned around in the doorway. He said defensively, "When I first got here, I went over there first. He let me in. Sometimes I stay there."

"Does he—" Max stopped, turned away, ran his hand through his hair. "Jesus Christ. All this time."

"What's the big deal? He gave me a place to stay. What's with you guys?"

I was surprised, too, because Richard hadn't said anything—and why hadn't he?—but I managed to say calmly, "It's fine for you to move next door while you finish up your studies with Max."

Max began, "I'm not sure—" but he was interrupted by Jason: "Yeah, I'm done here." He turned to Max. "It was a happy picture of Adam. Fucking Adam, who's like a stone around my neck."

We stood there, the three of us, Max and I watching Jason, Jason with his eyes closed, swaying slightly as if he might faint.

"I'm sorry," I said softly, "but if you've come here looking for absolution—"

"Fuck that!"

"It's too much to ask, you understand?"

"I don't want anything from you!"

"I think you do."

"Jesus Christ, I—"

"Because if you pushed Adam off a mountain—"

"I didn't push him."

"And you want us to say *It's okay, never mind—*."

"I didn't push him."

"It isn't okay. It—"

"I didn't push him! I dared him!"

He looked around at us, furious and desperate. We waited.

"You want to think it's my fault? Go ahead, maybe it was. Maybe I did kill him, maybe I'm responsible. Does that make you happy?"

"Take it easy," said Max.

"He was such a wimp! He wanted to go up to the lookout, but when we got there, he chickened out. It was the fucking wind."

Max said tiredly, "It's all right, Jason. That's enough. You don't need—"

"You don't know what I need! I dared him, do you understand? It was blowing like crazy and he wanted to go back down, but I dared him. He was always the brave one, doing scary shit but making me go first. But for once, I wasn't scared. I called him a chickenshit. I dared him to stand on the edge. We were both leaning out into the wind, it was like flying, and then the wind stopped or something. And he wasn't there."

In the silence we could hear the clock over the refrigerator ticking. Jason looked like the skin had been stripped off his face. I couldn't bear to look at him.

Max said, "You didn't push him, did you." It was a statement, not a question—the only comfort he could offer.

"I dared him. He was my best friend," Jason choked. "And now I carry him on my fucking back!" His voice was scratchy with grief. "You know anything about friends?" He glared at Max and me. He goaded Max: "Ask your best friend there, your faggot neighbor. Ask him about friends."

"Okay," said Max, lifting his hands in a gesture both appeasing and quieting. "Okay. Okay."

My own broken heart was breaking again. I took a step toward Jason. "I'm sorry you've had to—." But he'd had enough. He turned and was out both doors in seconds, slamming the outer door behind him.

I said, "Ah, shit."

Max roused himself and sprang after him.

I grabbed his arm. "Let him go." He stopped and looked at me. He unclenched his fists and when he took a deep breath, tears sprang to his eyes. I reached for him but he shook his head.

He said, "What have you done?"

Richard

It was snowing so hard, I'd left work after my two late-afternoon appointments, to finish work at home. I'd had a hard time concentrating anyway, felt churned up and angry, even jacked off at one point, which made me feel like a teenager, if not very relieved in my heart. But when I got home about five-thirty, I crawled into bed with a bowl of vanilla ice cream like a rebellious, unrepentant child, to watch "Run Silent, Run Deep," which is the best World War II revenge movie I know. Clark Gable plays an American naval commander who's obsessed with sinking the U-boat that wiped out all his friends, and nearly kills his current crew a half-dozen times in the process.

Thus refreshed, I worked in my back office for a while taking breaks only to replenish my chips and soda, till Alice called. We talked, I tried to cheer her up—after all, none of this was her fault—and around nine, I was just starting dinner when there came a loud knock on the door. Jocko was covered with snow as if he'd been walking in it for a good hour.

"What's going on? Are you locked out?"

He didn't answer. I got him a towel to dry his hair, turned up the thermostat, put on water for tea. Then I changed my mind and poured him a glass of wine instead. I imagined he might have preferred beer, but I didn't have beer, and he seemed to need not only warming but cheering up. He took the glass with a nod.

"I'm not a failure, you know," he said.

"I never thought you were."

He continued, "Not yet, anyway. Some people think so, like my dad. Mrs. Henry. She thinks I'm a major loser. She blames me."

I poured myself a glass. "For Adam's death."

He shrugged, as if it was useless even to discuss it. "Anyway, I'm done. But I don't know about the killing myself piece. It hasn't really been long enough."

I had begun peeling an onion, but now I turned to him. "Excuse me? Are you suicidal? Because I'm not a therapist, I'm an accountant."

He smiled. "Right. But you've probably thought about it. Right? Since you're gay and all."

"Actually, no." I found the implication insulting, but this wasn't the time.

"Well, I think it's bullshit anyway, I mean about its being the only truly serious philosophical problem."

"You're out of my league. I'm making spaghetti." I started chopping.

"It's not really a *problem*, anyway. You just go up into the mountains and don't come down."

I looked over my shoulder. "Would you *stop*?"

He didn't seem suicidal to me, he seemed rather energetic— unpredictably, unnervingly so. And what had happened to his cold? He still sniffled but showed no sign of being diminished by it, let alone flattened. *Youth*, I thought with some private eye-rolling. He wandered over to the other side of the counter with his wine. "Do you believe in God?"

"What's God?"

"Well, how about fate?"

"What's fate?"

"Come on, man. I mean, like do you think things happen because they're meant to happen?"

I glanced at him. He seated himself at the counter and picked up one of the red sequined high-heeled salt and pepper shakers and danced it along the counter's edge.

If only the answers could be found in kitsch.

He went on. "We did have some good discussions. I mean they were interesting. Like what if you're standing on the sidewalk and a little kid on a bike swerves to go around you, and because he just went out in the street at that moment, he gets hit by a car passing. Is that your fault?"

"I wouldn't think so."

"Okay, so that one's easy, right? But what if the kid swerves to get away from you because you've been mean to him and now he's afraid of you? Is it your fault then, because you were mean to him once before? Or what if you were like his friend and you make like you're blocking his way—you know, you're just playing—and he swerves and goes into the street and gets hit?"

"Does this have anything to do with you by any chance?"

He pushed his empty wine glass toward me. I slid a box of crackers toward him. "Dinner will be ready in ten minutes." I added ground beef to the sautéed onions and garlic and filled a pot of water.

He said, "So I ask *him* a question. If a girl comes onto me, am I responsible for my actions? He says what do I think? I'm like, okay, but what about her? And he pulls this book from his shelf. I don't know how he even knows where it is, his books are in this crazy order of how much he likes them."

"What's the book?"

"It's a kids' book. Kind of. But I don't see how kids would get it. It's called *Sir Gawain and the Green Knight*. You know it? Anyway, in the end this knight is a guest in this other guy's castle, and the castle guy goes out every night and his wife comes onto the knight. It happens three times. It's like a test of his honor."

"So what happens?" I emptied two jars of sauce into the pan with the meat and onions.

He gave a half smile, clicking the heels of the red boots together. "I'll tell you what would happen in real life. In real life you wouldn't stick out your neck to a crazy man dressed in green so he could chop off your head with an axe." He came around the counter and refilled his glass. I raised my eyebrows at him but said nothing. He raised his glass to me. He was feeling more chipper.

"Sex can be tricky," I said.

"You think?" He was looking again at my photo wall. I stirred the sauce.

I thought it best to change the subject. I said, "Don't you think the person driving the car bears some responsibility for hitting the kid on the bike? Or more precisely, to *not* hit the kid on the bike?"

Jocko returned to his seat and after a minute he said, "The problem is, the guy in the truck is like the wind. He's just going along doing his thing, driving his truck on the street. Little kids aren't supposed to ride their bikes in the street."

That puzzled me. The wind? I looked down into the spaghetti sauce I was stirring so hard and I thought, *he's like a man going down a whirlpool.* But... did he see himself as the driver in the truck, the wind, or the kid on the bike?

"Kids are not supposed to ride their bikes in the street," I agreed.

"But when you're driving, it's your job to watch the road and also look around. You drive past a playground, you make sure there aren't any kids about to run in front of you chasing a soccer ball or something."

But evidently he didn't want to talk about it anymore. He shrugged. "It doesn't matter now. Like I said, I'm done."

I dished out a large portion of spaghetti and slid it across the counter to him. I brought mine around and sat at the table a few feet away. "You've only been here two weeks. How come?"

He ate in silence for a minute. Then he said, "One, I fucked up. I mean, you were right. She's pissed about the picture. Two, he said I could go to the college for free if I was his son, and that freaked me out. Three, he's got this sexual harassment charge."

What? Wait. Back up. "He knows you're not his son."

"Right. But why did he say that? I felt like I got kicked in the stomach." He blew his nose again.

I brought the wine over to my table. I had to defend Max, God knows why. "He cares about you—"

"No," he interrupted. "That's not about me. It's about him."

I said nothing. There was so much more to it. Max, Max. What a mess.

"And I'm not a kid." There was an element of challenge in his voice, as if he were taunting me.

I thought to myself, *You sure aren't.* More like a young panther pacing in his cage, sleek and strong and ready to snap the neck of his keeper, bound out the door and take off into the night. He gave me a long, appraising look as if I'd spoken aloud or he read my thoughts. I broke away first. Was that when things shifted? Was that when some line was crossed?

290

"What was the sexual harassment charge?" I asked.

"I don't know. He didn't say much about it. He just kind of let it slip. What a hypocrite."

"How so?"

"I can't study good and evil with a fucking hypocrite."

"Hold on. Max is many things, but dishonest isn't one of them."

He stood up. "You think it's fine?" His face was dark.

I said carefully, "I'm saying, I doubt it happened. But I also think you're better off not idolizing him. Nobody's perfect, you know."

"I never thought he was." He moved to the end of the counter then wandered restlessly around the sun room. I had the sense he wanted to kick something and tried to lighten the mood.

"You think he's The Wizard of Oz and you're Dorothy—no offense—who's come to him for help when all you need—."

"You don't know what I need!" He stopped, then murmured something it was probably good I didn't hear.

I got up and collected his empty plate as I went by. "I know you have a lot more power than you think." I stopped myself from calling him Little Munchkin. This was serious business for him.

"Power," he echoed. He picked up the interlocking salt and pepper shakers that vaguely resembled humans and ground them together in a rather brutal fornication. "And there's a fourth reason."

"Okay."

"He thinks I should be in jail."

I almost laughed. "I doubt that very much."

"I heard him. I heard him telling Mrs. Henry that maybe I should be locked up."

"He couldn't have been talking about you. You know he teaches in the jail sometimes. He told me he took you with him. He was probably talking about one of those guys.”

“I don’t think I should be in jail.”

“Well, of course not! Jail is for violent criminals who need to be separated from the general public for reasons of safety. Max has taught me that much. Are you a dangerous criminal?”

“What if I am?”

“Oh, please. Okay, dangerous maybe, but not a criminal, eh?” I smiled in spite of myself. He didn’t smile back. “Listen, are you by any chance of the mistaken belief that more pain will make you feel better? Very primitive.”

“Maybe. But then, like, what’s the point of these things?” He jumped the porcelain cow over the moon and set it down. “Why not just little bottles?”

“Sorry, I missed the connection.”

“Don’t you get it? It’s like, why bother? If the only thing that matters is sex and death.”

Sex and death? I began washing the dishes. “Are you calling my salt and pepper shakers trivial?”

He went on. “Mr. Henry says you can’t make art out of suffering, like they’re parallel universes but not connected.” He observed the porcelain cow carefully. “It’s like, where’s the meaning? Books, paintings, movies, philosophy, dumb little things like these. If everybody’s suffering.”

This was the oddest seduction I’d ever participated in, if indeed that’s what it was. Was he teasing, taunting me, or actually trying to have a serious conversation?

“Well, I’m just an accountant, but maybe there is none.”

He tilted his head at me. “Mr. Henry says our job is to find meaning, or make meaning.”

I waited.

"I've been thinking about this all afternoon. Over here you've got Sisyphus doing this shit work of pushing a rock up a hill, right? And then over here you've got, like, these ugly navy battle paintings on the wall—sorry, but they are—and then over here you've got Mrs. Henry's thing she's making in the basement, it's like a collage with photographs and drawing on top, pretty random. And I'm like, why? What's she trying to do? *Something*, right? Something that matters. Because she totally freaks out when I just, like, add to it. I mean I get that it's her piece and she didn't want anyone touching it, but I didn't glue it down, I just laid a picture on top. It was like a suggestion. Not like an artist's statement. But it's like, where am I? What do *I* get to do? "

I set the last plate in the dish drainer and glanced at him—his damp hair, his young strong body, his obsessive playing with my salt shakers, his distress. He was trying so hard, but how could I help, besides offer ice cream. *Sex and death,* I thought, and smiled at myself. So ridiculously inappropriate. He glanced up and his open expression turned cold.

He said, "You and Mr. Henry are friends, right? What does that mean?"

"I wasn't laughing at you," I tried to explain. "I was laughing at myself. What you said is all true. Profound even. But I'm a simple guy. I watch World War II movies because they're so straightforward around good and evil. Life is a mystery anyway."

But he was no longer interested; it seemed he'd moved on to something else. He said, "You go way back, right?"

I don't usually dry the dishes but I needed something to do. He was so quixotic it was nerve-wracking.

"You do stuff together. Like Adam and me."

The inside of the pot was already dry, but I wiped it out with the towel anyway.

"You share each other's pain, right?"

That gave me a chill. There was something in his voice. I said lightly, "We have dinner, we go out for breakfast. We talk."

"But what did you do to deserve it?"

I watched him. He'd come around the counter into the kitchen and was re-examining the photos on the refrigerator behind me. I said, "Deserve what? The friendship? That's not how it works. You don't have to do anything." He turned to look at me and held my eyes.

Maybe that was the moment I should have asked him to leave, or found out why he wasn't at Max's and sent him to bed here if that was better. But I didn't, and the moment passed and it was too late.

Careful, I thought. *You're the grown-up here.*

"Maybe it's fate," he said with a strange intensity. "Maybe everything so far in my life happened in order to bring me to this moment, so I'd be standing in your kitchen talking about power and sex and death."

I turned back to the sink, thinking hard. I was fifty-five and knew how to take care of myself. My minimal sex life depended on monthly encounters with a casual friend in Montreal. I hadn't gone to bars since before Hecky, but even then I only had sex with men, not boys. But Jocko was not a boy.

And now he was standing close behind me. I set the plate and towel on the counter.

He reached around my chest, pinning my arms and grasping his wrist with one hand. I felt the pressure of his chest against my back, his thighs against the back of my legs. There was a violence in the embrace, if embrace it was, but I wasn't afraid. I thought, *Does he want to kill me?* And I thought, *No.* I breathed. But he didn't relax his grip.

Neither of us said anything. I waited to see what he would do. He was strong and hard where I was soft. I felt his hardness against my butt. The clock over the door ticked and the refrigerator hummed. He slid his right hand down my belly. I tightened reflexively—a mistake. It made my pants looser at the waist and he slid his hand inside them.

Again I wondered idly if he intended to hurt me. I thought I knew what he wanted from Max, but I had no idea what he wanted from me. I thought what was happening in that moment probably shouldn't be, but I couldn't have said why. There was something wrong, but what was it? Or maybe there wasn't. Now Jocko's hand covered my crotch, outside my shorts. He didn't need to wait; I'd already responded. Now he slid his hand through the open slit of my shorts and enfolded my flesh with his hand, not ungently.

If I were going to move away, now was the time. I was bigger, older, possibly stronger, given my bulk. I could have stopped him. For his sake if not my own. But I didn't want to. Once you start eating ice cream, it's hard to stop. Erections did not come as often or as easily as they once had. I closed my eyes. He worked me expertly, if a little hard, as if holding himself, rocking into me. His fierce grip around my torso relaxed a bit, as he understood I wasn't going anywhere. With his now free hand he unbuttoned my trousers. Still he pressed me hard from behind, now with his own vigor. I steadied myself against the counter.

I should have known it would come to this. I knew it, didn't I, the first time I saw him? But how could I have known? I could still stop it. There was a statistically significant chance he would ignore me, but I didn't think so. It was my house, my kitchen.

Max. Max.

The pressure behind me eased and I heard the unzipping of jeans. Did I want this? Yes. No. Yes. I gripped the counter. I felt his warm, quick breath on my neck. *Safe sex, you idiot*—but he was so young, what was the risk? He tugged at my trousers and my shorts; the cloth scraped over my buttocks. All other considerations flew from me.

"Fuck Mr. Henry," he murmured. "Fuck them all."

Okay, I thought, and then, absurdly, as he entered me, *I hope Alice doesn't walk in.*

Afterward I put away the dishes and tidied the sun room. Jocko had headed out into the snowstorm to make the short trip next door, I assumed. The last ten minutes we had said almost nothing; he asked me for money and I gave him some. I suspected this was for him the first encounter of its kind. I didn't try to make sense of it. He could have thought he was doing me a favor, or punishing me for something, or just venting his deep anger in a safe place, or all of the above, or none. Maybe he was just peeing on the floor as Adam had done so many years ago. It didn't matter. Overall the experience had been… distasteful but not unpleasant. No, that wasn't true. It was thrilling. It was delicious. I was embarrassed by it.

However, even if he was a sexual predator who knew exactly what he was doing, which I doubted, he was still Max's protégé. His goddamn Adam-substitute.

But I hadn't seduced him. Had I? No, definitely not.

Well, I had lusted in my heart. *Stop,* I chided myself. *It's not funny.*

Oh dear, dear, dear. But Max wouldn't know, unless Jocko told him. And why would he?

I needed to lie down. *You are* not *having a heart attack*, I told myself sternly. I retrieved a blanket from the guest room—the same blanket I'd given to Jocko—and returned to the sun room because I didn't want to go to bed, even with ice cream and a movie. What movie would do? "From Here to Eternity" where loving your buddy, and avenging his death, ends up getting you killed? "The Guns of Navarone" where Stavros tells Mallory in the end he no longer wants to kill him? "Midway" where the son survives, though badly burned, and the father crashes and dies?

For once they all seemed too simple, even for me. I lay on the couch in the sun room in the dark, replaying the earlier scene over and over, which did little to slow my heartbeat, and tried not to imagine Max's face.

In the eyes of fish, tears. Max and his Basho. At the time I'd thought the line was funny. Charming. Ah, the comedy of it all, the cosmic joke. I'd wanted to be Harold Bloom and instead I was the Queen of Ridiculous. And there I fell asleep.

Max

These are the horrible punishments I have found so abhorrent and yet fascinating. In my research I discovered others, but only the most esoteric were unfamiliar to me; that in itself says something about the acceptance of punishment in our world. The existence of such cruelties is better known than the accomplishments of Desmond Tutu or the Dalai Lama.

What extraordinarily complex creatures we humans are, to be capable of such extremes of cruelty on the one hand and compassion on the other. It is a mystery to me.

Contemplating them makes me physically ill, but I thought of them that evening after Jason bolted, as Alice and I circled each other like ghosts.

Keelhauling was practiced by brutal sea captains and involves throwing a sailor off the side of a ship and dragging him underneath it. Few survived this.

Lashing with a cat-o'-nine tails or a whip tears the skin from your back and leaves it hanging in strips. Caning on the buttocks is considered less harsh.

Burying a man up to his neck in sand condemns him to die of heat stroke if he's lucky, otherwise from thirst or an encounter with fire ants or vultures or a larger predator.

In crucifixion, one dies of asphyxiation.

Chopping off body parts—fingers or hands or ears or tongue—merely mutilates, though a subsequent infection can kill. Ditto branding.

Castration mutilates, stigmatizes more severely and limits future sexual development.

Stoning, burning, breaking on the wheel, boiling alive (practiced occasionally in rational New England) are worse than beheading and hanging.

On the other hand, the procedure known as hang, draw and quarter involved first hanging the prisoner, then cutting him down before he was dead, disemboweling him and finally cutting off his head and chopping his body into quarters.

These are some of the historically practiced punishments that involve imposing severe pain. Punishment requires either inflicting pain or humiliation or withdrawing comfort or pleasure. These are some that involve deprivation.

Withholding sleep induces psychosis, first, and ultimately death.

Locking someone in a cell deprives him of freedom and the opportunity for most productive activities but is widely considered among the least harsh of punishments. Solitary confinement, however, creates in most people disorientation at best, and may cause irreversible madness. Sanity requires interaction with others.

Shunning, banishment from a community and exile may damage the psyche and even lead to death if survival outside the community is too difficult. Banishment may sometimes be necessary for the safety of the group but in that case doesn't necessarily constitute punishment because the *intention* is not to punish but to safeguard the public's wellbeing.

Depriving someone of other intangibles—for example, love—can also be deadly. Newborn children and animals will die without adequate touch. Older children will choose physical punishment over emotional rejection.

An enlightened man does not withhold love any more than he condones keelhauling.

But what, then, does one do with one's pain?

Alice went upstairs to bed while I paced the living room, tried to read, had a beer and tried to think, and finally lay on the couch to at least rest. But I couldn't sleep, and after a couple of hours I got up. I told myself I just needed to make sure he was safe, though what I meant by that I couldn't have said.

Richard's lights were still on. I called several times but got no answer and concluded the phone was off the hook. I'd have to go over there. I tromped through the snow, now at least a foot high, and knocked on his side door several times, loudly. Why wasn't he answering? He had to be awake; he was meticulous about turning off all the lights when he went to bed. He didn't believe in leaving a light on downstairs, as Alice and I did. Rather than slog back through the snow to his front door which had the doorbell, I let myself in.

Was I concerned about what I'd find, barging in like that? I hoped I'd find them sitting at the table deep in conversation, or discover that Jocko had long ago gone to bed and Richard was at the table working on taxes. I didn't expect to see Richard rise from behind the counter like a ghost. He must have been sleeping, but it took me by surprise.

"Where is he?" I demanded.

"Who?"

"Jason. You know who I'm talking about."

He rubbed his neck as if he had slept funny. "I thought he was at your house."

"He said he was coming over here."

"He did come over here, but he's not here now."

"Is that the truth? For Christ's sake, don't play games with me."

He took offense at that, said coldly, "I've never lied to you, Max."

"That depends on how you define lying, I suppose."

"Hey, fuck you. And what are you doing here anyway? It's one o'clock in the morning."

"Let me try to explain it to you. We have a houseguest who happens to be sick, who left in a state of... distress, saying he was coming over here, and I'm worried about him and he doesn't have a cell phone. What kind of a kid doesn't have a cell phone? And now I find out he's not here, and we're in the middle of a significant snowstorm, and I don't know where he is."

"He's eighteen, honey. He's capable of shacking up somewhere else."

"Look, *honey*, I care about his whereabouts even if you don't."

Richard raised his eyebrows and spread his hands in exaggerated innocence, meant to irritate me.

I shook my head in disgust. But I was at a loss at what to do next.

Richard went on. "Well, let's see. He said he was going to kill himself if this didn't work out."

"It *is* working out," I said quickly.

"Of course."

I couldn't believe this. "What are you trying to do?"

Richard took a deep breath and seemed to reconsider. "Sorry, Max. It's late, and I'm not thinking. I've had a bad day." He picked the phone off the floor and replaced it in its cradle.

"*You've* had a bad day?"

He shrugged. The phone rang almost immediately. I grabbed it, thinking for some reason it might be Jason. But it was Alice.

"Is everything all right?" she asked.

"No. He's not here. I thought you were asleep."

"I heard you leave. Where is he, then?"

"Richard doesn't know. He thinks he might be suicidal."

"That was a joke, Max," said Richard.

I looked at him, incredulous. "A joke?"

Alice said, "I'm coming over."

"No, stay there. I'm coming home."

When I hung up, Richard said, "All right, not a joke. A stupid comment. I didn't mean it." He followed me to the door. "I'm coming with you."

I could barely look at him I was so furious. "Suit yourself."

Alice had thrown on sweatpants and a fleece bathrobe over her nightshirt. She handed Richard a cup of coffee which he took without a word. She asked him, "Why do you think he's suicidal?"

"I don't, Alice. It was a stupid thing to say. I thought he'd be here."

Alice said, "I know what I'd do if I were him and wanted to make a dramatic gesture. I'd go back up to Spruce Mountain."

"Yeah," said Richard.

"Take a bus or hitchhike to Plainfield, climb the mountain, scrabble out to the cliffs and freeze to death. There's a lovely symmetry to it, the prefect way to punish us all."

"It's not funny, Alice," I said.

"I'm not laughing." Indeed she wasn't; her arms wrapped around her as if she were holding herself together.

"We have to go after him," I said stupidly. I opened the curtains to the street to check on the snow. It fell thickly in cones of light under the lamppost across the street.

"Max, don't be ridiculous!" Richard said. "No one's going anywhere in this snowstorm. The roads haven't been plowed, there's no way he could get to Plainfield even if he wanted to."

"Do you know where else he might go?" Alice asked. "I checked his room: nothing."

Richard said, "He talked about a girl he'd shacked up with at the university, but I don't know her name."

I checked the pad where Alice and I write the messages left on our voice mail; Alice is an inveterate doodler and often I can barely read a message for all the designs inked around it. But there was indeed a phone number penciled in a different hand. It was almost too easy.

"You call," I said to Alice. "It's better—if it's a girl."

Reluctantly she made the call. "This is Alice Henry. I'm terribly sorry to call so late. My husband, Professor Henry, teaches at the university, and we were wondering—." She stopped. After a moment she said, "Wait, I'm putting you on speaker phone. Could you repeat what you just said?"

A young woman who sounded very awake said, "Sure. I just wanted to say I'm really sorry about my roommate. She just, well, she's kind of crazy. I mean, she *likes* Professor Henry. But he didn't do anything to her. She just complained really because he didn't treat her any differently than anybody else and she wanted him to. She has this huge crush on him, it's like an obsession, really. I just wanted to apologize for her, because I know she won't, but she feels really bad about it."

Alice raised her eyebrows at me. She said to the girl, "Okay. I really appreciate that explanation, but that's not why I'm calling at this hour. I'm actually wondering whether you know a boy named Jason Green."

"Um, no, I don't think so."

"Jocko," said Richard from across the room. "Ask her about Jocko."

The girl heard this. She said, "Oh, yeah. Sorry, I didn't—um, he stayed here a few nights, but I haven't seen him in a couple of days, I guess since, like, maybe Thursday? I'm not sure."

"All right, look, did he ever say, did he ever sound *desperate* to you, like, ah… We're worried about him."

"You mean like suicidal or something? Not really. I mean, you know he told us about studying with Professor Henry. That's what put my roommate over the edge, that Jocko had this special thing going that she would have liked. She was jealous. He said he was giving it six weeks and he didn't know what he was going to do, if it didn't work. He was pretty intense about it. But I mean, shit, we all feel that way, like, you know, what the fuck am I going to do if something doesn't work out. I don't think it meant anything."

"And you don't have any other idea where he might be?"

"Not really. I guess I can tell him you're looking for him if he comes by."

"Yes, would you, please? That would be good." She hung up gently.

"What do you think?" I asked Alice. "Should we call the police? Should we call his parents?"

Richard spoke up then with more vehemence. "No." Alice and I looked at him. "He's eighteen, guys. He's not *missing*. He's been out of sight for a few *hours*. That doesn't qualify as a missing person."

"His parents would be worried. They'd want to know," said Alice. She was trying to sound reasonable but she was chewing her knuckles.

"And what are they going to do? They can't get here even if they wanted to."

Richard sat on the couch under the windows. I stopped pacing and glared at him. Behind him the curtains were still open and I could see the snow under the streetlight. It was eerily beautiful. Alice moved to the kitchen and put on some more tea water.

"Anyway, he's not suicidal," Richard said.

"How the hell do you know?" I snapped. "How much time have you spent with him? What did you talk about? You think you know what's really going on with him?"

"Nope." He was irritatingly matter of fact.

"Asshole," I murmured.

He ignored that. "If I were eighteen and suicidal, I'd get a bottle of vodka and get nice and plastered in a snow bank. That would be an easy death. But he's got too much life in him. He's not depressed. He's angry. And sad."

Alice's head dropped. *Please don't cry*, I thought. I turned to Richard. "This is all your fault," I said slowly.

"Excuse me?" Richard put his cup down on the floor and stood up. "My fault? Did *I* take him on as an apprentice under the illusion I could help him understand the universe? Did *I* hold out some hope that he could get over a lifetime of grief by talking about Plato or God knows what?" He turned to Alice. "Was I the one who made him feel unwelcome, who jumped all over him when he made a clumsy attempt to connect with you around Adam? Was that me?"

I was almost choking. "All right! Enough!" He could belittle me, but not Alice.

Richard stood in the middle of the living room trembling. We faced each other like prize fighters. I would gladly have thrown him to the ground and banged his head against the floor. But I am a rational man and the room was small and full of sharp objects. Instead I turned to Alice, who stood with her fist at her mouth, leaning back against the counter as if she'd been struck.

She looked past me and dropped her hand. "Look, Max. There he is."

Indeed, he had appeared like a phantom under the streetlight and stood gazing at the house. With the lights on and the curtains open, we would have been as lit up as players on a stage. I grabbed my coat and rushed out.

Alice

I followed Max out, with Richard behind me. "Max, wait!" I called. He turned. "Let me. Please." He hesitated, but I caught up to him in those seconds and he must have seen the urgency in my eyes. He nodded. I hurried across the street, with the snow collecting in my shoes with every step. I stopped halfway across the street. In the meantime, Jason hadn't moved, except to shake his head periodically to get the snow off. He wasn't wearing a hat.

"Hey," I called. "Some snowstorm, eh?"

"Yeah."

"Are you coming in? We were worried about you."

"You shouldn't be."

"It's awfully cold out here."

"Yeah."

I came a few steps closer. "I'd like to apologize for—"

"You don't need to."

"Yes, I do, actually. I treated you badly. I was wrong, I didn't realize... and I'm sorry."

"It's okay." He paused. "I just came over to say goodbye. If anyone was still awake. What time is it anyway? I've just been walking around and shit."

"Late. Past one."

"Oh, wow. I guess I lost track of time." He shook his head again and the snow flew off and he laughed at himself. He had a lovely smile.

"Listen, I need to say something to you. Shh, wait. Wait. This isn't about Adam, this is about you. What you carry. You may not get this, but suffering is not redemptive. Do you understand what I'm saying? Nobody deserves to suffer. People suffer enough already."

His eyes were locked on mine; he was listening, but whether or not he took it in I had no idea. I brushed snow off my face. "So where will you go next?"

"My sister lives in Chicago. I have a bus ticket. He lent me the money."

"Who, Max?"

He shook his head and indicated Richard. "I never knew what to call him. We used to call him Uncle Richard, but that didn't seem right anymore."

"You're taking the bus tomorrow?"

He nodded, and he didn't seem in despair or suicidal. He seemed relieved. Something in me eased. I put my hand on his arm. "Jason, I'm glad that you came up here—honestly I am— and it's also fine that you're leaving. And I'm not your mother and Mr. Henry's not your father—and Richard for God's sake is not your uncle—but I must insist that you come inside and spend the night in our house where it's warm and dry. Why are you smiling?"

"You sound like Mr. Henry."

I nodded. "You don't have to say a word; I won't let Max interrogate or lecture you, I promise. And tomorrow you can hop on

308

that bus—if the buses are leaving, and if not, the next day. Please. Let us do that for you."

He looked at me for a long moment, then at my hand on his arm. I removed it. "Okay," he said simply.

He followed me to the house. I held up my hand to Max as we passed and he nodded and said nothing. Richard stood to the side. I took Jason inside, gave him a towel to dry his hair, urged him to make himself at home, and went upstairs and wept.

Richard

As he passed, he glanced at me, without malice or obvious acknowledgment of our connection. But it was there. I felt it as I had the first time he came into my house, and perhaps had felt when he was a child and I showed him how to blow a leaf, though I couldn't remember. I didn't expect ever to see him again, and that was fine. I wished him a good life.

Max, on the other hand.

Max had not followed Alice inside. He stood behind me. When I turned to him it was as if he were waiting for me. He said quietly, "You and I have some unfinished business."

I felt a clutch in my belly. But I said calmly, "And what is that?"

He walked a few feet into the yard, away from the driveway, and turned to me.

"What, you want to fight?" I said. "What is this, an old western?"

"Did you seduce him?" he demanded.

"Of course not," I said, a little defensively.

He lunged at me. I moved, and his fist just grazed my chin. I can't explain what happened next, it was so unlike me, wimp that I am. I hadn't hit anyone since third grade and was surprised I had it in me, particularly at my age and at the end of an exhausting evening. But I punched Max in the jaw. He stumbled backward. It took him a moment to grasp what I'd done—he was maybe even more surprised than I—and then he grabbed me in a bear lock and punched me in the stomach. I slugged him at the same time. We both went down.

"Fuck you," he said when he caught his breath.

We lurched to our feet and stood there panting and glowering at each other. He lunged at me again and I grabbed him around the chest and we struggled till we fell over. The snow helped some, but I hurt my knee. He'd landed on top of me; I fought to get him off. I outweighed Max by at least fifty pounds, but he was more fit. We struggled until he managed to lie above me, and then he pushed away and rolled off. I lay on my back panting, with my arm protecting my face from the snow.

"I think you broke my jaw," Max said. "I'll never forgive you."

"I didn't hit you that hard."

It was intensely quiet but for our breathing. Then Max said, "Nothing happens without the necessary causes and conditions. I had a chance there, and you ruined it."

A last burst of fury surged through me. God only knows where I got the strength. Max lay only a foot or so from me; I reared up and sat on him, pinning his arms with my knees the way I used to do as a young child with slimmer antagonists. He hardly resisted. I think he wanted to see what I'd do.

"I didn't seduce him," I said with effort. "But yes, that is what we do, us queers. You—" I stopped, saving myself from saying something I'd regret. The light from the house illuminated his face, exaggerating the lines and shadows; his eyes blinked away the snow. Even then, when I hated him, I loved him. I tightened my thighs over his arms.

"I didn't ruin anything," I went on. "He was out for himself all along. You—. There was nothing there to ruin." I eased myself off him. "Except a twenty-year friendship."

I picked myself up with a groan and limped off through the snow.

Max sat up, called after me. "All this time, you misled me."

True enough. I stopped. "I'm sorry."

"You always said I was more like a bear. Not a chief gorilla. I trusted you. All this time I could have been beating my chest and snorting and huffing."

Meaning what? I headed up my driveway.

"Richard!" yelled Max. I waited again. "All I wanted was to be a father."

Of all the thoughts careening through my head, none seemed worth saying. "I know," I grunted. I shuffled inside, unsure whether he'd heard me.

By unspoken agreement we skipped our shared breakfasts and dinners for the next couple of weeks. I had a lot of catching up to do and spent long hours at my office. I needed to file a few extensions, but the clients didn't mind. I might have had to anyway.

When I needed to decompress, I watched "The Great Escape" and "Bridge on the River Kwai," where everyone dies as a result of Alec Guiness's crazy obsession, and the horrified chaplain surveys the carnage at the end and says, "Madness, madness."

I didn't see Max, but I ran into Alice once in the grocery store. She told me Jocko had left the next morning as planned, and guess what, she'd been fired from her job. But she seemed in surprisingly good spirits about it. In fact, she was eager to tell me about a series of collages she was making that were obviously delighting her, using those "horrid" photographs from the catalogue on suffering and turning them into a strangely poignant celebration of Adam. I couldn't really see it—she described them as lighthearted, even funny—but then I admit a failure of imagination in such matters which is why I like my unsubtle battle paintings and my equally unsubtle war movies. It was clear Alice herself was happier than I'd seen her in a long time.

Furthermore, she said, she and Max had decided to take advantage of their temporary freedom and go to Japan for two weeks—and she was taking her camera. They'd found cheap last-minute flights and were leaving in less than a week. Max had abandoned his idea of a book about punishment and planned to write a series of lighthearted haiku about philosophy instead. It was the second time she used that word.

My own heart was not light.

I told her I was going to Florida as usual for a week after the fifteenth, and we promised to get together for dinner when we all came back. I wondered whether we actually would.

Tax Day finally arrived on a Friday—good timing. On Saturday I slept in and had a lovely, leisurely breakfast. I planned to work outside all afternoon—the day was wonderfully warm—and I was changing into my gardening overalls when I heard Max calling from the mudroom. I hurried downstairs, surprisingly eager to see him. Nervous, yes, and wary, but I took his appearing at all as apology. Or forgiveness. They seemed inextricably linked, but after all, he'd hit me first.

I gave him a cup of tea and we sat at the table in the sun room, bright with spring light. It was clear he had something to say.

"Why didn't you tell me he was here?" he asked, less accusatory than curious.

"Why didn't you tell Alice?" I had thought about this potential conversation, too.

"That's not the question. I should have. Married couples have certain standards of behavior. Certain expectations. As do friends."

"Especially friends who are like couples?" I hadn't meant to say that.

"We're not like a couple, man. We're friends. I love you, and we're friends."

I gazed at my tea, embarrassed.

"I love you," Max repeated. "And you shafted me. Why did you do that?"

I sighed. "It was stupid."

"Yeah, but why?"

I would have liked to change the subject, but this was probably my one chance to speak. He might as well know how small I was. "Because you have everything."

He shook his head, bewildered. Obviously he didn't think so. "One of the best things in my life is our friendship. You would just...ignore it?"

I looked at my tea; I should have made coffee.

"Did you—" he began. He ran his hands through his hair and pulled at his scalp, obviously struggling. The silence was uncomfortable but I wanted him to finish. He took a deep breath and dropped his arms. "Hell, it doesn't matter now. It's over." He nodded to himself and blinked a few times as if concluding an inner dialogue. Then he said cheerfully, "Alice says you're going to Florida tomorrow." I nodded. "We'll be gone when you get back. You know we're going to Japan for two weeks?"

"That's great."

"Alice is taking her camera."

"Nice."

"Yeah."

"Keep an eye on our house while we're away? I mean when you get back. You'll be back before we will."

"Sure."

"You have a key still."

I nodded.

He hesitated. "We're coming home on a Sunday morning. Do you, do you want to pick us up at the airport?"

"I'd love to." Tears pricked at my eyes. We'd done this for each other for years. "How are you getting there?"

"We'll take a cab; it's too early. Hey, wear sunscreen in Florida so we'll recognize you."

I smiled. It was an old joke about my fair skin, which never tanned at the beach or anywhere else.

"Okay, then." He stood up. I stood, too. He hesitated. We stood in the sun room a moment while he seemed to make up his mind, and then he headed for the door. I followed him. At the door, he turned.

"So," he said.

What else did he want to say? Was he waiting for me to say something? That I'd missed him? That I loved him? That I had tried to hurt him and in the small part of my soul was glad I had, because I no longer longed for him in the same way? I would always love him, but I could not have explained any of this. He gazed at me, in spite of his obvious desire to tread lightly, and I met his gaze. He was a beautiful man, and a good man, maybe the best I knew, but I no longer imagined we were young bucks naked in the locker room waiting for everyone else to leave.

Whatever I communicated to him, whatever he read in my eyes

or didn't read, evidently was acceptable. He opened his arms. We embraced, and there was nothing tentative or uncertain in the way he held onto me.

"Have a great trip," I said gruffly when he let me go.

"I'll tell you all about it over breakfast. Fleury's, first Tuesday in May."

When I came home from Florida I found in my accumulated mail a small package from Chicago. It contained a money order repaying my $200 loan and a DVD wrapped in brown paper with a note that said only, "Better than all those war movies." It turned out to be a documentary about whales, full of wonder and mystery.

The day before Max and Alice were to return, I got two postcards from Alice. One was of an older Japanese woman on a motorcycle wearing a big bonnet underneath her helmet, just the kind of image Alice would like. On the back she'd written, "Taking pictures!" The other was a photo of a small roadside shrine full of simple, almost formless, little statues called *giros* according to the caption. On the back of this one, Max had copied a haiku, the same one by Basho about the horse pissing by the pillow he'd first read to me only weeks before—or was it months? It seemed like a long time. Underneath, Alice had written, "See you soon. Love, us."

Love, us.

Love, loyalty, Harold Bloom. Nothing inevitable but death and taxes. What could I do for them? I determined I'd plant a new peony in their honor, a brightly colored Japanese late-season bloomer if I could find one. Then I put both postcards on the refrigerator and went upstairs with my ice cream to watch the largest creatures in the world romp with grace and beauty.

Fomite

Burlington, VT

A fomite is a medium capable of transmitting infectious organisms from one individual to another.

"The activity of art is based on the capacity of people to be infected by the feelings of others." Tolstoy, *What Is Art?*

Flight and Other Stories - Jay Boyer

In *Flight and Other Stories,* we're with the fattest woman on earth as she draws her last breaths and her soul ascends toward its final reward. We meet a divorcee who can fly with no more effort than flapping her arms. We follow a middle-aged butler whose love affair with a young woman leads him first to the mysteries of bondage and then to the pleasures of malice. Story by story, we set foot into worlds so strange as to seem all but surreal, yet everything feels familiar, each moment rings true. And that's when we recognize we're in the hands of one of America's truly original talents.

Loisaida - Dan Chodorokoff

Catherine, a young anarchist estranged from her parents and squatting in an abandoned building on New York's Lower East Side, is fighting with her boyfriend and conflicted about her work on an underground newspaper. After learning of a developer's plans to demolish a community garden, Catherine builds an alliance with a group of Puerto Rican community activists. Together they confront the confluence of politics, money, and real estate that rule Manhattan. All the while she learns important lessons from her great-grandmother's life in the Yiddish anarchist movement that flourished on the Lower East Side at the turn of the century. In this coming-of-age story, family saga, and tale of urban politics, Dan Chodorkoff explores the "principle of hope" and examines how memory and imagination inform social change.

Improvisational Arguments - Anna Faktorovich

Improvisational Arguments is written in free verse to capture the essence of modern problems and triumphs. The poems clearly relate short, frequently humorous, and occasionally tragic stories about travels to exotic and unusual places, fantastic realms, abnormal jobs, artistic innovations, political objections, and misadventures with love.

Carts and Other Stories - Zdravka Evtimova

Roots and wings are the key words that best describe the short story collection *Carts and Other Stories,* by Zdravka Evtimova. The book is emotionally multilayered and memorable because of its internal power, vitality and ability to touch both your heart and your mind. Within its pages, the reader discovers new perspectives and true wealth, and learns to see the world with different eyes. The collection lives on the borders of different cultures. *Carts and Other Stories* will take the reader to wild and powerful Bulgarian mountains, to silver rains in Brussels, to German quiet winter streets, and to wind-bitten crags in Afghanistan.

This book lives for those seeking to discover the beauty of the world around them, and will have them appreciating what they have—and perhaps what they have lost as well.

Fomite

Burlington, VT

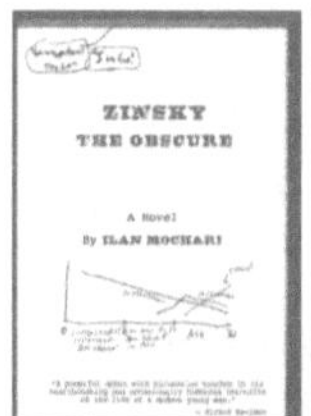

Zinsky the Obscure - Ilan Mochari

"If your childhood is brutal, your adulthood becomes a daily attempt to recover: a quest for ecstasy and stability in recompense for their early absence." So states the 30-year-old Ariel Zinsky, whose bachelor-like lifestyle belies the torturous youth he is still coming to grips with. As a boy, he struggles with the beatings themselves; as a grownup, he struggles with the world's indifference to them. *Zinsky the Obscure* is his life story, a humorous chronicle of his search for a redemptive ecstasy through sex, an entrepreneurial sports obsession, and finally, the cathartic exercise of writing it all down. Fervently recounting both the comic delights and the frightening horrors of a life in which he feels—always—that he is not like all the rest, Zinsky survives the worst and relishes the best with idiosyncratic style, as his heartbreak turns into self-awareness and his suicidal ideation into self-regard. A vivid evocation of the all-consuming nature of lust and ambition—and the forces that drive them.

Kasper Planet: Comix and Tragix - Peter Schumann

The British call him Punch; the Italians, Pulchinella; the Russians, Petruchka; the Native Americans, Coyote. These are the figures we may know. But every culture that worships authority will breed a Punch-like, anti-authoritarian resister. Yin and yang—it has to happen. The Germans call him Kasper. Truth-telling and serious pranking are dangerous professions when going up against power. Bradley Manning sits naked in solitary; Julian Assange is pursued by Interpol, Obama's Department of Justice, and Amazon.com. But—in contrast to merely human faces— masks and theater can often slip through the bars. Consider our American Kaspers: Charlie Chaplin, Woody Guthrie, Abby Hoffman, the Yes Men—theater people all, utilizing various forms to seed critique. Their profiles and tactics have evolved along with those of their enemies. Who are the bad guys that call forth the Kaspers? Over the last half century, with his Bread & Puppet Theater, Peter Schumann has been tireless in naming them, excoriating them with Kasperdom....*from Marc Estrin's Foreword to Planet Kasper*

The Co-Conspirator's Tale - Ron Jacobs

There's a place where love and mistrust are never at peace; where duplicity and deceit are the universal currency. *The Co-Conspirator's Tale* takes place within this nebulous firmament. There are crimes committed by the police in the name of the law. Excess in the name of revolution. The combination leaves death in its wake and the survivors struggling to find justice in a San Francisco Bay Area noir by the author of the underground classic *The Way the Wind Blew: A History of the Weather Underground* and the novel *Short Order Frame Up*.

All the Sinners Saints - Ron Jacobs

A young draftee named Victor Willard goes AWOL in Germany after an altercation with a commanding officer. Porgy is an African-American GI involved with the international Black Panthers and German radicals. Victor and a female radical named Ana fall in love. They move into Ana's room in a squatted building near the US base in Frankfurt. The international campaign to free Black revolutionary Angela Davis is coming to Frankfurt. Porgy and Ana are key organizers and Victor spends his days and nights selling and smoking hashish, while becoming addicted to heroin. Police and narcotics agents are keeping tabs on them all. Politics, love, and drugs. Truths, lies, and rock and roll. *All the Sinners Saints* is a story of people seeking redemption in a world awash in sin.

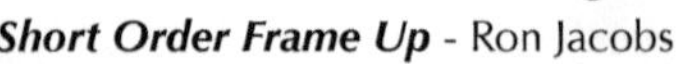

Fomite
Burlington, VT

Short Order Frame Up - Ron Jacobs

1975. America as lost its war in Vietnam and Cambodia. Racially tinged riots are tearing the city of Boston apart. The politics and counterculture of the 1960s are disintegrating into nothing more than sex, drugs, and rock and roll. The Boston Red Sox are on one of their improbable runs toward a postseason appearance. In a suburban town in Maryland, a young couple are murdered and another young man is accused. The couple are white and the accused is black. It is up to his friends and family to prove he is innocent. This is a story of suburban ennui, race, murder, and injustice. Religion and politics, liberal lawyers and racist cops. In *Short Order Frame Up*, Ron Jacobs has written a piece of crime fiction that exposes the wound that is US racism. Two cultures existing side by side and across generations--a river very few dare to cross. His characters work and live with and next to each other, often unaware of each other's real life. When the murder occurs, however, those people that care about the man charged must cross that river and meet somewhere in between in order to free him from (what is to them) an obvious miscarriage of justice.

Loosestrife - Greg Delanty

This book is a chronicle of complicity in our modern lives, a witnessing of war and the destruction of our planet. It is also an attempt to adjust the more destructive blueprint myths of our society. Often our cultural memory tells us to keep quiet about the aspects that are most challenging to our ethics, to forget the violations we feel and tremors that keep us distant and numb.

When You Remember Deir Yassin - R. L. Green

When You Remember Deir Yassin is a collection of poems by R. L. Green, an American Jewish writer, on the subject of the occupation and destruction of Palestine. Green comments: "Outspoken Jewish critics of Israeli crimes against humanity have, strangely, been called 'anti-Semitic' as well as the hilariously illogical epithet 'self-hating Jews.' As a Jewish critic of the Israeli government, I have come to accept these accusations as a stamp of approval and a badge of honor, signifying my own fealty to a central element of Jewish identity and ethics: one must be a lover of truth and a friend to the oppressed, and stand with the victims of tyranny, not with the tyrants, despite tribal loyalty or self-advancement. These poems were written as expressions of outrage, and of grief, and to encourage my sisters and brothers of every cultural or national grouping to speak out against injustice, to try to save Palestine, and in so doing, to reclaim for myself my own place as part of the Jewish people." Poems in the original English are accompanied by Arabic translations.

Roadworthy Creature, Roadworthy Craft - Kate Magill

Words fail but the voice struggles on. The culmination of a decade's worth of performance poetry, *Roadworthy Creature, Roadworthy Craft* is Kate Magill's first full-length publication. In lines that are sinewy yet delicate, Magill's poems explore the terrain where idea and action meet, where bodies and words commingle to form a strange new flesh, a breathing text, an "I" that spirals outward from itself.

Fomite
Burlington, VT

Visiting Hours - *Jennifer Anne Moses*

Visiting Hours, a novel-in-stories, explores the lives of people not normally met on the page—-AIDS patients and those who care for them. Set in Baton Rouge, Louisiana, and written with large and frequent dollops of humor, the book is a profound meditation on faith and love in the face of illness and poverty.

The Listener Aspires to the Condition of Music - Barry Goldensohn

"I know of no other selected poems that selects on one theme, but this one does, charting Goldensohn's career-long attraction to music's performance, consolations and its august, thrilling, scary and clownish charms. Does all art aspire to the condition of music as Pater claimed, exhaling in a swoon toward that one class act? Goldensohn is more aware than the late 19th century of the overtones of such breathing: his poems thoroughly round out those overtones in a poet's lifetime of listening."

John Peck, poet, editor, Fellow of the American Academy of Rome

The Derivation of Cowboys & Indians - Joseph D. Reich

The Derivation of Cowboys & Indians represents a profound journey, a breakdown of the American Dream from a social, cultural, historical, and spiritual point of view. Reich examines in concise detail the loss of the collective unconscious, commenting on our contemporary postmodern culture with its self-interested excesses, on where and how things all go wrong, and how social/political practice rarely meets its original proclamations and promises. Reich's surreal and self-effacing satire brings this troubling message home. *The Derivation of Cowboys & Indians* is a desperate search and struggle for America's literal, symbolic, and spiritual home.

Views Cost Extra - L.E. Smith

Views that inspire, that calm, or that terrify—all come at some cost to the viewer. In *Views Cost Extra* you will find a New Jersey high school preppy who wants to inhabit the "perfect" cowboy movie, a rural mailman disgusted with the residents of his town who wants to live with the penguins, an ailing screen-writer who strikes a deal with Johnny Cash to reverse an old man's failures, an old man who ponders a young man's suicide attempt, a one-armed blind blues singer who wants to reunite with the car that took her arm on the assembly line— and more. These stories suggest that we must pay something to live even ordinary lives.

Entanglements - Tony Magistrale

A poet and a painter may employ different mediums to express the same snow-blown afternoon in January, but sometimes they find a way to capture the moment in such a way that their respective visions still manage to stir a reverberation, a connection. In part, that's what *Entanglements* seeks to do. Not so much for the poems and paintings to speak directly to one another, but for them to stir points of similarity.

Fomite
Burlington, VT

Travers' Inferno - *L.E. Smith*

In the 1970's, churches began to burn in Burlington, Vermont. If it was arson, no one or no reason could be found to blame. This book suggests arson, but makes no claim to historical realism. It claims, instead, to capture the dizzying 70's zeitgeist of aggressive utopian movements, distrust in authority, escapist alternative lifestyles, and a bewildered society of onlookers. In the tradition of John Gardner's *Sunlight Dialogues*, the characters of *Travers' Inferno* are colorful and damaged, sometimes comical, sometimes tragic, looking for meaning through desperate acts. Travers Jones, the protagonist, is grounded in the transcendent—philosophy, epilepsy, arson as purification—and mystified by the opposite sex, haunted by an absent father and directed by an uncle with a grudge. He is seduced by a professor's wife and chased by an endearing if ineffective sergeant of police. There are secessionist Quebecois involved in these church burns who are murdering as well as pilfering and burning. There are changing alliances, violent deaths, lovemaking, and a belligerent cat.

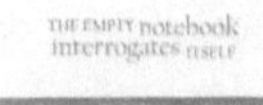

The Empty Notebook Interrogates Itself - Susan Thomas

The Empty Notebook began its life as a very literal metaphor for a few weeks of what the poet thought was writer's block, but was really the struggle of an eccentric persona to take over her working life. It won. And for the next three years everything she wrote came to her in the voice of the Empty Notebook, who, as the notebook began to fill itself, became rather opinionated, changed gender, alternately acted as bully and victim, had many bizarre adventures in exotic locales, and developed a somewhat politically incorrect attitude. It then began to steal the voices and forms of other poets and tried to immortalize itself in various poetry reviews. It is now thrilled to collect itself in one slim volume.

My God, What Have We Done? - Susan Weiss

In a world afflicted with war, toxicity, and hunger, does what we do in our private lives really matter? Fifty years after the creation of the atomic bomb at Los Alamos, newlyweds Pauline and Clifford visit that once-secret city on their honeymoon, compelled by Pauline's fascination with Oppenheimer, the soulful scientist. The two stories emerging from this visit reverberate back and forth between the loneliness of a new mother at home in Boston and the isolation of an entire community dedicated to the development of the bomb. While Pauline struggles with unforeseen challenges of family life, Oppenheimer and his crew reckon with forces beyond all imagining. Finally the years of frantic research on the bomb culminate in a stunning test explosion that echoes a rupture in the couple's marriage. Against the backdrop of a civilization that's out of control, Pauline begins to understand the complex, potentially explosive physics of personal relationships. At once funny and dead serious, *My God, What Have We Done?* sifts through the ruins left by the bomb in search of a more worthy human achievement.

Suite for Three Voices - *Derek Furr*

Suite for Three Voices is a dance of prose genres, teeming with intense human life in all its humor and sorrow. A son uncovers the horrors of his father's wartime experience, a hitchhiker in a muumuu guards a mysterious parcel, a young man foresees his brother's brush with death on September 11. A Victorian poetess encounters space aliens and digital archives, a runner hears the voice of a dead friend in the song of an indigo bunting, a teacher seeks wisdom from his students' errors and Neil Young. By frozen waterfalls and neglected graveyards, along highways at noon and rivers at dusk, in the sound of bluegrass, Beethoven, and Emily Dickinson, the essays and fiction in this collection offer moments of vision.

Fomite
Burlington, VT

As It Is On Earth - Peter M. Wheelwright

Four centuries after the Reformation Pilgrims sailed up the down-flowing watersheds of New England, Taylor Thatcher, irreverent scion of a fallen family of Maine Puritans, is still caught in the turbulence. In his errant attempts to escape from history, the young college professor is further unsettled by his growing attraction to Israeli student Miryam Bluehm as he is swept by Time through the "family thing"—from the tangled genetic and religious history of his New England parents to the redemptive birthday secret of Esther Fleur Noire Bishop, the Cajun-Passamaquoddy woman who raised him and his younger half-cousin/half-brother, Bingham.The landscapes, rivers, and tidal estuaries of Old New England and the Mayan Yucatan are also casualties of history in Thatcher's story of Deep Time and re-discovery of family on Columbus Day at a high-stakes gambling casino, rising in resurrection over the starlit bones of a once-vanquished Pequot Indian tribe.

Love's Labours - Jack Pulaski

In the four stories and two novellas that comprise *Love's Labors* the protagonists, Ben and Laura, discover in their fervid romance and long marriage their interlocking fates, and the histories that preceded their births. They also learned something of the paradox between love and all the things it brings to its beneficiaries: bliss, disaster, duty, tragedy, comedy, the grotesque, and tenderness. Ben and Laura's story is also the particularly American tale of immigration to a new world. Laura's story begins in Puerto Rico, and Ben's lineage is Russian-Jewish. They meet in City College of New York, a place at least analogous to a melting pot. Laura struggles to rescue her brother from gang life and heroin. She is mother to her younger sister; their mother Consuelo is the financial mainstay of the family and consumed by work. Despite filial obligations, Laura aspires to be a serious painter. Ben writes, cares for, and is caught up in the misadventures and surreal stories of his younger schizophrenic brother. Laura is also a story teller as powerful and enchanting as Scheherazade. Ben struggles to survive such riches, and he and Laura endure.

Signed Confessions - Tom Walker

Guilt and a desperate need to repent drive the antiheroes in Tom Walker's dark (and often darkly funny) stories: a gullible journalist falls for the 40-year-old stripper he profiles in a magazine, a faithless husband abandons his family and joins a support group for lost souls., a merciless prosecuting attorney grapples with the suicide of his gay son, an aging misanthrope must make amends to five former victims, an egoistic naval hero is haunted by apparitions of his dead wife and a mysterious little girl.The seven tales in *Signed Confessions* measure how far guilty men will go to obtain a forgiveness no one can grant but themselves.

Body of Work - Andrei Guruianu

Throughout thirteen stories, Body of Work chronicles the physical and emotional toll of characters consumed by the all-too-human need for a connection. Their world is achingly common — beauty and regret, obsession and self-doubt, the seductive charm of loneliness. Often fragmented, whimsical, always on the verge of melancholy, the collection is a sepia-toned portrait of nostalgia — each story like an artifact of our impermanence, an embrace of all that we have lost, of all that we might lose and love again someday.

Fomite
Burlington, VT

The Housing Market - Joseph D. Reich

In Joseph Reich's most recent social and cultural, contemporary satire
of suburbia entitled, "The Housing market: a comfortable place to jump
off the end of the world," the author addresses the absurd, postmodern
elements of what it means, or for that matter not, to try and cope and
function, and survive and thrive, or live and die in the repetitive and
existential, futile and self-destructive, homogenized, monochromatic
landscape of a brutal and bland, collective unconscious, which can
spiritually result in a gradual wasting away and erosion of the senses
or conflict and crisis of a desperate, disproportionate 'situational
depression,' triggering and leading the narrator to feel constantly
abandoned and stranded, more concretely or proverbially spoken,
"the eternal stranger," where when caught between the fight or
flight psychological phenomena, naturally repels him and causes
him to flee and return without him even knowing it into the wild,
while by sudden circumstance and coincidence discovers it
surrounds the illusory-like circumference of these selfsame
Monopoly board cul-de-sacs and dead ends. Most specifically,
what can happen to a solitary, thoughtful, and independent
thinker when being stagnated in the triangulation of a cookie-
cutter, oppressive culture of a homeowner's association; a
memoir all written in critical and didactic, poetic stanzas
and passages, and out of desperation, when freedom and
control get taken, what he is forced to do in the illusion
of 'free will and volition,' something like the derivative
art of a smart and ironic and social and cultural satire.

Still Time - Michael Cocchiarale

Still Time is a collection of twenty-five short and shorter stories exploring ten-
sions that arise in a variety of contemporary relationships: a young boy must
deal with the wrath of his out-of-work father; a woman runs into a man twenty
years after an awkward sexual encounter; a wife, unable to conceive, imagines
her own murder, as well as the reaction of her emotionally distant husband; a
soon-to-be-tenured English professor tries to come to terms with her husband's
shocking return to the religion of his youth; an assembly line worker, married for
thirty years, discovers the surprising secret life of his recently hospitalized wife.
Whether a few hundred or a few thousand words, these and other stories in the
collection depict characters at moments of deep crisis. Some feel powerless, overwhelmed—unable to do much to change the course of their lives. Others rise to the occasion and, for better or
for worse, say or do the thing that might transform them for good. Even in stories with the most
troubling of endings, there remains the possibility of redemption. For each of the characters, there
is still time.

Raven or Crow - Joshua Amses

Marlowe has recently moved back home to Vermont after flunking his first term
at a private college in the Midwest, when his sort-of girlfriend, Eleanor, goes
missing. The circumstances surrounding Eleanor's disappearance stand to reveal
more about Marlowe than he is willing to allow. Rather than report her missing,
he resolves to find Eleanor himself. *Raven or Crow* is the story of mistakes rooted
in the ambivalence of being young and without direction.

Fomite
Burlington, VT

The Good Muslim of Jackson Heights - *Jaysinh Birjépatil*

Jackson Heights in this book is a fictional locale with common features assembled from immigrant-friendly neighborhoods around the world where hard-working honest-to-goodness traders from the Indian subcontinent rub shoulders with ruthless entrepreneurs, reclusive antique-dealers, homeless nobodies, merchant-princes, lawyers, doctors, and IT specialists. But as Siraj and Shabnam, urbane newcomers fleeing religious persecution in their homeland, discover, there is no escape from the past. Weaving together the personal and the political. *The Good Muslim of Jackson Heights* is an ambiguous elegy to a utopian ideal set free from all prejudice.

Meanwell - *Janice Miller Potter*

Meanwell is a twenty-four-poem sequence in which a female servant searches for identity and meaning in the shadow of her mistress, poet Anne Bradstreet. Although Meanwell herself is a fiction, someone like her could easily have existed among Bradstreet's known but unnamed domestic servants. Through Meanwell's eyes, Bradstreet emerges as a human figure during the Great Migration of the 1600s, a period in which the Massachusetts Bay Colony was fraught with physical and political dangers. Through Meanwell, the feelings of women, silenced during the midwife Anne Hutchinson's fiery trial before the Puritan ministers, are finally acknowledged. In effect, the poems are about the making of an American rebel. Through her conflicted conscience, we witness Meanwell's transformation from a powerless English waif to a mythic American who ultimately chooses wilderness over the civilization she has experienced.

Four-Way Stop - Sherry Olson

If *Thank You* were the only prayer, as Meister Eckhart has suggested, it would be enough, and Sherry Olson's poetry, in her second book, *Four-Way Stop*, would be one. Radical attention, deep love, and dedication to kindness illuminate these poems and the stories she tells us, which are drawn from her own life: with family, with friends, and wherever she travels, with strangers – who to Olson, never are strangers, but kin. Even at the difficult intersections, as in the title poem, *Four-Way Stop*, Olson experiences – and offers – hope, showing us how, *completely unsupervised*, people take turns, with *kindness waving each other on*. Olson writes, knowing that (to quote Czeslaw Milosz) *What surrounds us, here and now, is not guaranteed*. To this world, with her poems, Olson brings – and teaches – attention, generosity, compassion, and appreciative joy. —Carol Henrikson

Dons of Time - Greg Guma

"Wherever you look…there you are." The next media breakthrough has just happened. They call it Remote Viewing and Tonio Wolfe is at the center of the storm. But the research underway at TELPORT's off-the-books lab is even more radical -- opening a window not only to remote places but completely different times. Now unsolved mysteries are colliding with cutting edge science and altered states of consciousness in a world of corporate gangsters, infamous crimes and top-secret experiments. Based on eyewitness accounts, suppressed documents and the lives of world-changers like Nikola Tesla, Annie Besant and Jack the Ripper, Dons of Time is a speculative adventure, a glimpse of an alternative future and a quantum leap to Gilded Age London at the tipping point of invention, revolution and murder.

Fomite
Burlington, VT

Screwed – Stephen Goldberg
Screwed is a collection of five plays by Stephen Goldberg, who has written over twenty-five produced plays and is co-founder of the Off Center or the Dramatic Arts in Burlington, Vermont.

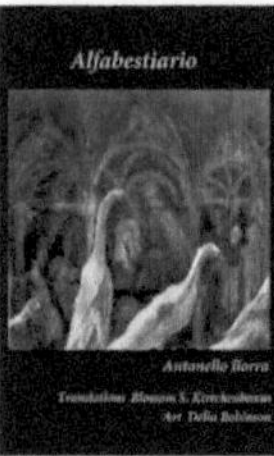

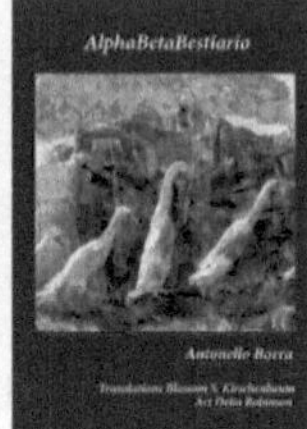

Alfabestiario
AlphaBetaBestiario - Antonello Borra
Animals have always understood that mankind is not fully at home in the world. Bestiaries, hoping to teach, send out warnings. This one, of course, aims at doing the same.

The Consequence of Gesture - *L.E. Smith*
On a Monday evening in December of 1980, Mark David Chapman murdered John Lennon outside his apartment building in New York City. The Consequence of Gesture brings the reader along a three-day countdown to mayhem. This book inserts Chapman into the weekend plans of a group of friends sympathetic with his obsession to shatter a cultural icon and determined to perform their own iconoclastic gestures. John Lennon's life is not the only one that hangs in the balance. No one will emerge the same.

Sinfonia Bulgarica—Zdravka Evtimova
Sinfonia Bulgarica is a novel about four women in contemporary Bulgaria: a rich cold-blooded heiress, a masseuse dreaming of peace and quiet that never come, a powerful wife of the most influential man in the country, and a waitress struggling against all odds to win a victory over lies, poverty and humiliation. It is a realistic book of vice and yearning, of truthfulness and schemes, of love and desperation. The heroes are plain-spoken characters, whose action is limited by the contradictions of a society where lowness rules at many levels. The novel draws a picture of life in a country where many people believe that "Money is the most loyal friend of man". Yet the four women have an even more loyal friend: ruthlessness of life.

My Father's Keeper - Andrew Potok
The turmoil, terror and betrayal of their escape from Poland at the start of World War II lead us into this tale of hatred and forgiveness between father and son.

Fomite

Burlington, VT

Unfinished Stories of Girls—Catherine Zobal Dent

The sixteen stories in this debut collection set on the Eastern Shore of Maryland feature powerfully drawn characters with troubles and subjects such as communal guilt over a drunk-driving car accident that kills a young girl, the doomed marriage of a jewelry clerk and an undercover cop, the obsessions of a housecleaner jailed for forging her employers' signatures, the heart-breaking closeness of a family stuck in the snow. Each of Unfinished Stories of Girls' richly textured tales is embedded in the quiet and sometimes violent fields, towns, and riverbeds that are the backdrop for life in tidewater Maryland. Dent's deep love for her region shines through, but so does her melancholic thoughtfulness about its challenges and problems. The reader is invited inside the lives of characters trying to figure out the marshy world around them, when that world leaves much up to the imagination

The Hundred Yard Dash Man - Barry Goldensohn

In dedicating this volume of poetry to his father, who was a championship runner in his time, Goldensohn compares the lyric poem to the hundred yard dash. Fans of Goldensohn's work will find poems chosen from previous published works, including *St. Venus Eve, Uncarving the Block, The Marrano, Dance Music* and *East Long Pond*, as well as a generous portion of new work.

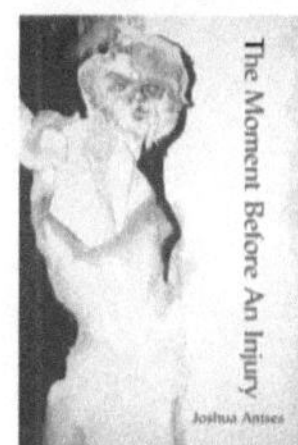

The Moment Before An Injury - Joshua Amses

At a glance, Acheron, Vermont contains all the people you expect to meet in an average New England college town. The bumbling, corrupt Sheriff Blivet, and his son Purvis, a junior paranormal investigator. Wilbur Broom, an alcoholic cinephile with a tragic past, and transfer student Denise, his mysterious and bewitching niece. And of course, local real estate magnate Joshua Castle, and his much younger, and far more ruthless wife, Jo. They all have secrets, and who better to compile them than Henry Hoffmann, blackmailer, tour guide, and adviser to Mr. Castle. In these capacities, Henry enjoys unlimited power and influence over the citizens of Acheron, until several strange events the week before Halloween put him at the mercy of the very people it is his job to control. The Moment Before an Injury is a novel of amoral ghosts, stolen dogs, creative revenge, petty criminality, vocational ennui, and the fragile politics of absolute power in a small town.

Drawing on Life - Mason Drukman Mason Drukman's collection—augmented by the artistry of Lisa Esherick—offers a fresh poetic voice that speaks with intelligence, clarity, humor and heart. His subject matter is life itself: culture, politics, family, death, grief, love and the Red Sox. Welcome to his special kind of poetry.

Fomite

Burlington, VT

Cycling in Plato's Cave - David Cavanagh
How we relate, how we know what we think we know, how past mingles with present, how a bike stays upright, how the butt can bear that puny perch – a lot more than pedals and wheels goes around in Cycling in Plato's Cave. Just like a bike, the poems are simple but have deftly moving parts that roll us along, offer fresh perspectives, and let us feel the air. And just like on a sunny Sunday in June, or is it September, or maybe it's cloudy and broody outside, it's all about the ride.

Writing a review on Amazon, Good Reads, Shelfari, Library Thing or other social media sites for readers will help the progress of independent publishing. To submit a review, go to the book page on any of the sites and follow the links for reviews. Books from independent presses rely on reader to reader communications.